DISILLUSIONED

BRIDGET E. BAKER

Purple
Puppy
Publishing

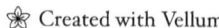

For Whitney

If you hadn't sacrificed our 'no-kids' vacation week to do a writing cruise, this book would not be finished. You have always been my strongest supporter in every way.

❧ I ❧

One week from today, I turn eighteen.

Six months ago, Mom mocked me mercilessly when I insisted I wanted stargazer lilies for the party. But she couldn't change my mind, no matter how many exotic options she suggested. Her disappointment in my pedestrian flower taste was nothing to the face she made when I told her I wanted bouncy houses. I thought it would be hilariously ironic to have stuff reserved for little kids at my party when I'm turning eighteen, finally an adult to the humans.

She and I spent hours planning this party, and it should have been epic. Elegant, posh, and delightful for the first two hours, and then the bouncy houses, the snow cone stands, the cotton candy comes out and everyone ditches their ball gowns to have some real fun. With everything awful that has happened lately, I should be excited about a party, especially one that's whimsical and different.

I'm not.

Because one week ago, on her nine-hundredth birthday,

my mom was murdered. So when her old chamberlain Larena, now my chamberlain, walks into the conference room with cake samples and dozens of new flower choices in vases, I practice the soothing breathing techniques Mom taught me.

I do not want a party for my eighteenth birthday at all. There's absolutely no way we can do the things that Mom and I planned, not for an empress. It's far, far too juvenile. Even I see that plainly. The idea of celebrating anything right now horrifies me. We haven't even had Mom's funeral.

When Larena spreads her arms wide, gesturing for the staff to place the cake on the conference room table, I close my eyes and shake my head.

"Before you throw me out," Larena says, "hear me all the way through. Your mother and I finalized all the details weeks ago. I've removed every part of the second round, as you mentioned, but it still leaves the bones of a wonderful party. All that remains is the final flower selections and the cake choices." She clears her throat. "It's not all about you. The people need something to look forward to with all that they've endured."

All that *they've* endured? My entire life has been turned inside out. And set on fire. I should be laughing right now, and arguing with my mom that I *meant it* when I said I wanted stargazers. She should be telling me that most people love chocolate cake, or even vanilla, but that I'm the only person who truly adores an orange cake with chocolate frosting.

I shouldn't be reconfiguring my birthday party while planning her funeral.

I can barely force out the words. "Cancel all of it."

Larena's lips compress and she sighs slowly. "I think that's a mistake."

"Why?" I ask. "Judica's gone, so the party is strictly for me. If I have nothing to celebrate, why should I?"

Larena purses her lips. "If you're not worried about general morale, consider this. Your mother would be disappointed if you didn't celebrate your existence. Her whole life changed when you came into it."

I destroyed her entire life. That's what she means. Thanks to her decision to keep me, her former heir was exiled. Thanks to me, she fought skirmish after skirmish. Because she kept me, she had to execute her best friend. My life has been a mistake since day one, and now thanks to a cosmic fluke, I'm about to be crowned Empress in her place.

"Fine," I say. "Throw a party. I'll even go, but I don't care what you pick for decorations, and I'm not going to dicker over the cake. Make it plain old chocolate, because this isn't about me, clearly."

Maybe I should make the decor for the entire party black. My twin sister Judica's either dead or she's about to attack me, and I probably won't know which until I'm blown to bits by a nuclear bomb or stumble across her corpse. A wave of exhaustion rolls over me. I'm not sleepy, but I'm so tired of this new life.

Noah strolls into the room as if on cue, his eyes taking in the haggard expression on my face. "You don't look so great."

"You should not speak to the queen like that," Larena snaps.

"Oh, sorry. You don't look so hot, *princess*." Noah winks at me. "Not sleeping well?"

I roll my eyes. "Not sleeping enough, probably, but I'm fine, really."

Noah takes a seat near the end of the table. "Are those

snacks for the meeting?" He picks up a fork. "Because I love cake."

He's so oblivious that he doesn't even recognize a cake tasting. "Sure," I say. "That's what they are. Why don't you try that dark one?"

"Chocolate? That's a little boring for me," he says.

I shake my head. "See the tiny chili pepper on top? That's chocolate spice." I lift my eyebrows. "Your mouth will burn for an hour."

"Sly, princess, but then you gave up the secret. You missed your chance to punk me."

"Punk him?" Larena asks.

"You know what?" I ask. "A solution has come to me. Noah, I'm putting you in charge of all details for my birthday party next week. You'll work with Larena to hammer out anything else she needs."

"Princess knows I throw a dope shindig."

Larena's nostrils flare. "Perhaps we can begin by not using the words 'dope' or 'shindig' under any circumstances."

"Oh." Noah folds his hands neatly in front of him. "It's one of those kinds of parties."

I shake my head. "If I must have a party, I don't want a fancy one." I think about the ice sculptures, edible helium balloons, and chocolate fountains at Mom's party not too long ago. I can't walk into something like that; I just can't.

"Dope it is," Noah says. "Tell me this, boss lady. Do you have any connections for electric bulls?"

I snort. "Not quite that wild. More like if one of your mom's garden parties and the one you threw after that track meet had a baby."

"I can do that." He turns to Larena. "Let's talk right after this meeting."

Larena looks like she's sucking on a lemon, but she says, "Yes, of course."

One less thing to worry about.

The doors open again, and this time several people walk inside. Edam pointedly ignores Noah and circles the table to sit right next to me. Balthasar takes the seat on my other side. Frederick stands by the door like he's here as a door guard. Inara trails in after the boys and sits directly across from me. Marselle waltzes through the door and takes a seat on the end of the table near Noah. Franco takes the seat on Inara's right, adjusting his already immaculate, bright red tie, and brushing the lapels of his suit before sitting down. Maxmillian is wearing a suit that looks exactly like Franco's, but his tie is sky blue and has a matching pocket square. Lark trails through the door last and sits in the only empty seat, between Marselle and Noah.

Now that everyone's here, I stand up. That might be unnecessary, but Mom used to stand.

"If you're here," I say, "it's because I trust you. For some of you, this is a promotion. For some of you, it may feel like a demotion." I glance at Balthasar, and he closes his eyes and shakes his head slightly. Good, he's not angry. "But I need each and every one of you right here where you are. At my coronation tomorrow I'll announce your names officially, but the real work has already begun. No one is operating under any delusions here that I'm perfectly prepared. I'm not. Mom left things in disarray when she passed, so we have a lot of cleaning up to do. But Alamecha is the first family for a reason, and we will rise even stronger for this period of chaos."

"This is your final Council composition?" Maxmillian glances around doubtfully, his eyes lingering on Noah.

"I'm sure I'll be adjusting things with time," I say, "but for now, yes."

"A human and a half-human?" Maxmillian asks. "What kind of message will that send?"

I expected someone to complain, but I didn't expect it to be Lark's uncle. "Angel is gone, her departure coinciding with Judica's. We don't know the circumstances yet, but it doesn't look promising. I'm delighted that Lark is willing to step in as my new Food Services Director, even without a lot of experience. As I'm sure you'll understand, I need someone I trust absolutely." His niece may not be fully evian, but I trust her a fair bit more than anyone else.

"What about your pet human?" Franco pins Noah with a glare.

"He's my new Human Relations Liaison."

"That's not even a position," Franco protests.

"Change is always hard." I pause to let that sink in. "And while I have nothing but respect for Mom's reign, I am not Enora the Second. I am Chancery Divinity Alamecha, and I disagree fundamentally with many of Mom's policies and laws."

"Your mother didn't create those laws alone," Franco argues. "All evian rulers worldwide agreed on many of them."

"They had their reasons when they established them, I'm sure." I meet Franco's eyes. I will not flinch, and I will not back down. "And I have mine now. You all know Alamecha's motto. *Accept the world as it is, or do something to change it.*" I spread my hands wide. "It's my turn to do something, and I won't shy away from what needs to be done, no matter how unpopular."

"What exactly are you planning to change?" Balthasar asks.

"I'll be changing a lot, but I will stagger some of it."

"Over decades?" Franco asks.

I shake my head. Sometimes I forget how old they all

are. Decades, *please*. It's hard, but I don't roll my eyes. "No, over several weeks."

Inara, Larena, Balthasar, Franco, and Maxmillian share nearly identically grim expressions. Noah, Lark, Edam, and Marselle, bless them, remain entirely calm. Frederick is so far away, I can barely see his face. He's behaving like he's not even part of my Council.

"Freddy, come sit at the table. I value your opinion. You're not here to guard the door."

His eyes dart from Balthasar to Edam and then back to me. "I'm not clear on what my role is."

"You were my mom's head guard. You're also mine. I'm simply adding that position to my Council, because I value your opinion beyond protection of my physical body."

"What's my position, exactly?" Edam asks.

"I apologize," I say. "I forgot that I hadn't already announced your formal positions. Larena, can you take these down?"

She pulls a pen from her pocket and nods.

"Balthasar will be my Warlord. I have severed preparation for war and offensives from the rest of the security protocols. I'm afraid with all that's coming, that position will be demanding enough. Edam will take over from Balthasar as my Chief Security Officer on all matters other than war. Larena will remain Chamberlain and will continue to administer all details of my household, including both the palace and all our other residences. Inara will serve as my Steward, and for now, also my interim Political Advisor." I was hoping to name Alora to that position if she agreed to move back to Ni'ihau, but in light of her recent actions, I'm not sure who to ask. "Lark will be my Chef, or Food Services Director for the formal documents. Maxmillian will step in as Alamecha's Operations Manager. His extensive history with managing the interests of his own family has prepared him admirably. I am not oblivious to the sacrifice he's making and I appreciate his willingness to join me. Franco will be my new Head of Governance to manage the human figureheads who rule our countries. Marselle will replace Angel as my Chief Intelligence Officer, but her official title will be Chief Technology Officer. She assures me she can handle the demands of both positions. You all heard that I have created a new position for Noah as my Human Relations Liaison."

"A bold and diverse cast for your Council," Inara says, "and an interesting mix of Mother's advisors and your own. Now that you've explained, would you care to enlighten us on your other plans?"

"This is a working list, but to start, I'll be modifying our laws and those of the nations we rule to provide humans with the same complement of rights as evians."

Franco leaps from his seat. "The vast majority of humans don't even know about us. Are you proposing we change that?"

"I haven't decided the best way to effect my plan yet, but we will set up a rigorous list of protections for humans. They aren't disposable, and it's wrong to treat them that way. Our purpose has always been to preserve the world and its resources, but we have lost sight of the obligation we have to all our subjects, especially the humans and half-humans."

Complete silence. Not a huge surprise, but disappointing all the same.

"Most of you haven't spent much time around them," I say, "which needs to be rectified."

"I've spent more than enough," Franco says. "They're untrustworthy, greedy, self-aggrandizing without support, violent, and duplicitous."

"I'm sorry, are you describing evians? Or humans?" I

raise my eyebrows. "*We are human*, you know. And they are evian. We descended from the exact same place, and I have seen each and every one of those traits you mentioned with distaste from my relatives, my friends, and my enemies."

Inara's eyes widen. "Are you saying we're *equal?*"

"That is exactly what I'm saying."

"You're wrong," Balthasar says. "Respectfully, this is an untenable position to advocate. You're only seventeen, and while you're bright and show a lot of promise, you have less experience with humans than any of the rest of us. Watching their entertainment has not given you a realistic view of how they will behave or who they are at their core."

I slam my hands down on the table. "I welcome intercourse, but I will not be patronized. I will not have you tell me that my core beliefs are wrong, especially in a condescending way that implies that my age renders my opinions invalid. Argue implementation with me, argue timing, but do not tell me that humans are dogs. Do not compare them to cannon fodder or pawns on a chess board. Do not imply that they are imperfect while we are infallible. It's simply not correct. Our ancestors are all the same. It's not their fault if they've suffered some genetic deletions, and it doesn't mean they have no value!"

I realize I'm shouting and moderate my voice. Mom never shouted. In fact, when she grew angry, her voice quieted, forcing her opponents to do the same. "I do welcome your input, but I will not budge on this point. Noah is here so that you can interact with a human and see that they are just like us."

Balthasar, Inara, Franco, and Maxmillian look at Noah as though I've deposited a bag of refuse at the table.

"Lest you think the human rubric is the only major change, let me tell you that evian society is corrupted in other ways, many ways, and I intend to course correct on all fronts. To that end, there will be no more sales or purchases of royal sons by Alamecha, period, full stop."

Edam maintains a completely blank expression, but his eyes sparkle with joy.

Inara clears her throat. "We can certainly enforce that for our family. Mother wasn't obligated to sell her children, or to buy others. She chose to participate, and her reasons for doing so remain valid. When you give birth to a female heir, how exactly will she choose a Consort that you can trust?"

"My heir, should I be lucky enough to have one, will marry whomever she chooses, just as I intend to do, without regard for what family trained them."

"And with all the other changes you're making, what if this heir falls for a human?" Inara glares pointedly at Noah, and I wonder whether she's asking about my heir or about me. But I'm certainly not the first evian, much less the first Alamecha heir, to like a human.

I scan the table slowly, meeting each Council member's eyes. "Like Lyssa? Like my sister Alora?" I try to moderate my voice, but it doesn't work. "I understand and respect the purpose of the requirement that an empress be the youngest daughter. It provides as much longevity in the rule as possible, and as much consistency in leadership too. I also understand the value in preserving the bloodline. My heir will be required to marry someone suitable, someone as close to seventh or eighth generation as she may find. But should she choose to abdicate and marry a human, I'll throw her the most beautiful wedding you've ever seen. Because becoming the ruler of a vast expanse of subjects should be *chosen*, not forced."

"And half-humans?" Lark asks.

"They will be welcome in my service, and welcome in this family. Always."

"What about one quarter evian?" Maxmillian asks. "What about one-eighth?" He grunts. "You'll degrade the line with this nonsense. Alamecha will be corrupted within a century, and what you perceive as justice will result in weaker and weaker guards. Our leadership in all branches will suffer if you allow those who are *lesser* to fill positions."

"Exactly what he said," Franco says. "These changes will spell the doom of Alamecha as we know it."

"Our requirements for obtaining a position will remain the same. The most excellent of the options will be chosen. Are you concerned that humans will defeat evians in performance, thereby being selected for elite positions?"

"I'm saying that they'll clog up the infrastructure with their petitions and complaints. Mark my words," Franco says.

I can't quite help my grin. "You're saying that degrading the line is a bad thing." I gesture around the entire room. "Alamecha is rotting with selfishness, greed, and manipulation. So if I doom the Alamecha we know by doing what's right, that's fine with me. The world we create will be so much more, and we will figure things out as we go."

"You won't announce anything today, right?" Inara asks.

"I won't announce a single thing until after the inauguration."

Cue the chorus of relieved sighs. They all have time to try and talk me out of these changes before I make them official.

I hold up my hand. "I welcome your feedback in the confines of this room. In fact, I demand that you share with me what's on your mind. Absolute honesty is what I want from my Council. But when we're in public, you will not question me. Speaking against any of these changes will be grounds for immediate removal. And if you don't stop, I'll consider it treason. Is that clear?"

Mouths click shut and heads nod all around me.

"Will you be naming a Consort?" Larena asks. "Because I'll need to prepare the Consort's chambers."

I shake my head. "No Consort yet."

"With Judica gone," Inara says, "your Heir is Melina."

Shoot. I hadn't considered that.

"She's not . . . strictly reliable." Inara shifts in her chair. "It would be wise to name a Consort soon."

"Duly noted," I say.

"What do we plan to do about Judica?" Franco asks.

I let her go after failing to kill her, and then she disappeared. I have no idea whether she fled, or was taken, whether she's alive, or dead. I don't know whether to send out search parties, or prepare for attack.

"I ask for honesty, and I'll give it in return," I say. "I probably made a mistake in sparing her life, and I certainly made a mistake in not detaining her in a holding cell. But what's done is done. I'll be spending quite a lot of time with Edam to discuss our next steps, and Balthasar to discuss our military assets in anticipation of a retaliation by my sister."

"You admit that you've opened us up to war with that rash, ill-conceived decision?" Franco asks. "And yet, you have no intention of altering course from other, far worse, decisions?"

Edam scowls, clearly ready to jump in and protect me. But I don't need his protection from my own Council. And if Franco is saying it to my face, others will be thinking the exact same thing. I far prefer someone who tells me his concerns to someone who foments discord behind my back.

"We've been at risk for war from the moment my mom was murdered. Didn't you see the other families licking their chops, salivating over Alamecha like a wolf circling an injured deer?"

Franco drops his gaze.

"I'm only seventeen, and I'm not perfect. None of us are. I'm going to do my very best, and you'll tell me when you think I'm making the wrong call. Then I'll decide, and we will all live with it."

"Since you aren't naming a Consort," Marselle says softly, "you should prepare yourself for the other families to be unbelievably annoying, thrusting their eligible sons at you until you name one."

"Yes, the ambassadors at court are about to get much younger and better looking," Inara says. "Thanks for that, at least."

I lift one eyebrow. "Hardly. They've sold all their sons."

Inara tuts. "Not quite. The empresses sell their sons, mostly, but many of their siblings don't. So there will be quite a few sons of other royal members of the family who would be excellent matches. If you haven't made your choice yet, be prepared for the parade of man-meat."

I hope she's exaggerating.

"I think we've covered enough ground for today. You should all begin sussing out what needs to be done in your particular sections, and tomorrow morning we'll meet again to prepare for the inauguration. Seven a.m. sharp."

When I stand up, Duchess hops to her feet too. Edam follows us through the doorway, the two guards stationed outside following us at a distance of ten feet. "You handled that exceptionally well."

"You think so?"

"Absolutely," he says. "You didn't get rattled, and you've begun establishing a level of trust. Excellent initial foray for a new queen."

"That's good to hear, because I have no idea what I'm

doing, and now I'm panicked that my changes will crumple Alamecha like a house of cards." I reach the door to Mom's room and freeze in front of it.

"You're brilliant, and brave, and merciful," he says, "and you'll figure out how to make these things work without breaking what your mother created. I know you will."

I swallow. "I hope your faith is not misplaced."

"It's not." Edam reaches for my hand and then drops his back at his side. "Are you going into her room?"

"Mhmm."

"Okay." Edam leans against the door. "Well, if we're hanging outside for a bit, may as well take care of some housekeeping."

I meet his eye. "About what?"

"If Frederick is head of your guard, but I'm in charge of security for the island, am I able to add guards to your detail?"

I roll my eyes. "Freddy will do fine handling my personal guards."

Edam's eyes burn into mine. "Fine isn't good enough."

"You two are cut from the same fabric." I glance at the guards behind us and lower my voice. "He already wants to beef up the guard and double the number on duty at all times. He's been analyzing the lists of guards to make sure the two on duty dislike one another heartily. He thinks it will increase their motivation and vigilance."

Edam bobs his head. "I agree. I'm happy to coordinate with him and pass off some of the better men on my force to help with that."

"Oh come on. I don't need two of you."

"Clearly you feel safe, standing in the hallway, too nervous to go inside your mother's room."

I close my eyes and see her body on the floor of the ballroom, blood streaming from her nose and mouth to form a puddle around her. And then a barrage of memories flood my brain: choosing clothing, eating snacks on her bed while we watch human television programs, training together in our private courtyard. The memories stream on and on and on.

"I'm sorry I said anything," Edam says.

"It's not about feeling safe from outside threats," I whisper. "I miss her so much that going into her room hurts."

"Take your time," Edam says. "I'm not going anywhere."

"You have work to do," I say.

"You're higher priority than all of that." He takes my hand in his and we stand together in front of Mom's door for several minutes.

Finally, I'm calm enough to push the door open and walk through. The massive stainless steel doors to her records sanctum in the corner looms larger than I remember. It's several feet wider than her spacious closet, and the entry pad outside the door face beckons me. I have what I need to enter, but I've been putting it off. Because no one but the current empress enters. I don't feel very regal, but that's not my hang-up, not really.

If I go in there, Mom is really gone.

"Thank you Edam. I needed the support."

"Anytime, anywhere, against anyone," he says.

I wish he could follow me inside, tell me what to do. Help me comb through the paperwork. "This part, I have to do alone." I walk across the room until I'm standing in front of the bio-scanner plate for the huge doors.

"I'll be out here, making sure you aren't bothered."

"Thanks." I press my hand on the bio scanner and a larger panel emerges from the wall. I press Mom's staridium ring into it. Then I key in Mom's code. *Divinity.*

The locks tumble and then come to rest. I twist the

huge four-pronged wheel and the door creaks and groans as it opens. I glance back at Edam, and he smiles at me. "You've got this."

More than seeing mother dead, or fighting and defeating my sister, or even finding Mom's ring, walking into the records room feels final. Mom will never train or teach or tutor me again. I blink as I enter the room. I'm prepared for it to be dark, windowless, and lead lined. Mom told me about some of the precautions to keep the records safe and they sounded extreme, excessive even. I imagined the room as a dark, dry, weatherless place. As if to compensate for the climate controls, the total lack of sunlight, the shield from sounds, nearly blindingly bright lights run up either side of the long room. Thousands and thousands of volumes of books and journals line the walls from the wood floors to the top of the ten foot ceiling.

I would have put this task off for weeks and weeks, but we have no real leads for Mom's killer. Zero. Which means my best hope for a clue is right here, in Mom's own letters and notes. With her funeral tomorrow, followed by my inauguration, I've got an excellent opportunity to confront many of those who were here for her birthday party.

I need to know where to apply pressure.

I sit in her leather wing chair and open the journal resting on the center of her desk. I scan through several days, noting that she records a surprisingly high level of detail about each day. What surprises me most is the amount of time spent on her feelings, her plans, and her hopes. I stop reading periodically to close my eyes and imagine her face. My memories, combined with her notes, bring her to life in a way she hasn't been for me since she passed away. Then one passage catches my attention.

I suspect that someone may be poisoning me.

I drop the book like it burned me. She suspected. Of

course she did, but why didn't she take action? Why not tell me? Why not eliminate all sources of any possible poison? I force myself to pick up her journal again.

I can't be sure, of course. Job ran a standard blood panel on me recently and found nothing, but I feel. . . suboptimal. My appetite is declining along with my energy level. I've spent quite some time reading mother's, grandmother's, and great-grandmother's accounts of their last few years. Most of my symptoms are also common symptoms of age, but I'm not yet nine-hundred. If I'm already aging, that doesn't spell good things for Alamecha's bloodline. Perhaps any suspicion of poison is merely wishful thinking. Perhaps I'm not suffering from any poison other than the ticking of time.

The next entry is dated ten days prior to her death.

I'm not being poisoned after all. My fatigue, my appetite shifts and my body aches have an explanation. A happy one, in fact. Against all odds, something strange and wonderful has happened.

I'm pregnant.

I want to tell the father, but I don't know how he'll take it, and then I'll have to explain too many other things. I might be better off letting him assume it isn't his. I can't even quite bring myself to write his name. I'll examine my reticence about this later. But for now, I'm more optimistic than I have been for a long time.

It sounds terrible, but I'm most excited about this baby for the hope that it might heal things between Judica and Chancery. Their anger and inability to get along pains me more deeply than any other wound of my long life. I would give almost anything to repair their relationship. A new heir would free them both and clean up the fallout from my decision to spare Chancery.

If it's a girl, I'm going to name her Sotiris, because she could be their salvation.

The next six pages have been torn out. I search for loose pages all over her desk and in drawers with no luck. Why would she tear out the rest? It had to be Mom who did it, since she's the only one who had access to this room.

I don't find the missing sheets, but I stop in front of a framed papyrus scroll. The prophecy.

In time of great peril, when the lives of women and men shall fail, the Eldest shall survive certain death to unite the families. She comes in a time of blood and horror, in a world overrun with plague and warfare. She shall command the stone of the mountain, be it small or large. Its power shall destroy the vast hosts arrayed against it. With the might and power of God, the Eldest shall destroy all in her path and unite my children as one. Only through her blood can the stone be restored to the mountain. Together, with the strength of her strongest supporter, she shall open the Garden of Eden, that the miracle of God shall go unto all the Earth to save my children from utter destruction.

Utter destruction. I close my eyes. I want nothing to do with this. Why couldn't Judica have been born before me? I don't want to be the Eldest, and I definitely don't want to destroy anything in my path. But I fear I've already fulfilled the first prong. Or at least, everyone seemed to think that fighting Judica would lead to my certain death, and yet, here I am. Maybe the destruction referred to the bomb I stopped from hitting China. Wouldn't that be nice?

Somehow, I doubt it.

Or maybe this entire thing was some whacked out delusion that people fixated on wrongly. That would be a lot of pressure off. . . Perhaps my rule will be uneventful and peaceful. Of course, if it's not true, then my drastically sweeping social and political changes might all fail. My position as ruler at all might be a tremendous mistake, if I'm not the Eldest like Mom thought. Judica is certainly better equipped to handle things from a competency standpoint.

How old is this prophecy, exactly? Without thinking about it, I take the frame off the wall and carry it over to the desk.

Before I can set it down to look at it closer, something flutters to the ground from the back. A white envelope.

I lean down to pick it up, but my hand stops, hovering over the words scrawled across the front in my mom's handwriting.

Chancery Divinity Alamecha

om wrote me two letters? Or was this a rough draft before she mailed the other one to Alora? If this is new advice, helpful information on how to rule, I really should have come in here days ago, before my confrontation with Judica or my selection of individuals for my Council.

I pick up the envelope, my fingers caressing the pressed paper. It's thick, like there's more than one page inside. I clear a space in the center of Mom's desk, and then I sit down before my unsteady knees fail me. I ought to rip it open. I have so many other things to do that I need to prioritize, but I can't. In fact, now that it comes down to it, I can't bring my fingers to open it at all.

Because this is probably the very last time I'll feel a direct connection from my mom straight to me. The last time she'll counsel me, or guide me, or help me pull sanity from the tangle of life. Her funeral is in the morning, and this letter feels like a hand from the grave, a final reprieve from the bone-crushing weight of ruling the first family.

Or what if it's not? What if it's nothing more than a

seating chart for my party? Or a list of things I need to train harder to learn? Or what if it's a sequence of stupid milestones like walking or mastering basic melodics harmonies, and the dates I hit them? It could be something inane, something irrelevant, something that doesn't matter. But it was hidden in a strange place for something of no value. Ultimately, the only way I'll know what Mom had to say is to open it.

My fingers tremble when I slide them under the flap of the envelope.

I force it open, slicing the pad of my finger in the process. Nothing in front of me even seems real as blood drips on the pristine white linen of the envelope. I'm no stranger to injury, but this reminds me of Mom's death for some reason. Unexpected, startling, juxtapositional. Mom was so energetic and pristine and perfect, and then, without warning, she was blood soaked and lifeless, almost from one blink to the next, just like my blood blossoming against this immaculate and snowy paper. Suddenly the whole thing feels wrong, like some kind of warning, some kind of foreshadowing of peril.

I drop the missive on the desk. I was fine before I found this message. I'll be fine without it.

The wall of recent journals beckons me. Mom labeled them on the spine, so I snag the second most recent one, immediately predating the one I just read. Maybe I'll find some clues to people who were angry at Mom or upset with one of her rulings.

I grab a notebook and jot down the names of the people from the first journal who could be angry. Dozens of people whose lives she adjudicated make the list. All of Lark's extended family, including Lark herself. Although, she was personally locked up most of the day that Mom was poisoned, so I doubt she's the culprit. On top of which, Lark's family didn't have a motive until the day before Mom died. Job says it took two poisons, one of which had been administered for at least weeks prior. That makes Lark's family extremely unlikely to have caused her death.

For the first time, I wonder whether it wasn't a combination of two different attempts that killed Mom. What if one enemy planned to kill her and began the slow dose poison, and another attacker planned to weaken her prior to a challenge or something similar? If that was the case, her death would be extremely difficult to pinpoint and even harder to punish.

I strike Lyssa's family from the list and return to my reading, creating a master list slowly. I need to have something to take to my meeting with Balthasar in a few hours. He's been spearheading the investigation, at Judica's direction up until now, but she's gone, all her work and suspicions with her. I hope she kept Balthasar somewhat up to date on what she found.

Every time I turn the page on the journal, Mom's letter beckons.

Finally, I pick it up again, my pulse pounding in my ears. What does she have to say? Why would she hide it behind a prophecy she said was about me? The missing pages make me wonder whether she was concerned that someone else could enter. Could her security have been compromised somehow? Could her murderer have removed something that condemned her or him?

I can't ignore evidence, not for any reason. What if she tore the pages off and put some of them here, in this very letter? I pull out the paper, a little disappointed it doesn't match the striped paper of the missing journal pages.

Dearest Chancery,

I hope I'll tear this letter up with a smile on my face one day soon. *I hope my suspicions will be proven wrong. But in case I'm not, in case my fears are realized. . .*

I have so many things to teach you and so many things to tell you. I would prefer to space the lessons out so that you can process the information in bite-size pieces, but in case that's not possible, I thought I should take a moment and draft a highlights reel.

You have such beautiful instincts, dear one. You have a heart the size of Paris. It's a real credit to you that you always put people first. You care so very deeply.

But you have to stop that nonsense immediately now that I'm gone.

If you're reading this, you're Empress in my place. I've died, as I feared I might. As a monarch you cannot consider the fate of the individual people involved in the problems you face. A question of treason isn't about Lark, or Lyssa, or Frederick. If we are at war, the determinations you make cannot be about the fate of the persons living in the combat zone. The laws you establish can't be created because of their impact on your friends or your family. You must look beyond those people and to the consequences, the policies, the fallout that will result decades and centuries down the road. I thought beheading my best friend might destroy me. I thought my heart might break beyond repair.

And I did it anyway.

If I hadn't taken that dramatic step, that irrevocable step, we would have barreled down a dangerous road. You make laws now, not decisions. You must consider the future consequences before you act, every single time. One of the reasons I played chess so often with Judica was so that she would learn to look beyond the next few moves. As a queen, you must see decades, centuries, and even millennia down the path. A small course correction will have rippling consequences for Alamecha and because of our pre-eminence, the world.

And your choices will be even more dramatic, because you have a Destiny.

I've shortchanged you I fear, my darling, because I never curbed your generosity or kind-heartedness. I didn't press you as a child, never forced you to accept the training you should have received. I didn't hone your mind and body like a blade as I did with your sister. I fear you aren't well prepared for the difficulties ahead. I'm sorry for that. I failed you, and I know there's not much I can do at this point other than entreat you to rectify those deficiencies at every opportunity.

Queens must not show mercy. They can't ever forget the needs of the whole when confronted with the one.

If you've been able to keep Judica by your side, through some miracle, she can help temper your decisions in this regard. She's an expert at looking dozens of moves ahead to what will follow. She always sees the big picture and acts upon that instead of worrying about the ramifications right now. Most importantly, she doesn't hang on to guilt and sorrow. You can learn a lot from that. Try consoling yourself with the twin comforts of justice and foresight.

But none of these are my biggest concern.

As queen, you can never make any mistakes. I'm going to say that again: You never make any mistakes, Chancery.

This will be especially difficult for you because you're naturally receptive to correction. It has made you an exceptional student. You take whatever criticism people dish out and then apply it going forward. It's one of your strengths, but with all things, our strengths are also our weaknesses.

You may not proceed in this manner anymore, not publicly anyway. I have made plenty of mistakes in my time. Most people thought keeping you was a mistake, but they were wrong. Sparing your life was my greatest blessing, my boldest and most intelligent move. No one directly saw how you blessed me, but you strength-ened me when I faltered, and now I know that saving your life was probably Providence. But I made many, many other blunders no one ever saw. I made dozens each decade, but I buried them.

You, too, will slip up, repeatedly. But as with me, your subjects must never know. Our people follow us because they have faith in us to keep them safe and maintain the rights and privileges to which they have become accustomed. If they lose faith in your ability to keep the wolves at bay, they will defect. And once that starts, it's nearly impossible to stop.

So whatever mistake you make, unmake it. Cover it up. Bury it. If that means people die, that's the price for maintaining control. And lest you feel like that means I'm a megalomaniac, it's not about the power, or the wealth, or the lifestyle. You see alphas everywhere in nature. The biggest, strongest, and scariest of the pack keeps the others safe, and prevents the members of that pack from arguing amongst themselves over their individual positions. Your role is vital and necessary and you must maintain it, regardless of the cost.

You might not have been born as an alpha, but it's time to transform into what your people need. Be perfect: That's all I'm asking. I know it seems like a tall order, but I believe you can do it. I'm not just saying that. I know it in my aching old bones.

I don't know how or when you're going to unite the families, and I don't know why it had to be you, but it has a strange sense of inevitability to me now. You should have died, and I spared you. Your flawed sister tried to kill you, and I banished her. Then your twin hated you, even though you weren't Heir, almost as if she could sense what would happen, what you truly are. As if she knew you'd displace her.

For what it's worth, great people very rarely strive for greatness from the outset. The remarkable evians who have changed the course of the future are almost always people who were in the right place to do the good the world needed at that time.

You will become what the world needs in order to do what must to be done. I know that's true. As always, failure is a choice. I know, Chancery, that you will choose to succeed.

I hate to leave you with a handful of platitudes, but our family motto has kept us on course for millennia. So I'll leave you with this now:

Accept the world as it is, or do something to change it.
Love,
Mom

I wish I had found this letter before announcing to my entire Council that I screwed up with Judica, but there's no recapturing that genie. Mom's faith seems misplaced. So far I've failed to kill my rival, released her to raise an army, and now I've created a Council composed of a half-evian and a human. My own Council thinks I'm insane.

What if they're right?

Perhaps I should phase in my changes more slowly. Maybe I need to think about the far-reaching impact of these changes and whether that long term impact will improve Alamecha or weaken us. I wish I liked chess. Like, even a little bit.

I think about Mom's letter while I train with Edam.

Whenever there's a lag in my discussion with Balthasar, I contemplate her words. Unfortunately, he hasn't really found any promising leads.

While I eat dinner and read through more journals, I hear them in my head on repeat.

And again as I review petitions, and governance reports, and career selections.

But after that, I need a break, a break from the past, a break from second guessing our future. So I lace up my Merrells and head for the door to my courtyard. When Duchess whines, I rub her head. "It's okay girl. I'll be back soon." Great Pyrenees don't really enjoy running, and I know she can't keep up with me, not with my current need for speed.

If I'm lucky, my guards won't notice I'm exiting through the back and I'll get to run alone for once. Other than my mom, the thing I miss the most about life before is the ability to come and go without much scrutiny.

"Your Majesty." Arlington's standing on the cobblestones of the courtyard near the wall.

I practically jump out of my skin. So much for my plan to escape alone and focus on nothing more than the wind and surf.

My eyes swivel to the other side of the courtyard to where Ralph stands with his hands at his side. "Why are you two out here?"

Ralph says, "Frederick has doubled your guard. He told us you knew."

I close my eyes. "He mentioned he wanted to, but it's really not necessary. I've been running around the island alone for years, not to mention the long rides I used to take on Napoleon. No one ever told me that riding my horse or going for a jog wasn't safe unaccompanied."

Ralph shrugs. "Our orders are to go with you, or detain you until Frederick can discuss it."

Freddy knew I'd be annoyed. I want to stomp my foot, but since I'm wearing sneakers, I'll look like a toddler throwing a tantrum. "I'm *Empress*. I'm going for a jog, and you two will stay put."

"What if I accompany her?" Noah offers from the other side of the gate at the back of my courtyard.

I sigh in relief. "Yes, I'll take Noah with me."

Arlington makes hurt puppy eyes. "He's a human."

Which is hardly better than taking a dog in their eyes. I grit my teeth.

"But we'll give you some space if you want." Arlington shrugs. "It's our job to keep you safe, Your Majesty."

And if I refuse to let them follow me, they'll be in trouble with Frederick. "Lag far behind," I say.

Noah opens the gate and I jog through it. I can pretend we're alone, right? I take off down my typical path.

"Whoa, Flash Gordon, ease up a bit for the pathetic human, por favor." Noah's practically panting behind me.

Right. I keep forgetting. "Sorry." I drop back to a pace I think he can sustain.

"Feel like talking about anything?" Noah asks. "Because I don't have a dog in the fight. I probably can't help, but I feel I should offer up my human opinion, now that I'm being paid for it."

I glance sideways at him.

"Wait, I am being paid right? Because Dad will lose it if I dropped out of school without a paying gig."

I laugh. He's worried about money. "Sure, we'll pay you."

"Phew."

"Speaking of your dad, where does he think you are right now?"

Noah chews on his bottom lip.

"What did you tell him?"

"I'm really super, duper sick," he says. "So I won't be at school for another few days. Those traitors call and tell him when I don't show up."

I hadn't considered this part. Noah's my age, but for humans that's not old enough to live on your own. "Um, do you need my help with anything? Should I, like, type up a job description or something?"

What if he needs to leave? Am I about to lose him to the mundane norms of the human world? It's not like I can kidnap a minor and keep him here. I mean, I could, but that's pretty awful. The idea of losing Noah makes my head spin. I want him to stay. I rely on being able to talk to him, because like he said, he doesn't have a dog in this fight.

Which makes me think of Cookie.

"Hey there, remember me? We were keeping this run slow for the human." He wheezes. "You know, so I don't die." Noah's face is bright red. "I can't answer your questions when you're sprinting away from me."

"Sorry," I say again. And then I recall Mom said I shouldn't admit my mistakes, which is basically an apology. Maybe that was Edam's point so long ago, when he told me not to apologize. I've only been striving for total perfection for a few minutes, and I'm already completely failing. Which I need to not do, because when I fail, I apologize, and that's another failure.

I hate all of this. Trying to be perfect is exhausting.

Noah's heart rate finally starts to come down a bit. "You asked," he says, "what you can do to help."

"Yes, right."

"My dad would be fine with me leaving that ridiculous American school if I could pursue my studies remotely, while working at a job that will hopefully provide room for growth."

"I thought he wanted you to step in with the family business."

"Our American interests, anyway," Noah says, "but he can't hand it off to me until he's confident that I'm prepared to handle something substantial. If I find a promising job on my own, that should be enough to keep him satisfied for a bit."

I'll talk to Larena. Surely together we can come up with something convincing.

By the time I return to the compound, I feel much better. I may have made one mistake and not known to cover it, but I know now. I'll have to hope my Council will be inspired enough by my future good decisions that they forgive me one oversight. Not that I can ask them to forgive me, obviously.

After my shower, Larena meets me to discuss a few hiccups that have cropped up with regard to Mom's funeral and my inauguration. By the time we hammer out the final details, I'm ready to drop into bed.

When I hear a tap on my door I groan. "Come in."

Edam opens the door and peeks his head through. "I checked the Queen's chamber, but it was empty."

I sink back against my pillows. "I can't use it."

"You'll get there, but there's no rush. If you mean to stay here for the foreseeable future, I'll let the guys know."

"Thanks."

At a tiny yip from behind the door, I bolt upright in bed. Duchess lifts her head beside me and growls low in her throat. I pat her head. "It's okay gal. It's only Edam and he'd never hurt us." Or at least, I'm pretty sure he wouldn't.

I swing my legs out from under the covers and straighten up to standing. "Why are you here?"

Edam pushes the door open and leans down to pick something up. "I thought you might be ready for this."

A tiny grey dog growls softly and then whines.

"It's a Weimaraner," he says. "They're very bright, and they love long runs. They also love to be right by their people."

"How did you—"

"I ordered him after what happened with Cookie. An old contact of mine breeds them, and since you love to run.
. ." He clears his throat. "He's finally old enough to be separated from his mother."

Separated from his mother forcibly, just like me. I close my eyes.

"I'm sorry," Edam says. "If it feels like a bad fit, I'll take him back."

I shake my head. "No."

"No?"

Edam's face falls. "I knew it was a gamble, and I'm sorry if it upset you."

My voice cracks when I say, "It wasn't a mistake. I'm happy, I swear."

"Oh good." Edam crosses the room and hands the wriggly ball of energy to me. "I figure you and Duchess can whip him into shape quickly."

Duchess hops off the bed, growling a little. When I place the pup on the floor, she bumps him with her nose. He spins in a circle over and over until he trips and falls into a pile on my rug. Duchess sits down, and if dogs could roll their eyes in exasperation, she'd have done it. She rests her face on her paws and watches the little dope with a long-suffering expression.

"Well, I'm sorry I interrupted you getting some sleep. I can take him tonight and bring him back in the morning if you'd like."

I shake my head. "No, I want him here."

"He'll need to get up and go to the bathroom every few hours," Edam says.

"I know."

"Okay, well, let me know if you need anything."

I grab his hand. "Don't go."

Edam turns around slowly, his eyes rising incrementally as well, until finally they meet mine. Something sparks there, something hot, something real.

My heart catapults into my throat and I can barely force the next words out. "What I mean is, if you don't mind, if you slept in here on the couch, we could take turns with him."

The smile spreads slowly across Edam's almost painfully beautiful features. "I'd be happy to stay here with him."

I climb back into bed, and Duchess hops up and settles next to me. Edam lays down on my sofa, and the fumbly puppy tries twice before he finally lands on his chest.

I stifle a laugh.

But when the wiggle worm licks his face, Edam shoves him into the small space between the edge of the sofa and his enormous body. The puppy isn't initially happy with that arrangement, but after a little reinforcement, he finally collapses with a small whuffle.

When I finally drift off to sleep, I feel safer than I've felt since before Mom died.

※ 3 ※

It felt like Mom's funeral would never actually take place, and in some ways, it kept me from truly processing her death. Every single morning since she died, I've woken up with an unfounded hope that maybe she's still alive.

No one holds funerals for people who are coming back.

I know that I should be looking for attendees who look guilty, or relieved, or exultant. I should scan the back of the room for people who turn up to gawk, but I can't do it. My brain feels almost foggy with grief, saturated with bone-deep sorrow. No matter where I look, my eyes circle back around to Mom's casket. At least Balthasar and Frederick are supposed to be watching the audience. Besides, we can review camera footage later.

Every seat is taken, and the areas around the seats are crammed with people standing. Mom was feared, but she was also loved and respected. Since the funeral and my coronation are happening back-to-back, each of the Five is formally represented as well.

I asked Balthasar to give her eulogy, and he does a beautiful job. He talks about Mom's brilliance, her magnificence in battle, and the ways in which she shaped and changed the landscape of evian leadership forever.

"Enora was a pioneer of the free will of people everywhere, both human and evian. She found ways to increase freedom while maintaining the prosperity of the entire population she ruled. She governed with grace, but also with an iron fist that never wavered. Her legacy includes sixteen powerful daughters, culminating with Chancery. I have known and trained every single heir, so it means something when I tell you that Enora and I both viewed Chancery as her most impressive accomplishment."

Balthasar lies much more convincingly than I expected.

As if he senses my disbelief, he continues. "For many of you, Enora's choice of Chancery as her successor was a shock."

That's an understatement. Since no one knew about the ring's reaction to me, even her closest advisors probably had to fight through their horror at Mom's change after she died.

"I'm sure some of you are still scratching your heads," he says. "But if you were present for the recent challenge Chancery fought against Judica, you saw how strong, intelligent, and capable Chancery truly is. Beyond that, if you know her at all, you love her. And while empathy isn't a commonly lauded evian value, it should be. Chancery's concern for others gives her a unique ability to see both sides of a situation, a skill she learned from Enora herself. I think it will become very clear to you all that in Enora's death as in her life, she served Alamecha in the best way possible, by choosing the strongest successor, if not the most obvious. Enora was able to change her path, change the trajectory of Alamecha in fact, the very second it became beneficial to do so, and she did that with her daughters, selecting the one who is right for Alamecha now. I hope all of you will join me in honoring Enora's memory by respecting and supporting her decision."

After he finishes and sits down, Inara was meant to share a few thoughts, but she doesn't stand up. I glance her way, and she shakes her head. She mouths the words, "I can't."

Mom deserves to have at least one of her children speak, so with nothing prepared, I stand up and walk to the podium. "You all knew my mother as Enora the Merciless, and certainly she earned that moniker. But it wasn't the fullness of the truth either."

All eyes are fixed on me. Enora's folly. Everyone has called me that as long as I can recall, and now here I am. Mom's replacement. "Each of us is incredibly complex. We reduce other people to labels so that we can understand them, but none of those labels truly do us justice, not really. For instance, everyone knows me as the girl who lived when she should have been killed. Each of you knows the risk my mother took in sparing my life, and you've heard about the fight it caused immediately after my birth. My own sister was banished as a result of Mom's decision."

I glance around the room, meeting people's gazes one at a time.

"I've been outspoken in my demands for mercy during petitions. You might even have called me the weak twin or the merciful one. You're probably all a little worried that you're being ruled by the B team."

Nervous laughter. Great.

"But Mom was such an innovator because she was always willing to discard rules that didn't work for her people and her plan for our future. She was never afraid to do what had to be done, no matter the cost to her, no matter the risk involved."

When I glance her way, Inara smiles at me.

"So today, I would like to share a story that exemplifies the real Enora Alamecha. When I was six years old, a bird flew into the glass of my bedroom. I raced outside, terrified the bird was dead. Unfortunately, my fears were realized. The rock dove's neck was snapped, its head at a strange angle. At the time, this felt like the most devastating thing that could have happened to me."

I tap the top of the podium. "Moments later I heard chirping coming from high in the banyan tree behind me. As sad as I was, it was nothing to the impact on that bird's children. With the death of the mother, the chicks in that nest were doomed to die as well. It felt so senseless, so desperately sad. Mom called me back inside. She told me someone else would take care of the problem."

I shrug. "I was old enough to know what that meant. Someone was going to disappear them. After all, I'd just learned that much of the food I ate came from animals someone had *taken care of.* I begged and begged Mom to let me climb into the tree and bring the nest down. Then surely someone would be able to take care of them until they could care for themselves."

More nervous chuckles.

"I scrambled up that tree like an expert, fueled by my burning desire to be a hero. I reached the nest and carefully dislodged it from the tree branches. I'm sure many of you can guess what followed. I couldn't climb back down as easily as I went up, and on top of that, I hadn't brought a bag, or a box, or anything to carry three squawky chicks down safely. I couldn't bring them down safely."

"I called to my mom. 'Help me, please!' But Mom simply shook her head. 'You took this path. It's your job to carry it to its natural conclusion.' I finally tied my shirt into a cocoon with a handful of clumsy knots and placed the nest inside, the chicks peeping frantically. But climbing down while trying to protect the front of my shirt proved to be harder than I imagined it would be. 'Mom! I'm going to fall!' I shrieked again. Her answer was the same as before. 'This was your decision, Chancery. I believe in you.' I kept climbing, but my clumsy hands were no match for branches slippery from dew, and I fell."

I wipe away a tear.

"Even though she insisted she wouldn't help me and told me that I was on my own, Mom caught me when I fell, and she did it in a way that didn't harm those helpless chicks. Mom knew that growth came from struggle and adversity, but she was also a kind, loving, generous mother, and she never wanted me to endure unnecessary pain."

I take a moment to clear my voice. "And even though she's gone, I still hear her in my head, shouting the same thing. 'This is your path, Chancery. I believe in you.' Although I know she's not here to catch me anymore—" I choke a little bit and breathe in and out deeply. "Even though she's not able to physically catch me anymore, she's still behind every decision I make. She spent the past eighteen years teaching me, and I'm surrounded with people who will advise me in her absence."

When I sit down, it feels as though a weight has been lifted. Mom is gone, but she's still all around me, in the things I've learned, in the legacy she created—like Balthasar said. I nearly drown in a sea of people wishing me their kindest condolences, and then I trudge back to my room to change for my coronation.

The queen is dead, long live the queen.

I've been thinking about this since my return, agonizing over what to wear. But now the moment is here, I know what's right. I pull the last dress I ever purloined from Mom out of my closet. The ivory Vera Wang, with full, heavily embroidered pink and gold panels comprising the entire skirt is the perfect selection. It's made with Mom's signature colors, and I want to signal that there's continuity here, the same strength guiding the wheel.

When I put it on, I think of how Mom looked wearing it, moments before I set off that first EMP and exploded my entire world forever. I call Varvara in to do my hair, and stare at my face in the mirror as she begins. After my trip to Trinity, I kind of liked the dark hair. I went back to it after I healed from the nuclear bomb fiasco. But when I look in the mirror, the face that stares back at me looks nothing like Mom's.

"Wait." I brush Varvara away.

I stand up and lop off my dark hair as close to the scalp as I can. Varvara's eyes widen. "We don't have much time."

"I'm aware. I'll be quick." I focus on my hair and grow it out in exactly the color of Mom's chestnut locks. Then I move to my eyes, shifting their color until it's an exact match for Mom's nearly violet eyes. Finally, I change my skin to the honey-gold color Mom favored. "Now I'm ready."

Varvara grumbles. "You couldn't have done this earlier? We're already behind schedule." She's always crabby. It's one of the things I like about her.

"I think you missed your calling in life," I say. "You should have been one of Snow White's dwarves."

"Excuse me?" She tugs a little harder than necessary.

"Never mind." I need to remember that evians never understand my human pop culture references.

Varvara is a whiz with hair, though. By the time she's done, I barely recognize myself as the Chancery I know. With my hair up in a combination of intricate braids and smooth, well-placed tufts, I look five years older, and the only thing that gives me away is the panic in the lines of my face.

As Varvara leaves, my new bundle of energy careens into the room, Edam only a few steps behind. I reach down so the puppy can lick my hand. "I'd pick you up, goober, but you might ruin the overlay on my dress, and I can't have that. Then everyone would realize that I'm an imposter."

Edam grabs the pup and picks him up and I follow the motion. I would have told you yesterday that nothing on Earth was more handsome than Edam, sweating in training gear, a sword clasped in capable hands, a glint of ferocity in his eyes, but I would have been wrong. Edam in a tux and holding a puppy short circuits the receptors in my brain, and I'm left staring dumbly.

"Any ideas for names?" he asks.

I shake my head like an imbecile.

"I was thinking Dart."

That brings me back to myself. "Dart?" I snort. "That's a terrible name."

Edam's eyebrows rise. "What do you suggest then? I'm heartily tired of calling him pup."

"He's energetic and bouncy and you picked this breed because he loves to run."

Edam nods.

"How about Red Bull?"

"Huh? He's grey."

Pop culture references again. Good grief. "It's a human drink they advertise a lot. The slogan is 'Red Bull gives you wings'—but really it's a quick way for humans to boost their energy when they're tired. And this little guy." I lean over and ruffle the soft, short fur on his head. "He always has lots of energy."

"He's your dog, Your Majesty," Edam says. "Speaking of majesty, you look absolutely stunning. Are you ready to go?"

I shrug. "As ready as I'll ever be."

Edam steps closer to me, Red Bull frolicking around our feet. "You know this is just a formality. You've been acting queen for a while now, so there's no reason to be nervous."

"Thanks." The tingly feeling that shoots up my spine when he steps inside my comfort zone zaps my eloquence. Hopefully he can't tell.

Edam holds out his arm and I take it. "Then let's go."

Noah meets us outside. "Hey, why does he get to escort you? You didn't get pressured into agreeing to marry him again, did you?"

Edam's arm tenses.

"Not hardly," I say.

Noah falls into step with me on my other side, my guards flanking us. "As a valued member of your Council, I think I should walk close, too. If I didn't, what kind of message might that send about my importance?"

I roll my eyes, but don't argue. I like having Noah around, and I suspect his childish complaining is as much to set me at ease as it is to stand closer.

I've walked down this hall to the throne room thousands of times, but I've always been headed for one of the smaller seats. Somehow, knowing I'm headed for the large central throne makes the entire hallway look different. When I walk through the side door, Edam and Noah drop back so I can walk up alone. I close my eyes and breathe in and out once, then again. I square my shoulders and ascend the stairs to the raised dais, Mom's ring sparkling on my finger, Mom's dress covering my body. It's easier to pretend she's with me when her belongings surround me.

Mom's throne is carved intricately from white marble, made to blend in with the ornate carvings that line the back wall, in the way Alamecha blends in among its human subjects. The motto of each Alamecha empress is carved into the side. Mom's motto, 'Failure is a Choice,' is carved into the stone in the very middle. A new quote has already been carved above it. 'The smallest light still vanquishes darkness.' I know what I'll see carved into the head of the throne when I circle around to the front. 'Accept the world as it is, or do something to change it,' the Alamecha family motto.

I'm trying, Mom. Heaven help me, because I need every scrap of help I can get.

I step into place in front of Mom's imposing throne. While I wait for Inara to cross to where I'm standing with the crown Mom almost never wore, I scan the audience. My sisters stand in an imposing row at the front. Magdelina, Margerite, Avina, Falin, Vera, Emmeline, Annekah, Danika, and Rivena. Although the vast majority of my living sisters came and Inara will stand behind me as part of my Council, I can't help thinking about the ones who aren't in attendance. Judica, Alora, and Melina.

I don't know Melina and opted against sending her an invite, seeing as she wanted to kill me when I was a newborn. But Alora was my closest family member aside from my mother, and in spite of her somewhat undefined betrayal, I wanted her here. I thought surely the sister I love most would have arrived for today's events with an apology and an explanation.

My feelings about Judica are so complicated, I can't decide whether I'm happy she's gone or devastated. I'm simultaneously relieved, angry, and mournful. But her absence certainly constitutes a glaring blight on my corona-tion. After all, I released her against the advice of every single person alive, and now she's splitsville.

Inara finally reaches my side. "It is my distinct pleasure

to stand before you all today," she says, her voice expanding to fill the room easily. "Chancery Alamecha has grown from a tiny newborn to the young woman standing before you in resplendence, and I couldn't be prouder of the ruler she has become."

"We are honored by her presence," the audience says.

"We recently held a funeral for Enora Alamecha, your ruler for eight hundred and seventy-three years. It was her desire that Chancery should become the next queen of Alamecha, ruler of the First Family of Eve."

"We are honored by her presence," the audience repeats.

My eyes recognize nearly every single attendee. I've interacted with almost all of them in small and sometimes large ways over the past seventeen years. But not all of them are friendly. Vela's Heir to the family of Shenoah, and her face is utterly blank. Melamecha from Shamecha purses her lips and tilts her head. Ranana from Adora scowls at me. Melisania from Lenora smiles so sweetly that it must be covering some deeply-felt contempt. But the biggest shock to me is Analessa's beaming face. I didn't expect her to be brave enough to come, considering Edam hasn't had any contact with her during the most tumultuous period in Alamecha's recent history.

Or has he?

I glance to the side of the room where Edam and Noah wait with the rest of my Council to be called forward. I don't think he's playing both sides, but how can I be sure? It was easier to trust his loyalty when we were far from the throne. Somehow being here, surrounded by my own family, I feel more alone than I did in New York.

"And now," Inara says, "I'll ask you to recite the Oath of the Empress." She circles around behind me and holds Mom's favorite crown over my head.

"I, Chancery Divinity Alamecha, solemnly swear, before God above, the demons of the world, and the angels who watch over us that I will govern the holdings of Alamecha, from Canada to the United States of America, from Puerto Rico to Cuba, from the United Kingdom to the Philippines, to the very best of my ability. I further swear to administer justice in all things." I quickly add my own stipulation. "Justice *tempered in mercy*."

The gasps after my amendment are satisfying. I'm not Enora, and I believe mercy should go hand-in-hand with justice. People may as well understand that immediately. It's not a mistake to forgive, nor is it a weakness to exploit.

"I hereby proclaim you to be Queen of the First Family, Empress of Alamecha, seven generations removed from Eve herself, Mother to us all. I admonish you to rule without fear under the sight of God." Inara places the crown on top of my head and steps back.

I shift toward the edge of the platform, closer to the crowd gathered. "As is customary, in my first act as queen, I will designate the members of my Council. I name Balthasar ne'Melamecha ex'Alamecha as my Warlord. I name Edam ne'Malessa ex'Alamecha as my Chief Security Officer. I name Larena Alamecha my Chamberlain. I name Inara Alamecha as my Steward and also my Political Advisor. I name Lark Alamecha as my Food Services Officer, and Noah Wen as my Human Relations Liaison. I name Marselle Alamecha as my Chief Technology Officer, and Frederick Alamecha as Head of my Personal Guard. I name Maxmillian Alamecha as my Operations Manager and interim Exchequer General, and finally, I've chosen Franco Alamecha as Head of Governance."

Murmurs of "No Consort?" and "Did she name a Consort?" flood the room, just as I knew they would, but I doubt if anyone will have the gumption to ask me anything directly. Each and every one of them will have the chance, because tradition dictates that everyone in attendance will bring me a token or gift and express their good wishes for my reign.

"Of course I'd be happy to meet with you sometime in the next month," I say to Benjamin.

"I would be honored to pose for a photo," I tell Giovanni and his adorable young son.

Only after every member of Alamecha has been received do I accept the well wishes from the Five. The rulers approach first, and I'm acutely aware how much these seemingly routine pleasantries matter. Inara takes up a position to my right, and Balthasar on my left, presumably in a show of support, but I suspect it may be to elbow me if I say anything untoward.

"My most sincere wishes for a long and prosperous rule." Vela's smile reminds me of a fox who recently devoured a house full of hens. "If you ever need an outsider's opinion, please reach out to me." She hands me a smallish box, and I lift the lid carefully.

An olive branch and a cell phone rest on velvet lining.

Vela leans closer. "You may call me freely with that phone, any time you'd like. I know our mothers have never gotten along, but I hope to set new precedents for our families. We are not our parents."

"No," I say. "We aren't. Although I respect my mother and yours, I sincerely hope we can improve the relationship between our families." The discord between Shenoah and Alamecha has been of great duration and terrible strength. If we can heal the breach, I'd be delighted and relieved.

"My gesture is sincere, but if you reach all the way down, you'll find another gift hidden underneath."

Below the olive branch, I find two sets of keys.

"If I knew you better, I might have gotten one or the other, but I wasn't sure which you'd prefer," Vela says.

I lift my eyebrows.

"Very few things clear my head like driving over a hundred miles per hour." She points at the keys. "Those are being delivered in the next few days. An Aston Martin Valkyrie, and a Bugatti Chiron."

"What colors?" Noah asks from a dozen feet away.

Part of me wants to slap him, but from past conversations, I know how much he loves sports cars.

"Red Valkyrie, black Chiron."

"Nice," Noah says.

Vela inclines her head to me so slightly that I almost don't see it, and she circles around and heads for the exit, presumably to join the celebration in the ballroom. Just before she disappears out the back, she turns toward me and offers what appears to be a genuine smile. I return it. Our mothers hated one another, but hopefully some grudges can die with Mom.

"Melamecha," I say. "Welcome to Ni'ihau, and thank you for coming." I'm surprised she came instead of sending her daughter Venagra, who's only two years younger than me, but perhaps she wanted to take my measure herself.

"I've noticed your mother's ring," she says.

I glance down to where it flashes angrily on my hand. I'm not sure how to address her implied question, because I'm not sure when to reveal my reaction to it, if ever. "Yes, it's a beautiful stone, as is yours." I look pointedly at the ring on her finger, which is barely illuminated at all, the refracting light is so gentle.

"Why does it flash like that?" She leans closer to whisper in my ear. "Is it the real ring? I hear there was some kind of complication, and wondered whether you recovered it."

I slide the ring off my finger and watch her eyes widen when it turns black. I slide it back on and the colors flash even more vibrantly. "It's authentic."

She waves her hand and her Consort, Michael, lugs a chest up the steps and drops it at my feet. "It's always frustrating to be stuck using jewelry and crowns fashioned in a completely outdated era by your mother or grandmother," Melamecha says. "Russia has a surplus of precious stones, so I thought I could get you started on fashioning pieces to your taste."

Michael flips the lid open to display the impressive cache of precious stones. Emeralds the size of my thumb, diamonds of nearly the same size, alexandrite, jade, amethyst, garnets, and even a few sapphires.

"What a thoughtful and generous gift," I say. "Thank you."

Melamecha tilts her head and I return the motion. She and Michael exit via the same path Vela took, but neither of them turns back around.

Analessa approaches next, entirely alone as she climbs the steps. "Chancery, you look magnificent. I'm sure you'll handle the many challenges you'll face with aplomb."

She's sure I will? Could she be any more condescending? And 'many challenges' sounds vaguely threatening. "I'm lucky to be surrounded by a very supportive Council," I say. "Including your brother Edam, for instance."

She flinches. Good. She hands me a box. I open it and lift a bundle of woven straps out. "Zeus?" The name's engraved on a gold plate on the side of a purple halter.

"You may know that I adore horses," she says. "And I heard you went riding often before your mother's passing. I've arranged to have a dozen of my best horses brought to your stable here, or anywhere else you'd like."

My eyes light up. She may be threatening and a little

prickly, but I do adore a good ride when I have time. "Thank you. What a thoughtful gift. I assume one of them is named Zeus?"

"Yes, he's the finest colt we've had from my most valued stallion, Cronus."

As a bonus, she gets in a subtle jab that she's stronger than me. But Zeus topples Cronus eventually.

"Don't read anything into that," Analessa says quickly. "I named him long before I had any intention of giving him to you." She drops her voice. "But you're in the middle of a viper pit, and I thought you should know you have allies. Your mother and mine were dear friends right up until her recent death. It's my hope that we will be the same." She glances pointedly at Edam. "And I know you value my brother's *friendship* already."

"I certainly do." I want to tell her that I value him far more than I trust her, but discretion is supposed to be the better part of valor. She is right that I need allies, and when I start making unpopular proclamations, I'll need them more than ever. Assuming her good wishes survive my rebellion against the evian status quo. "Thank you for this very generous gift. I'll love them, I'm sure."

"If you ever need anything," she says, "day or night, please call me."

I lift my eyebrows.

"I'm sure you have the main Malessa phone number, but Edam has my private line. Tell him to share it with you."

She's poking to see whether this surprises me, but I'm improving. I don't acknowledge that I knew, but neither does my heart accelerate, my perspiration spike, or my face twitch. "I so appreciate that offer."

She tilts her head in the same way Melamecha did, so I reciprocate. I don't recall Mother ever doing that, but I

BRIDGET E. BAKER

wasn't paying nearly enough attention to Mom's interactions with the Five.

Ranana walks up the steps and drops into a very slight bow. "Congratulations on your successful coronation." She gestures and two of her guards lift a very large painting onto the dais and carefully remove the brown wrapping.

When Botticelli's *The Birth of Venus* is revealed, I can't quite help my delighted gasp.

"I hope you like it," Ranana says. "Mother sends her condolences that she could not come to welcome the newest empress herself, but other pressing matters kept her at home. She didn't want her absence to be perceived as a slight."

I shake my head. "Not at all."

"She also felt that Venus resembles you in many ways. Botticelli was influenced by your mother when he painted it, you know."

"I had no idea." I study the image for a moment. I do see elements of Mom's face in Venus, although I certainly hope Mom didn't pose nude. The idea makes me smile. Mom would never have even considered that, especially not for a half-evian. "Frederick, please take this to my chambers."

He salutes me and bounces up the steps, along with Arlington, and the two of them reverently carry it out of the throne room.

Ranana scowled at me during the majority of the coronation. I'm baffled by her welcoming greeting and impressive gift. I watch her departure closely, but she doesn't spare me a backward glance.

Melisania strolls forward and takes the stairs slowly, not reaching the top until Ranana and all of her people are gone. She extends her hand to me, and when I take it, she

48

pulls me in for an embrace. "I'm very sorry for your loss," she says.

"Thank you."

"I wanted to do more than offer you a simple gift. I wanted to offer you something that might actually help."

I lift my eyebrows.

Melisania reaches into her shoulder bag and pulls out a thick sheaf of papers. "We trade a lot of food items, Alamecha and Lenora. We value that relationship, and I want it to continue." She hands the papers to me. "Look over these and compare them to our current trade agreements. You'll find that it's nearly thirty percent better for your bottom line than our current terms. I'm willing to extend you that courtesy for the first three years, until you're on your feet and in fighting shape."

"It'll take me some time to analyze—"

"Of course it will. I don't expect you to do anything today, or tomorrow, or even next week. Once you have time to evaluate what I'm telling you, sign and return the papers. I noticed you chose Maxmillian to handle this type of thing, and I heartily approve. He's a shrewd negotiator, and I promise, this will even meet with his approval."

"Thank you," I say again, and this time I mean it.

After Melisania heads over for the celebration, I breathe a sigh of relief. I'm stuck here accepting many, many more well wishes, but the most complicated are through. By the time I accept my last gold bar, fabulous diamond necklace, and overpowered sports car, it's time for me to head over to the celebration. I'm supposed to be happy that I'm the new empress. But really, I wish I could dismiss the people on my Council who are still hanging around to support me and sneak across the hall to my room to change into pajamas and go to bed. I'm sick of this kind of pomp in every circumstance. Like everything else, I'm discovering that it's thoroughly taxing. I wonder whether Judica hated these stupid parties as much as I do.

I wonder whether she's alive to hate anything.

"Larena," I say.

She makes her way to my side. "Yes, Your Majesty?"

"Did we hear anything from Alora?"

She shakes her head.

"Draw up a summons for Alora and see that it's delivered immediately. It should require she attend me immediately, with an explanation for past acts prepared. Tell her if she doesn't come to see me in the next three days, I'll bomb her out of existence, never mind the collateral damage. Her half-evian children won't survive something like that."

Inara's sly smile tells me she's pleased with my reaction. Maybe I'm learning, or maybe not. I really hope Alora doesn't call my bluff.

"Marselle?"

She's waiting near the door a few dozen yards away, but she hastens over. I lower my voice once she's close. "Any word of Judica or Angel's whereabouts?"

"I know you're worried that the two of them worked together to poison your mother, but I don't think that's likely. By all counts, no love was lost between your twin and Angel during the investigation. I think it's more likely that the same person took both, or one of them took the other."

I bob my head. "Balthasar said the same. I'm hoping Judica's alive, actually, and not in danger. But if she is, I want to figure it out ASAP."

"Understood," Marselle says. "I'll check in on my assets immediately and let you know." She turns to leave and I square my shoulders in preparation to join the party in my honor.

"Wait," Marselle barks.

I spin back around to face her.

"This isn't about Judica." Marselle stares at her phone. "But it is about Melina."

"What is it?" I ask.

"Unusual activity at her compound. Doubled guards and several bizarre supply orders."

"Like what?" I shift uneasily.

"Horse tranquilizers, for one, and a shipment of weapons."

I shake my head. "Why? Because I've been named Empress?"

Marselle shrugs. "No one has heard anything from her for years now. Your guess is as good as mine."

Great. I've been queen for an hour, and I may need to prepare for a civil war.

❧ 4 ❧

Puppy breath and a very sloppy tongue on my face wake me up. "Oh, come on Red Bull. It's too early for you to be slobbering all over me."

Edam insisted on sleeping on the sofa in my room again so Red Bull wouldn't ruin my night. Apparently he woke Edam up a dozen times the night before. "Blast." Edam leaps to his feet. "I'm so sorry I didn't hear him before he woke you."

Edam's looks aren't marred by poor sleep, bed head, or bleariness. He looks just as gorgeous as he always does, with his short blond hair perfectly styled, and his deep blue eyes clear and alert. Even his pajama shirt, clinging to his sculpted shoulders, chest, and abdominals, looks wrinkle free.

I glance down at my flannel shirt and pants and cringe a little inside. "I'll take him out. It's fine."

Duchess lifts her head when I sit up and stretches her paws out in front of her. She whimpers and wuffs softly as she stretches her back legs too, one at a time. I scratch her under her chin and swing my legs out from under the covers.

It's strange to have a dog that resembles a huge, shaggy white bear on my left side, and a bouncy, circle-spinning, tail-snapping bundle of silver muscle on my left, but it's calming somehow, too. "Thanks," I say.

"For what?" Edam yawns.

Oh great. Now I'm yawning too. "For Red Bull."

"You mean Dart?" Edam winks. "You're welcome."

By the time I open the back door, Edam's standing right behind me. "You're coming?"

He shrugs. "Why not?"

I walk through my back door and past the guards. I'm becoming more accustomed to them being everywhere, but it's still annoying. Edam and I walk to the furthest edge of the courtyard, where our view of the guards is obscured by riotously blooming hibiscus.

Red Bull pees, then frolics and frolics, chasing a butterfly that is confused about the time of day because of the courtyard light. Duchess watches him with one eyebrow raised, like she's somewhat embarrassed he's acting so goofy, and somewhat amused at the same time.

"It's so nice to see you smiling," Edam says. "I haven't seen much of that recently."

I duck my head, embarrassed.

"The duties of an empress can consume you," Edam says. "You need to make sure you carve out some time for things you enjoy."

"Like what?" I ask.

He steps closer and reaches toward my face. He casually tucks my hair behind my ear, but when his fingers brush the top of my ear, I shiver. "Reading, maybe. I used to see you out here reading a few afternoons a week."

"Or?"

"Riding Napoleon. Every time I saw you thundering down the beach, it took my breath away."

"Or?"

"Or anything else that makes you happy." He steps closer still, our faces separated by mere inches, our bodies nearly touching.

"Like eating tacos, you mean?" I ask.

He chuckles and his chest swells. "Sure. Like tacos, if they're spicy enough for you." He leans down slowly, his lips nearing mine and the air thickens around us until I can barely breathe. When his lips brush against mine, the shiver that races up my spine eclipses the one I felt before like the sun to the moon, like a habanero to a bell pepper, like a tiger to a tabby. His arms circle mine, his mouth consuming me, lifting me up, and devouring me at once.

I realize, for the first time ever, that his heart is racing too, his pulse much faster than usual. His hand trembles at my waist, bunching the material of my flannel pajamas tightly. I want him to yank me closer, to need me like I need him.

But his soft groan, low and urgent, is almost as good. My fingers tighten on his sleeve and wrap around the muscle of his triceps, pulling him closer, answering his desire with my own. The sound of water spraying in a place where there shouldn't be any water at all brings me back to reality and I freeze, speaking against his full lips. "What's that noise?"

Edam leaps backward. "Oh, no, Dart, no. Bad boy."

Red Bull peed on his foot. I can't contain my laughter. "That's what you get for calling him Dart."

Edam starts to laugh too, his pee-soaked foot already forgiven.

"Puppies are a mess."

Edam nods. "They sure are."

"Remind me again why I have one?"

"Because he makes you smile," he says, "and if we're lucky, he'll make you laugh like that again."

One of my guards clears his throat.

"Yes?" I ask. "Is anything wrong?"

Bellatrius walks around the hibiscus. "A message from Balthasar." She hands me a slip of paper.

"We really need to get that guy a cell phone and teach him to text," I say.

Bellatrius doesn't smile. Crap, what if it's serious? I unfold the paper and read the message: *Roman is gone.*

He doesn't say that Judica's alive, but he doesn't have to spell it out. When I hand the paper to Edam, the wheels in my head are already turning. If the man Judica chose as head of her personal guard after Edam left has vanished, it's because she summoned him to her side. It's too coincidental to be plausible that he disappeared for any other reason.

"We need to track his phone calls," Edam says, striding back toward the palace. "We can find her now."

"Stop," I say. "If my sister fled, I won't drag her back. And if she needs help, well, she chose not to call me about it. She called Roman." It shouldn't sting, that she doesn't trust me, but for some reason it does.

"What are you saying?" Edam asks.

"Leave it alone for now. If we have any evidence that she's attempting to raise an army, or if she joins forces with Melina or someone else. . ." I can't quite bring myself to name Alora. "Well, then we'll start talking about options. But for now, I told her she was free. If she ran as fast as she could away from here, well, I understand the sentiment."

Edam opens his mouth, and then closes it without saying a word.

"Tell Balthasar I'd like to talk with him over breakfast. We can discuss this then, if you'd care to come."

"I'll be there," Edam says.

The sun is rising on the horizon, so I don't even try to regain the sleep I lost. I run through my melodics forms instead, take a shower, and change into fresh training gear. I finally feel ready to discuss whether my first instinct was correct with regard to Judica. I put Red Bull in his crate and take Duchess with me to the breakfast room. I've been eating breakfast in the same room for my entire life, and until today, I didn't realize how much I have come to rely on the spread Angel laid for us.

We had four or five egg dishes, waffles, pancakes or French toast, and a platter of beautifully displayed fruit every single morning. Steaming cups of hot chocolate and coffee magically waited when I arrived, always. Carafes of fresh-squeezed orange juice, freshly pureed mango smoothies, and freshly pressed apple juice were always right next to them.

Today when I walk in, Balthasar is poking at a pile of brown-flecked scrambled eggs with a curled lip.

"Did you ask for those to be so . . . well done?" I joke.

Balthasar glances back at me. "Did it occur to you to check whether Lark has any culinary talent before naming her as your chef?"

I bite my lip. "She'll improve. I'm sure she will."

"She better, or I'm going to have to eat instant oatmeal and jerky in my room." Balthasar closes his eyes and scoops up a big bite of scrambled eggs. He chews with a truly pitiful expression on his face.

Edam takes the whole scene in as he walks in the door. "Lark's off to a bumpy start, then?"

"It looks that way. And there's literally no other food. Does she know we're ready for breakfast?" I ask Balthasar.

He shrugs. "She came in and asked me what I wanted a few minutes ago. Right before you arrived, one of her people brought this." He shoves an empty plate to the middle of the table.

"Was it good?" I ask, hopeful.

Balthasar opens his mouth and then closes it.

"Well, you ate it." I sit down. "I'll talk to her, but hopefully she'll bring more food soon."

"I wouldn't hold my breath," Balthasar mutters.

"I asked you to come here to discuss the Roman situation," I say. "My inclination is to let it go. If my sister needs his help, well, as my heir, she should have it. I take it as a good sign that she's likely alive."

Balthasar frowns. "I'm worried that it means she's trying to build a military force to challenge you."

"She can legally challenge me again as Heir in two months' time."

"Judica won't try the same thing that didn't work last time," Balthasar says. "She would change tactics."

"You think she's assembling an army to attack Ni'ihau?" I ask.

"I doubt that," Edam says. "It's not like her to sneak around, and I don't think she'd attack her own people, not now anyway. My guess is that after her defeat, or when reality sunk in, she decided life would be easier a little further from you."

"She should have requested leave," I say, "and asked if she could take Roman. I can't have people leaving their positions willy-nilly and flying all over the place with members of the guard. He took a jet, I assume?"

Balthasar nods. "Signed it out as official business of the Heir."

"So he definitely went to help her," I say. "That's good news. Even if she's going to try and stand against me, I'm relieved she isn't dead."

"I recommend you allow Roman three days to sort this and get in contact with us one way or another," Balthasar says. "If we haven't heard from him by then, we track them down and enforce our protocols."

"I agree," Edam says. "But no more than three days."

My stomach rumbles. As if on cue, the doors open and several servers walk through the door with Lark on their heels. "Sorry this is late. I swear I'll get better," she says. "But I brought pancakes *and* waffles, and only two kinds of eggs." She beams at me, but her eyes are tired.

I stand up and walk into the hall. "Follow me outside for a moment, Lark. Will you?"

"Of course Your Majesty."

Once we're in the hall, my guards catch my eye. They aren't looking at us, but they can clearly hear us. I'd prefer not to interrogate Lark about this in front of them. It'll spread like wildfire. I clear my throat and address them directly. "Balthasar and Edam are both within shouting distance and I'm standing in a main hallway. Please duck into the breakfast room for a moment and ensure the serving staff remains inside as well," I say. "I need a moment with Lark."

They disappear without argument.

"What's going on?" I ask.

Lark shakes her head. "Everything is fine." She runs a hand over her hair, probably checking to make sure it's all pulled back and no stray hairs could work their way into any food items. Angel used to do the same thing. It might have reassured me, the consistency of their actions, one chef and now another. Except when she does that, her sleeve rides up and I notice faint bruising on her wrist.

"We aren't going inside until you tell me what's going

on. That's not a request from your best friend. It's an order from your queen."

Lark's lower lip wobbles. "I'm so grateful to you for you championing me, but it might be easier if you placed me somewhere else and assigned someone else to this position."

"You mean you'd rather not be on my Council?" I can't keep the surprise out of my tone.

"Here's the thing. As the poster child for half-evian rights, I'm delighted for this chance. The visibility will surely help, as well as the visual of me standing at your side. But. . ."

"But being on the bleeding edge takes its toll."

Her eyes are sad. "What if I'm not strong enough?"

"The kitchen staff aren't pleased that a half-evian is their boss." In spite of my desire to keep this private, anger causes my voice to bounce off the walls, like rocks hitting pavement.

She shrugs but doesn't argue.

I duck my head inside the breakfast room where the kitchen servers are waiting patiently until they can return to the hallway their monarch is using. "Let's take a little field trip right now," I say. "To the kitchen. I just realized I haven't spent much time there since Mom—" I clear my throat.

The three of them bow and follow me out the door, my guards not two steps behind them.

I don't say a word as we walk to the kitchen. I don't slap anyone. I don't pull the sword off my back and do any of the things I want to do with it. I am not Chancery the Merciless. I am not Chancery the Avenging Angel. I am Chancery the Merciful.

The trouble is, I'm not feeling very merciful.

Lark trails behind me dutifully, as do the guards and her

servers, but Edam and Balthasar quickly fall into step beside me.

"What's going on?" Balthasar asks.

"Is something wrong?" Edam asks.

"I don't need back up for this, boys. Stay in the hall with the guards, please."

"Of course," Edam says.

I hang a left into the kitchen and raise my voice as loud as I can make it. "All kitchen and serving staff report front and center in the prep room. Immediately."

It takes a few minutes, but they all appear. "Stand in lines with the shortest in front. I want you to all be able to see me."

"Is something wrong?" a redhead I don't recognize asks.

I turn to Lark. "Is everyone here?"

Lark surveys the assembled personnel, counting silently. She nods.

"Great, we're all here. I'd like to tell you how much I appreciate your selfless service. I appreciate your hard work, your dedication, and your excellence. I don't always do a wonderful job of telling the people I rely on what their hard work means to me, but I know you strive to provide the very best of everything."

Their faces relax. Good.

"I didn't take the time to introduce you to your new head chef after the coronation yesterday. That was a major oversight on my part. My best friend Lark never planned to become a chef, but she makes some of the best soufflés I have ever had. And this morning, as I stared at my War Chief's pile of burned, poorly beaten eggs, lacking in garnish and presentation, I thought, 'Wow! How did my best friend in the entire world make such a mess of things?'"

I meet their eyes, one-by-one.

"That's when I realized that of course poor Lark didn't make those eggs herself—she has an extensive staff. So I'm here to inquire: Are you incompetent, or are you intentionally underperforming?"

Jaws drop. Eyes widen. Heart rates spike. The smell of perspiration hits me like a wall.

I unsheathe my sword. "You've seen Enora decapitate someone because they violated a single law. In fact, you recently saw her behead Lark's mother. That may have given you the wrong impression of the way of things. I'd like to set the score straight. I'll only say this one time, so listen closely. I am reversing Mom's positions on half-evians. I would never have executed Lyssa for sheltering the truth that I don't find to be disappointing or shocking about my dearest friend. I don't believe Lark has a single thing to be embarrassed or ashamed about. But I promise you this. I am enough like my mom that I *will* execute the next person I discover is not jumping when Lark says jump."

I step closer, and at least five of the staff flinches. "I will separate your head from your shoulders if you so much as imply that she is less than any of you because of her father's DNA. And if you burn eggs, or pancakes, or toast again in an attempt to make her look bad, I'll torture you before I do it." I slow down and over-enunciate each word. "Am I being clear enough?"

Wide-eyed faces nod.

"And in case you don't already know this, the cameras mounted in these rooms are active. If there's any question of what one of you said or did or whether you looked at her sideways, I'll be the judge, jury, and *literal* executioner. Let me repeat for those of you who aren't very bright: Lark is my best friend in the world, and she's your boss. Either of those things should be more than enough reason for you to follow her without complaint. Apparently some of you didn't understand the shift in the power dynamic in Alamecha, but I hope that this has cleared that up for you."

I sheathe my sword, pivot on my heel, and walk back toward the breakfast room. Lark practically chases me down the hall. I finally stop so she can say what she needs to say.

"How did you know?"

"I didn't know," I say. "In fact, other than a few times you and I played around with Angel making soufflés, I've never seen you cook a single thing."

"But back there—"

"You may not be an excellent chef, I have no idea. But you're bright enough to know not to send something like that out to the dining room. When I saw your bruises, I realized I've been an idiot. I'm sorry I didn't anticipate the kind of heat you'd be taking right now. It's scary to be the face of a movement." I touch her cheek. "But if anyone is strong enough to do it, beautiful enough, brilliant enough, it's you."

"I'm not sure."

"Give me a few more days, but if it's still too much, I'll reassign you, I swear." I can barely force the next words out. "Even if what you want is to be reassigned to New York, or Los Angeles, or somewhere that's not here."

She nods resolutely, and heads back for the kitchen.

"Can I just say how utterly awesome that was?" Edam asks. "I am *so* going to pull the video on that and watch it later."

Balthasar grins.

"What's so funny?" I ask.

"Your mother would be popping buttons, she'd be so proud right now," Balthasar says.

I pause at the door into the breakfast room. "I'm reversing her laws."

Balthasar shrugs. "You're queen. Enora knew you'd govern differently than she did. She turned the world on its head in her time, you know. You were magnificent in there, the spitting image of your mother when she was your age."

We go inside and eat surprisingly edible food. Maybe Lark had it under control and would have figured it out without me. Either way, they can be in no doubt that I support her now.

"Now that we've all had our share of excitement for the morning, I think it's time to develop a training plan for you, Your Majesty," Balthasar says.

"That falls under my purview," Edam says, "as Chief Security Officer."

Balthasar leans back in his chair and lifts his chin. "You may have the title kid, but you're in way over your head. I can ease you into this."

The vein in Edam's temple throbs.

I lay both hands on the table before he can leap across it. "Why don't we let Balthasar tell us what he has in mind, and his reasons, and then Edam, you will make the final decision. But of course, we all want the same thing—for me to catch up on everything I need to know in order to effectively govern."

"And for you to be able to protect yourself," Balthasar says.

"Right," I agree. "That too."

"Well," Balthasar says, "then I think your biggest liability right now is your inability to engage in combat with more than one enemy at a time. Very few people will send an attack force of one in your direction."

Edam shakes his head. "She's remedial in pain, healing, poison, and torture training. Those should come first."

Balthasar rolls his eyes, just like every irritated high school girl on human television programs. I will not laugh at my War Lord. I will not laugh at my War Lord, even when he acts like a baby.

Mom would totally have laughed. The pain of missing her claws at my lungs until I struggle to breathe.

"We can't delay multi-opponent," Balthasar finally says. "Because it's the biggest threat. I say you spend an hour on that every day, half an hour on individual combat, and then half an hour each on the others. That will barely leave her time to do everything else she needs to accomplish."

"We can't work her to death, either," Edam says. "She needs to have some unscheduled time."

"I don't disagree," Balthasar says. "In fact, I've been thinking about that. She should be dating. She needs choices in order to choose the right Consort, and if she's spending every second training with you, how will she ever find any?" Balthasar smirks.

Check and mate, old man.

Edam's eye twitches, but he doesn't disagree. At least, not out loud.

"What exactly is the point of multi-opponent?" I ask. "I mean, I get why you want me to learn it, but what are the basic principles?"

"You need to learn to distract the group and focus on one person at a time, disabling them before moving to the next," Edam says. "As well as knowing positioning and defense strategies when you're in a bind."

"So it's sort of like the healing and pain training, in that I'm learning what things to focus on and what to ignore, all without losing my focus."

"Very good," Balthasar beams. "Shame on your mother for keeping your training mostly to herself."

"Edam, I'll block off two hours a day for training, and you can split it out any way you'd like," I say.

Edam nods. "That will be sufficient, or at least, I'll make it work. We may combine some disciplines to save time."

"Wait, like what?" I ask.

Edam's smile looks at least half evil. "Well, pain training goes hand-in-hand with multi-opponent, obviously."

Arlington throws the door open and runs through it, panting. "I have a message," he says. "It's urgent."

"Where is it?" Balthasar asks.

Arlington takes another deep breath and stands up straight. "It's not written." He blinks several times. "Malessa is attacking Puerto Rico."

Balthasar swears, leaps to his feet, and roars like a lion. "How dare Analessa do any such thing?"

I close my eyes. I knew the Five would test me, but I had hoped for a little more time before they did. Then the full import of the words sink in. "Wait, Malessa?"

Arlington nods.

My eyes slowly slide around the room until they meet Edam's. Yesterday his sister told me she knew I'd handle the many challenges coming my way with aplomb. Now she's attacking me. I should be worried about my people, my holdings, whether others might attack, and whether she's part of a coordinated attack across my holdings by more than one family.

But all I can think about is whether Edam knew, and how I can possibly trust him when he denies it.

5

"The majority of the bases we've had in Puerto Rico over the years have been decommissioned," Balthasar says. "Mostly because our aircraft no longer need it as a stop-over."

"So what was left?" I ask. "What exactly did Malessa do?"

Zira takes over at this point, one muscular arm extending to point at a map projected on the wall. "As we understand it, Analessa's main force struck Fort Buchanan and the Muñiz Air Force Base simultaneously."

I close my eyes. "Do we have a casualty count?"

"Preliminary estimates only," Zira says.

"And?" I ask.

"Somewhere between eight and ten thousand, but they're all humans."

I grit my teeth. All humans, said with relief, as if they don't really count. How am I supposed to change the way my people value humans? It's a pervasive mindset, too, taught to them since birth, which is centuries for most of them.

I'll have to do it the same way I would eat an elephant, I suppose. One bite at a time.

"I have pressing business." I stand up. "Please discuss our options and when I return, I'll hear your suggestions for how to react and choose from among them." I spin toward Zira and place my hands on the table in front of her. "I expect these options to minimize casualties, regardless of whether we're talking evian or human. Is that clear?"

She gulps. "Clear."

"Good."

Edam jumps up from the table and follows me out.

"I think they'll need your input in there," I say.

He puts a hand on my arm. "Where are you going?"

I yank my arm back. "I'm sorry, am I accountable to you?"

The hurt in his eyes cuts at me, but what if it's all part of his act? "No, of course not."

"I'm going for a run, okay? It helps me think."

He nods. "I'm happy to accompany you."

So he can tell his sister how upset I am? I shake my head. "They need you in there. I'll be back shortly."

"Take guards and be safe," he says softly, his eyes wounded.

"I will, I swear."

The second Edam disappears back into the War Room, I call for a guard. "Bellatrius?"

She steps closer.

"Find Noah and bring him to my room. Tell him we're going for a run."

"Yes, Your Majesty." She bows and sets off at a jog down the hall. One of the advantages of the new four guard schedule is that they don't balk at leaving me when I send one to carry a message.

When Duchess and I reach my room, Red Bull is a

whiny mess. I take him outside for a break. As I watch his antics I think about Edam bringing me a puppy. Sleeping in my room to take care of him. I think about the times he's trained me, the times he's joked with me, the way he watches over me.

Edam couldn't have been involved or even aware of his sister's plan. He couldn't, not now, not anymore. Right?

After I change into running clothes and shoes, there's a tap at my door.

"Come in," I say.

Noah saunters through the door. "You called, princess?"

Bellatrius arches an eyebrow imperiously. "She's not a princess. She's Empress of the First Family."

"It's fine," I say, "really."

Bellatrius crosses her arms over her chest and raises one eyebrow imperiously.

"Noah and I are going for a run. Two guards will trail us," I say, "and two will remain here with Red Bull. I shouldn't put him back in his kennel right now, and he can't wander around alone."

"Puppy sitting?" Arlington asks.

"It's what I need right now," I say.

"Three of us accompany you, and one of us stays," Arlington says, bargaining for my safety.

I toss my hands into the air. "Fine, whatever."

Noah follows me through my room, into the courtyard, and out the gate.

"Why'd you want to bring me along?" Noah says. "Feeling a little out of shape? Need an excuse to slow down a bit?"

"I noticed you were getting a little squishy around the middle," I say. "Figured with the amazing food around here, you could use the workout."

"Ouch," he says. "But seriously."

I listen to the slap of our shoes on the sand for a moment. "Malessa attacked Puerto Rico."

"Attacked sounds bad, but I'm afraid I don't entirely understand what you're saying. Who, exactly, is Malessa?"

"I'm sorry," I say. "I'll send some materials to your room for you to study, basics about evian life."

"Okay, but for now, maybe a little primer."

"Of course," I say. "Malessa was the second youngest daughter of Mahalesh, who was Eve's youngest daughter. She was given one of the pieces of staridium, the stone cut from the mountain, by Mahalesh herself. Alamecha, my ancestress, was given this one." I hold up my ring to show him.

"Okay."

"Analessa is the current leader of the Malessa family. She's also Edam's sister."

"Right," Noah says. "The one who he was talking to before your mom passed."

"Correct, and now his sister's attacking one of our protectorates that isn't well defended and doesn't have many resources. It's clearly a statement, or the throwing of a gauntlet, if you will."

"Sure," Noah says. "My family does the same thing."

"Excuse me?" I ask.

Noah shrugs. "They don't, like, attack anyone, obviously. What I mean is, when Dad wants to acquire a business, he usually starts with one of their weakest holdings. Then he systematically applies pressure to other vulnerabilities until they topple like dominoes."

"You think Analessa won't stop with Puerto Rico." I start jogging again.

Noah follows me, breathing heavy by the time he catches up.

I slow down, but only a hair.

"I don't know Edam's sister, so I can't really say. But if I were attacking you, I wouldn't."

I swear under my breath and immediately feel guilty. Mom hated crude language. The crutch of the uneducated, she always called it.

"But what about Edam?" I ask. "How do I know whether I can trust him?"

Noah doesn't answer at first, and I think maybe he didn't hear me.

"What about—"

"I'm thinking," he says. "Give me a minute. Slow human brain, remember?"

"Okay."

"Here's the thing." Noah reaches the top of the highest point in Ni'ihau and stops to look out over the ocean spread before us. "I want to tell you that Edam's probably a spy for Malessa, because I completely understand your concerns. And it's no secret that guy bugs me. But."

"But what?"

"I can't tell you that."

"Okay."

"I've seen how he looks at you when you're preoccupied." Noah turns a little more, casting shadows over his features. "He pines for you."

"I don't understand."

"He adores you," Noah says. "His fury is immediate and real when someone else disparages you, or hurts you. He would mow them all down with his swords if you'd let him. Turn them into some kind of nasty potpourri."

"I don't doubt that he has a crush on me," I say. "My question is, can I trust—"

Noah cuts me off. "No, I must not have been clear. Edam does not have a crush. That boy is one hundred and fifty percent head over heels. He's in love with you, so for him to betray you to his sister? I don't know. He'd have to have multiple personalities or something."

"You think I can trust him?"

Noah sighs melodramatically. "I wish I didn't, but yes, I think you can trust him. I really, really doubt if any of this had anything to do with him."

I'd feel better about Noah's assessment if it wasn't exactly what I wanted to hear. If I've learned anything from my mom, it's that a queen can't believe in something just because she wants to. "I better head back," I say. "I've got training later, and some big decisions to make about how to handle this attack, but this was very helpful. Thanks."

"Speaking of your training," Noah says. "Who knows about your super powers?"

"My what?"

Noah points at the ring on my finger. "Who knows what you can do with that?"

I shake my head. "Inara, Judica, and you. And anyone else they've told, I suppose."

"Holy moly, really? That's it? What about Edam?"

"He may guess something—he knows what everyone else does. Mom hadn't chosen me, then there was an EMP, and then Mom picked me. He also knows I used something to knock out that bomb over the Pacific."

"Why not tell everyone? Maybe the other evian queens would be less likely to attack if they knew. Didn't you say it had some kind of epic meaning for your people? Like there's a prophecy or something?"

"Mom believed it did, but I wonder whether that wasn't wishful thinking. I'm not convinced it even lines up with the promises of the dumb prophecy by Eve. But even if it does, I'm not sure that *I'm* the Eldest it mentions. It would be ridiculous of me to announce something to the other rulers that I'm not even positive about myself."

"You're scared."

I splutter. "Are you kidding?"

"Not at all, but I've known you for a while now. When you want to avoid something, you make up a lot of straw man excuses. They always sound just like this."

"Excuses for not telling every evian ruler on the first day of my rule that I expect them to bow at my feet? Come on, Noah. That's not reasonable."

He stops and points at my ring. "This isn't reasonable. You took out three planes with nothing but that rock. Four if you count ours, not to mention the first blast that convinced your mother."

"I appreciate your input on that," I say. "But it's not the time to run around issuing ultimatums to the evian queens, not when I'm being attacked. A fight I'm actually losing at present."

"Are you at least training with it?" he asks.

"Training with what?"

"Chancery." Noah stares at me for a minute. "Think about this. If I gave you a sword and said you can activate a fire power, and a poison power, and an ice power on it, but it was complicated to figure out, would you stick it into a sheath on your back and never give it another thought?"

"An *ice* power?"

Noah huffs. "Focus. That's all made up, but that ring isn't. You're wearing something that to anyone else is a nice piece of jewelry, but for you, *it's a weapon*, and you're not even studying how to use it." He shakes his head. "You're definitely scared, because you should be investigating this."

He's right. Maybe I blocked the whole concept since the only work I've done with it was with my mom, right before she died. "I probably should, as soon as I get things under control."

"I know you're stressed, and I know I'm suggesting you

toss one more obligation on the pile, but I really think this should be near the top of the list. Whether you believe this came from God or not, it's clearly got some kind of value. If that prophecy you're so dismissive of turns out to be something, you'll need to know how to use the gift you were given."

"Duly noted," I say. "I suppose there's no time like the present to get started."

Noah's eyes light up. "You're going to practice with it right now?"

I nod. "But not here. Down in the bunker Mom set up. Then whatever I do won't decimate the rest of the island."

"Oh good. I'm glad you have a plan."

"Would you come with me? Be my trainer for this?"

"Will I help you figure out the limits of your super power?" Noah throws one fist up in the air. "Heck yes I will."

With Noah's help and suggestions, I manage to refine my range a little. We don't discover any new powers, and I still can't always control when or where my attempts result in a fire, but I can feel the difference between the two—the EMP and the heat blast. Noah has no idea what I'm doing, but he's pretty handy with a fire extinguisher, so I don't burn the bunker to the ground.

"I absolutely have to report for my training and make some kind of decision about Puerto Rico," I say. "But thank you for the perspective."

"Sometimes it helps to have friends in low places," Noah says. "And for what it's worth, I trust you to make the right decision. Unlike the people who have been trained their entire lives, you still remember how to listen to what your heart says."

"Which is why I make so many mistakes," I say softly.

Noah bites his lip. "At the risk of sounding unbearably

cheesy, I've seen you sad, angry, scared, happy, and nervous. But no matter the circumstances you've faced, or the magnitude of the stakes, you've never done the wrong thing."

"Except when I didn't notice my mom was sick. Or when I let Judica escape and start to build an army." I shake my head. "Or how about when I left Ni'ihau alone to disable the planes and die out there. It didn't even occur to me to turn the planes around and fly away from the target."

"That might be your most impressive trait of all," Noah says. "You don't have to come up with all the answers yourself. You listen to the people around you and think things through before acting."

I also tell the people around me when I make a mistake, undermining their confidence in my abilities. My entire Council thinks I'm a complete screw up. And what's worse, I agree with them.

"Thanks," I say.

Noah shrugs. "You don't believe me yet, but you will. Good luck today."

The War Room is packed when I return. Balthasar's gesturing and Edam's drawing lines on a white board.

I clear my throat. "So, about those options?"

Edam shakes his head. "We aren't ready yet. We need another hour or so, and a little more information that we should have shortly."

"The kid's correct," Balthasar says. "But I don't need him here. He's not in charge of war. I am."

"Maybe this is a good chance for Edam to work with me on my training then," I say.

"Multi-opponent training falls under my purview," Balthasar says. "Because it's combat training."

I throw my hands up in the air. "You can't be everywhere all the time."

He grunts. "Fine. Go with him." He pins Edam with a hard stare. "But don't screw this up."

I duck back into the hallway and Edam follows. I'm relieved he didn't punch Balthasar on his way past. The last thing I need is to have my top military minds challenging one another.

"Why do you smell like Noah?" Edam asks.

"Because he's pretty heavy handed on the cologne?"

Edam grunts exactly like Balthasar just did. "Went for a run with him, did you?"

"It's nice to have someone to talk to about things. An outside observer."

"And you can't trust me, since my sister's the one attacking." Edam's voice is flat, his eyes guarded.

"Your sister is attacking me, yes."

Edam's shoulders tense. "I had no idea, Chancery, I swear."

"I want to believe you."

"What can I do?" he asks.

I shake my head. "There's nothing you can do."

"I'll lead the team that wrests control back," Edam says. "Then you'll see I have no qualms about fighting Analessa, none at all."

"I don't even care about regaining Puerto Rico, unless Analessa makes things worse for the people there. Mom and I disagreed fundamentally about her failure to provide support and infrastructure to the local people."

"That." Edam stops in front of the arena, his fingers touching the door handle. He turns around, pivoting inside of my personal space. "That's the reason I'm one hundred percent behind you. I have no contact with my sister, and I haven't, not since I broke up with Judica."

"Wait," I say. "What is the reason?"

"You want to do right for the people your mother

neglected. You never grow complacent about things because it's how they've always been. You may be wrong sometimes, but when you are, you admit it and move on."

I'm wrong sometimes. His words are like a slap in my face. I've already failed my mom, and it's been one day since my coronation. Everyone on my Council accepts it as fact that I mess up, that I'm wrong, that I'm borderline incompetent. How can I ever hope my people will respect me, or follow me, or obey me when they see me as a bumbling do-gooder?

"Thanks." I push past Edam into the training arena. "So what's first, boss?"

"Multi-opponent," Edam says. "With Judica's guards, since they aren't likely to take it easy on you. That way we should be able to combine pain training with the multi-opponent strategies."

"Okay."

Edam clearly planned this earlier, because Barrett and Dante walk through the door a few seconds later. Barrett sports a meaty build, with heavy muscle across his chest and over his shoulders and back. He's only an inch or two taller than me, so our reach will be comparable. Dante's even taller than Edam, but his frame is leaner, too. Both of them have shaved the sides of their heads since I last saw them to form a sort of thick Mohawk.

"What's with the hair?" I ask.

The men share a glance. "Nothing," they say at the same time.

Which means it's definitely something.

"Answer her question," Edam says.

Barrett shuffles his feet and looks at the ground. "Some of us wanted to show Judica that we support her."

Ah. So anyone who shaves their head like that would support my sister if she stands against me again. "Thanks for making it easy for me to know who I can't trust." Not that I expected her personal guard to be driving the welcome wagon for me.

Dante says, "I would never, ever betray Alamecha and you are our queen. But Judica is still Heir, and we stand with her."

"Even if she stands against me," I say.

"It's part of our law," Dante says. "That the Heir may sometimes need to stand against the queen, for the good of the family."

Edam pulls his sword, his shoulders tense, his mouth strained. He's ready to cut them into confetti. Noah might have been right.

I open my mouth to tell them I'm glad that my sister has supporters. I don't want her to feel like an outcast. But then I recall my mom's words. I can't make any mistakes. I can't show weakness. I can't do the wrong thing. "We have some training to do now," I say. "But we will discuss this later."

I'm done blurting out whatever I feel. Before I address this, I'll spend some time figuring out what I should do or say about it. I can't afford any more mistakes. Not a single one.

Edam sheathes his sword and the guys noticeably relax. "Normally we will practice with weapons," Edam says, "but for today, it's going to be hand-to-hand." He directs his attention to me. "We will gradually increase the number of fighters and the intensity of the weapons until you can handle five or more, but for today, three men without weapons will be challenging enough."

I unbuckle my sword sheath and lay it on the ground at my feet. Barrett does the same with his axes, and Edam with his swords. Dante doesn't seem to have a sword or an axe or anything at all, really, until he starts pulling knives from his boots, his belt, and his back. Three guns also appear from somewhere. The man is a walking concealed weapons depot.

We climb into the ring one at a time. Edam points at the center of the ring and I stand there.

"Your guiding principle in this style of fighting is that you can only truly engage one person at a time," Edam says. "You want to pivot, circle, back up, or advance as needed to keep from being attacked on several fronts simultaneously. You land any strikes you can to delay their hard hits, and manipulate them into an area where you can limit them to single access."

I bob my head. That makes sense.

"And never let them put you on the ground. It's better to absorb multiple strikes than let them knock you down, because it's practically impossible to get back up once you've fallen."

"Understood."

Edam cues the start, and I know what I'm supposed to be doing—figuring out how to get myself out of the middle as quickly as I can. My ring flashes particularly bright and somehow I feel like I ought to crouch. So I do. Barrett's hook swings right over my head, and I pivot and sweep his legs. Overextended from swinging wide, he topples forward to the mat. I shift out of his way, but Edam and Dante haven't been merely watching idly.

They both come at me, Edam from the side, and Dante from directly in front of me. I block Edam's jab, forcing it right into Dante. I step back away from Barrett, and Edam takes the lead, with Dante falling behind him.

"This is fun," I say.

Of course, the guys take that as encouragement. I should have kept my big mouth shut.

Edam hammers me with punches in the solar plexus,

knocking the wind out of me so quickly I can barely track what he's doing. I barely notice that Barrett's standing again before he's swinging wide to hit me from the side. I stumble back, evading Barrett and breaking free from Edam, but I'm playing defense.

I can't win by defending, no matter how well I do it.

It's only a few moments before Edam puts me into the mat and the other two pile on, kicking me repeatedly.

"That's enough," Edam says. "Pain training is one thing. Punching bag is another."

I breathe a time or two, and force myself to stand back up. "Well, that sucked."

"You did really well for your first time," Dante says.

"She actually did." Barrett's voice holds begrudging respect, which means more than all the praise in the world from a friend.

"So what do I need to improve?" I ask.

"First, let's talk about what happened with that very first move," Edam says. "Did you hear Barrett coming? How did you know to duck?"

I can't really tell them that my ring inexplicably warned me and I somehow understood it. "I guess so," I say. "Some of this is instinctual for me."

"Your instincts are amazing," Dante says. "Keep listening to them."

We do hand-to-hand on the next round as well, and I last another thirty seconds before Barrett snaps my arm. "You don't have to pull the plug at first break," I say.

"I know," Edam says, "but we're barely getting started. I'd rather not overload you at the outset."

"You can't take it easy on me," I say. "There's no time to ease me in."

The third time, they take my words to heart. Edam and Barrett draw my attention to the front, distracting me so that Dante can headlock me from behind. I completely pass out and wake up a moment later, once I've recovered from blood loss and repaired my windpipe from the interrupted air flow.

I sit up, the spots in front of my eyes clearing out, and that's when it hits me. "I know what to do about Puerto Rico," I say.

Edam offers me a hand and I leap to my feet.

"What?" he asks.

"They're expecting us to move against them to retake it."

He bobs his head. "Because it belongs to us."

"They'll be ready for anything we cook up. Instead, we should pick one of their small holdings and steal it from them. Something better than Puerto Rico, something that they won't expect, but something that will hurt."

"Not a bad idea," he says.

I grin. "And at the same time, we kidnap your niece DeLannia. Analessa won't see either of those coming, and she'll be forced to beg us to release her Heir. We only agree to return DeLannia when she vacates Puerto Rico. She was the aggressor, so we demand she gives us back our land, but we keep hers without retaliation. She started it, and we finish it by coming at her in an unexpected way." I cross my arms over my chest. "She needs to learn that she can't dictate the terms of engagement."

Edam's not the only one smiling when I finish, and for the first time since Mom died, I feel like I'm figuring this out.

6

"It's not a bad strategy," Balthasar says. "But if we do that and she's prepared at all, we'll hemorrhage troops."

"But your way," Inara says, "we'll lose a minimum of a hundred evian soldiers and an unknown number of humans to retake Puerto Rico. Iceland on the other hand is a frozen rock, and it'll be hard to pin anyone down there."

"Is Iceland our best bet?" I ask. "I mean, we could still pursue somewhere else. Besides, Iceland has a couple hundred thousand citizens, but Puerto Rico has three million, give or take. It hardly seems like a fair exchange."

"Iceland is self-sustaining," Edam says. "And Puerto Rico needs a lot of support, especially on the infrastructure."

"You're letting yourself get bogged down in small details," Balthasar says. "This is about politics more than warfare at this point. The Five will all either test you like Malessa has done, or they'll watch to see how you respond. Your idea to take two things and force yours back is brilliant, but the details of size and population are less critical."

"Then we're agreed?" I ask.

Heads nod all around.

"Good. Edam and I worked up some ideas for how to take Iceland and kidnap DeLannia," I say, "but Balthasar calls the shots on the approach, obviously."

"I'll need to spearhead Iceland," Balthasar says.

"Which leaves Edam to take point on the abduction of his niece." I watch his expression closely. "Will that be a problem? Kidnapping your sister's Heir?"

Edam shakes his head. "Not at all."

"What if I told you we might have to kill her?"

He blinks repeatedly.

"I'm not saying that," I say. "It was mostly a test. We're on the same page here. She's a bargaining tool, nothing more."

I try not to focus on how distasteful I find the entire premise that Analessa would trade her daughter's life for that of three million humans. Thinking about it merely enrages me. Although, if I had a daughter, I might do the same, I suppose. I know Mom would have.

"Whatever we're doing," Balthasar says, "we need to do it soon. It's been nearly twenty-four hours since Puerto Rico was taken. We can't delay much longer."

"You're right," I say. "I'm going to review some records in Mom's sanctum, and when I emerge, we'll finalize the plans for each leg of this campaign. Each of you need your timelines and troop selections in place. We move on them first thing tomorrow."

"Or perhaps late tonight," Edam says.

Balthasar's face flushes. "I've already told you—"

I walk out in the middle of their argument. They'll have to settle into their new roles on their own. I can't spend every second jumping in to mediate fights between the two of them.

I walk through the door to Mom's room and look around. It still hurts just to stand here, but eventually I'll need to remodel the room and make it my own. That thought makes me want to curl up and cry. For now, I pad across the floor like an intruder, stopping in front of the solid metal doors to key in the code.

A knock startles me and I type the access code wrong. The keypad bleats angrily at me and flashes blue.

"Who it is?" I ask irritably.

Noah opens the door. "I'm sorry to bother you."

"What do you need?" His face alone calms me down. He wouldn't be in here if it wasn't something important.

"Larena asked me to come and get you. Your sister is here."

Ice fills my belly. "How many troops did she bring with her? How did she arrive, exactly?"

Noah holds up his hands. "I'm so sorry I wasn't clearer. It's Alora, and she came with only a handful of people. Three, I think."

It takes me a moment to change gears. "Right, Alora. I summoned her."

"Yes you did."

"Okay." My mind spins furiously. I should be holding a public hearing. I should allow my subjects to watch my interrogation, but I can't do it. I haven't made what she confessed on the plane trip over public, so no one expects anything. And if she admits to treason publicly, I'll have to behead her. . . I shudder. I can't do that, I know I can't. "Bring her to me."

"Here?" Noah asks. "To this room?"

"Yes." Maybe it'll rattle her, and if she had anything to do with Mom's death, I will behead her without remorse. Okay, without much remorse.

I pace while I wait, until the frenetic activity annoys

me. Then I sit on Mom's bed, and hop right back off. I sit down at Mom's desk and swivel around in the chair. Great, now I'm four years old.

I stand up again. At least if I met her in the throne room I wouldn't wonder where to sit or how to greet her. What do I want Alora to feel? Because that's probably the heart of my confusion. What is my goal?

Mostly I want to hug her and sob against her shoulder. I want her to swoop in like she did after Mom died and save me.

But that's not what Alamecha needs, and it's not realistic. I can't run around forgiving everyone for everything, even if that's what I want to do. We'll become a target for everyone. I need to hold a position of strength in the family and in the public eye. I glance around the room. I could sit on the edge of Mom's canopy bed, which is a patently absurd idea, but every other place in the room is the same height. There's no place that clearly screams, "I'm the boss."

Mom met with plenty of people in here, and she terrified them sometimes. I think back on those memories to try and figure out how she did it. But I realize it wasn't about her location. Sometimes she sat in her chair, sometimes on the edge of her bed, sometimes in an armchair, but no matter where she was, a sense of confidence, control, and sometimes even borderline menace rolled off her.

She spoke calmly. Nothing rattled her. Basically she was the opposite of me. Fake it until you make it, right?

Footsteps coming down the hall echo back to me through the crack in the door. I rush to the sitting area and take a seat in one of the armchairs. Relaxed, that's the goal. I'm utterly relaxed. Of course, this is precisely when I realize I still haven't spent any time or resources investigating the attack I suffered in New York. Which means I'm not one hundred percent positive what Alora even confessed to doing, or why she might have done it. I'm so sick of life barreling past at the speed of light, always scrambling to catch up.

That doesn't change the fact that I couldn't be less prepared for this meeting.

When Alora, Noah, and Frederick walk through the door, it takes every shred of strength of will I possess not to leap to my feet and fly into her arms. She looks exactly as I recall, from her long, straight, dark hair, to her tawny golden eyes, full of affection and delight to see me. But I can't run to her. She's not the place of refuge I thought she was.

She betrayed me.

"You finally came." I force my shoulders to relax and lean back slightly in my chair. I don't stand to put us at eye level. I don't express any excitement to see her, either.

"I'm sorry I wasn't here for your coronation or Mother's funeral. I wasn't sure how I'd be received."

I lift one eyebrow, but don't say a word.

"My absence made things worse."

I still don't speak.

"When I received your summons." Alora holds both hands out toward me, palms up. "I wanted to come anyway. I would have come anyway."

"Before or after I was attacked by each of the Five?" I ask softly.

She closes her eyes. "I'm so sorry."

"Did you have a hand in that attack as well?" I ask.

Her eyes widen. "There's already been one?"

Noah circles around to stand behind me on my right, and Frederick takes up a spot on the other side. As if Alora notices Noah for the first time, she sniffs. "Wait, this is the human from Trinity."

"It is," I say.

"You brought him here with you?" she asks neutrally.

"He brought me here, if we're being literal," I say. "I've made him my human liaison for as long as his family allows him to stay. But we're going off topic."

Alora gulps and glances back at Noah again. Then her eyes dart back to mine. "You want to know how exactly I betrayed you?"

"I know you sent that hit team that almost killed Noah and me on the East River," I say. "But what I don't know is why you did it. Did you really mean to kill me?"

"They had orders not to actually kill you or anyone else," Alora says. "It was a major miscalculation on my part. I should never have done it, but at the time I thought you were floundering. It was the only way I could think to encourage you to be bold, to take action."

"My sister's impending plan to nuke China wasn't enough?" I ask dryly.

She shakes her head. "We didn't know about that. You were waffling back and forth between abdicating and returning home to fight your sister. I knew which you wanted to do, but I wasn't sure what you'd choose. Since you couldn't pick one, you weren't preparing for either."

She doesn't mention that I was considering making Edam my Consort, which I appreciate.

"I thought that making a decision would help you move down the path toward whatever was best for you."

"You shoved me the direction you thought best. You knew I'd think the attack was from Judica." My voice is flat, emotionless. Eerily like Mom's.

"No," she protests. "Not at all. I had no idea what direction you might take, but it was clear that you felt safe in

New York, complacent even. I wanted you to know that nowhere is safe, not really, not ever."

"Losing my mother, my dog, and my best friend's mother in the space of a day had already taught me that lesson far better than an attack on my life could. Didn't that occur to you?"

Alora drops to her knees. "I'm sorry, Chancy. I truly am. All I've ever wanted to do was to help you. Maybe what I did was utterly wrong, but I didn't mean to cause you any real harm. I was trying to galvanize you in your decision. I knew Judica wouldn't hesitate to kill you, but to believe that yourself, you needed to see that she would take out a hit on you."

My big sister did what she did because I was so dithering and weak she felt she needed to force me into a position of strength. She knew I'd struggle to do what needed to be done, and she took steps to strengthen me in ways I couldn't have myself.

My flaws are the reason Alora did what she did.

"You might have ordered them not to kill me," I say. "But they could have easily taken Noah's life."

"They called to tell me a human was there. I told them to ignore him. It was Judica who was the problem, and you needed to see how vicious and merciless she really is."

"But my twin didn't take out that hit," I say. "And when she had the chance to kill me, she didn't take it. I almost failed to see that, thanks to your subterfuge." I step closer and look her dead in the eye. "I almost killed our mother's daughter because of you."

A tear wells up and rolls down Alora's cheek. "I was wrong. You knew her better and saw her clearer than I did. Thank goodness for that."

Or maybe, in light of Judica's immediate departure, Alora was right and I should have eliminated my rival permanently. But I can't admit that, not now. I can't be weak any longer, not to anyone. "I valued your counsel, but even more than that," I say, "I valued your friendship."

Tears roll freely down her face now. "I hope you'll value it again."

"I'll do my best to forgive you," I say. "And I won't charge you with treason."

Her eyes fill with hope.

"But I have one condition."

"Name it," she says.

"When Inara was born, you bowed out of evian politics because you hate them. But it wasn't because you weren't excellent at them, and I need your skill. I'll do my best to forgive you, but you have to earn my trust back. You must give up your life outside Alamecha and rejoin the fray. I need every supporter I can find, and you're one of my strongest. Leave your hideout and join me here. Be a part of my Council."

The struggle on Alora's face is clear, but she doesn't have any other option, really. She knows she committed treason, no matter how good her intentions. Besides leveraging her experience, I'll also keep her close enough to watch.

"I'll do it," she finally says. "I'll stay here with you."

"Perfect," I say. "Then I'm delighted to welcome you as my new Exchequer General." Inara will have to pull double duty as both my Steward and Political Advisor until I trust Alora enough to send her out to handle sensitive negotiations.

Alora forces a smile, which prompts an actual grin from me.

"From now on," I say, "if you think I need a good shove in the right direction, please come and shove me yourself. Don't send armed mercenaries."

"I'll try to remember that."

"And for heaven's sake, stand up." The second she does, I stand too, dragging her into a hug.

"Thank you," she says softly. "For being merciful in ways Mother never was."

Her compliment feels more like a criticism, thanks to Mom's letter. "I better get you caught up." I step back. "Yesterday, Analessa attacked Puerto Rico. It crumpled like a ball of tin foil."

"Oh no." Alora scowls. "She didn't even give you one day?"

I shake my head.

"She should be ashamed of herself."

"Edam and Balthasar are working out the details," I say, "but she'll be expecting me to take it back. Instead of doing that, I plan to attack Iceland and kidnap DeLannia at the same time."

"Brilliant," Alora says. "Then you can use DeLannia to get Puerto Rico back, while keeping Iceland. You win."

"That's the idea."

"How will you actually pull both of those things off?" Alora asks.

"We have dozens of ideas, but we're struggling a bit with integrating a two prong attack."

The door to the bedroom bangs open. Frederick unsheathes his sword and Noah pulls a gun.

Inara holds her hands up. "It's only me. But Chancery, you should come quickly. A jet recently radioed."

I lift my eyebrows. Jets come and go daily. If they notified me of every one, I'd never get anything done.

"It's the plane Roman took when he left."

"Only one jet is approaching?" I ask.

Inara nods.

I spring to my feet without even thinking about it and race for the landing strip.

Edam and Noah somehow both know what I need, and they fall in beside me, not slowing my approach at all. When I stop, they both wait patiently on either side of me, utterly still. No bickering, no arguing, no maneuvering.

The similarity between this moment, as my guards gather around to wait for a jet that probably holds my twin, and my return four days ago isn't lost on me. I wonder whether Judica's as nervous as I was. I wonder whether she's scared.

Not Judica, surely. But does she wonder how I'll greet her? She should. I'm not sure how I feel myself. Am I angry? Scared? Nervous? All of the above?

Finally, the jet appears on the horizon. I reach for Edam's hand and then Noah's, taking comfort from the knowledge that I have supporters. Diverse, powerful, intelligent people who support me and my rule. I try not to panic, but this is a moment of truth for me. I stupidly allowed my sister her agency, and her departure could go down in history as my first and most catastrophically stupid blunder.

If Judica and Roman aren't on this plane, if it's a message from them that she has joined forces with Melina against me, or if she's working with Analessa. . . it would cut the legs out from under me. I might never recover. I think back to the videos I watched of Judica. I was brashly confident that I understood how she felt and I could predict how she would react. I thought I understood what motivated her. My belief in her hatred was unfounded. I came to believe that she hurt as badly as I did, our circumstances forging us into opposing entities in ways that neither of us wanted. And when I spared her life, she turned around and surrendered. The Judica I thought I knew my entire life would never have done that. It confirmed my belief, my discovery. Or so I thought.

What if I was utterly wrong?

The landing gear deploys. The plane lowers more and more and more until finally it hits the ground, slowing rapidly as the engines engage their reversers and the powerful brake system halts it right in front of me. My heart leaps to my throat and I let go of Noah and Edam and clasp my hands together, standing alone as a monarch should.

The stairs are put in place, and I watch the exit closely.

I finally recognize the feeling I couldn't pinpoint. I'm hopeful. Hopeful that I was right. Hopeful she has an explanation for her departure, hopeful she returned to support me, to fulfill the prophecy as Mom thought she would. Roman walks out first, and then Judica follows, her eyes scanning the area nervously. She doesn't look like an attacker or a conqueror. Hope soars in my throat that she's not a threat, that perhaps she's returning to Alamecha on her own.

For the first time since Mom died, there might be great news. I should stand calm and stoic. I should make her come to me and beg forgiveness for disappearing without any word about her intentions. Excellent monarchs never cede power to anyone, and they never yield to another for any reason, especially not in public.

But everyone already knows I'm a terrible monarch. Before I have time to stop them, my feet race toward the stairs. Once I'm close enough, I throw my arms wide and hug a very shocked Judica.

"I'm so glad you're alive," I whisper, tears running down my cheeks in the most un-regal display I could possibly imagine.

Judica's probably disgusted with me, but all she says is, "I'm alive."

She may not be giddy to see me, but she doesn't pull away either. After a brief moment, her arms circle around behind my back. It's the first time we've ever hugged, and I need it more than I've needed anything in a very long time. What's funny is that five minutes ago, I didn't even know I needed this. Or maybe I simply never dreamed it would happen.

"I'm sorry you were worried," she whispers. "I didn't mean to scare you. I should have called you or had Roman tell you where I was."

I release her, since it's odd to be hugging, much less talking while we're hugging. Actually, anything combining hugging and Judica would probably seem bizarre.

"What exactly did happen?" I ask.

"Oh," she says. "I didn't realize you didn't know."

I stare at her.

"Angel knocked me out and took me to Melina."

I gulp. "Melina, our older sister Melina?"

Judica nods. "This is likely to be a lengthy discussion."

"And you need to get food and clean off." I gesture for her to precede me. "Don't let me stop you. But as soon as you're ready, I'd love to include you in the discussions we've been having."

Her eyes widen. "What discussions?"

"Before we can talk about all this, you need to go get cleaned up, and I want Job to evaluate you." And as happy as I am to see her, I should probably vet her story before I update her on every single development in her absence. Why would Melina kidnap her? Why would Angel work for Melina? And where is she now?

Judica's dog Death starts barking from the other side of the complex, and comes flying toward us, tongue lolling.

When he reaches us, Judica crouches and lets him lick her all over her face. Gross.

"A lot has happened while you were gone. I didn't realize you left against your will," I say. "So I held Mom's funeral and my coronation without you. I'm sorry for that."

"Don't be," she says. "You did what you should have done."

"I hope so." I hate how unsure I sound.

"How did the Five take your coronation?" she asks. "I wish I could have been here to watch them."

"You can certainly review the feed," I say. "I should probably look over it as well."

"You haven't had time?" she asks. "Why not?"

I forgot how sharp she is, picking up every last cue. "It has been a busy few days." I wave Larena forward. "But why don't you head for your room now, and I'll send Job to evaluate you."

I should prepare a list of questions to ask her or something. I'd like her input on my plan for Puerto Rico, but first I need to make sure her story checks out.

"You don't trust me yet," she says. "I understand that, believe me."

"It's not that I don't trust you," I lie.

"Check the feed for my room," she says. "You'll see that the last person who came inside was Angel."

I shake my head. "The feed has been erased."

"I should never have restored Angel's security clearance. I have so much to fill you in on, especially about my investigation into Mother's death."

She's here. She wants to help. No matter how much I drill her for details, ultimately it will come down to whether I believe her intentions.

"Look, get checked and cleared," I say. "And then we'll talk."

"Something happened." She frowns. "Something bad. What is it? Someone attacked? Which family?"

I sigh. The rest of the world may already know. It can hardly be concealed, Analessa's actions. "Yesterday, the day after my coronation, Analessa attacked and took Puerto Rico."

Judica's eyes flash.

"Don't worry. I have a plan in place."

"You can't delay your response," she says.

"I know that." I want to tell her the details, and I realize I'm proud of my idea. She might be impressed by my creativity. Alora was.

"You're going to attack her elsewhere?" she asks. "Or do you plan to try and retake Puerto Rico?" Her eyebrows rise. "Or both?"

I can't quite suppress my smile. She was involved in every decision Mom made for too long to shut that off. "We will talk before I do anything, I promise."

"Both of those are a mistake," Judica says.

A mistake? Her words hit hard. "How so?"

Her grin is at least half evil. "You're destined to be the Queen of Queens. You can't be squabbling in the mud over tiny gains and losses like a pig."

My eyebrows climb up my forehead. "I'm sorry. Queen of Queens?" Did Mom show her the prophecy?

"Ever heard the phrase 'Go big or go home?'"

"I'm surprised you have," I say.

"You shouldn't worry about retaking Puerto Rico, or attacking some other worthless holding, not when you're the rightful ruler of the entire world. No, let Analessa think she's taken Puerto Rico. Because you're going to take every single thing she owns, and that's just the beginning."

7

Edam and Balthasar have done the impossible. They've worked together long enough to come up with a perfectly timed plan of attack that would carry off both prongs of my idea simultaneously.

"We finally worked out the details," Balthasar says. "And now you tell me we aren't doing any of it?"

"I'm only saying that we should pause the plans for now." I implore Edam with my eyes.

"Judica returned not even an hour ago, and she's got a few ideas to contribute to the entire plan of attack," I say. "I need to spend some time talking to her, and once I have, I'll make my final determinations."

"Well, once you're done braiding each other's hair," Balthasar says, "maybe you can let us know whether you're trashing the entire offensive we've worked out."

"You won't talk to your Empress like that," Edam says. "Or I'll remove your tongue and we'll have a reprieve while you regrow it. I hear tongues are the most painful organ to regrow, but if you can think of a worse one, I'd be happy to remove that instead."

Balthasar's nostrils flare, but he snaps his mouth shut.

I could kiss Edam right now for supporting me in front of Balthasar, especially when I know he's not keen on listening to anything Judica has to say. "I'm heading over to talk to her now. I'll let you know my decision the second I've made it."

Indecisive and inconsistent, that's me. I really suck at this queen thing so far. It'll be a miracle if any of my Council still respects me by the end of this week.

Balthasar crosses his arms over his chest and leans back in his chair. "I'll be waiting with bated breath."

I let my hands shake until I'm already in the hall. It's hard to ignore the disapproval of someone who raised me.

"Chancy," Edam says.

I pause and turn. "Yeah?"

"Did you want me to come with you or stay here?"

"Come along, but I'll have you wait outside, if that's okay. I think your presence might agitate her." I hope my eyes convey my unspoken apology.

"That's a smart call," he says, following me down the hall. When we reach the door to my room, he wraps his hands around my forearms, tugging me close. "You're navigating a very complicated maze exceptionally well. It's a lot, and it would be overwhelming for anyone, but remember to use your head as well as your heart. You may be ready to forgive her right away, but she's had a lifetime in training as a viper."

I allow myself a single heartbeat to breathe in his support, and then it's time to move ahead. "Thanks, and I will keep that in mind." I squeeze his hands once before letting go and heading into my room. I need to sort through my feelings and thoughts. Judica said I can't become a Queen of Queens without starting as I mean to proceed.

What does that even mean?

It's not like I can simply tell the Five that I'm taking over. Then there's the fact that I don't even want to take over. The idea of ruling Alamecha makes me want to cry, but the idea of trying to rule the whole world makes me want to sprint for the nearest exit, then get on a boat, and disappear forever.

Not for the first time, I wish this dumb ring had reacted to Judica. "You chose the wrong sister, dummy," I say aloud.

It doesn't react in any way. Of course it doesn't. It's a ring, not a fairy or a leprechaun or a genie trapped in a stone. It's not magic. It's science we don't understand yet. If Mom can see me where she is, she's hardcore rolling her eyes right now.

A single loud rap on the door startles me, and I stand up. "Come in."

Judica pushes through the door, and I fold my hands in front of my body, unsure what to do with them, or even how to stand. "Did Job clear you?"

"I was undernourished and a little dehydrated. He made me eat platters of food and drink gallons of juice, but otherwise, he says I'm completely fine." She steps through the door and stops near it, her hands shoved into her pockets. I've never seen her put her hands in her pockets, not in eighteen years. Could she be as uncomfortable as me?

I gesture to the sofa Edam has been sleeping on. "I'm glad you're okay. Now I won't feel bad badgering you to tell me exactly what happened. From our end, you disappeared while I was gone disarming the bombs you aimed for China."

"Once you trust me, I'd love to hear how you managed that." Judica's facial expression holds more respect than I've ever seen directed my way.

"Tell me how you got off the island." I sit on one side of the sofa.

She perches on the edge of the other. "I think I need to go back further than that. I botched the investigation of Mother's killer," Judica says. "I spent a lot of time interrogating Angel, and because Balthasar had taught me to follow my gut, I let her go. Like an idiot."

"Why did you let her go?" I ask. "Just because you had a feeling?" That's not like her at all. Judica's all about facts and hard logic.

Her brow furrows. "Nothing cleared her, but the more time I spent thinking about her involvement, the less it made sense to me. Angel poisoning our mother was too obvious. She certainly had means and control, but ask Balthasar. He and I both dug and dug and couldn't find any motive at all. Beyond that, she told me about a vow she made to Mother to protect the family, and she seemed passionate. When I threatened her family, she didn't even flinch or stress in the slightest. I took those things to mean that she hadn't been involved."

"Now you think that's wrong?"

"The day I left, she brought me my tray. It was laced with tranquilizers of some kind. She drugged me and took me to Melina."

"You said that before. She took you to Austin?" I shake my head. "But why?"

Judica closes her eyes and bites her lip. She inhales through her nose several times. "It never even occurred to me during my investigation that she'd be working for Melina. As far as we knew, they had no connection at all." She frowns. "I still don't have a motive, not really, or anything that connects Melina to Angel, but I saw Angel when I woke up, while I was in transit. She definitely took me to our older sister."

I think about how involved Angel was as we grew up. Perhaps she was even more interactive with Melina. Perhaps a friendship grew between them. "We are at such a disadvantage, being so young," I say. "There are so many things that have happened, so many past interactions people have shared that we know nothing about."

"Nine hundred years of life is a very long time to create grudges, hurt feelings, and buried anger," Judica agrees. "And Mom didn't exactly treat everyone with kindness."

"Why do you think Melina killed Mom? Isn't it possible she simply took you, but didn't harm Mom?" I want to believe her. For the first time in my life, Judica is here, ostensibly trying to help. But for that very reason, I'm struggling to accept her help. She could have snuck away, developed a plan, and come back here to put me off my guard. It's possible she's planning to rule through me, by convincing me to do what she wants done, and then challenge me in two months. Or even something much more devious.

"I accused Melina of Mother's death and she didn't deny it."

"You denied it, and I didn't believe you," I say.

Judica leans back against the sofa. "Melina knew things she shouldn't have known. Angel was working for her, and if you'll recall, she challenged Mother after you were born."

"What did she know?" I arch one brow.

"She wanted me to confirm why Mother changed the Heirship documents." Judica's eyes are unsure, almost scared when she meets my gaze. "You and I both know what you did with Mom's ring." Judica glances at my hand. "Did Mother mention anything else, like any old stories or a prophecy?"

I want to tell her everything, but I can't. Not yet. She could be fishing for information.

"Melina thinks Mom changed the heirship documents because of a prophecy. She said it's from Eve herself. It says an empress will be born who will rule all others, basically."

"What did you tell her? Did you confirm that I reacted to the stone?"

Judica shakes her head. "Absolutely not. I told her nothing. If she'd known that, she would have killed me."

"Excuse me?"

"She wants to be some kind of helper for you, also mentioned in the prophecy, and once she's sure you're the empress named, she's planning to pledge her support."

"Why would she need to kill you?" I can't quite keep the disbelief from my tone. The prophecy says nothing about eliminating rival sisters.

"She has seen the twin dynamic as an issue from the beginning, and believes God spared you on the day we were born. She thinks I'll only get in the way of you fulfilling your destiny." Judica shrugs. "She might be right. I haven't exactly helped you up until now. She thought killing me would be a favor for you."

"I don't believe that," I say. "For what it's worth, and neither did Mom. She did change the heirship documents because of a prophecy from Eve, a secret one, something Melina shouldn't have known about. It was Mom's *only* reason for replacing you with me."

"So Melina was right." She closes her eyes.

"About that, anyway," I say. "Yes. Mom never would have displaced you, except for my reaction. In all other ways, I'm far inferior."

Judica opens her eyes and shakes her head. "I don't agree." She opens her mouth, and then clicks it shut.

"What?" I ask.

"Mother always told me she had another good option if I didn't live up to my training potential."

"She *what?*" Mom wouldn't say that.

"You've always been a valid option, at least, in Mother's eyes you have. She trained us differently, but you had strengths I lacked."

"Obviously the reverse is also true," I say. "You have many, many strengths that I don't possess."

Judica shifts on the sofa, like I've made her uncomfortable. "Angel told me that she made a promise to Mother to always do what's best for Alamecha, no matter what. And Melina has this prophecy that says, 'With the might and power of God, the Eldest shall destroy everything in her path—'"

I cut her off. "You're starting in the middle."

"Excuse me?"

"Is that the beginning of what Melina showed you?"

"Uh, she had it tattooed on her arms, so yeah."

"Tattooed on her arms?" I find that very hard to believe. It's practically impossible for an evian to be tattooed. The body typically absorbs the ink within a few days.

Judica shrugs. "Look, don't ask me how. I saw it there, and I read the words right off her body."

"She sounds unstable."

Judica laughs, the sound like a sea lion barking. "That's an understatement. But look, if you've heard the prophecy, Mother must have believed you were the Eldest too. Now I'm wondering if maybe Angel believed she was working for Mother in delivering me to Melina. Maybe Angel wanted me out of the way, and couldn't bring herself to do it."

"If Angel thought she was helping Mom, then she didn't betray her, at least, not in her mind."

"Maybe not," Judica says.

"So then maybe Melina didn't kill Mom after all."

Judica's lips compress.

"What makes you so certain Melina killed Mom?" I

mean, I want to know. I just don't want to pin all my suspicions on the wrong person. Again.

"She held me captive in my underwear," Judica whispers. "She could have killed me right there. She would have, if only she could confirm her suspicions." She turns to face me. "She would have killed our mother without the slightest hesitation. I actually think if we can figure out who witnessed Mother changing the documents, we can find a trail that leads to Melina. I believe she gave the final kill order after Mother chose you as her heir. Melina's entire life has been dedicated to finding this Queen of Queens."

"If she thinks she's supposed to be my supporter, I think she's wrong."

"You do?" Judica asks.

I nod.

"Why?"

"Mom wanted us to work together. The full text is, 'In time of great peril, when the lives of women and men shall fail, the Eldest shall survive certain death to unite the families. She comes in a time of blood and horror, in a world overrun with plague and warfare. She shall command the stone of the mountain, be it small or large. Its power shall destroy the vast hosts arrayed against it.' It sounds like Melina doesn't have that first part. But then it continues with what you heard. 'With the might and power of God, the Eldest shall destroy all in her path, and unite my children as one. Only through her blood can the stone be restored to the mountain. Together, with the strength of her strongest supporter, she shall open the Garden of Eden, that the miracle of God shall go unto all the Earth to save my children from utter destruction.'"

"I did hear only the second part."

"Mom said only the queens had access to the prophecy

and it has always been that way. I wonder how Melina knows it."

"It does say you'll destroy all in your path." Judica bites her lip.

"It doesn't sound very good, does it?"

"You think I'm supposed to be this strongest supporter?" Judica asks.

"Mom did," I say. "I thought maybe you could be the Eldest. I'd make a better supporter than ruler."

Judica shakes her head. "I can't command the stone, and you're older than me. Clearly you're the Eldest." She pauses, her mouth open. "But if Melina kills me, she could step into that position."

"I'm glad she didn't." I'm surprised how true that is.

"You are?" Judica swallows. "You wouldn't have been a little relieved?"

I scoot a little closer on the sofa. "I was relieved when you returned. Truly." It has not been a good week for me, but it sounds like Judica's week has been just as rough. "Why did Melina let you go if she wanted to kill you? Or did Roman get you out?"

"Neither. I escaped."

"Then you called Roman to bring you back?"

"I called him when I was planning to—" She coughs. "Melina is our sister, but Chancery, you have to believe me when I say she's not sane. She needed to be stopped."

My eyes widen. "Did you kill her?"

Judica looks down at her feet. "No, sorry, poor tense choice. I tried, but she has too many people there on her compound. I wouldn't have survived the attempt."

I breathe a sigh of relief.

"You're glad she's alive." Her voice holds no emotion whatsoever.

"I'm more glad that *you're* alive, dummy," I say with a smile.

"Oh."

There's so much to address here I don't know where to start. "I'm glad you didn't kill her in some kind of kamikaze attempt. Also, going forward, I believe that killing siblings is something we should discuss before actually doing. I'll be sure to share this rule with Melina and Alora and Inara. I feel like we could all benefit from a little more talking and a little less beheading, generally speaking."

Judica frowns. "So you don't plan to eliminate her?"

"Not today," I say. "But we can discuss it further. My preference would be to talk to her about this before pulling any triggers."

"She isn't safe." Her eyes flash.

"Speaking of keeping me safe, I'd like to talk to you about a position on my Council." Because I may not entirely trust Judica yet, but she is wicked smart and well trained. Her advice might really help.

"I heard the spots are all filled." She leans against the wall and crosses her black booted feet. "Although I hear Inara has two assignments."

"I could assign you to be my Political Advisor." I tap my lip. "But I had another idea."

"That sounds ominous."

I arch one eyebrow. "There has been a great deal of bickering between Edam and Balthasar, now that I split that role. I'd like to eliminate that and find you a place fitting of your skill level."

"Oh?"

"I'm naming you my Chief Strategist. My War Lord, my Political Advisor, my Operations Manager, my Exchequer and my Head of Governance would all report directly to you."

Judica meets my eye and I can't read her expression at all. Until she bursts into tears.

"Oh no," I say. "You don't have to do it. If it was rude of me to ask, I'm sorry."

"How can you invite me to essentially lead your Council?"

How? "How could I not?" I ask. "You're much smarter, stronger and more devious than I am."

"I've failed you and Alamecha repeatedly," Judica says. "I freed Mother's killer, and I failed to eliminate Angel and Melina both. I lost to you in the challenge, but long before that, I was awful to you. So horrible, over and over."

I shake my head. "Life isn't fair, and things aren't always perfect. I think Mom tried her best, but I think she frequently made things worse." I think about Melina. "I wish I could go back in time and do things better, but I can't. All I can do is try to set things right now wherever possible."

A memory of a song rises up in my mind. Something about a blackbird singing at night. The face that looks down at me smiles. Flawless dark skin, golden brown eyes, shimmering nearly-black hair that falls past her shoulders, high cheekbones, full lips, white teeth.

"I think——" I pause. "I think I've seen Melina before, and she was good and kind to me. I wonder if I could meet with her and mend the fences torn down when she and Mom fought."

"I recognized her, too. That threw me at first, but Chancery, she's not like you, and she's not even like me. Something is off about her."

"How can you be sure?" I ask. "I mean, no offense, but you weren't around her for very long, and threats notwithstanding, she didn't actually kill you. You threatened to kill me, too, if you'll recall."

"It's not the same."

"How so?" I ask. "Explain how it's different."

"She only held off on killing me to get confirmation that you were here, safe and sound."

A familiar rap on the door interrupts us.

"Come in, Inara." She may as well know, too.

"Judica!" Inara rushes to her side and hugs her.

"I'm fine," Judica says, "truly."

"I've heard a rumor," Inara says, "that you're with Roman."

Judica has perfect control of her emotions. She never blushes, looks embarrassed, guilty, or afraid. Her heart rate remained almost entirely steady as we discussed Melina's attempt to murder her. It remained steady when we discussed the prophecy. But one little mention of Roman by Inara, and Judica's entire face flushes bright red, her heart rate spikes, and I smell sweat.

Judica likes Roman. That makes me smile, probably too broadly.

"We can discuss all that later," Judica says. "For now, we need to focus on Chancery's plan for countering Analessa and dealing with Melina."

"Wait, what about Melina?" Inara frowns.

We fill her in.

She shakes her head. "We shouldn't move too quickly there."

"She kidnapped me within the walls of this palace," Judica says, "and her people here were working on confirmation of Chancery's abilities."

"How would she have any idea of what went on with that EMP?" Inara asks.

Judica looks skyward. "Think about it. A huge EMP knocks out the island. We specifically explain it's a drill. Mother dies shortly after, and surprise, surprise, the Heir ship documents are different. Melina may have been working with whoever helped Mother change the documents, or perhaps she doesn't actually *know* anything, but she suspects. We should assume that based on the sequence of events, many people have theories."

"Mom made me promise not to tell anyone," I say. "About the ring or the prophecy."

"Not to put it too bluntly, but Mother's dead," Judica says. "She obviously handled this all wrong."

"You think we need to make the prophecy public?" I ask. "Because the queens kept it secret all this time."

"Obviously not secret enough," Judica says, "because Melina has half of it tattooed on her forearms. I'm still not sure how she made that happen, but it was silvery, almost, or at least, it was metallic looking."

"Metal ink," Inara says. "It's painful, but the body can't absorb the heavy metals quickly."

It shows some real dedication, I suppose.

"I think you should ignore Puerto Rico," Judica says. "We eliminate Melina, and then you issue a proclamation to every queen of the Five, announcing that you're the Queen of Queens."

"That sounds smart," I say sarcastically. "Make them attack us all at once—get things over with quickly."

"Before we make any big decisions," Inara says, "maybe we should discuss some things about Melina, and her father Eamon, too."

Eamon is also my father, of course. And he's someone I've heard virtually nothing about.

Inara crosses the room to my computer monitor. She taps through screen after screen until a video populates. "This is right after your birth," she says. "These files are top level security clearance only."

Judica and I crowd around the screen.

Melina's singing, just exactly as I recalled, about a blackbird in the dead of night. Her voice is magnificent. I'm in her arms, cooing. After she finishes the song, another memory crowds into my mind.

"Wait," I shout. "Stop!" I don't want to watch it.

But the video feed rolls along. Melina takes a blanket and covers my face with it. "Shhhh," she says. "Hush now."

My arms and legs flail, but she keeps the blanket pressed against my face. "This is the only way," she says. "Mother can't do what needs to be done. I don't want to do it, but if she won't, I don't have a choice."

Enora, Judica in her arms, rushes into the room. "Melina! No."

Melina backs up a step, but keeps the blanket over my face. "You can't keep her, Mother. You can't. You know that as well as I do, but you're not thinking straight."

Inara runs through the door after Mom, sprints across the room and snatches me from Melina's arms. "This isn't your decision to make," she says. "It's Mother's."

Melina's eyes flash. "She made the wrong one."

"Only history will tell," Inara says.

"I'm telling you now. If we don't learn from history, then what's the point? I know it's hard," Melina says. "So blame me. I can take it."

"You're the reason I needed a new heir in the first place," Enora says. "You're *flawed*."

Melina stiffens as if Mom slapped her.

I gulp in deep breaths in Inara's arms, my skin pinking up.

Melina's voice is soft, so quiet I can barely hear the words. "I am exactly who I was always meant to be. You can't ignore the hard truths, and you can't pick and choose who and what to love because it fits your worldview. Love is many things, but convenient isn't one of them."

"I don't need or want your help," Enora says.

"You do though, more than you realize," Melina says.

Inara backs away from Melina, taking me closer to Mom.

"You never meant for me to have your throne, no matter what, did you?" Melina asks. "Not from the second you found out."

"I won't lie and say I wasn't relieved to discover I was pregnant again," Enora says.

Melina's face flushes and her nostrils flare. "I challenge you, Enora Alamecha, for the good of our family. I challenge your leadership, your competence, and your abilities."

Enora's face falls. "Your sisters aren't even one day old. You're challenging me now?"

"You've left me no alternative," Melina says. "I take no joy in this."

"So be it," Enora says.

The video stops.

Melina tried to smother me. Mother saved me, and Inara saw it all.

"We've always known Melina was a threat to you, Chancery," Inara says. "But she stopped any attempts at harming you when you were barely two years old. Now I suspect that she found a fragment of this prophecy and changed her focus."

Inara makes Melina sound as obsessive and unhinged as Judica does, but she didn't look unhinged in that video. She looked betrayed. She looked wounded.

"What did she mean when she said 'from the second you found out'?" I ask. "Found out what?"

"I think from the second she discovered she was pregnant," Inara says.

I shake my head. "Of course Mom didn't mean for Melina to rule once she discovered she was having another girl." It doesn't make sense. Is Judica right? Is she unstable?

"Why didn't Mother kill her?" Judica asks.

Inara sighs. "There's more to the story." She gestures for us to sit down.

I settle lightly on the edge of my bed, and Judica takes my desk chair.

"You know Mother remarried, quite a few years after her first Consort, my father, Althuselah, died. She married a man named Eamon."

"Our father," I say.

"Even so. Eamon was handsome, vibrant, passionate, and intelligent. All of those are very good things." Inara's voice sounds almost wistful. "Enora had vowed never to remarry after Althuselah died, but Eamon reminded her of how she felt so many centuries before, I think. She longed to have someone again, and she missed having passion in her life, and hope for her future."

Eww. I do not need to hear about this. I must make a face because Inara laughs.

"The point is," Inara says, "Mother married him without much forethought and without knowing much about him."

I don't want to hear anything terrible about my father. I just don't, but I never seem to get what I want, not these days.

"Eamon was flawed. He had suffered a major deletion in his DNA that wasn't clear to any of us until after they married. He was a zealot, obsessed to the point of madness with his causes. He believed the human Bible was literally true, every word. He wanted to save humanity, even at the expense of all evians. He called it our duty." Inara looks at me pointedly.

"Why does his belief constitute evidence of a major deletion?" I ask, somewhat testily.

"He passed that single-mindedness along to Melina." Inara looks out my window. "I loved Melina like my own daughter, and Enora and I trained her together. Eamon even helped when he had the bandwidth to lend a hand. She was brilliant, precocious, talented, and Judica, for what it's worth, she's the most talented swordswoman I've ever seen."

Judica scowls.

"It's good you didn't try to kill her. You'd likely have been killed instead, I swear it." Inara takes a few ragged breaths. Clearly she loves Melina still.

"When Mother wouldn't kill you." Inara looks at me. "And then they fought, Melina could have ended Mother's life, but she didn't. She left instead, disgusted with how far she had gone, how terrible the path she had taken. Mother and I hoped that insight, that shred of sanity, would grow. We hoped she could be saved."

"Are you saying Mother exiled her because she was insane, and Mother hoped she'd recover somehow?" Judica asks.

"That's exactly what I'm saying."

And Judica and I have the same father. The same flawed father.

8

"I wonder whether we should call a Council meeting?" I ask.

Judica shakes her head. "You can't put this kind of information out to that many people without losing control over it."

It's sad that I can't trust my own Council, but she's right.

"You need to set up a team to eliminate Melina immediately," Judica says. "I volunteer to head the whole thing."

Hold a grudge much? "I want to talk to her before we do anything. . . permanent."

Judica rolls her eyes. "I'm telling you, that's a waste of time. Did you not see the video where she tried to smother you? She's worse now. She was absolutely planning to kill me."

"But you said she was doing it to help me," I insist. "She's not the only sibling who has been a little misguided. I'm not going to budge on my requirement that she give up her intention of killing you, but I think I could talk to her safely. And I want to interrogate her about Mom's death."

Inara sits down on the edge of my bed, eyes on her hands.

"Do you have any input?" I ask her. "Since you're the only one who really knows her."

"I'm afraid I haven't known Melina for quite some time."

"But you spent years and years with her. You helped raise her," I say. "Can she be reasoned with? Could we bring her around by showing her the whole prophecy? Maybe she would acknowledge that Judica has a part in it."

Inara shakes her head. "I wish I knew. I feel like anything I tell you would be too emotional to be beneficial. I love Melina." She looks up and meets my eyes. "The thought of killing her guts me. I don't think I could do it, even if you ordered me to."

"You vote against the strike team, then?" I ask.

Inara nods. "I guess I do. So far, she's taken Judica, but hasn't done anything else."

Judica practically explodes. "Are you two not listening to a word I say? *Angel* took me to her. I accused her of killing Mother and she never denied it. She would have killed me too, if I hadn't woken up early from her sedatives, knocked out two guards in my underwear with only the aid of a spoon. I know Chancery never wants to harm anyone, but Melina's a legitimate threat. She may be our *largest* threat, since she's in the USA, and has been hatching who knows what plot right under Mother's nose this entire time."

"Okay, let's consider. You want me to kill Melina, and then what?" I ask. "Send a letter that looks utterly insane to every one of the empresses, demanding them to acknowledge me, a seventeen year old girl, as their rightful ruler based on the fact that I can set off an EMP?"

"You're right." Judica's eyes practically crackle. "As long

as you see yourself as a teenager with nothing to offer, as long as you're totally unsure of your own value, no one else will take you seriously either."

No mistakes. I can't make a single mistake, or I'll ruin everything. And now Judica wants me to up the stakes.

"What exactly do you propose we say?" Inara says. "Because any way we word it, that will essentially be a declaration of war."

Judica smiles. "Yes, yes it will."

She's wanted this her entire life. Even the thought of watching Alamecha take over the other families fills her with unbridled joy. I wish I felt even one iota of anything other than dread over the prospect. "I don't want to be Queen of Queens," I say. "I don't even want to rule Alamecha."

"Well, fate doesn't care what you want," Judica says. "And it doesn't care about me at all, clearly, but whining won't help. If Mother's prophecy is right, this isn't about what you want, or what you need, or what your heart yearns for. It's about saving the world from *utter destruction*."

Why do I always sound so whiny? Since when did not being power hungry become such an epic flaw? "Let's say I send out a declaration, or a proclamation, or whatever. Do I send it out to every evian we know, or just to the empresses?"

"Everyone," Inara says.

"Only empresses," Judica says at the same time.

Why can't anyone ever agree? "Explain."

Judica begins pacing. "Think this through. If we want to enrage the world, yes, we tell everyone. If we tell only the queens, the ones who have known about this prophecy all along, they might actually listen. They have the power to make the decision, so why bother upsetting everyone else? You can't retract information once it's out there."

"I disagree," Inara says. "The empresses are the ones who lose if they acquiesce to your demand. They're the ones who have absolute power, and they'd have to give it away. Our only hope of bringing them to heel is if their people demand it. The empresses will see this as a declaration of war, and not a single one of them will share this with their people. But if you're the one who tells the people about this threat, exposing a prophecy their own empresses kept from them, and if you're the solution to that problem, and their rulers can't deny it. . . Then you have a real shot at them having no choice but to follow you."

I flop onto my back on my bed and stare at the ceiling.

They're both right. And that means they're probably both wrong.

"I need to think about all of this."

Judica and Inara both stand up and walk out, without saying another word.

Edam pokes his head in a moment later. "Are you okay?"

I grunt.

He walks over to me. "You look. . . stressed."

"Ding ding ding, give the guy a prize."

"Huh?" Edam doesn't watch human television, so he has no idea what I'm saying.

"Never mind. Can you send Noah in? I need to talk to him."

Edam's face falls, but he obeys.

I wish I could talk to Edam, but he'd agree with either Inara or Judica, and then I'd probably choose that path. I need to make this decision myself, and the person with the highest likelihood of seeing outside of the evian box is the non-evian.

Noah's voice is unsure when the door opens. "Chancery? Did you want to talk to me?"

I sit up and wave him in. "I did, thanks."

"You do know that your mother's rooms have an office and a small meeting room for exactly this sort of thing," he says.

I chuckle. "I do."

"Because if you keep inviting me into your bedroom, I might get the wrong idea."

I laugh out loud. Noah's an idiot. "I need an unbiased person to talk to me about my options."

"Okay." He sits down next to me. "What's up?"

"Judica's back."

"I saw that," he says. "She's a real peach, huh?"

"She's. . . evolving. But that's one of the reasons I asked you to come in here." I fill him in on how Melina took Judica and wants to support me, but that the support means she wants to kill my twin. "Inara wants me to spare Melina, at least until I've had a chance to talk to her myself, and she thinks I need to send a proclamation to every evian I can contact, telling them about the prophecy and declaring myself the Eldest."

"And Judica wants to eliminate Melina, and send the proclamation to only the rulers?"

I nod.

"What do you think?" he asks.

"I don't know." My hands shake. "I don't know what to do, Noah, and I'm pretty sure that whatever I do will be wrong."

Noah makes jokes all the time. He's always got a funny quip, or a snarky comment, but not now. He puts his hand over mine, and the trembling stops. "You haven't made a wrong turn yet."

"Oh, but I have. So many."

"Like what?"

I swallow. "I failed to save my mom. I should have seen

that she was ill and done something. I was so busy worrying about my stuff that I didn't even notice."

"Don't you think she knew she was sick, or possibly being poisoned?" Noah asks. "But it was long term, and she hadn't identified the source. That wasn't your job."

I think about her journal. She suspected.

"You can't see everything all the time," he says. "What else you got?"

"I ran," I say. "When she died, I didn't stand and fight. I ran."

"Would you have defeated Judica if you had stayed?"

I shake my head. "I hadn't figured out melodics and I didn't know her well enough even if I had." If she had been unwilling to kill me, maybe. But she was so angry with me, and we didn't understand each other. "I don't know. But probably not."

He shrugs. "So running was the right move."

"I released Judica," I say. "And she disappeared shortly after."

"You saved the village she targeted, and she was kidnapped while you were preoccupied. That's not on you."

"But it is," I insist. "All of it is. My judgment isn't great."

He squeezes my hand. "What has you all keyed up?"

I wish I could tell him about Mom's letter, but that would be another mistake, over-sharing with the human. "I have all these decisions to make, and I'm not qualified to do it. Inara and Judica are both much better able to handle this stuff, but when they disagree. . ." I flop backward on the bed again. "I don't want to do any of this."

Noah taps my hand, his finger brushing the top of my staridium. "I don't know what it means that this stone reacts to you. I'm guessing no one does."

I close my eyes.

"But it's significant, Chancery. Whatever has stolen

your confidence, you need to find it again. Alamecha looks to you, which alone is tremendous. But judging from that prophecy, you've got a longer path beyond you than sitting on your mother's throne."

"Maybe."

"Judica's point that you need to begin as you intend to carry on is a good one. She may be a little over-eager on the killing Melina bit, in my opinion, but she has seen her more recently than any of us. Certainly confirmation bias is real, but if someone tried to kill me, I might not give them the benefit of the doubt either."

"I can't do it," I say. "I was absolutely positive Judica killed Mom, but she didn't. I can't order a hit on Melina on the basis of circumstantial evidence."

"That's one issue solved. You reach out to Melina, and at least offer her the opportunity to defend herself."

I feel calm about that decision. "Good. Thank you."

Noah shakes his head. "Don't thank me. You made that decision yourself."

I did. He's right.

"What about the proclamation?" he asks. "Do you even want to do something like this? You don't have to. Judica's point is solid, but it doesn't mean that's your path. You could simply proceed as you meant to before she returned."

"I love the idea of my two pronged attack, taking Iceland and getting Puerto Rico back. But even if things go flawlessly, which they never do, at the end of the day, nothing of real import will have changed. Nothing."

"What do you think needs to change?" He lifts one eyebrow.

"So many things. How evians treat humans, how they treat half-evians. How they treat royal sons. The entire purpose for evians is off course."

"You're saying they." Noah's head tilts. "Are you not evian?"

I shake my head. "I am, of course I am, but I don't want any part in all of that. It's *wrong.* My mom did a lot of good. She changed the way humans were treated and how we govern them, but it wasn't enough, not by a long shot. And the way Mom and all the empresses allowed women to be horribly and systematically repressed among humans so that the humans are led by testosterone-blinded—"

"Hey there. Testosterone blinded fool right here." Noah's eyebrow arches. "Look, you're only seventeen. You have plenty of years to accomplish all your lofty goals. But if you make your claim now, you might change the things you hate about the evian world and the world at large much sooner than if you wait for your secret to come out on its own, which it will eventually, mark my words on that."

He's probably right. "Judica and Inara seem concerned only about me ruling all the families, but maybe it's not about that. Maybe it's about leading the existing rulers to change things that matter."

"And?"

"I need to win over more than just the rulers if I want to remake the fabric of our communities. Inara's right. The empresses will never hand over control unless they're forced. They must have no other choice."

"What worries you about that?" Noah asks.

"Mom and all the other empresses throughout time have kept the prophecy a secret. I wish I knew why."

"Power?" he asks.

I shrug. "I don't see how hiding it gives them more power."

"Knowing something others don't is a classic power play," Noah says.

I wish I knew whether it was that simple.

"Instead of sending a proclamation to the other empresses," Noah says, "what if we made a video and sent it to every leader and every member of Alamecha? It would spread like wildfire, I imagine."

"They'll think the video's a fake," I say.

Noah grins. "That's why you demonstrate for every member of Alamecha present, including any spies, and all ambassadors for each family. They'll vouch for it. I think it'll be enough."

"I'll turn myself into a huge target," I say.

"And that's different than the status quo, how?"

I suppose it's not.

I stand up. "If I'm doing this, I may as well do it."

Noah jumps to his feet. "That's the spirit."

I glance at my ring. I wish Mom was here to tell me whether this is the right decision. But she's not; I'm alone. It hurts more than it usually does right now, standing on the edge of a precipice, full of doubt and fear. Before I can change my mind, I walk toward the door. Noah follows a step behind me.

When I pause with my hand on the doorknob, Noah whispers. "You've got this. Truly. I know you feel alone, but you aren't."

"Can you bring Lark?" I say. "She can help me pick what to wear."

Noah smiles. "Absolutely."

He ducks out the door, but before it can close, I step outside. Edam's still there. "Hey."

"You doing okay?" he asks.

"I am now. Can you send someone to ask Inara and Judica to have everyone brought to the throne room in ten minutes?"

"Everyone?" Edam asks.

"Every single person we can squeeze into the room, but

leave a path ten feet wide down the middle of the room. And have your people bring every fire extinguisher they can find."

Edam's mouth opens, but then he shakes his head.

"Don't worry," I say. "It'll make sense soon enough."

He glares down the hall where Noah just disappeared, but doesn't argue with me.

I'm rummaging around in my closet when Lark arrives. "Chancy? What's going on?"

"I'm going to have to wear my birthday dress a little early," I say. "And I need to order a wider selection of gowns right away."

"You mean the Oscar de la Renta?" Lark's eyes light up.

I pull it out of the closet, take it out of the bag, and slide it off the hanger. It's a shimmery purple fabric that complements my eyes with the way I'm copying Mom right now. The bodice is laced with enormous, sparkly, perfectly cut amethysts, and the full skirt features clusters of stones at intervals, sewn on to the places where the fabric is bunched.

"What's going on?" Lark asks.

I shed my pants and shirt and pull the dress on. I spin around and Lark zips me up.

"Bring a camera with you." I grab Mom's crown and settle it over my hair. "You'll want to remember this moment, I imagine."

Lark follows me out the door and sprints down the hall to her room. I march straight to the throne room, Edam next to me, Arlington and Frederick only a pace behind. "What's going on?" Edam whispers.

"You'll see soon enough."

He doesn't ask whether Noah knows, and I'm grateful. When I reach the throne room, over a hundred people are already gathered. More pour in as I climb the steps, a continuous stream. I sit down on my throne and fold my hands across my lap.

Inara and Judica appear shortly after, and I gesture at the smaller thrones next to me. Inara takes the one I used to use, and Judica sits in her typical spot as Heir. My entire Council stands in the front row. There aren't any chairs set up, since I didn't plan to do this. The next five minutes stretch like taffy, pulling and pulling and pulling. My hands tremble and I still them. My pulse races and I slow it. My breath hitches and I calm it. But finally, the room is full to bursting. Edam, Frederick, and Arlington successfully maintain a ten foot path in the center of the room.

I really hope I don't screw this up. I haven't practiced this part nearly enough to have confidence in my ability.

But at some point, something has to go right for me. I stand up and walk to the edge of the raised area. "You all know that my mother changed her heirship in the last minutes of her life. Many of you have speculated about the possible reasons. Today I'm going to tell you. If you have relatives who aren't in attendance," which every single person in this room does, "you're welcome to videotape my announcement for them."

Hundreds of phones immediately appear. Perfect.

"Today I'm sending a message to the Five, but I'm including my people and theirs in the transmission. The time for secrecy has passed, and I believe this will impact the lives of all of us. For millennia, empresses have known about a prophecy given by Eve herself."

Murmuring fills the room.

"You're wondering why the prophecy was never made public, I assume, because I wondered the same thing." I shrug. "I don't know the answer to that. My mother did what all the empresses before her had done and kept it hidden. But today, I'm sharing it with all of you. Later today, I'll have it transcribed in the original Adamic, and also in English for distribution. But for now, I'll recite it for you."

I clear my throat and close my eyes. I want them to focus on the words and not on me. Then I recite the prophecy.

Murmurs spring up the second I stop talking. No one knows quite what to make of it. I can relate.

"I'm sure you're confused, unsure, and doubtful. I felt all of those things and more. But you see, there's a reason I heard this prophecy before any of you did. It's the same reason Mom changed her paperwork and named me as Heir."

I hold up my hand, the staridium flashing on my hand like fireworks. The little bucket in my head is full, and it pulses right alongside the flashes. "I tried on Mom's ring with her blessing, but with no idea what might happen." I breathe deeply in and out. "I discovered that this ring behaves differently on me than it does on anyone else."

"In what way?" Balthasar asks from the front row.

"I blew a hole in Mom's wall the first time I ever put it on my finger. I set her room on fire, too."

"How do you know it won't react to anyone else like that?" Davina yells from the back. "None of us have ever worn it."

My mouth turns up into a smile. "Now that's something to think about. But for now, in case you doubt that it reacts to me, I feel a demonstration might be in order. The prophecy says the Eldest will command the stone of the mountain. This staridium is the stone from the mountain, and I do command it."

I point at the people lining the empty space in the middle of the room. "If you don't mind, can you all take one more step backward?"

They're packed in like sardines, but I don't want to burn anyone. They shift another six inches or so on either side. I lift my hand and form it into a fist with the ring facing outward. I focus on one square of wood paneling at the back of the room. I don't want to set off an EMP, or even let the world in on the fact that I can. I don't want to knock out our electronics—that was obnoxious and expensive. No, I need something splashy, something visual. I need to do something I've only ever done on accident.

I think about the pool of energy, the bucket. I dip into it, and it's not hot like I worried it would be at first, or electric either. It's cool, almost refreshing. I shape it into a ball in my mind, then I roll it around and around, spreading it into a larger ball, and then finally, I thrust forward, straight at that panel in the back of the wall, clenching my hand into an even tighter fist.

A fireball the size of a basketball flies out of the ring and slams into the wooden panel I targeted, burning straight through it, and traveling beyond into the utility closet. "Fire extinguishers!" I shout.

Edam and my guards run across the room, liberally spraying everything that's burning. Every mouth in the room is open, every eye wide. But the light on the ceiling is still shining. I threw a fireball without setting off an EMP. I'm learning. I can't quite help my smile.

But I can't stand here smiling like an idiot all day. This is my moment.

"I am the eldest twin by a few seconds. I command the stone of the mountain, and I demand the other stones Mahalesh provided be returned to me. I am the Queen of Queens foretold by Eve. I will give each of the Five two weeks to come to terms with this information, but if they refuse to surrender and relinquish their rings to me, I'll come and take them."

9

"Well you certainly kicked the hornet's nest," Judica says.

She's right. Although I left the throne room quickly, I was there long enough to see the shock, hear the surprise and smell the stress and excitement of my people. I also watched them text and call others—within seconds, the videos of my fireball and proclamation spanned the globe.

It's a completely different world than the one Mom was born into.

My Council sits around me, filling every seat at the large boardroom table Mom made for Council meetings. I'm lucky she made it big enough for guests or it would never fit all the new positions I've added.

"I think it was brilliantly handled," Inara says.

"Of course you think that," Judica says. "She did exactly what you suggested."

And now I'm about to tell them my plan to visit Melina, which is also the opposite of what Judica suggested. I wish I could think of a way to smooth that over.

"I've called you all here—"

"A little late, if you ask me," Balthasar says. "It would be nice to get a heads up before these types of announcements."

"I'll certainly keep that in mind in the future," I say. "But for this particular move, it needed to shock everyone in the room."

"Well, you certainly did that," Franco says.

I don't frown or slam my hand down or scowl. "I'd like to talk to you about what we can expect, in light of my announcement."

"Well, you've blown our plans with Iceland and Puerto Rico all to pieces," Balthasar says. "I hope you weren't planning to pursue that."

"No, I decided to go another direction," I say.

"What you did with that ring was outright unbelievable," Edam says.

"Why didn't your mother tell me what was going on with that EMP?" Balthasar says.

"I think she was hoping to train me a little more before we reached this point," I say, "but that ship is already out at sea. I'm here, I'm queen, and if I'm supposed to unite the families, I can't fall into the same petty squabbles that have consumed the Five for centuries. Judica helped me to realize that." Perhaps if I recognize her major contribution, she'll be less upset that I'm ignoring her advice otherwise.

"What about Melina?" Judica folds her arms.

Maybe not.

Everyone turns to look at her.

"Melina, with Angel's help, stole Judica right out from under our noses," I say. "The only reason Judica returned is that she managed to escape. Ingenuity and skill beyond what most of us possess brought her back to us."

Judica frowns.

"My twin believes we should eliminate the threat Melina poses, and I agree." I tap my fingers on the table. "Our difference comes in the way in which we believe we should go about accomplishing that. Judica would like to send a strike team to take her out. She has offered to head that team, and while I recognize the reasons behind that suggestion, I still believe that's a little premature."

"She killed Mother," Judica says. "I'm positive." She lowers her voice. "And she tried to kill me."

I splay my hands flat on the table. "I was absolutely positive that you killed Mom. I was wrong then, and you might be wrong now. Until I've met with her and evaluated her story myself, I won't terminate her life."

Judica groans. "This is a huge mistake. Melina and I are nothing alike."

"I agree it's a mistake," Inara says. "You can't leave Ni'ihau, not right now, not after the grenade you just lobbed at our rivals."

"I won't move on her until I'm positive," I say. "I won't."

"Then send me," Inara says. "We were always close."

It would be much simpler, but I can't be sure of how I feel without meeting her myself. "I can't do that either."

"Summon her here," Edam says. "Then you can evaluate her without risk to yourself."

"But will she come?" I ask.

"Give her that option, and by the time we hear back, maybe we'll know how the Five are reacting to your demonstration," Edam says.

"We don't need time to know," Balthasar says. "You've just declared war on the Five. They will respond in kind."

"I'm sorry if you're upset," I say. "I should have consulted with you at least. It wasn't my intention to start a war we can't win."

"You mistake my meaning." Balthasar grins from ear-to-ear. "Don't apologize to me. I've been preparing for this my entire life. Our armies are the best in the world, by far."

"Oh." I blink. "Well, that's good to hear, I suppose."

"The next few weeks will be some of the most exciting of my life," Balthasar says.

"Right. Well." I catch Inara's eye. "Send a summons to Melina. Tell her she has a week to report to me voluntarily, or I'll come and find her myself."

"May I recommend something?" Maxmillian asks. "Don't say you'll come to her. Then she has no incentive to appear. Threaten to bomb her out of existence."

"There's no way I'll carry through on that threat, and I won't threaten something I wouldn't follow through on. But you can tell her if she doesn't appear, I'll send a tactical team to retrieve her."

"Better," Judica says.

"Agreed, then," I say. "And on to the next item of business. We've got a war to prepare for."

Judica interlaces her fingers and stretches. "I wouldn't have advised this, but now that it's here." Her grin looks eerily similar to Balthasar's. "Alamecha is strong. Maybe even strong enough to force this."

"Perhaps Judica and Balthasar should go over preliminary plans for the different ways this could all go down. In the meantime, Marselle and the rest of you will do your very best to obtain information on how the Five are taking this news. I'd love to assemble anything we can that will prepare us."

"But when they refuse your demand, Alamecha will squash them like bugs," Balthasar says.

"We've been working on a number of scenarios to crush each family for years," Judica says.

Squashing people sounds like a tremendous death toll. They should not be smiling. "I don't want to squash anyone," I say. "I merely want to make sure we're prepared to stave off the utter destruction, not cause it myself."

"Sure, right," Judica says. "That's our goal too."

I frown.

"Does anyone else see the irony that we wait six thousand years for this Queen of Queens," Judica says, "and now that she's here, she doesn't have any desire to govern?"

"It may be the precise reason she was chosen," Marselle says.

"Chosen?" Judica snorts. "Okay."

The rest of my day melts in a never-ending round of meetings. Eventually, I break away to spend a few minutes training with the ring in the bunker. After all, if I'm telling the world I can use it, I'd better be able to use it.

"It seems like a lot of hurry up and wait," Noah says. "I mean, you send out this huge, amazing, unbelievable thing into the universe, and then no one replies."

"It took me days to process it myself," I say. "I expect they'll spend today not believing it's real, and then the next day or two determining whether it might be. Then they'll need to figure out what their options are."

"I guess," Noah says. "But I swear, my stomach would be eating through its own lining if I were you."

"Luckily, if mine does, it heals itself right back up."

Noah sighs wistfully. "Of all the evian bonuses, from super strength to brilliance to limitless energy and physical excellence, the one I envy most is the ability to heal."

"I wish I could give them all to you."

When I emerge from the bunker, half a dozen guards are waiting for me.

"What's wrong now, Bellatrius?" My heart accelerates. Has one of the Five replied?

"There's someone asking to see you," she says.

"Who is it?" I ask.

She shakes her head. "Not to see you, Your Majesty." She points at Noah. "The plane that's circling is requesting to land so they can see Noah Wen."

"Aww crap," Noah says. "I forgot about the tracker."

"What tracker?" I ask.

"When my parents sent me off to study in the United States alone, they gave me a jet."

Right, and we used it. Actually, I kind of destroyed it. "The one we flew here with, I assume, and then took nearly to the coast of China."

"We blew up the plane, but my parents could access the flight pattern remotely."

I close my eyes. "They'd have seen that it was destroyed."

"And my last location," Noah says. "Prior to the explosion."

"Which means they aren't sure whether you're alive or dead. Have you been messaging them?"

"Of course," Noah says. "I'm not a complete dunce. I sent them several texts."

"Texts?" I slap my forehead. "Electronic messages anyone could have sent? And now they know you blew up their plane." I shake my head. "I'm surprised they didn't show up sooner."

"They only check the report on the plane weekly," Noah says.

"It doesn't send an alert when it malfunctions?"

Noah shrugs. "This is my first time destroying an unbelievably costly jet, believe it or not."

"Noted." Time to smooth over a few parental feathers. "Allow them to land, and then show them into the Council boardroom," I tell Bellatrius. "But make sure they don't see the throne room. I doubt that would go over without causing a lot of other questions."

"Probably not," Noah says. "Good call."

"I'll change clothes and meet you in the boardroom," I say. "Is there anything else I need to know?"

"My dad loves hot tea."

"I was thinking more along the lines of, 'My dad hates when people call him by his first name,' or something like that, but I'll make sure the tea caddy is stocked." Noah turns to head for his room, but I grab his arm. "Hey, I didn't even ask you before and I'm sorry. Do you want to go home? Because I can find a replacement. You can go back to normal life."

He leans toward me like he's telling me a secret. "Wild horses couldn't drag me away." Then he presses his lips against mine briefly. My heart hammers in my chest, but only my guards can hear it, thankfully.

I step back and regroup. "Alright. Good to know."

Noah winks at me and jogs down the hall to his room.

I change into a plain but well-cut business suit and head for the conference room. Noah meets me just outside the door. "Ready for this?" he asks in Mandarin.

I've met nearly every powerful human in Mom's employ, from Presidents to Prime Ministers, Chief Justices and even dictators. How bad could this be? I open the door.

An outrageously tall man with broad shoulders and short, black hair is pacing from one end of the board room to the other.

I clear my throat and he spins around, pinning me with a glare. "And who are you? I demand to speak with the person in charge here." His English is perfect, with no hint of any accent. Impressive.

"You are speaking to the person in charge," I say in Mandarin. "My name is Chancery Alamecha." I glance around and realize Noah didn't follow me in the room. Good grief. What a coward.

"My son flew here on Friday. I demand to know where he is." Even though I replied in Mandarin, he's still speaking in English. His melody is staccato, and there's a harmony I can't quite distinguish.

Fine, I'll switch to English, too. "You're looking for Noah Wen, I understand."

"So you do acknowledge that he was here." He stops pacing and pins me with dark brown, commanding eyes. He's accustomed to being obeyed with alacrity. That much is clear.

"He did arrive here on Friday, just as you said."

"Where did he go from here?" His chest heaves, his heart hammering inside his ribs.

Suddenly I recognize it. The notes I couldn't make out. He's terrified. Texts notwithstanding, he believes his son is dead.

"Haven't you heard from him?" I ask.

"Not with anything verifiable."

I could strangle Noah. "Mr. Wen, your son is alive and well, and he's here with us. I am terribly sorry that wasn't clear to you. I assumed he was in communication with you regularly." I raise my voice. "Please send Noah into the boardroom immediately."

Noah darts around the corner, hands in the pockets of a very nice suit I didn't pay much attention to before. I wonder where he found that. Larena must have really taken a liking to him. "Hello, Dad."

I'm expecting a bear hug, or maybe some tears. I am not expecting Mr. Wen to straighten his shoulders and begin berating Noah in lightning fast Mandarin.

Noah bows his head without a word. Where's the Noah I know?

I speak Mandarin, but I'm missing every other word, he's talking so fast.

"Outrageous. . . mother . . .sick to death. . .not the. . .responsible adult. . . immediately."

"Excuse me," I say.

Mr. Wen stops mid-diatribe and turns to me. "Thank you for returning my son. We will not impose on your hospitality any further. He will be coming home with me right now."

"Whoa." I hold up both my hands. "Noah can't leave."

"Why ever not?" Mr. Wen asks sharply.

"He didn't tell you the honor he has received?" I ask.

Mr. Wen slowly turns toward his son.

"He must have been wanting to surprise you," I say. "He was sent to the United States to develop contacts, was he not? To pave the way for you to broaden your company's holdings into new markets? Western markets?"

Mr. Wen nods stiffly.

"My company, Mr. Wen, is the single largest company in the United States. We own Zongran, Peters and Company, and Xavier Enterprises, to name a tiny few. Our interests are broad and extensive and reach into almost every aspect of business in the Western Hemisphere. We approached Trinity School about hiring an intern, someone we could trust to assist our top personnel with the ins and outs."

"And you chose a foreigner?" Mr. Wen's voice practically drips with skepticism.

"We did not," I say. "No, in fact we chose a student named Logan Calvert."

Mr. Wen points at Noah. "That is not Logan Calvert."

"When we announced our decision, your son approached us and told us we were making a mistake. He told us that he had twice the skill and insight of Mr. Calvert, and he told us that he also had extensive holdings in China. He implied heavily that he might be able to encourage your investment in our operations in the future, as well as locate and point out inefficiencies. He said if he learned enough, he might even be able to foster partnership and trade arrangements between the United States and various Chinese interests. Some of the other leaders have been concerned he overstated his influence, but I had faith in his claims. Enough to give him a chance here."

"And that won you over?" Mr. Wen glances at Noah with begrudging respect.

"He's here, isn't he?" I put one hand on my hip. "But now I'm wondering whether the autonomy your son bragged about might have been grossly exaggerated, if you chase him around like a dog herding chickens."

Mr. Wen shakes his head. "He didn't lie to you, Ms. Alamecha. He has a wide degree of autonomy with our western holdings. I'm ashamed to admit this, but I've been nervous for more than a day now that he perished. You see, we tracked his plane and it went down somewhere in the ocean, not too far from China. And when we reviewed his messages, they were. . . vague."

"I understand emotional transference all too well," I say. "But I fear I must take responsibility for the fear you endured as well. In my carelessness, it didn't occur to me to reach out to you myself in spite of hiring a minor. Shortly after you arrived, we rooted out a few corporate spies, and they managed to hijack your plane. We caught up to them, but they chose to drown rather than be captured. Of course my organization will reimburse you for the cost of the loss."

Mr. Wen's eyes widen. "That sounds terrible, and I couldn't possibly accept. Our insurance will need to coordinate with you, but the plane was covered."

"I'm also happy to inform you that your pilots were resting here when the plane was taken," I say. "You can take them home with you, and your son too, if that's what you'd like to do. But if he's allowed to stay, we'll be very happy to continue his training. He's proven very clever and has already been helpful."

"Of course he can remain," Mr. Wen says. "This is the whole reason we sent him to the United States." He beams at Noah, who perks up a little bit.

"The internship is set to last six months. At that time, we can discuss our business relationship moving forward together."

Mr. Wen offers his hand, and I take it. "This was a very successful trip," he says. "But before I leave, can I speak to someone a little older? Perhaps your boss?"

I don't roll my eyes. "Of course," I say. "Let me see whether I can find our CEO. She's wandering around here somewhere."

Alora fills in as the CEO of Alamecha Corp. beautifully and after a half dozen cups of tea and a few minutes alone with Noah, Mr. Wen re-boards his plane.

Noah follows me back to my room. "I'm sorry about that," he says when I reach my door.

I walk through and wave him inside. "It's fine," I say. "I'm just glad he was relatively easy to convince."

"You're pretty persuasive when you want to be," Noah says.

"Speaking of, you really shrink down when he's around, huh?" I'm smiling bigger than I meant to, and I wipe it off my face.

Noah scowls at me. "You weren't raised by him. My dad's scary."

"I can see that. He almost had me quaking with that tongue lashing he was giving you."

"He thought I dropped out of school to follow a girl to Hawaii," Noah says.

Oh. "Well." I giggle. "You kind of did."

Noah leans closer to me. Our bodies are only inches apart, standing in the middle of my room. "I did."

"So he wasn't totally wrong," I say.

"But he thought I had a crush on you."

"Oh," I say. "Then I guess he was wrong."

Noah nods his head. "He sure was."

I hold my expression steady. I won't let on that I'm disappointed. I will not. I have too much self-respect for that.

"I don't have a crush on you, Chancery. You know that, right?"

I bob my head up and down jerkily. "Of course. I mean, yes, I know that."

"Comparing how I feel for you to a crush would be like saying Romeo had a crush on Juliette."

"Um, they died."

"Every day I spend here, a human walking among all these perfect, deadly specimens, I could die."

He's right.

"I don't have a crush on you because I'm in love with you, Chancery Divinity. Your fire, your empathy, your humility, they all combine in an unbelievable way. You're perfect, and I'm utterly unworthy of you, but I love you anyway."

When he kisses me this time, I lean in to it. My heart soars, but it also cracks, just a little. Because he's right, about all of it.

10

When Frederick stabs me in the thigh with a dagger, I accidentally shoot a teensy, tiny fireball at him. It sets his shirt on fire, which quickly spreads all the way up to his neck. I still haven't heard from Melina, and it's been twenty-four hours. We haven't heard a word from the Five either, and I might be a little on edge with all the waiting.

"Whoa, whoa," Edam says. "That's not okay."

"I'm so sorry," I say. "I didn't mean to do that."

Frederick drops to the ground and rolls until the fire goes out, but the smell lingers. "It's fine, Your Majesty," Frederick says. "You really should use all the abilities you have when fighting more than one opponent."

"No, she really shouldn't," Edam says. "She can't rely on always having something we don't understand."

"I'll always have it on," I say, "so shouldn't I learn to use it?"

Edam scowls. "But what if you lose it, or it stops working? It's sloppy to rely on anything other than yourself when fighting."

"Fine, fine," I say. "I won't shoot off any more fireballs."

Edam runs his hand through his hair. "Add that to the list of things I never expected to hear while training new fighters."

"Will do," I say.

In the middle of my next fight, two guards rush into the room. "Your Majesty," Franklin calls. "You're needed urgently."

Edam, Frederick, Dante, and Desmonda step back immediately and wipe their blades clean on their clothing.

"What is it?" I ask, healing the slices on my formerly exposed left side as quickly as I can.

"There's a plane hailing us, requesting permission to land."

"Who is it?"

"Vela, Your Majesty."

Adika's Heir. Second in line for the throne of Shenoah, the sixth family. A thrill of excitement runs through me. This will be the first response we've received, and it's being made in person. Bad news would come via some other communication channel, right? I'd be even more excited, but Shenoah, more than any other family, hated Mom. I struggle to believe they'll surrender to me without a fight, no matter what kind of magical rock performance they witnessed. Of course, Vela could be here to request a demonstration in person, and that I can definitely provide.

"Sorry to cut this short," I say, "but I need to go fling a few condoned fireballs. Probably."

"I'm coming with you," Edam says.

"As am I," Frederick says.

Frederick didn't leave Mom's side for more than three centuries. Old habits are hard to break. Luckily, Edam likes him. I think he trusts him, too. Mostly.

I rush down the steps and toward my room. "You might want to change clothing as well," I say.

"Not a bad idea," Edam says, sprinting past me to his quarters.

Frederick shakes his head. His shirt is half gone and what's left is charred and melty. The gap that burned now displays a wide expanse of perfect man chest. "If Vela happens to ask me what happened." He wiggles his eyebrows.

He's going to be my living witness. Smart.

I duck into my room while he stands outside the door with my regular door guards. What should I wear? Something welcoming? I pick up a tan sheath dress and matching jacket with pink backstitching. It's sort of concierge Barbie. Which is clearly a little too friendly for a meeting that may very well turn confrontational. I wish Lark was here—she always knows what I should wear. I consider pulling a Judica: black pants, black shirt, black boots.

But I'm not my sister, and I never will be. I'd look ridiculous.

I settle on a dark blue silk blouse and black dress slacks, without a crown. Because that's just pretentious. I adjust my ballistic necklace and touch up my lipstick.

I'm as ready as I'll ever be.

Edam's already waiting in the hall by Frederick. He changed into a navy blue button down shirt, the top two buttons undone to show a hint of his beautiful chest, with dark pants and matte black leather shoes. We look almost like we planned it.

"You look," Edam says, "breathtaking."

I force myself not to smile or run down the hallway toward the throne room. "Thank you," I whisper. "You look pretty good yourself."

"It's a good day to conquer another family, don't you think?" he whispers.

I smile this time, but I shake it off. "We have no idea why she's here," I say. "No idea at all."

"She wouldn't have flown this far to tell you no."

"It's not Adika," I say. "She sent her Heir. But we'll find out why she came soon enough."

Moments after I reach the throne room and sit down, leaving Frederick and Edam to stand between the smaller thrones and mine, one on either side of me, Vela is escorted into the room. She's flanked by a dozen men, all wearing swords on their backs. I straighten up in my seat.

"Good morning." Vela's long, dramatic gold earrings sway as she speaks. "My mother viewed your video yesterday."

"And she sent you here to provide me with an answer, I presume."

Vela compresses her lips and nods.

Uh oh. "What exactly does your mother have to say to me?"

"Adika Shenoah, daughter of Malimba, granddaughter of Sethora, great granddaughter of Jericha, great great granddaughter of Sela, great great great granddaughter of Avina, who was daughter of Kankera, who was daughter of Adelornamecha, who was daughter of Shenoah, who was daughter of Eve herself, sends you a message, Chancery Alamecha, seventh daughter of Eve."

I've aged a year. Why Shenoah always insists on naming the entire lineage from Eve down in formal situations, I will never understand. I memorized all of that at the age of two. I could recite it to her. "And what is Adika's response?"

"My mother refuses your demand that she surrender. She refuses to part with the stone that was passed from Mahalesh to Shenoah, as a gift from a beloved sister. She refuses to serve you, seventh daughter of Eve. But she does not wish to be at war with you, either."

Oh, wonderful. She really did fly all this way to tell me no. "Why didn't your mother call me to share this? Wasn't she worried I'd be upset? I don't think I'd send my heir to deliver a refusal." I lift one eyebrow with displeasure.

Vela's guards all draw their swords as though I threatened to kill her. Good grief.

"She sent me to deliver the message as a show of good faith," Vela says. "My mother doesn't believe you have the conqueror's spirit, or the grit you need to enforce your demands, no matter what types of tricks you're able to perform. She's not even convinced your display was real. Computer animation does all sorts of things these days, after all."

My ring flashes brightly on my hand and Vela's eyes drop.

"It's no trick." I hold up my hand and shape a small ball, so small, so controlled. I launch it at the ground beneath her feet. When it strikes, it explodes in a shower of sparks. "You can at least reassure your mother that I can do what I say."

"I never doubted you."

"But your mother—"

"My mother sent me to refuse you, but that's not why I agreed to come."

Wait, what?

"I have a different purpose," Vela says. "I came to talk to the Eldest. I am not my mother."

"Your mother is barely over five hundred years," I say. "It's unlikely you'll be her successor."

"My mother does not serve Shenoah. She does not make decisions for the good of her people. It's time she is removed from her throne."

I glance back at Vela's guards. Not a single one flinches, or even looks surprised. This isn't the first time they've heard her say something like this.

"I think we should reconvene this meeting in the board room," I say. "Any chance your watchdogs will put away their claws?"

Vela bobs her head and her guards sheathe their swords. "I hoped you'd say that."

I walk down the steps and out into the hall, Vela and her entourage only a few steps behind me. We pour into the conference room, but as we do, every member of Vela's guard eyes Frederick and his burned shirt with caution and understanding.

"Training exercise." Frederick shrugs. He's a genius.

I sit at the head of the table, and Vela moves to take the other side. She touches the back of the chair, and changes her mind. She strides toward me.

Edam reaches for his blade, and I stop him by placing a hand on his arm.

Vela pulls out the chair right next to me. "I'm not here to fight with you," she says. "I only brought them," she gestures at the men behind her, "because they wouldn't agree to let me come alone."

I can certainly understand that. Edam stands right next to me, with Frederick on my other side. I want to roll my eyes at them, but this kind of intimate meeting with a rival has to be their worst nightmare.

"Why did you come?" I ask.

"As I mentioned, my mother doesn't care about our people."

"You care about the humans you rule?" I ask.

Vela frowns. "Excuse me?"

Okay. "Then you mean the evians of Shenoah."

She lifts one eyebrow. "Of course that's who I mean."

"Continue," I say.

"She does what she wants, when she wants to do it, and she doesn't think about the cost to the rest of us. She's a terrible ruler."

There's a reason she and Mom didn't get along. "What do you propose to do about it?"

"As it turns out, my mother isn't as. . . vigilant at preserving secrets as she should be. I had seen that prophecy before you read it. But seeing Mother's eyes bulge when you read it aloud." Vela shakes her head. "It was magnificent, what you did."

"Thank you."

"And you're exactly the kind of ruler I'd like to be."

Which means she's not interested in surrendering to me.

"But I don't mind taking orders either, not if they come from someone I trust."

Ah.

"And I heard that you defeated your sister, Judica."

I nod.

"But you didn't kill her."

"That's correct," I say.

"I can defeat my mother in combat," she says. "But I don't think I could bring myself to kill her."

"Okay," I say, still waiting for the details of her offer.

"I propose that I challenge my mother and defeat her. You have troops standing by locally to support me, in case the people of Shenoah prove to be more loyal to Adika than I believe they will be."

"And?"

"And the second I've deposed my mother, I'll pledge to you," she says. "I'll surrender her ring to you, and take an oath to serve you. But surely you'll need someone to administer things in each family. You can't intend to maintain a day-to-day presence across the entire globe."

She's right. I can't possibly manage every detail, and she knows Shenoah. She's aware of how the entire continent of Africa operates. "All of that sounds acceptable to me, but I have some clarifications."

She inclines her head. "I expected that."

"Unlike you," I say. "I value human life."

"Human life?" The incredulity in her voice is palpable.

"I believe humans are as much the children of Eve as you and I. They may be further removed, but it doesn't impact their value. If I appoint you as my Regent for Shenoah, I'd expect you to transition every government to a freedom model."

Vela swallows hard. "That can't be done overnight. I agree with your mother that providing humans the illusion of freedom increases their productivity, but—"

"I'm not talking about the illusion of freedom," I say.

"What do you mean, then?" she asks. "If I might be blunt."

"I believe humans should have rights, and they should be able to govern themselves, much as we do. Eventually, I think they should know about us, and understand the power dynamic between us. Obviously we live longer, and we have capacity to do some things they can't, but it doesn't make them worthless."

"That's. . . controversial," Vela says.

I don't disagree. "Very."

"I'm assuming that's not the only thing you mean to change," she says. "Any other startling plans I should be made aware of?"

I shrug. "That's probably the worst of it, but I also believe half-humans should be allowed to live among us. I believe it shouldn't be a crime to have split parentage."

Vela's mouth snaps shut.

Before I can say anything else, Frederick steps forward and clears his throat. Inserting himself in a conversation like this is a new thing with him. Maybe he's taking his elevation to my Council seriously. "Go ahead," I say.

"I'd like to know why," he says. "Why come to Alamecha and offer a surrender? Your mother hated Enora for centuries. Alamecha stole your humans and clapped them in chains. Not to mention every atrocity of war. The bad blood between our families runs deep, and yet here you are, promising to hand over your crown to Chancery if only she'll help you supplant your mother. Is it because you know you'll be replaced otherwise?"

The muscles in Vela's face tense and her shoulders stiffen. "Everything you say is true, charred guard. I stand to lose every scintilla of power I now possess the very second my mother becomes pregnant with another female."

"Is that why you've come to me?" I ask. "You'd rather lose Shenoah to me than lose your place in line?"

Vela shakes her head stiffly. "I saw with my own eyes how much Enora doted on you as a child. I'm young, but I'm much older than you. My mother may have more daughters. She probably will, but I saw something else in you. Something I recognized—the lack of any desire for power. I've never wanted my mother's job. It's miserable and never-ending and depressing."

"So you don't want to rule?" I ask. "And you'd rather pass things off, but you think I'd be better for your people than your mother?"

"All of that is true, and there's more." Vela's shoulders relax. Her eyes shine. "Your mother has been gone for a week, and you've survived a challenge without killing your rival, and now you've shared the prophecy with the world. Your mother was a great woman, undeniably impressive, strong and intelligent, but cruel, too. You may look like her, but in the reality of your rule, I believe you're nothing like your mother. You are, however, someone I respect and admire. Just like you, I'm nothing like my mother. I'm offering this at great risk to myself, because I think it's the right thing to do, and I always try to do the right thing once I've identified what that is."

"Trusting you at your word is a real gamble," I say. "You don't know me very well, and I know nothing about you."

"I might not have come at all," Vela admits. "In spite of all the evidence supporting what I'm telling you now, and after seeing you wield the power of the staridium, it still might not have been enough for me to risk my family, my future and my own very long life."

There's something else going on here, but I can't think what.

"A character witness I trust spoke on your behalf. You don't know him, but he has followed you and your sister very closely from the day you were born. He also knew your mother and had fond memories of her."

Who is she talking about?

"Moses, it's time."

The tallest guard with the broadest chest and the largest sword steps forward, separating himself from the others.

Moses. The name is familiar, but is it really him? Is this enormous warrior really my older brother?

"I told Vela to take this gamble." Moses' voice is deep and rough, but his eyes are steady.

"You're Moses?" I can't quite believe it.

When he smiles, I see Mom in him and I know. He's telling the truth.

"I told her she could trust you," Moses says, "and that my mother changed. She tried to break out of the mold with me. She wanted to keep me, but seeing me grow hurt her too badly. She gave me up when I was barely two weeks old. But she kept you, and you changed her. I came to court several times over the years and watched you with curiosity."

"Why did you believe him?" I ask Vela. "What significance does my brother have to you?"

"I took him as my Consort last month," Vela says. "We're married."

"I hate that," I say.

Vela scowls and Moses frowns.

"The sale of children. Boys raised among people who don't love or care for them. I hate it all."

Edam puts a hand on my shoulder. "Chancery's going to abolish the practice."

"Are you serious?" Moses asks.

"Deadly serious," I say.

I glance back at the men behind Vela, and every single one of them is looking at me with something akin to hero worship.

"It's wrong. When you choose a Consort, it should be a choice for both of you, not only for the Heir. As things are set up now, the Heir has all the power, and the men are little better off than slaves. It's disgusting."

"We agree with you," Moses says. "And we aren't the only ones."

I hadn't considered that.

"Will you support me if I challenge my mother?" Vela asks.

She's so young, barely more than a decade older than me. I want to believe we can do this, that we can make a difference, change the shape of the evian world, and the human one too. I think about her gift to me at my coronation. She's been thinking about this for a long time. The olive branch is proof.

Accept the world as it is, or do something to change it. It might be a mistake, but if I don't take the risk, I'll never know.

"Yes," I finally say. "I'm with you."

❧ 11 ❧

I spend the next two hours going over details with Vela, but she can't stay too long or her mother will suspect.

"It's time for me to go," she finally says.

I walk her to the landing strip where her jet waits. "I'll be thinking of you," I say.

She reaches for me, and I meet her halfway. We clasp arms, my palm on her forearm, my fingers wrapping around her arm tightly, and hers doing the same. The shake of equals.

Vela begins to ascend the steps of her jet, her guards following right behind her, all save one.

Moses turns around and walks toward me.

Edam places his hand over a dagger casually. If I didn't know him so well, I'd think he was just shifting slightly.

"Chancery," Moses says. "I know you don't need to hear this from me, and I know to you, I'm probably nothing."

I shake my head. "To me, you're my displaced brother. I'm glad you've found joy, but if you hadn't, you'd have had a place by my side."

"I would have taken you up on that a few months ago," Moses says. "Love changes you, though."

Edam swallows hard next to me.

"If anything ever shifts, you're welcome here with me. Alamecha is always available to you."

"Would you extend that offer to all the sons of Enora and Alamecha?" he asks.

"I will. My brothers and nephews are all welcome, always. But I won't stop there. Any of the displaced children of Eve are welcome with me, no matter what family they hail from, always."

Moses smiles at me, his eyes sparkling with hope. "I'll remember that."

"Good," I say. "I mourn for the loss of all my brothers, and my sisters' sons too. It was a special opportunity for me to meet you. You've grown into a very fine soldier." I reach my arm out toward him.

He takes it, and then pulls me closer, wrapping me in a nearly rib-cracking hug. "I'm proud of you, sister. Prouder than you know."

His words soothe a part of my heart I didn't realize was injured. I don't cry when the jet flies away, but if I wasn't surrounded by guards, I might have. Seeing my brother drives home to me that I still don't know who poisoned Mom. She's been dead ten days and her killer is still free. In fact, other than Judica's belief that Melina killed her, I don't have any leads.

It would be nice to believe Judica, that she knows who killed Mom, but I'm not convinced. I can't decide whether I'm being open-minded, or stupidly optimistic, hoping it wasn't her own daughter, my full sister, who killed Mom. I return to my room, but instead of going inside, I walk past it to Mom's room. It's time to dig back into her correspondence and journals. There must be something in here that will give me an idea. Judica meets me at the door before I can enter.

"You might say no to this," she says, "and I completely understand if you do. But I would like permission to enter Mother's records room. I spent days searching for leads on the investigation of her death. If I could read her journals, it might trigger something."

I was agonizing over not making progress, lamenting that I had no time and this possible solution falls into my lap. Is it too easy? Empresses do not allow anyone to enter their records room. It's a violation of the rules, again. But I need some help.

So it really comes down to whether I can trust her.

Two weeks ago, I'd have turned her down flat. She was stabbing my hand with forks. A week and a half ago, she practically decapitated me during a training session. But we've moved beyond that. She was taken by our older sister and nearly killed, and when she could have fled, she returned home to help me without any idea of how I'd receive her. I believe she didn't kill Mom, and I believe she's hurting. Even so, I'm not one hundred percent positive our goals are the same. Not yet.

"How about I go inside and grab some of Mom's journals and bring them out to you?"

She smiles. "That's a great idea."

I press my ring into the opening and then press my hand to the scanner for the finger prick. Then I enter Mom's password, Divinity. I don't ask Judica to look away.

"Her password was your name?" she asks softly.

"It was," I say. "I need to change that. Thanks for the reminder."

"Why did she love you more?" Judica asks, her voice so soft I barely hear it. "What did I do wrong?"

I turn around to face her, astonished at the misery in

her eyes, the terrible, all-encompassing sadness. "She loved you just as much as she loved me."

"Never mind." She sits at Mom's desk in the sitting room off her bedroom and begins browsing through some correspondence.

I duck inside the records room and grab a box of the most recent journals and carry it out to her, but before I can push for more information, one of my guards opens the door from the hall. "Your Majesty?"

I always hated being called Your Highness, and now that I've graduated to 'Your Majesty', I hate it even more. I wonder whether the titles exhausted Mom too. "Yes, Fesian. What now?"

"Two messages have arrived for you. One from Adora, and one from Shamecha."

I glance at my sister.

Judica meets my eye, her body utterly still. She heard. "Do you want me to go with you?"

I shake my head. "They're messages, so I can guess what they'll say."

She leans back in her chair. "We knew it was unlikely that any of them would simply hand control over to you."

Did we? I hoped someone would. More evidence of my incompetence, I suppose. "I'll be back."

If I drag my feet on the way to the command center, well, no one can blame me. Inara and Alora are waiting.

"We were here when the messages came," Alora says.

More like they've both been camped out here since I released that video. "It's fine." I hold out my hand.

Alora places two envelopes on my palm.

"They sent these via normal channels?"

"No, they both arrived via messenger plane," Inara says. "But the planes arrived within minutes of one another."

They're likely in contact, which doesn't surprise me.

They've been allies more often than not over the past few centuries. I open the envelope on the first missive.

Chancery:

Parlor tricks notwithstanding, I find your claim that you are the Eldest spoken of in Eve's prophecy to be exceedingly premature. Shamecha does not relish the idea of war with Alamecha, but if you attempt to press your claim, we will defend ourselves. Rest assured, we have not allowed our military force to dwindle like some families. We will consider any further proclamations or declarations on your part to be an act of war and proceed accordingly.

Melamecha

I hand the letter to Inara. "As expected."

Inara holds it out so Alora can read it at the same time.

"It's not as bad as it could be," Alora says. "We aren't at war, they just aren't surrendering."

"But not much time has passed," Inara says. "That's why we made this public. Their people will know exactly what you claim, and they'll see this war coming. I doubt they'll appreciate Melamecha forcing them into a bloody or protracted altercation with the strongest family for the sake of maintaining her sovereignty."

"Time will tell," Alora says. "I wouldn't panic yet, certainly."

I open the next envelope.

Chancery:

Parlor tricks notwithstanding, I find your claim that you are the Eldest spoken of in Eve's prophecy to be exceedingly premature. Adora does not relish the idea of war with Alamecha, but if you attempt to press your claim, we will defend ourselves. Rest assured, we have not allowed our military force to dwindle like some families. We will consider any further proclamations or declarations on your part to be an act of war. We will proceed accordingly.

Lainina

"Wow," I say. "They aren't even attempting to hide their

alliance." I pass the second letter to Inara. "This is verbatim the same letter."

Alora shakes her head. "I had no idea they were still this friendly."

"I'm unsurprised," Inara says. "They've been together far too often lately."

"Applying pressure tends to shore up friendships," I say. "Common enemy and all that."

"We only have two more to hear from at this point," Alora says.

The rest of the day passes slowly. Judica finds nothing helpful, and neither do I. When I finally drop off to sleep, I spend all night tossing and turning. Between nightmares of the Five attacking and slaughtering my people, and Red Bull whimpering to get out of his crate, I barely sleep at all. Finally I walk to my door and open it.

"Where's Edam?"

"I'm here." His deep voice drives all thoughts of sleep from my mind.

"Your dumb dog won't stop whining."

His mouth turns up into a smile. "My dog?"

"You know what I mean. What are you going to do about it?"

He turns toward the other guard. "Call for the alternate for the door."

Arlington reaches for his radio, and Edam walks into my bedroom. "Nice pajamas."

I glance down at my pink fleece pants covered in fluffy white clouds. "Shut up."

Edam walks straight over to his couch and opens Red Bull's crate. He picks him up and puts him on his stomach. The traitorous little whelp goes right to sleep.

I wish I could. And eventually I do.

But the next morning is more of the same. Hurry up

and wait. I train. I meet with Balthasar and Judica to discuss our strategies if every family turns me down. "It's like a game of dominoes," Judica says. "Taking out the first family will be hard, but once we do, they'll all fall one at a time."

"It might not be quite that simple," Balthasar says. "But once you overcome one, you can use their resources to chivvy, entice, and intimidate the others. Once we've successfully overcome two other families, no single family will be able to stand against us."

"Which means our best bet is to wait for Vela," I say.

Balthasar nods. "Correct."

"Should I worry that I've heard nothing from Malessa and Lenora? I mean, we're already sort of at war with Malessa."

"They picked a fight," Judica says, "but you escalated. You ignored their parry, and countered with a death strike. Now it's their move."

Larena walks through the doorway. "Were you just talking about Malessa?" she asks.

"We were," I say.

"Speaking of the devil, Analessa's in a plane not too far out. She's requesting permission to land."

Whoa. She came herself? Presumably with her ring.

"Granted," I say.

Judica smiles. "This should be interesting."

"Do you think she'll turn me down?"

Balthasar shrugs. "This is all unprecedented. None of us has any idea what she'll say or do, but I certainly didn't expect her to appear in person."

We all head for the throne room. I don't bother changing. She'll have to be fine with me greeting her in training gear. I regret my cavalier decision the second Analessa breezes through the door. She's only brought two guards with her, and her Consort, Daniel. Her ivory dress hugs her every curve and bells out around her knees. It would be impossible to walk in, except that it's slit up to her hip. She looks stunning, commanding, regal and yet also completely at ease, as though she's not worried at all to be so outnumbered in enemy territory. Like we're old friends who go back centuries.

"Chancery, darling."

"Darling?" I ask. "You attacked Puerto Rico, stole my property, and killed my people." Her smug smile and carefree manner pisses me off. "I ought to kill you and take your ring right now."

She laughs. "I love it! You don't waste any time, which is quite refreshing." She reaches the raised part of the dais and puts her hands on the edge, catapulting herself up to the same level as me, her ivory heels clacking against the tile, not a hair or a tuck of her dress out of place. "I abhor posturing."

I stand up. "Do you?"

She smiles and looks sideways. "Oh fine, you got me."

"Why are you here, Analessa?"

"I apologize." She beams at me, and then makes eye contact with each member of my Council in turn. "I didn't mean to protract this, not at all. I thought the purpose for my presence would be obvious." She takes a small step toward me, placing a ring bedecked hand on her thigh and glancing at the staridium purposefully. "I'm here to surrender."

I could kick every single one of the people behind me who gasp like they can't believe it.

"We've been allies for the better part of a thousand years. How can this surprise you, really?" Analessa sits down on my former throne and puts her head on her hand. "I have terms, of course." She looks down at the ring on her finger. "I mean, I have always adored this ring. I won't just hand it over for nothing."

"What exactly do you want?" I ask.

"I'll remain the regent of Malessa, of course."

I expected that.

"And I'll be on your Council, obviously, in a permanent capacity. My Council position and regency over Malessa will be hereditary, passing to my youngest daughter upon my death. Not that any of that would allow me or mine to ever countermand your rulings or laws."

I incline my head. "Go on." Get to the part where you take away everything you've just offered.

"And you'll name Edam your Consort, and produce an heir as soon as possible. I don't even care whether you use *in vitro* to accomplish that, although judging from the looks I've seen you two share, I doubt it will come to that."

I meet Edam's eyes. He looks as shocked as I feel.

"Until you've produced an heir of your own, I'll be your Heir. And that's it. Pretty simple, really."

12

Balthasar's words ring in my ears. If I can take one family down, they'll all follow. An image of Judica flicking a domino and an entire row cascading across the tile flashes through my mind.

Analessa is handing me a domino, and all I have to do is marry a man I care for deeply.

I should say yes immediately.

"I need time to think about it."

Analessa stands up and walks past Edam, patting his cheek. "Of course you do. I'm not in a terrible rush. Think it over, and maybe take Edam out for a test drive, and then give me a call."

As quickly as she breezed in, Analessa flows from the room. She heads straight for her plane without a backward glance. She didn't ask for a demonstration or try and talk me into anything. She's so sure her offer will be accepted, she didn't even bother.

Alora and Inara both open their mouths, like they have insights to offer. Only, I don't want to talk to anyone about it. I practically run down the steps and then down the hall to my room. I'm fast, but apparently Edam's faster. When I open the door to my bedroom, he's there, one of his enormous arms rippling as he blocks my entry.

"We need to talk," he says.

I shake my head.

"Fine. If you don't want to talk, that's okay. But hear this before you hide in there. I had no idea she was coming. I haven't had any communication with my sister since before your mother died. I swear that to you, on anything you'd like. I didn't have anything to do with this, and as far as I know she has absolutely nothing to gain from encouraging you to marry me. I certainly have no intention of doing a single thing for her, ever."

He's so earnest, so concerned, and I know beyond a shadow of a doubt he's telling the truth. I should be relieved. I should feel a sense of peace, knowing that I can simply say yes to a man to whom I'm insanely attracted, and whom I respect. I could marry the best looking guy I've ever seen, the bravest, the toughest, and possibly the most devoted.

This should be such a simple decision. Why isn't it?

I reach for Edam's face and pull his head down toward mine until our foreheads touch. "I care about you, Edam. I do, maybe more than you know. But this isn't a small thing. It's forever. Can you try and understand that?"

His right hand lifts my chin until my face is turned toward him, like a daisy toward the sunlight. His other hand wraps around my waist pulling me against him. Strength, power, and confidence all radiate from him, and why wouldn't they? He's an unparalleled fighter, a gifted strategist, and he has the looks of Adonis himself. His lips press against mine, and my heart takes flight. I could fall into Edam and let him take care of me. He would keep me

BRIDGET E. BAKER

safe, he would guard my back, and he would treasure my heart.

I have no doubt about any of those things.

But what will happen to me if I do that? I can't rely on someone else. The Queen of Queens can't take the easy way out. I break off the kiss and push against his chest.

"I know it's not a simple decision," Edam says. "I know that. I won't fault you if you turn her down, not for a second."

He leans against the wall as I close the door.

What's wrong with me? Why can't I simply make this decision? I'm sure my mom would urge me to do it if she were here. When my door bursts open a moment later, a furious retort rises to my lips. I can't be rushed.

Judica stands in the doorway. "You said yes, right?"

I push the door closed. "I haven't decided yet."

"You've been mooning over Edam for at least a year."

My jaw drops. "You knew I liked him when you started to pursue him?"

She rolls her eyes. "You're so naive. Mother told me he was the best of the lot, but that wouldn't have been enough alone." She pauses, but then forges ahead. "You may as well know that I pursued him *because* you liked him."

Fury bubbles up inside of me. "I hate you."

Judica smiles. "If you'd told me that last year, we might not have made such a mess of things."

"Excuse me?"

"You still don't know anything about me," Judica says. "I hate everyone and everything. That's my default feeling, and for the first time, you're speaking my language."

She's right. I still don't understand her at all.

"Tell me why you don't want to take Analessa's offer."

"I'm not even quite sure why she's making it," I say. "I mean, what does she get out of it?"

"Ah, I can help there. She saw your video, and she believes it. She thinks you're the Eldest from the prophecy, which means she's got a decision to make. She can oppose the prophecy and back the losing team, or she can get on board first, which will assure her a spot on your Council, as well as winning your trust, or at least a facsimile of it."

"But then why demand I marry Edam?"

"She's clearly noticed you favor him. She'd have to be blind not to see that, honestly. And if you marry her brother, he's sure to feel some affection for her. But beyond that, she gets to displace me, and if something goes horribly wrong, she has leveraged her willingness to join Alamecha into *owning* the First Family. And one more thing. Since you'll be married, to someone of her choosing, the world knows you're hers. And beyond that, she'll have eliminated the best bargaining chip you had to offer other families, your Consort position. It's brilliant, really. She came up with all of this in less than twenty-four hours. She could teach a master class on politics, but of course, she never would. Analessa's not interested in giving back."

"Would you take the offer if you were me?"

Judica curls her lip. "In case you didn't notice, Edam and I didn't suit."

Thank goodness.

"But even so," she says, "I might say yes. Or I'd counter with another Consort, maybe one of her sons."

"You'd toss Roman over just like that?"

Judica flinches. "What do you know about Roman?"

"Nothing," I say. "Sorry."

"Look, the point is, you have an opportunity here to take the first family in a very, very simple way, with no casualties."

I close my eyes, and imagine saying yes. I imagine a life with Edam. Something about it appeals to me greatly, but something is off. "I can't bargain with my uterus. Surely that's not something the Queen of Queens would do."

Judica sits down on my bed. "Are you kidding me right now?"

"What?"

"This isn't about the prophecy or your integrity."

"It's not?" I ask. "Then what is it about?"

"Hmm." Judica drums her fingers on her knee. "Let's see. He's about six foot two inches, so about two inches shorter than Edam, but not short by any means. He's got black hair, black as sin, in fact, but sky blue eyes. Eyes you could fall into, if only he weren't so bloody *human.*"

"Whoa," I say. "You think I'm hesitating because of Noah?"

Judica stands up. "You're clearly lost in a big old pile of denial. Come see me when you've navigated your way out. Okay?"

"Let's say I agree to marry Edam," I snap. "What about the other families?"

Judica puts a hand on her hip. "We've been over this. If Analessa falls in behind you, the others will go down, especially if Vela comes through. With three families behind you, the others will fold like a laptop."

"Or they'll ally together and I'll have caused the worst war the world has ever seen."

"Sure," Judica says. "Or that."

"Here's the thing," I say. "Things that are forced together never hold."

"You don't even want to fulfill the prophecy," Judica says.

I'm prepared to tell her she's wrong. I'm prepared to say that of course I do. But she's right.

I don't.

"The whole thing is kind of ridiculous," I say. "I mean, if

it wasn't for that dumb thing, I'd have abdicated after I realized you didn't kill Mom and walked away."

Judica's laughter shocks me.

"What's so funny?"

"Even now, even after I've accepted that I lost to you, I have a burning, consuming desire to rule our people. The irony is too great. I've never believed in God a day of my life, you know. I figured that we're able to rule all the humans of the world because our ancestors unlocked the truth: too many generations passing breaks down our DNA and we're all hurtling toward the same ending. Genetic explosion. I figured that when that happened, some new species would take our place."

"You don't think God created Adam and Eve?" I ask.

Judica shrugs. "Does it matter? No one's seen hide nor hair of him or her since, so worrying about whether it was cosmic coincidence or divine intervention is a massive waste of time."

"But now that I have no desire to rule?"

Judica throws her hands into the air. "You hate everything about it, but it *has to be you*. You're the only one who can use the stupid ring. You're literally hurling fire balls and pulses of electromagnetic fields and who knows what else!"

"It's not like the rest of the prophecy makes sense," I say. "I mean, I didn't survive certain death."

"Didn't you?"

"Excuse me?"

"Well, first there's the fact that Mother should have killed you, and barring that, Melina tried to kill you. But let's pretend those didn't happen." Judica shakes her head. "You didn't know about the betting?"

I lift one eyebrow. "Do I want to know?"

"Probably not," Judica says. "But it sounds like you need

to know. Before you returned home, the odds on our fight were four hundred to one."

People were betting on which of us would win? Why does that surprise me? I shouldn't be shocked by anything anymore.

"And I could have killed you during that challenge," Judica says. "And I'm not someone who cedes a win. Ever."

"But you did to me," I say.

Judica nods. "I hadn't heard or read the prophecy, but I played right into it. You survived almost certain death not once, but at least three times to take control of Alamecha, just as it said you would."

"Let's assume that part is true. It's not like this is a time of blood and horror," I say. "And the world isn't overrun with plague and warfare."

"Isn't it?" Judica asks. "Mom sheltered you from too much. Afghanistan, Syria, Yemen, Mexico, Somalia, Iraq, Boko Haram, Sudan, Libya. I could go on."

"Those are wars caused by poor management of their holdings or disagreements between empresses."

"All of which you can rectify if you take over," Judica says.

"But there's no plague," I say. "Vaccinations have seen to that."

"Heart disease, cancer, mental illness, obesity, malaria, tuberculosis, and diabetes. Plagues. Should I continue?"

"Fine, I suppose depending on your interpretation of things, this prophecy could apply during any time in the last five thousand years."

Judica sighs. "The youngest female always leads. You're the youngest and can rule, but you're also the Eldest. Explain that as a commonplace event. Or what about commanding the stone cut out of the mountain? That's clearly a reference to staridium, and you and I both know I can't do anything with it."

"Try again." I pull the ring from my finger and hold it out to her. "Now you've seen what I can do with it, maybe you can too. I feel a sort of bucket in the back of my mind. That's not quite right, but I can't think of any other way to explain it. Then I can sort of dip into the bucket and pull out what I need."

Judica raises both her eyebrows and shakes her head. "No thanks."

"You said you wish you could rule! You're obviously better qualified. So just try it, okay?"

Judica opens her mouth to argue and then snaps it shut again. She snatches the ring from my hand and slams it onto her finger. She and I both watch it carefully, like somehow we'll see a secret in its facets.

The same pastel color begins to blink inside of it that I always saw with Mom. Judica scrunches up her face, and then she closes her eyes. She licks her lips and opens them again. "I don't feel anything at all."

"I didn't either, not at first."

"It doesn't even look the same on me."

It's not flashing like it does for me, but maybe that doesn't matter. "Keep trying."

"How long will I have to stand here looking like a wannabe idiot before you admit it?" Judica snarls.

"Admit what?"

"That you're the Queen of Queens. That someone, or something, or science, whatever, has chosen you, and you can't just bow out. You're going to have to accept it before you can start making the decisions you need to make."

I look away from her accusations and out the window at the ocean waves.

"You're too good a person to walk away from the prospect of utter destruction," Judica says.

"Maybe you handle things until something bad happens," I say. "And then I can step in if it ever gets to that point."

Judica pulls the ring off and holds it out to me. "You're the only one they'll follow, and it's precisely because of that dumb prophecy that they'll do it. They just won't like it, so you're going to have to bully and badger and chivvy them into it."

"I hate that part," I say.

"But this one family, the second most powerful after Alamecha, that one you can waltz right into running. Surely you can't fault the method on this one."

"You realize Analessa probably already has half a dozen people lined up to assassinate you if I say yes."

"Of course," Judica says. "That's part of the fun."

"You really are deranged," I say.

"Possibly, quite possibly. But the point is that, for the first time ever, we'd be in a position to eliminate the fighting, all the war, and spread out resources to wherever they're needed. We wouldn't need to hoard technology or medicine, or anything at all."

"Yeah, yeah," I say, "you're all about the benevolence."

Judica stiffens. "I may be scary and abrupt, but that doesn't mean I'm a monster."

I know she's not. I shouldn't have baited her.

"Whatever my flaws, I'm pragmatic," Judica says. "So I can tell you to take Analessa's deal, no matter how you feel about the human. Besides, he's a human. So if you want to keep him, do it. It's not like Edam can really do anything about it."

But I don't have to take the deal, not absolutely, because there's always Vela. I'll almost surely rule Shenoah at the end of the week, and as Judica said, once the first domino goes down. . .

A hard rap on the door spares me from arguing with Judica. "Come in," I say.

Inara's face in the doorway is strained, her lips compressed.

"What's wrong?" I ask.

"A message has come from Shenoah." Inara hands me a piece of paper.

"What's wrong? Our troops were in position," I say. "I checked with Balthasar earlier."

"Our troops were in position," Inara says. "That's true."

I glance down at the paper.

Vela was not a traitor before your proclamation. I lay her death at your feet. You aren't the queen from the prophecy, you're a greedy, spoiled little girl, and I'll take pleasure in killing you and razing Alamecha to the ground.

-Adika

I close my eyes in horror, but when I open them again, Inara's staring. "What happened to our troops?"

She shakes her head.

"None of them survived?" Hundreds and hundreds of humans, and half a dozen evians. It's a blow, but not devastating by any means.

"All of our troops were killed," Inara says. "But a plane did arrive, a passenger jet full of refugees."

"Excuse me?" I ask.

"Wait, refugees from where?" Judica asks.

"Moses," Inara says, "and others like him. He says there are thirty-something other men whom Adika had purchased from various families, but I haven't allowed anyone else to deplane."

"Why not? Of course they're welcome in Alamecha," I say.

"It's not that simple," Inara says. "Vela failed. This could be a plan by Adika. We need these men to be vetted. They've all been raised by another family. Their loyalty is, at best, problematic."

I lift my eyebrows. "Thirty? That's an awfully large group."

"That's true. Probably some of them are from Dahlia's stable of men."

"Don't call them that," I say. "They aren't animals."

Inara shrugs. "Breeding stock, basically."

"That's exactly the kind of attitude that we need to change," I say. "These men have fled without the benefit of families or friends, and they're risking their lives coming to a strange place because of a promise I made to my own brother."

"I apologize," Inara says. "My point was that there are loyalty and logistical issues with simply welcoming them here."

"We can repurpose guest quarters, surely," I say.

"The kitchen staff provides meals for anyone staying in guest accommodations, which will become onerous quickly if they're permanent residents."

Details, so many details. "I better go greet them." I have no idea what to say to them, especially Moses, who just lost a spouse.

I trot out the door and down the hallway, Edam and my guards trailing behind me.

"What's wrong?" Edam asks.

I fill him in quickly, finishing just as I reach the landing strip outside. It's raining, water puddles quickly turning to mud holes all around me. A large group of men are standing in the rain in a huddle near the bottom of the stairway.

"Moses," I say.

His head turns my direction, eyes cutting to my very

core. I've seen that look before, in the mirror after Mom died. Without thinking, I rush toward him, and I don't know whether I wrap my arms around him or whether he embraces me first. His arms tighten until my ribs creak, which is when Edam steps uncomfortably close.

Not that Moses is even aware of anything going on around him, much less subtle intimidation cues.

"I'm so sorry," I whisper. "So very sorry."

"I didn't know where else to go," he says.

"You did the right thing," I say. "You're welcome here, all of you. We will find you a place among us, I swear it."

"Uh, Your Majesty," Balthasar is standing a few yards away.

I finally extricate myself from Moses and step back. "Yes?"

"Another plane is hailing us." Balthasar points.

A larger plane circles above the island.

"Who is it?" I ask.

"It's another plane from Shenoah, and they claim it's more than fifty men. They're calling themselves the Motherless," Balthasar says.

"Why are you out here, and not Larena?" I ask.

He shrugs. "Fifty trained guards just showed up on our doorstep thanks to a military maneuver gone wrong. We lost all our troops on the ground. This is what high alert looks like."

Before I can even answer him, I notice Larena jogging toward us, her arms pumping. "Your Majesty!"

"Yes?"

She shakes her head. "We can't simply accept nearly a hundred evian males from another family. We don't have a place for them."

"I agree," Balthasar says. "We can't take a risk that they're a ploy by Adika, for one."

"Debrief them," I say. "You and Edam should be more than capable of handling that together. And Larena? Come up with possible solutions for housing, because I won't turn them away."

Larena and Balthasar exchange sour expressions, but neither of them argue with me. I guess for now, that's enough.

🎇 13 🎇

Yesterday two families turned my demands down flat, but I had a plan to take over one, and an offer to ally with another. That offer's still on the table, for a short period of time, thankfully. All three of my sisters in residence have converged to tell me in no uncertain terms that I'd be a fool to turn it down.

Which means I really, really need to figure out what I'm going to tell Analessa tomorrow.

"I'm canceling the birthday party," I say.

"Why?" Alora asks. "You need this."

I lift my eyebrows. "Vela and our people are all dead. I need cake and gifts and dancing?"

"Alamecha lost its monarch *on her birthday,* and then the heirs tried to kill one another. After that, one of them was *kidnapped,* and the other declared herself Queen of Queens," Inara says.

It's been a busy week.

"They need something normal," Alora says. "They need to be reminded that you're seventh generation, a leader who has been groomed and prepared, Enora's daughter.

They need a reminder of what life is like when things are good. You can't cancel this party. You can't. We haven't opened it to the outside, and that's enough."

"I have nearly a hundred men from Shenoah here," I say. "That seems pretty 'outside' to me."

Alora shakes her head. "They're defectors. They're joining you, the Queen of Queens."

"Stop saying that," I say.

Every single one of them has requested asylum here, and I couldn't turn them away any more than I could turn Moses away. It's not going to endear me to Adika, but it seems like we're not destined to get along in any case.

"Besides," Inara says. "The party will be a perfect place for you to send a message to the world. We'll live stream a few portions of it, knowing the Five will be watching. You and Judica need to stand united, and put the rumors and insinuations to rest. Can you do that?"

Judica nods. "Of course. In fact." She sits down and pulls the high ponytail out of her hair. "How about you get a clip right now of Chancy braiding my hair."

I kick her chair.

Of course she stands up gracefully before the chair topples over. Judica hasn't had a clumsy day in her entire life. "Fine, we keep the party, but can we at least tone it down a little?"

Alora's smile is patronizing. "Of course, Your Majesty. I'll cancel the elephants and the eighteen cannon salute right away."

"Moses is waiting for you," Inara reminds me, gesturing toward the adjoining door from my bedroom to Mom's.

I avoided using Mom's office for as long as possible, but it's really the only appropriate place to talk to Moses. Especially since Edam and Frederick won't leave me alone with him, and both my bedroom and the throne room seem like inappropriate alternatives to ask him about the details of what went wrong. "Fine. Fine, I'm going." I duck through the adjoining door into Mom's room, and walk to the exit into the hall to tell my guards I've changed rooms. "Over here guys," I say.

"Nicely done," Frederick says. He and Nelson jog down the hall to stand outside Mom's doorway instead of mine.

"I'll be in the study," I say.

Frederick tries to walk inside with me, but I block him.

"I'll be fine. It's only my brother."

"Who may or may not have an agenda," he says.

"Edam *and* Balthasar cleared him," I say. "It's fine."

"I disagree." Frederick scowls as he takes up his position right outside the door.

"Duly noted." I push through the doorway and into Mom's office. "Moses."

He stands up and crosses the room to hug me. "Chancery. Thank you for welcoming us here. I didn't know where else to go."

"What happened, exactly?" I ask. "If you feel up to talking about it."

He stares out the window that overlooks the ocean.

"Moses?"

"I can talk," he says. "Or at least, I should make myself talk."

"Okay," I say.

"Adika knew," he says. "It's as simple as that. I don't know whether it was one of our people who told her about Vela's plan, or whether it was someone from Alamecha."

"How do you know she knew?" I ask.

"Vela hadn't even challenged her yet when she——" He chokes and then clears his throat. "We returned home, went back to our quarters, and then went down for dinner, like always. Adika greeted her daughter with an embrace, which wasn't abnormal, but when Vela pulled away, Adika was holding a long knife." His voice drops to a whisper. "She stabbed her straight through the throat and severed her spine."

"She didn't suffer from Vela's aversion to killing a family member, clearly."

Moses shakes his head. "She did not."

"How did you escape?"

"We didn't escape. Adika let us go," Moses says. "She told us we could take her smallest jet if we were gone within ten minutes. She told us it was our only opportunity to leave, and that anyone disloyal who stayed would be eliminated."

I understand a little more why so many of the guards fled. Even if they hadn't been disloyal, the fear they might be found wanting was enough to expedite their departure. "I hope she doesn't kill anyone else."

"I'm surprised she allowed another jet to leave," Moses says.

"The men from that aircraft claim they weren't given permission, but they weren't shot down either, so they took that as permission."

"How long can we stay?" Moses asks.

I splutter. "What do you mean?"

"I appreciate you taking us all in, but I know they can't all stay forever."

"You misunderstand," I say. "I've proclaimed myself Queen of Queens. That means every evian on earth is my subject, so they should all be welcome in any case. But beyond that, you're my brother. You'd always be welcome here. And even past that, you and Vela tried to win Shenoah for me. I wouldn't repay your attempt, whether successful or not, with a short show of support followed by an eviction notice."

"We can stay. . . permanently?"

I bob my head. "Of course you can. I'll ask you all to swear to Alamecha tonight, and anyone who's willing to do it may stay. Forever. We'll find you jobs and provide housing until you can integrate."

Moses pulls me close for a hug again. "Thank you."

"Of course, if any of the men would rather return to their mothers, I am fully supportive of that as well. It's high time this unnatural practice ended."

Moses' eyes tear up.

"I would never have sold you," I say. "And you always have a place here. Mom regretted selling you from the moment she did it. I imagine many other mothers feel the same way, but of course, if they don't, the men are welcome here."

"Since they aren't here to tell you, let me express my gratitude for all my brothers," Moses says.

"We've been discussing the guest quarters," I say. "We have plans to add a central kitchen and mess hall where you can take turns making meals. It's not fair for me to ask the kitchen to provide meals around the clock for all of you."

"I completely understand," Moses says. "And we all know how to cook, so that shouldn't be a problem."

"Perfect," I say. "Also, by way of warning, I'm hosting a big party tonight. I'm eighteen today. I tried to cancel it, but my advisors tell me that's a bad decision. I'm sorry if it feels inappropriate."

"We heard about that," Moses says. "And we'd like to come, if that's not a problem."

Oh. "No, I'm sure that's fine," I say. "I'll make sure we have enough food for all of you."

Edam's standing by Frederick outside my door when Moses leaves. "Do you have a moment?" he asks.

"Of course," I say, as though I haven't a care in the

world. Meanwhile, my palms sweat, my heart races and my eyelids flutter. Which he can smell, hear, and see, obviously.

I am so dead.

I back away from him as he shuts the door. The backs of my legs bang into the leather sofa along the back wall of Mom's office, and my knees betray me. I fall onto my butt.

"I think we need to talk," Edam says.

My throat is drier than the Sahara. "Sure."

"My sister has backed us into a corner." Edam crosses the room and drops down in front of me on one knee.

My heart freezes. I'm pretty sure I need it to beat. I should also be breathing. Because my brain needs oxygen, doesn't it? Is he proposing? I blink and blink. Maybe that will restart my major bodily functions.

Edam's voice comes out gritty and deep. "I hate corners."

"Me too," I whisper.

"But I love you. You know that already."

I nod.

"You need to breathe." Edam takes my hand in his. "And you really need to calm down. I'm not proposing to you right now, I promise, even if I am kneeling. I'm only crouched down because you sunk into this seat over here."

"Right, obviously." I swallow.

Edam's eyebrows rise. "Is it obvious?"

"No, I guess it's not." I stammer. "The thing, well, the thing is, that I don't know what the thing is."

His gorgeous, perfect lips lower toward mine, and his hands cup my face. His lips touch mine, kicking my heart back into high gear, my pulse pounding in my ears. Every single nerve ending in my body suddenly comes alive. I feel the leather underneath my fingertips, the rasp of his beard against my chin and cheek, the heat radiating from his chest, his face, and his hands. My fingers tighten against the top grain leather and his mouth moves against mine.

I think I love Edam, too. So why does the prospect of marrying him terrify me to my very soul?

Edam pulls back and stands up. "You like me, even if you don't love me. I'm okay with that. I could wring Analessa's neck for trying to force something between us." He inhales deeply and slowly. "But I want you to turn her down tomorrow."

"I—how—I can't—"

"I know you need Malessa behind you. I know my sister's evil for her stipulations, but I know her pretty well, I think. I believe that she'll drop her conditions, or at least, that one condition, if you refuse. I think she believes she's helping me. She must know my loyalties are entirely to you. She hasn't heard from me since she told me to drop Judica and pursue you. She has tried to contact me and I've ignored her entirely."

"I—"

Edam presses a finger to my mouth. "I'd also like to ask to be your date for the party tonight. Nothing would make me happier."

I nod dumbly.

"I know you well enough to know that you're not ready to get married. You're not ready to pick one person to be with for the next thousand years, and I'm not in a hurry. Okay? That's all I wanted to tell you. I'll fight for you against any and all enemies, and that includes my stupid, pushy sister. But I also have enough pride that I don't want you to choose me because your hand is forced." He drops to one knee again. "When you say you want to marry me, I want your eyes to light up with joy. I want your heart to soar. I want to plan for children together, so many children, rooms and rooms full of them. But not because you're honoring some kind of demented bargain. I think after everything that has happened in your life, you deserve to marry for joy and no other reason at all. Don't give up on that dream, not for me, not for a prophecy, and certainly not for my sister."

"My life may not be my own," I say. "Not if my mom's right about that prophecy."

Edam smiles. "You're the Queen of Queens. I've seen it from the very beginning, but the beauty of that is that it's destined. You can do this however you need to do it, and it will still happen. So be true to what you know is right. You have that luxury."

Do I? Is that how life works? Or do we have to do what needs to be done, even when it cracks our dreams and our hopes and our joy in half? Utter destruction. That's what I'm supposed to save the world from. When that's on the line, does my readiness to get married really factor into the equation? "What if I decide to tell Analessa yes?"

Edam frowns.

"What if I tell her I will marry you? What then?"

His eyes spark. "I would never deny you. If I thought you wanted this." He gulps. "I'd be delighted."

"Then I say yes, to you escorting me to my party tonight. I say yes to being your date. And I'll be considering my decision. As soon as I know what I plan to tell your sister, you'll be the first person to know."

Edam pulls me to my feet. When he kisses me this time, he's slower and even more electrifying than before. When he leaves, my fingers feel just a little bit numb. I walk back to my room to eat my lunch tray in a bit of a daze.

"Earth to Chancery." Noah's sitting on a chair in my room, staring at my plate.

"Oh, hi," I say. "What are you doing in here?"

"I asked Larena when I could talk to you and she said your only free minutes are while you're eating, so." He points at my food. "Lunch, and me."

Right. "I'm sorry. Things have been a little out of hand lately. Are you here to talk to me about the troops we lost? I've already told Alora to notify their families and provide them—"

Noah shakes his head. "I already saw that. I thought the benefit you sent for each of them was very generous."

"Oh. What are you here for, then? It's not about the Edam thing, is it?"

"No. That's your decision to make, and I'm sure it's not a simple one. Look, I just need your authorization on something small."

"Huh, okay, what is it?"

"I ordered you a birthday present," he says. "And it's in Kauai, but they can't ship it over here without your signature. It's not like Amazon delivers here, you know. You're a hard lady to shop for."

"A present?" I ask.

"Right. I mean, I'm not like Santa Claus or whatever, but I pride myself on giving the people I care about something to tell them how I feel about them on the day of their birth."

"You had something made for my birthday."

"Yes, you're eighteen today," he says. "Try to keep up, princess."

I smile. "That's so nice."

"I try." Noah scratches his nose. "But you know, you're my boss. So I kind of have to get you something or people will talk."

"What is it?"

"Sign here," he says. "And you'll get it in like an hour. Those ferries are actually pretty fast."

I roll my eyes, but I sign.

"Now, if you could tell Larena to squeeze me in so I can give it to you, that would be awesome."

"I'll let her know," I say.

"I'm sorry things are crazy right now," Noah says. "Have you heard anything from your sister?"

"Melina?" I ask.

He bobs his head.

"Nothing. She has until tonight, but I don't have high hopes she's going to suddenly show up and apologize profusely. I mean, stranger things have happened, but it doesn't seem likely."

"Why wouldn't she?" he asks. "I mean, if what Judica says is true, she supports you. She wanted to kill your potential opposition. She wants the foretold role of super-fan, right? So why isn't she pedaling over here on her big wheel to be by your side as quickly as possible?"

I don't even ask what on earth he's talking about. With Noah, I frequently don't know. "I doubt it's that simple."

"It never is. But you'd think she'd at least respond."

"You think she didn't get my message?" I ask.

Noah shrugs. "The most obvious solution is sometimes the right one."

"I could send another."

"If this one went awry. . ." He shrugs.

"Then the next probably would too. If someone is trying to keep me from talking to her. . ." I bite my lip. "Who would do that?"

"If I had any real ideas, I'd already have shared them," Noah says. "But if I were you, I might make time to visit my sister myself. Find out if she's crazy and unhinged or just misunderstood."

"I guess. But if she's crazy and unhinged," I say, "I might never get to the next part."

"True," he says. "So you'll need to think about it. Just a lowly human's two cents, that's all."

"Thanks," I say.

After Noah leaves, I stand in the hallway between Frederick and Dante. Why didn't Noah even mention Analessa's offer? Why didn't he try and talk me out of taking it? He said he loved me, but he didn't even try to kiss me.

Judica's bootsteps in the hallway drag me out of my reflection. They sound exactly like they always did, the clicking of Death's claws right beside her, but they don't cause the same anxiety anymore.

"Happy birthday, J," I say when she turns the corner.

"J?" Her head tilts sideways.

"No?" I ask. "What about Jude? I kind of liked the idea of having nicknames."

She scrunches her nose. "Not Jude, but I'll think about J," she says. "But I also want to talk to you about something."

Of course she does. I open the door into my room and wave her through. At least Judica wants to talk instead of stabbing me. Mom is probably beaming down on us from above. I close the door behind her.

"I wanted to say happy birthday," she says. "I don't think I've ever really said that."

"You did on our ninth birthday."

"Ouch." Her hand clutches at something underneath her black t-shirt. "Look."

"At what?"

"No, I don't mean look at something. I was trying to tell you to listen to me." Judica begins pacing.

"We've made a lot of progress," I say. "Don't feel like you need to force things. I mean, *not poisoning me* is enough for this year. I don't want to press our luck."

Judica pivots on her heel and turns toward me abruptly.

"I kept this you know." She pulls a necklace out from under her shirt. "See? I've worn it for nine years."

The infinity pendant I gave her on the same day she tried to kill me. My mouth drops open, but I have no idea what to say to her. Why would she keep it? Hate wasn't a strong enough word for what she felt for me. Contempt is closer. "I'm super confused."

Judica paces again. "I know. Here's the thing, okay? I didn't ever mean to kill you that day. I know you thought I did, but." She stops again, and clenches her hands into fists. "Mother thought I was going to kill you, and you did too. And I did kill your dog and I'm so sorry." She breathes in and out. "I don't know the right way to say I'm sorry. But I am. Okay?" She turns to face me again, her eyes meeting mine and darting away again. "I felt. I feel, not I felt. I feel really bad about it. Even still, now, I feel bad."

Something inside of me that kept me going—when Pebbles died, and Cookie died, and then Lyssa died, and Mom died and my entire world was turned upside down—snaps. I drop to the floor, doubling over, my nails digging into my palms. It can't be true. Judica felt a lot of hate, and pain, too. But she couldn't possibly have been hurting as badly as me. She couldn't have wanted to be my friend all this time. It's not possible. It's not. She's learning now how to be a sister. She's improving, and growing and learning, but she wasn't hurting like me.

Because if she was *good* all along—if we wasted all this time, if all this hostility was for nothing?

Tears stream down my cheeks. "No."

Judica swallows and nods her head once. "I don't expect you to forgive me. I know it was horrible, but I only poisoned those cookies thinking you'd be sick for a little bit and I'd get some time with Mom alone. I was a selfish, spoiled kid, and I thought your life was easy compared to mine. I never thought Pebbles would eat them and die. I'm not trying to reopen old wounds, and I don't mean to hurt you again, or upset you, or make things worse. I'm just not good at this at all. I'll go." She sprints for the door.

I crawl across the floor and grab her ankle. "Stop."

She sinks to the floor next to me, pulling her knees into her chest. "I want it to be me," she says.

The Queen of Queens. She hates that she's got to watch me rule when she's better equipped. "I do too," I say. "I wish I could give this to you." I take Mom's ring off and throw it across the room.

"No." Judica crawls across the floor on her hands and knees and retrieves it. She places it in my hand slowly. "Not that. You don't understand." She gulps. "I want to be your number one supporter. I've been total crap up until now, and I hate it." She shakes her head and a tear streaks down her cheek. "I killed your dog." She balls her hands up and presses them to her face. "You thought I killed our mother. I was so awful to you that you believed I would kill our mother."

Judica bawls next to me like a baby, and the world is upside down and the room doesn't have enough air and fish can fly. All of those things seem equally likely in this moment.

"I don't even blame you for thinking that," she says. "I let you think I was evil, like the devil herself. I treated you —" She hiccups. "So badly. So very badly."

She kept the necklace.

"I wanted to tell you today that you can trust me," she says. "I wanted that to be my birthday present. I wanted to tell you that no matter what, no matter whether you heed my advice or ignore it, no matter how hard things are, no matter what anyone says or does, or who you kiss, or—" She tosses her hands in the air. "If you decide that you want to marry *Roman.*" She chokes on the word. "If you do, it's fine. I'll deal with it, okay? Because I love you. You may be the only person in the world I really, truly love, and I will do whatever you need. I will support you in whatever way necessary. If you can just forgive me."

"I can't forgive you," I say.

Her face falls, her chest heaves, and her hands tremble. She opens her mouth, but no sound emerges.

"You're unforgiven Judica, but only because I'm beginning to think you never did anything that needed forgiveness in the first place. I won't forgive you, but I want to *understand* you, if you'll help me to do it."

❧ 14 ❧

A loud banging on my door prompts me to scramble to my feet. I don't know why leaning against Judica and crying feels like something I should hide, but she reacts the exact same way. Maybe because it's so new and utterly foreign.

I wipe away any residual tears and hope my face isn't blotchy. "Yes?"

Balthasar opens the door and glances from Judica to me and back again. "Is everything okay?"

"I was going to ask you that." I brush off my pants.

"I don't see any blood spatter, so I guess you two are alright." Balthasar stuffs his hands in his pockets.

"We're fine," Judica says. "What did you need so urgently?"

"Right." He turns toward me. "There are three planes hailing. All three will arrive within the hour."

"Why?" I ask. "We specifically didn't invite anyone else."

"One of them contains two of your sisters, Magdalena and Magerite. But the other two are not invited, and they aren't Alamecha jets." Balthasar frowns. "One is from Shamecha, and one is from Adora."

We knew this would happen. I was just hoping we wouldn't be bombed on my birthday. Evians suck. "I assume our defenses will prevent the bombs from hitting Ni'ihau. Is that incorrect?"

Balthasar shakes his head and my stomach ties in knots.

"Wait, why would they hail us to let us know they're attacking?" Judica asks.

That is strange.

"No, it's not an attack, or at least, I don't think it is," Balthasar says. "Each plane contains several dozen evian men. Refugees. They're calling themselves the Motherless, like the Shenoah men did."

"Wait, are you serious?" Judica asks.

Balthasar nods. "We need to decide what our position is, because it appears we may be inundated by royal sons from the past few centuries, none of whom appear to love their adoptive families overmuch."

"I don't get it," I say. "I thought they'd want to return to their own families. I thought they were upset they had to leave."

Judica smiles. "Their families didn't want them. And they clearly don't feel like they have a place in their adoptive homes either. You're probably the first person in millennia who has cared about them at all."

I think about Edam. Any of the men Mom bought so Judica would have options who weren't the one person she chose, well, they'd suddenly be without purpose. They could join her guard, which would be heavily weighted with men as a result, or they could try and find other positions, but they'd have missed the typical age for finding a placement, and everyone would know they weren't Alamecha born.

They're utterly alone.

"But they think you will make a place for them," Judica says.

I will, and I do understand them. "Fine," I say, galvanized in my decision. "Tell them they're welcome here. I'll coordinate with Larena, and unfortunately you and Edam will have to vet more people, but I won't turn them away. If they feel like they can accept a place among us, we'll make one for them."

Balthasar looks like he wants to argue, but he doesn't. "Yes, Your Majesty." He marches through the door as though the planes actually harbor bombs. I hope he's wrong.

When I reach the arena for my training session, I'm expecting three or four opponents at least. I'm surprised when Edam's the only one present.

"Change of plans today," he says. "I figured you deserved a break for your birthday."

I don't have time for any breaks at all, but I don't chastise him. His heart's in the right place.

"Also, I've got a surprise for you," he says. "A birthday present."

And now I'm glad I didn't complain. "What is it?" I rub my hands together.

"Here." He hands me a long object, thin, and wrapped in dark brown paper, tied with a string.

The second my hand connects, I know just what's inside.

Mom gave Judica her first sword on our ninth birthday. My twin received some kind of blade every year thereafter, from knives to spears, to long and short swords of various disciplines. She received a balanced set of katanas last year.

But no one ever gave me a blade, because I'm not a warrior.

"I thought it was high time you had your own weapons, made for you. You've gotten quite good, and while your mother's first gift from Althuselah is a fitting sword for you to use, I wanted you to have options."

I tear off the paper to reveal two beautifully balanced, ornately tooled swords. One blade is dark with a light, silvery inlay snaking up both sides. The other blade is silver with dark decorations clawing their way up the blade's face. The two blades are mirror opposites of one another, counterbalancing one another perfectly. I look more closely and realize the creature climbing both blades is a dragon, one breathing fire, one breathing ice.

"For a twin on her birthday," he says. "I may not understand exactly how, but you and your sister are working in sync now and it's a wonder to behold. I hope you'll be able to learn to wield both of these together with half as much grace as the two of you are currently managing in your interactions."

"Thank you," I say, my heart swelling with gratitude. Even though Mom is gone, so many people have stepped up to make my birthday a positive experience. Of course, after Edam spends the next hour hacking away at me, some of those good feelings wear a little thin. "Good to know you won't let me slack off, even on special occasions."

He shrugs. "Can't fall behind, can we?"

I guess not.

Larena is standing at the doorway when I finish. I wipe the blood from my face onto my sleeve. "What's wrong now?" I ask. "Are the refugees all hacking at each other? Is there a giant bloody melee on the front lawn?"

Her eyes widen. "What?"

"Never mind," I say. "What's wrong?"

"Nothing that I know of," she says. "But a shipment has been delivered for you, from Kauai."

"Oh!" My present from Noah, I bet. "Where is it?"

"We had it delivered to your room," Larena says. "I wasn't sure where to put all of it."

I hope it's five hundred roses. Or maybe a dozen song-birds. No, I know, piles of diamond necklaces. I'll say this for Noah, he keeps things interesting. I race to my room and throw open the door, but nothing looks out of place.

I should have made Larena follow me to my room and explain. I prowl around, checking things out methodically. Jewelry box is untouched. Bed looks like it always does, which is good because anything to do with that would be creepy. Desk looks no different. Window and view, not modified. After a moment, I give up, deflated. Then it hits me.

My closet.

I push through the doors and it's plain to see what he sent. Dresses, dozens of them. Full skirted ball gowns. Slinky eveningwear. Dramatic statement pieces. But at the front, a gold sheath dress with delicate pink embroidery along the bodice that trails down the fabric along the slit. Mom's colors. Noah must have guessed because of the colors of Mom's room. It's perfect for tonight. It shows I remember Mom, but I'm moving ahead without her. I'm grown, I'm queen, and I have things under control, but I won't forget who prepared me. A tiny paper is pinned to the bodice.

A queen needs a splashier wardrobe. Before you didn't want to be noticed, but now all eyes are on you. You've got this: warrior, diplomat, humanitarian, rebel.

Happy birthday.

-N

I put the dress on, noting the thigh sheath and gold bands in back with which to lash a sword. Thinking of Noah explaining that to a dressmaker puts a smile on my face. I slide one of my new birthday swords from Edam into place and stare at my reflection in the mirror. It fits me perfectly, as though I stood through a dozen fittings. I don't even recognize the woman in the mirror. She's not quite Enora the Merciless, nor is she Chancery the overly-merciful. The woman staring back at me can do what it takes, even if it's hard, even if it's scary, even if it seems impossible.

Of course, once I take this dress off, I'm the same person inside that I've always been. Who am I kidding? I'm terrified and I hate this and I've only been at this crappy job for a few days. But hopefully this dress will help me fake it for this stupid celebration I didn't want to attend at all. In that regard, at least for the next few days, Noah's gift might keep me alive better than Edam's sword.

And in this moment, I admit that I'm hesitating to marry Edam because of Noah.

Not because I think he's a viable option for a future husband. I mean, I *know* that as the queen of all evians, I can't marry a human. I couldn't possibly produce an heir with Noah who could rule after me. But the fact that Noah makes me smile tells me that I'm not ready to commit to anyone else. I'm only eighteen. If I was human and it would have any impact on me at all, I couldn't even drink alcohol, at least, not in our biggest principality, the United States.

One glance at the clock tells me that it's time for me to report to my own party. Edam's leaning against the doorframe when I open the door. He has always looked amazing in a black tux, but tonight he practically hurts my eyes.

"Happy birthday," he says, his voice low and quiet.

"Thanks," I say.

When he shifts to offer me his arm, I notice he's got two swords strapped to his back. I wonder how many other weapons he's wearing underneath that tux. I'm not even surprised that he's armed to the teeth to escort me to my birthday party. Edam's always been unbelievably lethal above all else.

"Are you expecting an attack?" I joke.

"I'm always expecting an attack."

"At my birthday party?" I remember what happened at the last party we threw and inhale. "Mom didn't die of an attack, exactly."

Edam squeezes my arm. "I know. It's just that you've invited a lot of outsiders, and you know I'm completely supportive of your position on that issue, but it's a risk."

"You and Balthasar interviewed them all," I say.

"I didn't have time to do a thorough investigation on anyone yet," he says. "The research on their past is ongoing. My understanding was that accepting them was a show of trust more than anything else."

He's right, of course. At a certain point, I have to do the right thing and hope it doesn't kill me.

When we reach the ballroom, I realize that's an easier concept in theory than in practice. I stop at the doorway to wait for Judica, but I can see everything clearly from here. The decorations are exactly what Mom and I discussed a few months ago, other than a few changes Larena and Noah made. At least the lily and rose mixes are as stunning as I knew they would be. Nightfall roses and night rider lilies for Judica, and stargazer lilies and white roses for me. Notably, although the flowers and centerpieces are all what I chose, they now feature crowns as a central decoration in the stargazer/white rose arrangements. The food platters, ice sculptures, fondue stands, and five tier chocolate fountains were executed perfectly, bravo Lark, but other things are. . . different.

The largest change is the hundred and eighty or so men we didn't anticipate who are lining the walls in their finest clothing, each one of them trained to become a Consort, each one of them prepared to attack and kill on command, each one of them boasting the finest DNA and the purest bloodlines. Each one of them is a question mark, a liability, a principled risk.

I'm sick of thinking about people as liabilities. It's no wonder my mom was a little sharp around the edges.

"Sister," Judica says. She's standing arm-in-arm with Roman, which is going to be a big enough shock to the family in and of itself. But instead of her usual black, she's wearing a white gown, and Roman matches her in a white tux. It sets off his deep brown skin handsomely.

"You two look stunning," I say.

"And yet, I think all eyes will be on you," she says.

My cheeks heat embarrassingly. I have got to get my emotions under control.

"Don't worry," she says. "Even the blush is becoming on you. The caring empress, the one everyone adores."

For the first time ever, I don't sense any ridicule in her tone. I can't tell whether she's changed, or whether I have. Either way, the smile I give her is genuine.

"Ready?" I ask.

She nods and gestures for me to enter first. I focus all my attention on keeping my heart rate steady, and my feet from tangling in the bottom of this immaculate gown or the strappy Louboutin wedges that came with it. Every single one of the Motherless doubles over into a full bow when I pass.

Once I reach the front, and Judica takes her place to my right, I lift my arms in welcome. "Thank you all for attending our eighteenth birthday celebration. It's an Alamecha event from start to finish. Mom and I decided months ago not to invite any of the other families, and I saw no reason to change that in the past week. Tonight we're celebrating that Judica and I were born eighteen years ago, and that Mom didn't cut my throat, I suppose."

Everyone laughs.

"But we're also celebrating that our family has survived a devastating period of upheaval. I've done my share to add to the unrest, what with my recent proclamation and fireballs and whatnot. And as you all know, I've always held different views from those of my mother and my twin. Actually, I've held different views than most everyone."

Murmuring.

"My views aren't always popular, and I understand that. But I expect my people to uphold my laws and policies. One new position is that Alamecha will no longer participate in the purchase or sale of male royal children. My Heir will choose her spouse from among the men she meets in any walk of life. It is obviously my hope that she will choose wisely, but I will not limit her to a small batch of options, nor will I encourage what I see as a barbaric practice of removing children from their proper families for any reason."

I pause to let that sink in.

"Last week I met my older brother Moses for the first time. He was sold to Shenoah many years ago, and I never had the opportunity to interact with him in any substantive way. I only met him because he was chosen to wed Vela, formerly Heir for Adika. I told him when we met how I felt about everything I've recently explained to you. He knew my feelings, and when Vela was killed, he and the other men who supported her came here as refugees, looking for a place with Alamecha. I welcomed them with open arms. All ninety of them."

More murmurs.

"You can look around for yourself and see that there are more than ninety newcomers here at my party. That is because there are also thirty-seven men who bravely escaped from Shamecha, and fifty-three who bravely escaped Adora. They have also requested asylum with Alamecha. Although Edam and the Security team will be conducting ongoing investigations into their backgrounds to ensure that all is as it seems, I am pleased to say that we are prepared to welcome them with open arms. They will have a home with Alamecha for as long as they want it, and we will find them employment and a place to live. I am not just empress of my own family, but empress of every evian and human on earth. I could do no less than welcome those who have not been cared for properly."

Rumblings, louder this time. I can even make out many of the exclamations. Some are happy, most are shocked, and a few are displeased.

"That's not all," I say. "Although I know this is a substantial policy shift, I have one more offer that needs to be announced."

The gathered crowd quiets.

"I'd like every man who was ever purchased by Alamecha to step forward and approach me at the front of the room."

It takes some time, but dozens and dozens of men who are present find their way to the front. Many of them are close in age to Edam and are men I know fairly well. Some of them are older, a few of them much older indeed. Tall, short, bulky, lean, but all of them warriors.

"The men who have been asking for asylum call them-selves the Motherless. I know that is not the case." I make eye contact with each of them in turn. "You all have moth-ers. Your mothers may have felt obligated to sell their sons, as did mine. They may have longed to keep you. They may long to see you still." I swallow slowly. "I don't care much what regrets they harbor, and you don't owe them anything.

But if *you* wish to return to your mothers, if you wish to know them, or if you wish to contact them and wait to see whether they look forward to your return, I make you a blanket offer to do that. Ask them if they want you to visit or return permanently, and make plans to go home, this week, this month, this year, or any year to come. You don't have to decide now. But do it through formal channels. Let Edam know you'd like to reach out, and then inform us if and when you're leaving. I ask that you respect your family here, Alamecha, but I invite you to return home to your mothers. We will wish you nothing but the best, and send you home with any belongings and assets you have amassed in the time you have spent with us. Be motherless no longer, if you desire it and your biological family wishes to welcome you back. You, like all the others, have a place here with me. But you are also welcome to find a place in your biological home if you prefer. A great wrong was done to you, and I can't set it right, but I will do my part to allow you to find whatever home you envision for yourself."

Loud conversations erupt left and right, but this time I do nothing to stop them.

"Enjoy the party!" I signal the band to begin playing, and offer my hand to Edam to lead me out on the dance floor.

"That was very well done." Edam's eyes see only mine, his hand in mine, and his other on my hip. He guides me adeptly, spinning me across the dance floor. "You are doing everything I knew you would."

"I hope it goes as smoothly as it possibly can," I say. "I'm sure it will make a lot of work for you."

"Probably far less than you imagine," he says.

"What do you mean?"

"I doubt any of those men will actually leave Alamecha."

"Why not?" I ask. "I thought you said they're unhappy here."

He beams at me. "It's not that they want to leave the only home they've ever known. It's that they want the choice to leave."

"They want agency," I say, "and I'm giving it to them."

"Which is why they're unlikely to ever leave your side," he says.

"And it's why I can't take your sister's deal," I say.

Edam smiles. "I knew you wouldn't."

My mouth drops.

"You can't start off your rule as Queen of Queens by letting another ruler dictate the terms."

He's right. I can't. Judica didn't see that, but surely she will. "I'm glad you understand."

"I understand you better than you imagine," Edam says. "But I'm fine waiting for you to figure that out."

When the song ends, Edam refuses to relinquish me. We dance two more rounds without speaking, but my fingers tingle where they meet his. When the third song ends, Moses is waiting for me. "May I have this dance?"

Edam passes me off with a bow. "Keep your eyes open."

Moses bobs his head.

"I'm surprised you came," I say.

My older brother looks so much like Mom it hurts for me to see it. "I wouldn't miss my own sister's birthday party. It's the first one I've ever been invited to attend."

"I'm sorry about that," I say. "If I'd known—"

He squeezes my hand and whisks me into a circle. "Don't apologize to me. Vela would be very impressed with you, you know, and I'm extremely proud."

I will not tear up. I will not cry at my party.

"What you did up there, it's very overdue, but it feels really good. To feel safe somewhere, to feel like I belong, it's not nothing. And it's not because you're actually my sister. It's more than that. It feels like, for the first time, someone made an effort to understand how we felt, and beyond that, you're making an effort to fix things."

I've never had a place, not really. I've never belonged, so yes, I understand the need to fit in somewhere. "I hope I'm handling things right. I wish there was a guidebook for some of this, but that prophecy is uselessly obscure and particularly vague."

Moses laughs. "It is. It definitely is. But I'm here to ask for a favor."

Another favor? I lift my eyebrows.

"I think you'll like this one. The Motherless would like to make a request of you after this song, publicly."

"All hundred and eighty something of them?"

Moses nods. "Even so."

"Alright," I say. "I'll hear them, as long as you think this is something that shouldn't better be handled in private."

"It may take some time," he says. "But I think it'll be worth the effort."

After the song ends, Moses leads me back to the front of the room. The band has realized that something else is happening and switches to playing instrumental music softly.

"The Motherless have asked me to speak for them," Moses says. "And we have a petition to make to Queen Chancery."

I nod.

Moses raises his voice. "We have conferred, and all one-hundred-and-eighty-one of us would like to join your personal guard, Your Majesty. You will face significant opposition in bringing your dreams for the future of all evians to fruition, and we would pledge our lives to keeping you safe so you can fulfill your destiny. With as new as you are, we understand your personal guard is understaffed. We'd like to fix that, and we're all prepared to swear an oath to you tonight."

Joining Alamecha requires an oath to the family, but joining my personal guard requires a lifetime oath to me, personally. It's too much. I shake my head. "You haven't had enough time to think before making that kind of decision."

"We knew it when you welcomed us here," Moses says. "I knew it, and so did my men. I've been assured that the men from Shamecha and from Adora feel the same. This is our birthday gift to you today, the promise of our service, our loyalty, and our lives, as long as you live."

I open my mouth to refuse, but Alora catches my eye. She shakes her head. I can practically hear her voice in my head. These men are offering me their lives. They're pledging me the greatest thing they can offer, and if I refuse it, I'm literally refusing them. I didn't ask for it. I feel outrageously uncomfortable accepting it, but I must. "Thank you," I say simply.

"I understand your concern that we haven't all thought this through," Moses says. "Or that some of us feel pressured. To reassure you, we'd like to make this pledge to you individually tonight. You may then judge each of us, to determine whether we mean it and accept or decline us into your service."

"I don't want to bog down the celebration for anyone else," I say, "but I'll set up in the front alcove and do just that."

Moses beams at me.

A hundred-and-eighty-one oaths takes a really, really long time. Hours later, when I've spoken to the last, I stand and stretch. Edam's busy recording the final new additions to my guard.

"Are you too tired to dance?" Noah asks.

I haven't seen him for the entire party. I wasn't sure he came. I spin around. He looks taller somehow, his tux a perfect fit for his lean frame. "Of course I'll dance with you." I ignore the irritated look from Edam.

Noah offers me his hand and I take it. We cross to the dance floor where dozens of couples still spin around. Noah integrates us into the midst of the chaos perfectly, not that I'm surprised. "Those giddy schoolboys hogged your entire party," he grumbles.

"I hope accepting them wasn't a mistake," I say.

"As long as you do your due diligence in interrogating them," Noah says. "Any of them could be working for another family. Edam was, you recall."

"I think it'll give him additional insight into researching them," I say. "And I've tasked him and Frederick to handle it. They won't drop the ball, I'm sure."

Noah lifts one eyebrow. "I would like to offer my help, if they'll take it."

"Sure, I'll let Edam know. And I want to thank you for the dress," I say. "It's perfect, and so are the others. It meant a lot. What a brilliant and thoughtful gift."

"It's no lifetime pledge," he says. "But I'd make one of those too, if it made any difference."

All hundred years of his life. I believe he would pledge it all to me. The notion of Noah aging and dying while I'm still young and strong hurts my heart.

"I hope you still had a little fun." His right hand tightens on my hip, drawing us close enough that our bodies touch from chest to hip.

A thrill races up my spine and I wiggle my shoulders in response. "I'm having fun now."

"That counts," he whispers, the breath from his words warming my face.

How am I so attracted to a human? If anything, I care

for him more, long to kiss his lips even more now than I did in New York. It makes no sense, because I'm acutely aware of what a bad fit he is for me. Something about Noah has grown since New York. He was king of Trinity, the most popular kid at the school, and the richest. I worried he'd be eaten by the swordfish in Ni'ihau, but somehow, he's grown into this bigger tank. He doesn't seem intimidated at all. He's completely at ease, exchanging barbs with evians as though he isn't infinitely more breakable than all of them.

But his personal growth doesn't change anything. He can never be more to me than an advisor. When the song ends, Edam is waiting for me, his hand outstretched.

I take it. "Thank you for a lovely dance, Noah, but it's getting late. I better call it a night."

"Have you decided what to tell Edam's sister?" Noah asks, swinging big, asking in front of Edam.

"I'm turning down her offer," I say.

Noah beams.

"Only because I asked her to refuse." Edam smiles smugly. "I don't intend for anyone to pull the strings when we decide to marry."

"No," Noah says, "I doubt anyone will force Chancery to marry someone she doesn't love utterly and absolutely."

"Exactly," Edam says, but his smile is gone.

"I'm Moses," my brother steps in front of me. "I don't believe we've been introduced, but with the way you were spinning my sister around on that dance floor, I suspect we should have been."

Noah grins. "I'm Noah Wen, human liaison on Chancery's Council."

Moses raises his eyebrows. "Delighted to meet you, and understanding a little more why she created that position."

"Why do you think she did it?" Noah asks. "I've been trying to figure it out myself for quite some time."

"Somehow I doubt that," Moses says. "But I hear I'll be joining you as Director of the Motherless."

"Congratulations," Noah says. "I look forward to seeing you more regularly."

"Absolutely," Moses says. "And if you ever want some training tips and whatnot, let me know. I'd be happy to teach you some self-defense basics."

"The more armed guards around Her Majesty, the better," Noah says.

"Exactly," Moses says.

"I doubt Noah's going to be much help if it comes to that," Edam says. "A single stray bullet could end him. We'd be better served ordering him a coat of head-to-toe chain mail. At least he can't stab himself with armor."

"You wouldn't think an evian prince would be so threatened by me," Noah says, "but there you have it. Edam and I are not the best of friends."

"I see that," Moses says. "Well, I'm going to stay neutral in this conflict, boys, so I'll wish you a good night."

"Edam was just taking me back to my room," I say.

"Where I'll be sleeping," Edam says.

"Covered in puppy drool, from what I hear," Noah says.

I roll my eyes. "I can manage Red Bull myself tonight."

Noah snorts, but I put my hand in Edam's before he can react. "Let's go."

When we reach my room, I pull out my cell phone. "I have Analessa's phone number. My response is due tomorrow. Do you think she'll be awake right now?"

Edam bobs his head. "They're eleven hours ahead of us in London, so it's the middle of the afternoon there."

On the day of my deadline. I hit talk.

"Chancery," she answers. "I'm so happy to hear from you."

"Actually," I say, "I—"

"Stop right there, Chancery. If you're starting this conversation with 'actually,' I must intercede. I hear things are about to become a little bumpy for you. Why don't we extend the deadline on this for a few days, hmm?"

"Excuse me?" Bumpy? What has she heard?

"Don't turn me down yet," Analessa says. "Think about my offer a few more days, okay? In the long run, seventy-two hours won't make a difference. I'm offering to pledge you my entire family, and my demands are quite small. I know the fourth, fifth and sixth families have turned you down, and I hear the third is up in the air."

She's well informed.

"So let me wish you a very happy birthday and let's leave it at that."

"Uh, okay," I say. "Though I doubt it will make a difference."

"Oh, a few days can often make a world of difference," she says. "So how about you call me back a week from today."

Seventy-two hours has turned into a week? I exhale. "Alright. I'll think on it for a week."

"Smart girl. I knew there was a reason that ring chose you. Be safe, be strong, and consider wisely."

"I will. Talk to you soon," I say.

"Absolutely." Analessa hangs up.

"She is the most patronizing person I've ever met, hands down," I say.

Edam nods. "She's insufferable, but you didn't let her bait you. You handled that nicely."

"What do you think she's talking about?" I ask. "What will change my mind? Does she know what the third family will say, do you think?"

Edam shrugs. "She's crazy. It could be nothing, or maybe she's heard something. No idea. But the point is, it won't hurt to let her stew for a few more days, and she has warning that you're likely turning her down. Let her wonder where that will leave her, because Chancery, she sees it."

"Sees what?"

"She knows you're the queen from the prophecy. I think the others would see it too if they'd pull their heads—"

"I don't even know whether it's true," I say. "Or whether I even believe in that stupid prophecy at all." I sigh.

I wish I knew. I wish I had some kind of faith in something, like my destiny or my path. All I have are my niggling doubts and my mom saying that I can't ever let anyone see me make any mistakes.

"Well, my birthday wish most certainly didn't come true."

Edam steps closer and kisses me softly. "How about now?"

"Ha. That was nice, but I was hoping for a crystal ball."

Edam laughs. "That's a blow to my male ego, but unfortunately, I don't have one of those."

"No one does, sadly. I suppose I'll have to wait patiently to figure out what Analessa is talking about."

As it turns out, I don't have to wait for very long.

❧ 15 ❧

I'm in the middle of training when the third family invites me to visit them to discuss possible terms of surrender.

For the first time ever, my entire Council agrees on something. They absolutely, positively insist that I cannot leave Ni'ihau. Unfortunately, I happen to think they're all wrong.

"How am I supposed to make any determinations without being there myself to judge their honesty? Furthermore, I'm the only one who can decide what I might accept and offer alternatives I would consider."

Inara scowls. "The Empress can't leave the safety of Alamecha."

"Mom left periodically." I cross my arms.

"Mother never issued a proclamation that declared war on anyone who didn't surrender to her." Judica points at the map on the wall of the war room. "You're at war with three families right now. Active war. This could be a synchronized ploy to draw you out."

"Or it could be a good faith offer to join me," I say. "You

told me that once I take the first family, I'll be on my way."

"You have the first family." Judica glances pointedly at Edam.

"Analessa agreed to give me another week," I say.

"But she came to you when she did that," Edam says. "Instead of demanding you go to her."

"They aren't insisting I go there," I say.

"That's right," Inara says. "They invite you to send a delegation. One I will happily lead in your place."

"And for the reasons I've already enumerated, that won't work for me. I need to hear their proposal myself." I put my hands on my hips. "I can't be safe every second. It's not viable."

"This is an unnecessary risk," Moses says. "And we know nothing about what they're planning to offer or their motivations. Send someone you trust."

Moses has been on my Council for all of ten hours and he's already freaking out right alongside the rest of them. The problem is that every member of my Council thinks they're the one I should trust, when really there are only two people I trust completely. One's a human, and one's a half-human, which makes them entirely unsuitable emissaries in the eyes of the world. I want to scream, but I settle for clenching my hands into fists instead.

"Has it occurred to any of you that they might have invited me in order to see a demonstration of the ring themselves?" I look around the room, pinning Balthasar, Inara, Alora, Marselle, Edam, Judica, and the rest of them with a glare one by one. "If I don't go, if I send an emissary, why should they trust that I am who I say I am?"

"They've seen the video like everyone else, and they'll have heard testimony from evians who were here," Balthasar says. "Everyone has some kind of agent living here, not to mention their ambassadors."

"What about you?" I ask Noah and Lark. "Do you think it's unreasonable of me to want to go?"

My half-human chef and my human liaison look at one another and then back at me, both of them reticent to meet my eye. Good grief, really? Them too?

"Fine." I throw my hands up in my hair. "Fine, if you all think it's a senseless risk, I won't go. But I need to think long and hard about who to send, because right now you're all at the bottom of my list."

I storm out of the room and down the hall. I'm a dozen paces from the Council room by the time my guards catch up. Edam's rotating the new additions in one at a time, but that means I'm now plagued by five guards at all times instead of only four, and they're threatening to add another now that we have more manpower. Each assignment includes one man Frederick and Edam trust, one they're unsure of, one of the Motherless, and two bonuses. None of them work very well together. In fact, if I were attacked, they'd probably trip over one another's feet and stab me in the back.

I try not to complain, but I swear, nothing is easy anymore.

Of course, two seconds after I slam the door to my room shut, someone comes barging through. I can barely go to the bathroom these days without being interrupted. I suppose all of this prepared my mom for having a toddler. I spin around, ready to let whoever followed me have it.

"You need to rant a little more, or are you done?" Judica asks.

I collapse onto my bed and flop back onto the pile of pillows. "I'm not sure."

"Well, let me know when you're done." Judica crosses her arms and stares at me. "I'll wait."

"If you're just going to stare at me until I'm finished, I

guess I'm done."

"Perfect, because I think I have a solution to your problem."

I sit up straight in the bed. "Are you kidding me right now? You thought, hey, Chancery's furious at all of us. But if I trot after her, I can probably pester her into choosing me?"

Judica taps her foot, and the corner of her mouth turns up.

"What? What's your solution that doesn't simply end with me sending you as my ambassador?"

Judica smiles. "Now that you've asked me nicely, I'll tell you."

Oh for heaven's sake.

"I think you should send me."

My head is going to explode. All the blood is rushing there, and I'm so sick of people telling me what to do that it is going to cover the room with gore, I know it. "Judica." I fume. I stand up and then sit back down. I wonder what she'd do if I punched her in the nose.

"You didn't let me finish before you got all furious and twitchy," Judica says.

"I haven't said or done a thing," I say.

"It's kind of funny to watch you when you're angry. It's a little like watching an angry baby elephant."

"When have you ever—"

"What I think is that you should send me, because then you can go yourself."

I do not explode. I do not scream. I do not punch her. "First of all, if you support my going, then why in the world did you argue against it so vehemently in that Council chamber? What is wrong with you? Are you losing your mind? And secondly, you know that there's no way I can go myself *and* risk my Heir."

Judica stares at me, the maniacal grin never wavering. She shouldn't smile. It doesn't suit her. I grit my teeth. "Just explain yourself. I'm sick of being a twitchy baby elephant."

"For the record, I didn't change my mind," Judica says. "But everyone else was so adamantly against you going that I pretended to be against it as well."

"That makes no sense. You're not afraid to disagree, not with anyone, ever. In fact, if I'm a twitchy baby elephant, you're practically Oscar the Grouch."

"Excuse me?"

"Never mind," I say. "But please finish your explanation." Before I stab you with a hair pin.

"I'm not afraid to disagree, which is exactly why no one will suspect anything when you select me as your delegate."

"I am still so lost. Do you want me to go or you?"

"Yes." Judica's smile widens. "See? Even you don't suspect. Our last eighteen years have been like the training ground for this."

"For what?"

"Chancery, dictators all over the world use doubles."

Oh. "You're saying I send 'you', and then I go *as* you."

She shrugs. "You can hear their request, and you can judge what you think about it, but no one will suspect you of being there, so they won't attack you."

"One major flaw. If anyone on earth is more likely to be attacked than me, it's you. Literally everyone and their brothers all hate you."

She doesn't even flinch. "But they don't gain much by killing me, not anymore, so I think you're safe. And in fact, my reputation might help you in the negotiations."

"It might." Also, it might be fun to be Judica for a few days. Pretend not to care, pretend to hate everyone, and hide behind black, black, and more black.

"I wonder whether we could pull it off," I say.

"Who would you send to accompany me?" she asks. "You have to maintain the front around whoever goes, and I have to be able to maintain it for everyone here."

"Obviously we'll have cell phones," I say. "In case something goes wrong. And I would expect you to let me know if we hear from Melina or anything else of significance happens."

Judica nods. "Of course."

"And you can't order a strike on Melina while I'm gone."

She doesn't admit she was considering it, but she doesn't protest either. Good heavens. Can I really trust her to take my place? What else might she do that I haven't even contemplated forbidding? I arch my eyebrow and pin her with my most vicious baby elephant glare. "You have to act like *me*."

"Insipid? Indecisive? Inordinately kind? Flirty? I think I can manage those."

"I'm not insipid." I frown. I wonder whether, underneath her contempt, she's looking forward to being nice for once. It might be good for her, to have people actually like her. "What about Roman?"

She stiffens. "What about him?"

"I could bring him with me. You know, so I can really sell it."

"You could." She won't meet my eye.

"Would that bother you?" I step closer. "To think about me spending time with Roman? Holding his hand? Kissing his—"

She looks out the window and I suppress a smile. She really, really likes him.

"Fine," I say. "I'll take Noah and Edam, and I'll leave Roman."

"You don't need to take your boys with you. I swear I

won't make a move on either of them." Her lip curls with disgust.

"I'm worried about the opposite," I say.

"Oh please. If I put a little distance between you and that human, I'd be doing you a favor. I have no idea what you're messing around with there, but it's not going to end well for anyone, mark me."

"Well, it's my mistake to make."

"Whatever."

"If I take them with me, or, you know, with you, then we *know* nothing weird will happen." I cough. "Like Noah falling down a well or accidentally being fed to a shark."

"Do you have a pry bar handy?" she asks.

"For what?" I quirk my eyebrow.

"Because that's the only way you'll get Edam away from this island. He's not going anywhere you're not."

I tap my lip. She's not wrong. "Well, if I order him to leave, he'll have to listen."

"Task him to keep me in line." Judica's grin is pure evil. "And if I flirt with Roman a little to make sure he's loyal, well, I'll do it when no one else is around."

"You're cracked," I say.

"That's why you love me," Judica says.

"Do not torment that poor man," I say. "He loves you down to his toenails and he's going to slap you as me if you flirt with him."

Judica has never looked more tickled. She really is twisted.

"Fine, so I announce that you've bullied me into sending you in my place. Everyone rejoices. Then I pull Edam aside and beg him to watch you for me. And I send Noah to temper Edam, and make sure he doesn't agree to do something awful to humans. I require that all three of you sign off on any kind of deal."

"Are you sure they won't immediately spot you?" she asks.

"Do you think Roman will?"

Judica shrugs. "It's not like Roman will interact with you at all anyway."

"That's true enough, and I'll be seeing them every minute, essentially." *Can I pull this off? Maybe I ought to leave them here. It's not like Judica will flirt with Edam or kill Noah. Would she?*

"I suppose the question is, how well can you act, sister?"

"Maybe that will be our litmus test," I say. "Because if we're doing this, now is the time. We switch places, and I march out of here as you."

"And if everyone buys it, then we move ahead with confidence."

"I'll be there and back by the day after tomorrow," I say. "Easy. And hopefully when I return, we'll have a second chunk of staridium."

"Do whatever it takes," Judica says. "Because you've got three families arrayed against you right now. It's looking less like a hammer and an anvil, and more like a pack of wolves circling the island."

"Great imagery," I say. "Thanks. Now how do we do this?"

Judica walks across the room to my mirror and stares at herself. "I always wear my hair up and out of my face. Braids, high ponytails. Mitigate the risk it poses if I—"

"If you suddenly find yourself embroiled in hand-to-hand combat. Can't let any assailants grab a fistful of hair."

"Yes, exactly," Judica says.

I don't laugh. She didn't even realize I was mocking her. "Well, I like to wear my hair down so that if anyone attacks me, they're sure to defeat me quickly."

Judica turns to face me.

BRIDGET E. BAKER

"No reason to drag things out," I deadpan.

Judica eyes widen slowly, and she turns back toward the mirror.

"I'm kidding, Judica. I like my hair down, but it's not because I'm hoping to lose a spontaneous attack I may pick at any point by being a complete jerk to everyone. It's because I don't wake up every day assuming someone will attack me. Isn't that why I'm surrounded by guards, guards, and more guards?"

"They're like armor. You hope it protects you, but you don't count on it unless you want to die."

I snort.

"Do you want to die?"

I don't even dignify that with a response. "Look, try to look at this as a mini-vacation. You don't have to scowl at anyone or anything. You can wear your hair down, suck at your training, and generally slack off, okay? You'll be fine. But do not, under any circumstance, kill anyone without texting me about it first. Having your hair down should help with that, since you'll be struggling to survive such a debilitating blunder."

"Shut up."

I stand next to her in the mirror and pull my hair up into a high ponytail on the back of my head. "Wow, this really showcases my stellar cheekbones," I say.

"Duh." Judica pulls the hair tie out and lets her ponytail down. "Why did you have to lighten your hair so much?"

I shrug. "It is what it is."

"I suppose so."

I pull scissors out of my drawer and lop off my hair, growing it out in the jumble of colors our hair grows in naturally, blonde strands mixed with brown, red, and even a few black. I trim up the ends, catching them all in a bag. "At least the color on yours is simple."

"How do you grow it that fast?" She asks.

"Lots of practice in looking as different from you as possible?" I hand her the scissors.

"Thanks." She scowls, but she lops her hair off and screws her eyes up until she's squinting in the mirror.

"What are you doing?" I ask.

She turns and puts a hand on her hip, her hair still shorn close to her head in patchy blotches. "What do you think I'm doing?"

"Do you. . . need to poop?" I ask.

"These scissors are pretty pointy," she threatens, jabbing them in my direction. "I'm pretty sure I could kill you with them. Especially with your hair down like that."

"It's not that hard," I say. "You're making it harder than it needs to be. Close your eyes."

"Why?" she asks.

"Stop arguing about every single thing."

"It's who I am," she says. "You should be practicing."

I sigh. "Fine, but in the interest of learning to be me, try being less obstinate for a moment. Now, close your eyes and relax your shoulders. Then think about your hair brushing against your shoulders."

She opens her eyes. "Is this a joke?"

I shake my head. "Close. Your. Eyes."

She does, but she sighs melodramatically first. "Fine. My shoulders."

"Think about how you wish your hair was brushing against them. Your long, mostly blondish hair, with darker colors peeking through on the lower layers. Imagine how it would look if your hair fell down past your shoulders, and then think of it lowering, lowering, lowering."

Her hair finally sprouts, not as fast as mine, but light-years quicker than it was growing before. "Shoulders," I say, "and beyond. You can do it."

"Of course I can do it," she snaps. And then, thankfully, she does. She trims up the ends and then closes her eyes again to grow it a little longer.

"Now our eyes," I say.

"If you didn't change your eye color all the time like a vagrant," she complains, "we wouldn't be in this mess."

"Vagrants are people who don't have a home and they're almost exclusively human, which means they can't change their eyes—you know what? Never mind. The point is, people likely wouldn't be as quick to buy this swap if I didn't alter my appearance from time to time," I say. "Because you haven't changed your look, well." I pause and think about it. "Actually, have you ever changed a single thing about your appearance?"

"I don't care what I look like. That doesn't mean I can't change it if I need to," she says.

I glance at her eyes and shift mine to the cerulean blue of our natural state.

"Now I don't have anything to look at," Judica grumbles. "What color were your eyes?"

"I've been missing Mom," I say. "I was copying hers." I focus and shift them back to the almost-violet color of Mom's eyes.

"How do you do that so stinking fast?" Judica asks.

I wait this time until she has matched mine, and then I shift back to the bright sky-blue.

"Do you ever wonder what Dad looked like?" Judica whispers.

"Excuse me?" I ask.

"Never mind."

I touch Judica's arm. "No, wait. I'm sorry, the question just surprised me. I figure we got our eyes from him, since Mom's are closer to purple than blue."

"I don't actually care what he looked like," Judica says.

"But sometimes I think about him, and I wonder why we don't even know. Mother couldn't have shown us a single photo?"

"I wish I knew more about him too. It's bizarre that Mom didn't talk about him, not even a little."

"It's infuriating," Judica says.

"I wish I'd met him," I say. "Even once would have answered so many questions. I mean, I know Mom felt like marrying him was a mistake, but we wouldn't be here if she hadn't, so."

"She hated him."

"I know."

"I won't do that," Judica says. "Marry someone only to despise them later."

"That's why I'm dragging my feet," I say. "I don't want that either. And a thousand years is a long time. A lot can change. I'm sure Mom liked him at first."

"You can always kill him off I suppose," Judica says.

A terrible thought occurs to me. "You don't think Mom did that?" I ask.

Judica shakes her head. "No. It wasn't in her to do that, I don't think. And although she despised him and blamed him for how things went wrong, she also seemed sad when he came up, like she missed him. I think if she'd done something that terrible, we'd have sensed guilt or anger."

That's true.

"Well, we better change our skin," Judica says. "Then we need to trade clothes."

"Right," I say. "Hey what about Death?"

"You'll have to leave right away," she says. "Just go to my room and throw some things in a bag and hope he doesn't freak out."

"Where is he, anyway?" I ask.

"I took him out and then had breakfast," she says. "And

I took him back to my room after my training and before I went to the Council meeting."

"It's early," I say. "How did you already finish all of that?"

"I like the hour before the sun comes up. It's my favorite time."

"Okay, Dracula." Which reminds me. Her skin is light, almost pearly. I shift mine from the sun-kissed golden hue of toasted honey to the bleached out alabaster Judica favors in a matter of seconds.

It takes her nearly ten minutes to darken hers. I don't laugh. Or not much, anyway.

"These boots are uncomfortable," I complain.

"Are you kidding me?" She shakes my Brooks at me. "Are you twelve years old? Who wears sneakers?"

I sigh. "I love to run, remember? I went for a jog before my training."

"I'm sorry. That was the last of my snark, I swear."

I hope she can do this. I stand up and walk to the door, and Judica's hand touches mine hesitantly. I turn around. "I know this is important," she says. "I didn't suggest it lightly. I can do this, and I will. I won't complain, I swear."

I pull her close for a hug to see whether she'll grumble about it. She doesn't even pull away. Not for a few seconds, anyway. I'll take it.

"Alright," I say. "Are you ready, Chancery?"

Judica bobs her head. "As ready as I'll ever be."

"Wait," I gasp. I yank the ring off my finger and pass it to her.

"Crap," she says. "People will notice immediately that the ring's not flashing."

I shrug. "No one pays attention that closely. Trust me."

She gulps. "I hope you're right."

Me too.

❧ 16 ❧

My guards follow a few paces behind Judica like I prefer, but her guards are noticeably absent.

"Uh, where are your guards?" I ask.

"I told them they were dismissed before I came to propose this," she says. "I didn't figure you'd want them following us around if you agreed."

No guards at all? Once we tell the Council and I ditch them, I'll be free? I clomp down the hallway a little lighter, a little freer, and that's when I realize that I walk differently in Judica's boots. More confidently, and somehow, bolder. I feel different in her clothing. Less nervous and more sure of myself.

"Easy tiger," she hisses.

"What?"

"You're practically strutting."

"Newsflash," I hiss back. "You strut."

Judica's mouth drops open. "Take that back."

"Yes, Your Majesty," I say. "Whatever you say, Your High and Noble, Esteemed, Most Excellent Majesty."

"Oh shut up," she mutters.

We walk back into the Council room. I'm a little annoyed that none of them have left. Were they talking about what to do while I was gone? I channel my irritation into what I think is a Judica-esque scowl.

"I'm glad you're here because that makes this easier," Judica says. "But I can't say I'm pleased you've been hanging around in here, presumably discussing the merits of a decision that isn't within your purview to make." She cocks her hip and glares each member down.

Easy there, Judica, or they'll figure us out in the first two minutes.

"But since you're here, I may as well let you know my decision." She sticks her lips out in a weird little pout.

I do *not* pout.

"I hear your objections for what I believe they are," she says, "and I appreciate your concern for my safety. I've decided to send Judica in my place, but she can't make any decisions on her own."

Before anyone can move from grumbles to complaining, Judica continues. "No, I'm sending two other delegates who will each hold equal weight in accepting or countering any proposals. And of course, no final decisions will be reached without my approval." She glares at me.

Oh good grief.

"Also, instead of meeting them at their home base," she says, "we'll be relocating somewhere else. Neutral ground. I'm thinking somewhere in Hong Kong."

"Who are you sending?" Balthasar asks.

"Yes, who are the two delegates who will accompany Judica?" Alora asks.

"Edam," she says pointedly, "and because of the location, Noah. He will be an asset in more ways than one."

Noah's mouth drops open. The rest of the Council explodes in an avalanche of objections.

"A *human?*" Balthasar and Inara ask at the same time.

"He's not safe outside of this compound," Alora says. "He's barely safe *inside* of this compound."

"Is that wise?" Marselle says.

"Your Chief Security Officer should remain present in Ni'ihau," Maxmillian says.

"Outlandish at best," Franco says.

"Enough," I shout, barely recalling that I'm not me. "None of you have the authority to argue about this. She's not going herself, which is what you were all freaking out about, so deal with her terms."

Lark gulps and stares at the floor. Hey, maybe people are buying this after all.

"You better get your stuff together," I say, glaring at Noah and Edam. "Wheels up in twenty minutes."

"I better go with you, to review some last minute suggestions," Judica says.

Which is code for, she needs to show me what to pack and ensure Death doesn't disembowel me when I walk through her door. "Fine, whatever."

We march back out and down the hall as quickly as we can. It's not fast enough to keep Edam from racing after us, unfortunately.

"What are you thinking?" he asks Judica.

"I'm thinking that I trust you," she says.

Edam glares at me. At me! "Why not just send me, then? Why does *she* need to go?"

"I trust her too," Judica says. "And she's well equipped to handle a situation like this."

"Then send her and Balthasar, or Moses."

"Actually," I say. "It might not be a bad idea to send a group of guards along."

"That's smart thinking," Judica says. "Let's include twenty of the Motherless as an honor guard."

Edam's jaw drops. "Why would they go with your *sister* when they've pledged to you?"

"Because I tell them to do it," Judica snaps. "And because this is my envoy. If I can't be there, they can d— darn well keep my Heir safe."

"Okay," Edam says. "I guess I'll go pack."

"Yes," Judica says. "Do that. Quickly."

He leans toward her. "I'm going to miss you."

Judica's eyes widen with what looks a lot like panic. "It'll only be a day." She scrambles away from him and bumps into me. "Uh, be safe."

"Be safe?" Edam shakes his head and heads down the hall.

"It's a good thing he's coming with me," I say.

"Yes." She shudders. "It really is."

"He was your *boyfriend* for months," I remind her. "How is this so hard?"

She shivers. "It is, okay? I don't know. We weren't all that affectionate, honestly, and I only really picked him because Mother said I should, and because. Well. I don't know."

"Because I liked him," I remind her softly.

"I don't feel that way about you anymore, so it's easier to acknowledge the way I really feel about him, okay? We better get packed." She jogs down the hall toward her room.

I stand near the door while Judica packs a bag for me of things she would take. "And hey," I say. "Watch the swearing when you're being me. I actually listened to Mom when she complained, remember?"

"Right. I know," she says. "You were Princess Perfect."

"That was definitely you, not me."

She hands me a suitcase. "Here. You're ready."

"You didn't forget the Eau de Evil spray, right?"

She rolls her eyes.

"What about basics like a bra? You gave me deodorant, right?"

"You might want to skip that," she says. "Keep everyone a little further away."

It takes me a full three seconds to realize she's making a joke. Judica is making a joke.

"It's all in there," she says with a sigh. "Trust me."

"Fine." I take the bag from her and stand stiffly, unsure how to say goodbye. A month ago she glared at me while I rolled onto a plane with Mom. Ten days ago, I literally ran away from her while she hurtled threats about killing me. A few days ago, I wasn't sure if I'd ever see her again. And today, I'm leaving her in charge of Alamecha, trusting her assurances that she won't wrest the throne from me, or bomb anyone, or destroy anything beyond repair.

Of all the things that have changed in my life in the past two weeks, this is by far the best one. I'm just not sure how to say that without offending her. She closes the space between us and hugs me of her own volition. I'm so surprised that I drop the suitcase.

"I know," she says.

Somehow, that's enough.

Death bumps our legs and we both spring free. I pick up the bag and head for the door.

"Can you make sure you feed Duchess and Red Bull?" I ask. "Edam won't be here to do it, so."

"Right," Judica says. "Of course."

"Alright, well, keep your phone on you," I say.

"Duh." She holds her phone out to me. "We need to trade."

"Right," I say. "And be careful around Roman."

She nods. "Will do."

"Should I text him something?" I ask. "Like, 'miss you' or I don't know what?"

Judica shakes her head. "I'm not clingy."

"Right." I clear my throat. "Of course not."

I rub Death on the head, and he doesn't even try to bite my hand. I wave at Judica and head down the hallway and toward the runway, breezing right past my guards like they don't see me. Because they don't see *me,* of course. Noah's standing completely still up ahead, and I very nearly call out to him before I bite my tongue. Judica would *not* call out to my pet human.

This is going to be hard.

I march quickly, passing him brusquely and continuing on toward the jet. Even though I know he thinks I'm Judica, it's strange when he doesn't say a word or try to stop me. The absence of my gaggle of guards may be the strangest change of all.

"Judica," a man standing near the stairs to the jet says. He's powerfully built, but only a few inches taller than me. His hair is pulled into a low ponytail, and he's wearing the uniform of my personal guard. It takes me a second, but I place him. Ibrahim, from Shenoah. He came with Moses, one of the Motherless.

I lift my eyebrows. "That's me."

"It's uncanny, the resemblance between you and your sister." The man's dark brown eyes scan me, as if checking for injuries. "You look and sound and smell exactly the same."

"Uh yes, it's uncanny," I say. And talking about how I smell is super odd. "I assume you're coming with us?"

"Edam says Her Royal Highness requested that twenty of us accompany you. I volunteered."

"Oh, well, thank you," I say. "I appreciate your willingness to do whatever needs to be done."

"It's not about the glamour," he says. "It's about being useful. This seemed like a real opportunity to prove myself."

I stare Ibrahim in the eye. "I really hope it's not, because that will mean things have gone very poorly. But I am glad you're along to see that they don't."

"I heard you liked a good fight."

I set my suitcase down so the ground crew can load it. I cross my arms slowly. "I enjoy a good match, yes, but not when I'm representing an entire nation and a disagreement could lead to a war."

"Right," he says. "And of course I hope things go smoothly in this case."

Sure he does. Young men can be so stupid, ridiculously desperate to prove themselves. Testosterone does odd things to the male brain. "Well, we'd better board." I shift past him and climb the stairs to the plane. I notice Noah's only a few steps behind me.

Edam's already seated when I reach the top. "Melisania has agreed to the Ritz Carlton," he says. "She's *en route*, or will be shortly."

"Perfect," I say. "Are we prepared to leave?"

Edam nods and conspicuously pulls out a book.

"This doesn't have to be weird, you know," I say.

He glances back up at me, eyes guarded, maybe even a little confused.

"We dated," I say. "And that's weird now that you and my sister are—" I cough. "Whatever you are. But things between us are over, and I've moved on."

"Congratulations," Edam says gruffly. "Roman is a good man."

"Thank you. He is." Or at least, I assume he is, since both Edam and Judica seem to think so. I wonder why she didn't go for him first. I maybe should have asked her a little more about that, since Edam seems to know him. Of course he knows him. They were raised together. Ugh.

I thought I knew so much about Judica and had made so much progress, but apparently I still have a lot to learn.

"Hong Kong, I hear." Noah slides into the seat next to me. "How's your Cantonese?"

"Passable," I say.

Noah's eyebrows rise. "Really?"

I have no idea what languages Judica can speak. She could have learned anything in the past few weeks, so there's no way Noah could know either. "I never learned Mandarin, but I've been studying Cantonese lately."

"You have?" Noah asks. "Did Chancery make you?"

I roll my eyes. "She can't *make* me do anything."

"Right, no, of course not." Noah tilts his head. "I'm human, and I know how you feel about us. Trust me when I tell you that I dislike you every bit as much as you despise me. But we do have to communicate well enough to survive this trip, so I'm going to set aside my personal feelings and act like I respect you."

Interesting. I've never seen this side of Noah, the in-it-to-win-it side. I always sort of assumed this was a joke to him. "What's your deal here anyway? I mean, do you think this is like a real job?"

Noah lifts his eyebrows. "A job?"

"Are you trying to make a real life for yourself here? Or what do you hope to gain?"

"If by here, you mean in Ni'ihau, at Chancery's side, then yes. I do hope to make a life here. If you mean on this jet, trying to manage the idiotic impulses of her twin sister, then no. I don't aspire to do *this* a second longer than I absolutely have to."

Wow, Noah's a little pricklier than I realized. I figured he just felt safe with me, but this is sort of like challenging someone armed with a nine millimeter when you're holding a water gun. "Impressive rhetoric for a human."

"We may not live as long," he says. "But we're just as good as you."

"Patently untrue," Edam says. "We're smarter, faster, stronger, and better looking."

Noah shrugs. "I have to work harder than you, but I'd say Chancery finds me as attractive."

Edam rolls his eyes, but I wonder whether he knows it's true. "I could regrow my *arm*," Edam says. "I could kill hundreds of humans before they realized what was going on."

Noah shrugs. "The humans you could kill? They're still people. You're not better because you're stronger."

"Really? I think that's exactly what 'better' means. But then, maybe we're short circuiting because of the 'smarter' part."

"Don't you think that people who are stronger should care for the weak?" Noah asks calmly.

Edam opens his mouth and then closes it again.

"Of course not," I say. "It's not the tiger's job to care for the rabbit." Except, I think it is. Noah's doing a pretty decent job of defending my position.

"That's a false dichotomy," Noah says. "Evians aren't tigers, and humans aren't rabbits. We're the same species. Our hopes and dreams are the same. Our DNA is compatible, as evidenced by Chancery's Chef Lark. So do you think a strong tiger should protect the weaker ones? Or what about the juvenile cats? That's the real question."

I'm so used to Noah cracking jokes that I never gave him quite enough credit for his mind, which is clearly very fine. "You've given me something to think about, rabbit."

Noah should smile at my lame joke, even if he doesn't

find it that funny. But instead he narrows his eyes at me and juts out his bottom lip.

Disengage, Chancery. He's going to figure you out. I put every ounce of disgust I can muster into my voice. "I should have brought a book."

One of the men sitting behind me hands me one. *Complete Cantonese: A Teach Yourself Guide.*

"You know what kills me?" Noah asks.

"Pretty much anyone on this plane, and half a dozen things that wouldn't hurt me," I say.

Noah scowls and I remember that Judica almost never makes jokes. "You could probably learn the basics of any language in the time it takes you to fly to the country that speaks it."

"It takes us many weeks to perfect a new language," I say.

"Weeks." Noah grimaces. "But in a few hours, you'll be essentially competent. You recall every single thing you read. Everything is so *easy* for you, and instead of gratitude for that, you take it entirely for granted. You've got so much more time than we do, and you don't even *need* the extra time."

He's right that humans have much less time, and that greatly limits their opportunities. I suppose that considered that way, Noah's willingness to help me means more than an evian's. His year of service is comparable to ten or more of an evian's life.

"Most humans still waste as much of their time as they possibly can," Edam says. "Reading, watching television, and laying around drunk or stoned."

"Wow, can I interest anyone else in a horrible overgeneralization?" Noah asks.

I almost tell them to knock it off, and then I remember Judica would probably sit back and watch Edam slit Noah's throat with a smile on her face. Or maybe she wouldn't really go that far, but right up until that point, she'd egg them on. "It was funny at first," I say. "Watching you two bicker like small children. But now I'm annoyed. I'm going to read through this little primer and I don't want to mediate any more squabbling. Got it?"

"You're not my boss," Edam says.

What a baby. "No, I'm not, and I'm eternally grateful for that. I actually pity my sister, dealing with the two of you." The chuckles from the men around me make me smile.

"We're not this bad when she's around," Noah says.

Now it's my turn to laugh.

This time Noah narrows his eyes at me suspiciously. I dive into my Cantonese textbook. It's pretty basic, but it explains a few things in a new way. Another one of the guards, Gideon, has several texts. I read two of those before we get close to landing. Long flight.

"Do you know what time the meeting will start?" Noah asks.

"Of course not," I say. "We'll get that information once we land."

Noah beams at me. It takes me a moment to realize why. He asked me that question in Mandarin, which Judica definitely doesn't speak. And I've been focusing on Cantonese for this flight, so I can't even pass it off as something I recently picked up.

I swear under my breath.

"That won't help either," Noah says, still speaking Mandarin. "Why the ruse?"

He knows. I glance around. Any of these guards could understand us. I have no idea who speaks Mandarin.

"About needing to learn a language you already know, I mean?" He lifts his eyebrows, and I realize he understands that we may not be speaking privately. "Were you worried it would tip off the rest of the family to your plans to conquer China, Judica?"

I clear my throat. "Right. Yes, that was it. But you've caught me. I studied things on my own."

Noah winks at me, but doesn't press the issue further. I wonder if anyone else has figured me out. I glance around, but Edam's engrossed in reading something, seemingly paying no attention to me or Noah. None of the Motherless seem to care about me at all, either.

Our plane lands without incident, and we load up into Suburbans immediately. I told Judica to put Inara in charge of all the details of making this happen. Normally Mom and I didn't stay at hotels, but Melisania would never agree to meet us at one of our private properties, and we would never agree to go to one of hers. In fact, using one of our hotels is pushing it, but I'm sure Balthasar could not be dissuaded on that point. And Melisania is getting pretty much exactly what she wanted: a personal envoy to discuss her terms.

If I were traveling as myself, I'd feel obligated to make small talk with the guards. After all, they've pledged themselves to my service, so I should get to know them. But as Judica, I have to glare at everyone. It's kind of fun if I'm being honest. And Noah, to his credit, isn't acting any differently than he was before. In fact, he doesn't insist on riding with me, and neither does Edam. We each take different SUVs, even though I'm sure that about killed Noah. But I'm probably safer with seven evian guards than if one seat was occupied by a human. He may have realized that.

Our ambassador in Hong Kong greets me in the lobby of the Ritz Carlton. "Fùnyìhng," she says. "Welcome to Hong Kong." Agnes doesn't bow but offers me a handshake instead. I recall reading that bows aren't common here, because most people still favor typical Western greetings. Or maybe she's welcoming me in the way to which I'd already be accustomed. She's been here for more than a decade, so it could really be either.

"Thank you, Agnes," I say.

Her eyes widen and I recall that Judica hasn't met her.

"My sister told me you'd be here," I say. "She sends her regards."

Agnes bobs her head. "Please tell Her Majesty how delighted I was to hear of her ascendency. And the video I saw of her reaction to the ring." She gulps and drops her voice to a whisper. "It's like magic."

It really is, but her comment reminds me of a conversation I had with Mom and I struggle not to cry. At some point, these bizarre bouts of unpredictable sorrow will have to fade. Or maybe that will mean I've forgotten her. The thought makes me sadder still.

When my conversation skill lags, Noah jumps in for me. "I'm Noah Wen. Nice to meet you."

Agnes glances from Noah to me and back again.

"Yes, he's a *human*." I shrug. "Chancery inexplicably likes him. She added a Human Liaison to her Council." I curl my lip.

Agnes lifts her chin. "Beyond time for an empress to value her human subjects, I think."

Interesting. There are more human sympathizers among the evians than I knew. The thought lightens my heart.

"Show me to the conference room?" I ask. "When will Melisania arrive?"

"Not for quite some time," Agnes says. "I've been instructed to show you all to your rooms. You should have the night to prepare, and the meeting is scheduled to take place at eight in the morning, local time."

I nod. "Very good."

Edam and the other guards can't get to their rooms fast enough, but of course, Noah follows me. Not that anyone notices, since I'm not me, and no one is tasked with guarding me specifically. Ugh. When he stops in front of my door, I spin around.

"What's your problem, human?"

"I think we should discuss it inside your room, you psychopath." His eyes flash and I've never wanted to grab his lapels and kiss him so badly in my life.

"Fine."

I let him inside and toss my bag on the bed, fisting my hands so I don't do anything stupid.

"What could you possibly be thinking?" he asks the second the door is closed. "This is monstrously unsafe."

"Hello?" I ask. "Thin walls."

"Nice try," he says. "Agnes said we were assigned evian rooms. I'm assuming that means they're soundproofed, *Your Royal Highness*."

I scowl. "Look, it's my decision, okay? And no one, other than you, knows anything. I'm safe."

"Oh sure, and no one wants to kill your beast of a sister?"

"I thought of that," I say, "and right now, I'm a much bigger risk to everyone than she is. I think after that Queen of Queens thing, most of the other empresses would welcome plain old savage Judica with a fruit basket and an aromatherapy candle."

"Oh, well, if you think that, then never mind. I withdraw my concerns." Noah points at the corner of the room. "But I'm sleeping in here on the floor."

He's sleeping in my room. My heart races, but thankfully he has no idea. "Oh good." I infuse my voice with all the sarcasm I can muster. "I'll have a human in here to keep me safe."

"It's better than nothing," he says. "And I have weapons now. I've been doing a little training, you know."

"Excuse me?" I ask.

"Your sister Alora thought it was a good idea for me to learn a few things, seeing as I'm swimming in the deep end."

I lift one eyebrow. "The pointy end goes out." I yank my sister's swords out of the sheath Judica wears across her back. "But what would you do if I came at you with these?"

Noah's eyes flash. "Why don't you try it and see?"

Heat floods into my cheeks. I do want to go after him, but not with my swords. I gulp. "You don't heal." Which is my reservation in truly kissing him, too. My brain keeps reverting to the memory of Edam crumpling my doorframe with his hand.

What if I crumpled Noah?

"How is Alora teaching you anything? The only way I'd consider it is if we wrapped my swords in cardboard and bubble wrap."

"You people are majorly lacking in creativity. Ever heard of practice swords? It's what the rest of the world uses."

"But we need to practice healing as much as we need to practice attacking," I say.

"I don't get better at healing," Noah says. "The more I'm injured, the worse I wind up."

"Which is why you shouldn't be training at all." I sigh. "Look, if it makes you feel better, sure, you can stay here. But there are guards on either side of me, and Edam's across the hall. If there's a problem, scream bloody murder as you run for help, okay?"

"I'm not sure anyone will come to save you, *Judica*,"

Noah says. "I mean, that's how I knew, right? You weren't nearly as awful as she'd have been about the human thing. And then, as if that wasn't obvious enough, you said you had a lot to think about." He laughs. "Like she will *ever* consider that humans have any value."

"You never know," I say. "She's young, and she's learning. She's not nearly as bad as I used to believe she was."

"If you say so," Noah says.

I'm so exhausted that while Noah's in the shower, I pass out. My alarm wakes me up far too soon.

"Ready to meet some Lenorians?" Noah's already dressed in a freaking suit. He's like the poster boy of trying too hard. And for that matter, how is he surviving on so little sleep?

"Lenorians is *not* a word," I say. "Please don't say it in front of Melisania."

"Duh," Noah says. "But wouldn't it be a hilarious nickname? Lenorians. It sounds like, I don't know, Delorean. A car that was ahead of its time, which makes them sound like a whole people who are ahead of their time. And maybe they are. They're considering surrendering to you, right?"

"I have no idea what you're talking about, but this could just as easily be an ambush. That's the fear, right? That's why Judica's here instead of me."

"Ugh, you are so evian," he says.

"Oh my gosh, I liked you better when you thought I was Judica," I say.

"No, you didn't," he says. "You can admit it. You're relieved that I know."

"But you were really serious when you thought I was her," I say. "Like, bizarrely serious."

"You like my jokes," Noah says. "But I know they're not

always appropriate. Do you think my dad taught me nothing?"

"We never talked about him," I say, "but we should have. He is one *intense* guy."

"No kidding." Noah stuffs his hands in his pockets and I take that as my cue to get dressed.

By the time I'm ready, we're almost late. Two minutes until we're supposed to be in the conference room, which stresses me out a little bit. When I open the door, Edam's staring at me. "Uh, morning," I say, before I remember I should be frosty.

Noah pokes his head out from behind me.

"What the—" Edam says.

"It's not what you think," Noah says.

"There's absolutely no way Judica would spend the night with a human," Edam says. "So what I think is that. . ." His mouth drops and he swallows, his Adam's apple bobbing. He blinks several times. "You're not Judica."

"Oh," Noah says. "I might have underestimated your intelligence. Maybe it is *exactly* what you think."

A muscle in Edam's jaw pulses.

"Please keep your voice down," I hiss. "And come with me. We're late." I stomp in Judica's designer black combat boots down the hall toward the conference room. Judging by the emptiness of the hallway, we're the only ones cutting it this close.

"Why?" Edam asks.

"Why do you think, meathead?" Noah smirks. "Humans are supposed to be the slow ones."

"We can talk about this after the meeting," I whisper. "But for now, not a word."

Noah and Edam are scowling at one another when we walk into the conference room, so at least that's going right. But when I look around, I know every one of the fifteen faces that swivel toward us. I glance at the clock. I'm two minutes late, and Melisania still isn't here.

"Where are our other five men?"

"Two in the hall," Gregory says.

"And the other three?" Edam asks.

"Downstairs," Gregory says. "But I don't see why you need to know. We're doing our job."

"Where in the world is Melisania?" I don't need to fake my irritation.

"They're delayed. Should be here in the next five to ten minutes," Ibrahim says.

I plop into a chair. They make me fly all this way to meet them, then they set a time, and now we're all sitting around waiting for them to show up. It's infuriating because it makes me look like the petitioner. And the novice. Which I suppose are both true in their own way.

I'm watching the door, which is why I don't immediately recognize the noise coming from outside the window. After all, you expect to hear helicopters when you're in the tallest hotel in the world. Since the Ritz Carlton in Hong Kong is located on the top seventeen floors of the one hundred and eighteen floor International Commerce Centre, we're pretty high in the sky. I'm sure helicopters fly by this conference room regularly.

But this one is flying close. Much closer than it should.

I finally turn to see what's going on, and I'm staring at the window when some kind of projectile shatters it. I leap to my feet, backing toward where Noah's standing in the corner of the room when a grenade clatters through the hole in the window. Edam leaps in front of me, but I've barely registered the cause of the noise before Ibrahim leaps on top of it.

A split second later, it explodes. And so does Ibrahim.

Military grenades combine equal parts pentaerythritol tetranitrate and trinitro-toluene. TNT may be one of the most stable explosives, but when it goes off, it packs a punch. The shrapnel tears into Ibrahim's body, or what I can make of it. His back shudders and blood pours across the floor.

"Protect her," Edam orders, pointing at me and incidentally blocking the grisly view.

Another window shatters as the helicopter moves slowly to the right.

"Why are you protecting *her?*" Gregory, the leader of the Motherless unit, asks tersely. "We have no idea who's attacking or why. They could be targeting you, or they could be here for Melisania."

"It could *be Melisania,* you idiot," Edam barks.

"And Judica's the Heir of your Empress," Noah says. "Chancery tasked me with keeping her safe myself."

Edam grunts. "The human's right. Protecting the Heir is our purpose. Now move." He glances back at me. "Are you alright?"

I nod and pull my swords from their sheaths.

The other two windows of the conference room shatter in sequence, and hooks fly up to latch on to them. Clearly they have a line of attack secured somewhere down below. More armed troops stream in through two of the three doors that open into this room. The Motherless have already closed the third, with two men holding it closed and four more working to close the second door.

Edam barks at Gregory. "Leave a few around Judica. Send the others to close those doors."

"Who will handle the windows?" Gregory asks.

Edam's eyes shutter. "The windows are mine."

"Alone?" Gregory's eyes widen.

"Worry about yourself," Edam says.

Where is Melisania? Are these her people? Is that why she's late? I scan the faces of the attackers, but I don't recognize any of them—not that I can see much of their faces. Evians are streaming through the doors, all wearing black from head to toe. A third hook flies through the furthest window, and the first attacker climbs through the nearest, also black clad.

Every single attacker that comes through a door or window surveys the room, searching. Until they see me. Then they start forward.

They're tasked with killing me or taking me. I wonder which, but I hope I don't find out soon.

"Who's attacking?" Noah asks from the back corner. He's standing behind a chair, like that might keep him safe.

"No idea." I wish I understood their purpose—it would tell me how much danger I'm in. I wish I'd brought Mom's ring. A few fireballs might level the playing field right about now.

Edam's holding his broadsword with his right hand and a wicked looking dagger in his left. "Keep her safe," he says to Noah. "Even if all you can do is throw yourself in front of her." Edam spins away from me and hurls his dagger at the furthest hook, knocking it loose and sending whoever's hand just reached over the windowsill to their death, hopefully. Then he sprints across the room toward the closest window. I wish there were a few Motherless free to help him. By my count five attackers have climbed through the windows and another is coming over the middle window now. Which leaves only Gregory and Rothgar to defend Noah and me. Everyone else is already fighting more than one assailant.

We should have brought more guards.

Edam parries several blows from his two closest opponents to slice viciously at an attacker coming through the first window, shoving him backward, and slicing the rope before he can secure a handhold on the windowsill. When Edam heads for the middle hook, a woman in black with a high ponytail is climbing in, and five men circle Edam, blades drawn.

My heart in my throat, I almost don't realize there's a threat right next to me.

Noah's grunt draws my attention. Noah has somehow maneuvered around me and is pointing a gun at an enormous man in black tactical gear advancing on us. I spring forward to save him, my right sword arcing sideways to part the man's head from his shoulders before he can cleave my favorite human in half. Blood spray triggers my gag reflex, but I inhale deeply and spin around to make sure our corner remains safe. One of our two guards is down, the other is actively fighting.

Why are all of these people targeting me?

Or rather, Judica. Who wants Judica dead badly enough to come after us here? Maybe Melisania invited me so she could deal me a serious blow before attacking Alamecha.

Losing Judica would be devastating, now that we're on the same side. Or maybe she's attacking here and at home, splitting me and Judica so I'll be easier to take out. My hands shake at the thought.

A small but quick swordswoman with double blades like mine slips past Gregory next. I meet her blow for blow, but I don't make any progress on defeating her until a gunshot rings out behind me and she flinches. I seize my window and sever her spine. A shudder of revulsion runs through me. I wish I really was Judica. Killing people who are attacking her wouldn't slow her down, that's for sure. Not that the swordswoman is dead, but it should take her a long while to heal a severed spine.

Noah fires off a shot into her skull at point blank range and my jaw drops.

"She was healing," he says. "A blow to the brain will take her much longer to heal. Can't have her coming back to do more damage."

"I'm not sure she can even heal both," I say.

Gregory renders our entire discussion moot when he decapitates her a few seconds later. "Can't have her coming back at all, you morons." He spins around to deflect a strike from another attacker. "They're trying to kill us, or hadn't you noticed?"

I close my eyes. This isn't happening. All this death, it can't be real. How do I live in this world? I hate that it has been forced upon me. I hate every second of it.

A huge thud in front of me forces my eyes back open. Gregory has fallen, blood gushing from his leg. I spring into action without thinking, parrying strikes by two attackers who made it through the defending Motherless in front to injure Gregory badly.

Before I can kill either of them, Edam shouts and hits one in the throat with a dagger. He ducks and dodges two confrontations to reach my side and ends the other assailant too. He moves so quickly I can barely follow. It's like he's on fast forward. I glance back at the windows—all the hooks are gone, and the attackers dispatched. Edam advances, eliminating the other attackers one at a time. Several of the Motherless in front of us are dead or badly injured, but Edam doesn't pause his momentum, apparently unconcerned about the lack of support.

His muscles bunch, the sweat on his shoulders shines, his blade flashes. Suddenly the music behind his movements sweeps over me in a wave. The melody of his attack crashes against my senses. He's slaughtering the people who would kill me, but my horror evaporates in the beauty of destruction. An aria to end violence, an arpeggio to decimate aggression. The walls are covered with gore. The carpets are soaked with blood, but on and on Edam goes, eliminating everyone who wants to harm me.

When he kills the second to last attacker, the final one stops. She sheathes her sword and holds her hands outward. "I surrender." She's tall, and her head is shorn on one side. A dozen earrings pierce her visible ear, starting in her lobe and climbing to the crest of her ear.

"It's too late for that." Edam's voice rasps. "You tried to kill Judica."

"That was our sole purpose," the woman says. "But why do you care?" She shakes her head as if she's baffled. "According to our intel, you don't even like her. This should have been a simple maneuver, eliminating an isolated opponent."

I can't see Edam's face, but he advances on her steadily, and she backs toward the window, her steps erratic and jerky.

"Why did you all risk yourselves for her?" she asks.

"My queen ordered me to protect her," Edam says. "I protect and serve, always."

"Clearly," the woman says. "But you're defending the very person who has been blocking our message for your queen."

"I don't understand," Edam says, slowing in his prowl.

"Of course you don't. I serve Melina, your queen's other full sister, and her truest supporter. Judica's a viper she's holding to her bosom. Tell her that, if you will. Tell her Melina has tried calling, has sent electronic communications, and has sent messages via messenger. She believes none of them have reached Chancery."

Edam glances back at me, his eyes wide in a face painted with blood spatter.

"Tell me your message," I say. "I won't block it, not this time."

The woman laughs. "Not with this many witnesses, you won't. But as extra insurance, I promise you that if Melina doesn't hear from Chancery by this time next week, she's going to kill your little pets. William and Ambrosia will both die by my hand."

Who the heck are they?

"And what's the message Melina hasn't been able to get through?" Edam asks.

"Melina wishes to join your queen. She demands only a place on her council and death to her twin, as prophesied from the beginning."

"What prophecy says I'm supposed to die?" I ask. "And why would my sister kill me? Even our mother knew we needed one another."

The woman shakes her head. "Not one another, no. Your sister needs *Melina*, her other full-blooded sister."

I lift one eyebrow. "What makes you think that is so?"

"I know it's so. Because your father located the rest of

the prophecy. He would have given it to your mother, but she had lost her mind by that point. He trusted it to the only person he could, his daughter Melina. The only way your sister can become the Queen of Queens as prophesied is with the information Melina has located." The woman glances at Edam. "I trust you'll ensure your queen hears everything this time around."

"My queen will hear it directly from me." Edam bows.

The woman's golden eyes flash once before she leaps out of the far window.

An image of her proud face, her flashing eyes, her warrior's arms, falling one-hundred and eighteen floors to the concrete below guts me and I race toward the window in horror.

But she doesn't fall to the ground.

She lands in the open door of a tilted helicopter in a move I thought only happened in CGI action scenes. My heart slowly descends from my throat as I survey the room.

Eight of the Motherless still have heartbeats, but twenty-three attackers sent by Melina are dead. All to send me a message of support that Melina has been unable to convey thanks to someone blocking it in my organization. I close my eyes, my heart at once shattered and pulsing with rage.

The sound of a clearing throat in the doorway pulls my attention away from the carnage. I have no idea what my face looks like, but it's likely to be spattered with blood and who knows what else. I can guess this based on the expression on Melisania's face when I meet her gaze.

"You're late," I say.

❧ 18 ❧

Melisania swallows hard and stumbles back a step. "I am so sorry. They detained our flight at the jet way. But now, I'm beginning to wonder whether that wasn't planned."

Melina.

I inhale deeply. "I'm sure Agnes can move us to another, less—" I gulp. "Another conference room to talk."

Melisania bobs her head. "I'll communicate with Agnes, and she can let you know where we're moving. In the meantime, please see to your men and clean yourself up. I'm deeply sorry we weren't here earlier."

She looks more sincere than I expect, but she has also had a long time to perfect her acting skills. I nod, and march toward the door. "Edam, see to the Motherless."

He shakes his head. "I won't leave your side."

I sigh. "So be it." I spin around. "Gregory?"

He's sitting up, his eyes focused inward. "Spinal cord repaired." He groans. "Working on my leg now."

"Can you see to your men?"

He nods. "I'll report to your room in ten minutes."

"Fine." I stride out, Noah and Edam flanking me.

Melisania watches our interactions without comment.

I walk back to my room stiffly, images of the small battle assaulting me every time I blink. I shake my head and try to think of anything else.

Like the fact that my twin is hiding things. She has been home for days, and she's already blocking messages and preventing me from communicating with Melina. I wasn't injured in Melina's attack thanks to the efforts of Gregory, Ibrahim, Holden, Edam, and countless others. My body is fine, but the knowledge that Judica is keeping secrets flays the abused corners of my heart.

When we reach my room and I pull out a flimsy plastic keycard to swipe it open, something inside of me breaks. The only thing separating me from the illusion of safety my room provides is flimsy plastic. Which means I may as well stand in the center of town with a sign, "Please kill me."

Nothing is safe when grenades are being lobbed through windows and helicopters are hurling swordsmen through after them.

Laughter bubbles out of my chest and I drop the card before I can even use it. I wish I could stop the laughter, but I can't seem to even slow it down.

Noah bends down to grab my card and swipes it for me. He opens the door, and I follow him through.

The door has barely closed behind me when Edam's arms wrap around me. I collapse against him, my face against his neck.

"I'm sorry," he whispers. "So sorry."

"For what?" His apology helps me finally stop laughing.

"Several of them made it through to you." His voice is low, urgent. "They never should have gotten close."

"You're not magical," I say. "You can't do every single thing in the world alone."

"I froze," he says. "I stood there assessing for an eternity. I put you at risk, and I almost failed you." His arms around me tighten. "And then at the end, I nearly gave you away."

"To that woman?" I ask. "I don't think she was that insightful, honestly." I lean against him for a moment longer, and then I pull back.

Edam's hands shake, but he releases me.

"I need to shower," I say. "And so do both of you."

"I'll grab my things," Edam says, "but I'm showering in here with my sword close by."

"If you run out of that shower naked," Noah says, "I swear I'm shooting first, then asking questions."

My laughter returns, but this time it's less manic. "I'm glad you're both okay," I say.

"Me too," Edam says.

When Edam crosses the hall to grab his things, Noah sits next to me on the edge of my bed. He takes my hand in his. "I'm sorry I didn't do anything." He looks at our hands. "I'm sorry I'm so useless."

"You were ready to attack that huge guy," I say.

"You mean the one you saved me from?"

I squeeze his hand. "You're learning," I say. "You told me yourself. Most people train for years and years before their first fight." I drop to a whisper. "If we're being honest, other than my fight against Judica, that was my first real fight."

"You did well," Noah says.

"I hated it. Every single thing about it."

"Including that stupid bomb," Noah says.

I think about Ibrahim. He wanted to make a name for himself. I'll remember him, but he won't ever do anything again. All those lives lost, utterly wasted. A tear streaks down my cheek.

"I am so sorry about Judica," he says.

I realize he meant the metaphorical bomb the woman dropped at the end of the attack. About my twin. The one that did more damage, at least for me. Has Judica really been lying to me? Keeping all the information a secret, pretending that messages are being sent to Melina, when she's preventing me from receiving communications? How many other things are being kept from me now that I'm resting, carefully protected, inside Ni'ihau?

Can I trust anyone?

Edam re-enters the room, and I have a sinking feeling that the two people I can trust, really trust, are in the room with me. One is a human doing an internship and crushing on his boss, and the other has been committing treason against Alamecha for a decade.

I'm doomed.

When I shower, flashes of death and destruction and gore bombard me. I also keep seeing Judica sobbing in my room—and her face when she shows me that she kept the necklace. Was it all an act? Was she playing me for a fool? The melody I feel inside me confirmed it—she didn't try to kill me when we were children, she does support me now. But why go against my express orders? Why block my messages? I sit down by the drain and bawl. I'm not sure how long I sob like a baby, but eventually Edam taps on the door. "Are you okay?"

I'm spoiled. I'm entitled. I'm a complete brat. Seven of my men died today. Two dozen others died, too. And I'm alive, one of the lucky ones, and here I am, hiding away to cry. I'm not worthy of their sacrifice, but I want to be. I have a job to do, and it's time for me to do it.

I stand up, finish cleaning myself, and towel off. When I open the door, Edam walks past me and into the bathroom.

"Does it always happen that fast?" I ask.

"What? A battle?" He shakes his head. "Not always, but usually. Fight scenes take a lot longer when portrayed by Hollywood than they do in reality."

"We lost so many men," I say. "Way too many."

"There are always casualties," Edam says. "This is a war, you know."

Thanks to me and my stupid proclamation, it is. And there will be many, many more to come. So much for not making any mistakes. I want to run home and curl up in a ball and cry more. I nod my head, because what's the point in broadcasting that I'm hurting?

Edam's fingers lift my chin until I'm making eye contact. "They attacked you. All you did was defend yourself. I know it's eating you up inside. You should have hidden. I'd have protected you."

"I'm Judica," I say. "Remember?"

Edam shrugs. "The Motherless are sworn to you. They'll keep your secret if they figure it out, so that doesn't worry me. But I hate seeing you in pain."

He doesn't understand that the whole sequence hurts me. The deaths of the people attacking hurt nearly as much as the loss of my supporters. They're all people, my people. All the death is senseless.

"You'd feel just as guilty even if you hadn't killed anyone yourself," he finally says.

I nod tightly.

"I can't spare you from the ugliness in the world," Edam says. "But I believe you're strong enough to see that you're not the problem." His fingers brush against my cheek before he turns and closes the door.

I collapse against the bed while I wait for him to finish.

"Edam's right, you know. I don't say that a lot, but he's right this time," Noah says.

"You couldn't even hear what he said," I say.

Noah shrugs. "Maybe not, but I'm sure it was something like, 'I'd die for you, Princess, if only I wasn't already bulletproof and so fabulous I can't be killed. But don't beat yourself up about how awesome I am. You deserve every last bit of it.'"

I roll my eyes.

"Look, my dad taught me how to shred companies when I was only three years old. He'd walk me through what was wrong with something, and we talked about how to fix it."

"That's kind of messed up," I say.

"Sort of like your torture training," Noah says. "But less blood."

Good point.

"All I'm saying is, I'm familiar with the idea of sustaining short term pain to prevent long term disaster. I know you're blaming yourself right about now, but this is on Melina. You defended, princess. You didn't attack."

"You sound like Edam."

His jaw drops and he presses his hand to his chest in mock horror. "Shut your fat mouth."

I shrug. "You're both right, but I can't get the images out of my head."

Noah shakes his head. "Me either. For that, I've got nothing."

Edam emerges, his shirt clinging to the defined line that bisects his chest. With his hair wet, his eyes look impossibly huge and devastatingly blue. They remind me of the ocean outside my bedroom in the morning.

"Oh man, what was in that soap?" Noah asks. "Because it made you ugly. And not like, 'I'm a pug and I'm so ugly I'm cute.' Just straight up ugly."

"Excuse me?" Edam asks, bewildered.

I shake my head. "Noah's babbling. Go shower, Noah,

so we can get this stupid meeting over with. I need something good to come out of this."

"I don't want to use the same soap as him," Noah says. "What if it makes me slightly less gorgeous? I'm human. I need every edge I can get."

I shove him off the bed. "Go already."

He stumbles to the bathroom, hobbling the entire way.

"I do not understand half of what that guy says," Edam says, once Noah's in the bathroom.

"It's okay," I say. "He's doing it for me."

"What?" Edam sits next to me, but on the opposite side Noah was on.

"When he thought I was Judica, he acted completely different."

"Less obnoxious." Edam's brow furrows. "So he did believe you were Judica?"

I tilt my head and stare into Edam's painfully beautiful face. "Of course he did."

He looks down at his hands.

"You thought I told him, but didn't tell you?"

His head bob is slight.

"No, Edam. He just figured it out sooner. I think you were so busy ignoring me when you thought I was her that you didn't really *look*."

Edam's shoulders are broad and strong. His brow looks carved from marble. But his lip trembles and his voice is small when he says, "He stayed in here all night."

"No," I say again. "Not like you think. He figured the swap out and confronted me. Then I showered and passed out. He slept on the floor, actually." I touch Edam's hand. "I swear."

"I hate that Analessa tried to force you to make me your Consort. I hate it."

"You wanted to protect me, and she thinks it's a good way to ensure her family is represented."

"But it's making you push me away." He stands up. "We can talk about this later. I'm sorry for making things about me. Again."

I stand up too, happy to deal with anything other than slicing people into pieces. "I would be lucky to have you as my Consort," I say.

"But it has to be your choice," he says. "I'm sick of everyone else getting involved."

"I did choose to bring you along on this trip," I say. "And it's a good thing I did. You were so busy apologizing that you didn't give me time to say thank you." I stand up on my tip toes and wrap my arms around Edam's neck, my hands winding through his wet hair. I pull his head down toward mine, one inch at a time.

When our eyes meet, it's as though the horror from today burns away. All I see now is his eyes, lit from behind, like a torch burning underwater. His hands splay across my hipbones and haul me closer, but not close enough.

Never close enough.

He carved his way through every single person who raised a sword against me. He never looked back then, and he doesn't regret it now. He'll do whatever it takes, every single day, torching his own heart, burning his soul to the ground to keep me safe. But he surrenders that ferocity when we're alone. His eyes are completely clear, devoid of anger, fury, or fear when they look into mine.

Our first kiss combined our desperation and need and soothed my pain. But not this kiss. This time Edam lowers his head slowly. Something inside of me unfurls, like the great and powerful wings of an angel, one at a time, while his eyes burn through mine. When his lips finally meet mine, they're gentle, soft, full of questions.

Like a prayer.

Because both of us need saving. His hands cup my face, and mine tug gently down until I'm cupping his as well. His jaw works under the skin of my palms, the rasp from his beard abrading my fingertips, his lips pressing against mine softly but insistently.

Until, in a blink, my panther growls. He's hungry and inpatient. He bites my lip and I moan, and he lifts me up. The hunger is still there, simmering beneath the surface. He tosses me onto the bed and steps toward me slowly, stalking me.

"Uh, what's going on?" Noah asks.

I scramble up until I'm sitting again. "Nothing." I cover my mouth in case it's bruised at all. "Nothing at all. I'm ready to go when you are."

Edam schools his expression into neutrality and I've never been more proud of him. But when Noah walks past him, he whispers, "I really freaking hate you, human."

I snort. I can't help it.

"Thank goodness I shower quick," Noah hisses as I stand up next to him. "Or you might be married with three point two kids."

"Maybe you should have taken a little more time," Edam says. "I think I can still smell you."

"Enough," I say. "We're going to confront the leader of the third family. You two will treat me like you would treat Judica, and you'll treat one another as though you're allies."

Edam's eyes clear immediately. "Yes, Your Majesty."

"It's really sad that he's not even a little sarcastic with that," Noah says. "But point taken. I'll be on my best behavior." Noah crosses his heart and grins at me. "No more smiling at all."

I walk from the room, Noah and Edam falling in next to me on opposite sides. Gregory is waiting down the hall.

"Four of the five Motherless who weren't inside the room survived, and with an infusion of blood from Melisania, Ibrahim is actually recovering. Voron, too. Which means we have fourteen of our original guards still alive."

A pang of guilt claws at my heart—I should have more closely checked my own people.

"You seem unhappy," Gregory says, "but with twenty-five dead evian attackers, those numbers are solid."

"She's not upset in the way you think," Noah says. "She feels guilty."

"You did exactly what you should have done," Edam says. "You were the target. You should have returned to the room to recover."

"Absolutely," Gregory says. "I merely thought you'd like to know that we were able to save more than we expected. I've already called to let your sister know what happened and that you're alright."

"You called Chancery?" I ask, my tone sharp.

"Of course I did," Gregory says, a note of warning in his voice. "I was sure you'd want her informed. Of everything." His eyes flash. He thinks I'm the risk—that I'm the one who may be keeping secrets. It was a bold move to call my sister and tell her right away, while I could retaliate, and then to tell me he did it.

Gregory is a good man.

But now Judica knows that I know. My nostrils flare, but I manage to keep my tone normal. "That saves me the time of calling her. I can't believe Melina's messenger implied that I had kept anything from her. It's nonsense, of course." I hope I won't be flying home to a coup, thanks to Gregory's honest diligence. It occurs to me for the first time, like a moron, that I might have handed her what she already wanted. She could kill me and no one would lift a hand to stop her. Because, of course, they believe she's me.

She's the queen of everything.

But I can't think about that now. I'll meet with Melisania, find out what she wants, and think this all through before I fly home.

Gregory leads me to the new conference room, conveniently located on the same level as my room.

Melisania is waiting when I arrive, which is a nice change. She stands. "Judica, well met."

I incline my head slightly. I'm not in a very giving mood, thinking of six of my men dying and contemplating the loss of twenty-five other Alamecha evians. "I am glad you're hale and hearty. However, I think you'll understand when I say I don't feel inclined to draw out our meeting here with any unnecessary pleasantries."

"I completely understand. And I want you to know that I came in good faith. I watched the video your sister sent, and I've had eye-witness reports to verify that it wasn't fabricated. I'd like to see your sister in person, but I worried that bringing this on to her soil might complicate things." She lifts her ring where the staridium sparkles on her finger. "I do believe she's the queen of the prophecy. It's pretty clear that something is different about her. She should have died at birth, but your merciless mother spared her. Which makes her the Eldest who is also an empress." Melisania shakes her head. "I should have thought of it sooner. But if that wasn't enough, the stone reacts to her. And she managed to turn you into a supporter when you initially wanted her dead, right?"

Judica supports me now, or at least, I thought she did until an hour ago. I'm not sure of how convincingly I can lie right now, so I grunt. Let her make of that what she will.

"Obviously she has some things to clean up within her own family." Melisania sniffs. "Did I hear that this was a hit team intended to kill you, sent by your older sister?"

"Early Intel agrees with that assessment. I haven't ruled anything out yet. Including people who came conveniently late but should otherwise have been present and in the middle of the attack themselves." I pin Melisania with a stare.

"I think you'll find that I am exactly what you see presented here today. If I wanted you dead, I would have had ample opportunity when we came upon you, wounded and broken."

I sit up straight in my chair. "I didn't receive a single scratch. And I'd dare you to try to harm me with Edam here, but I think you already know that."

Melisania smiles broadly. "Bravo. Everything I thought you would be. I feel better than ever about my proposition."

"Then spit it out," I say.

"I will." She clears her throat. "But a bit of friendly advice first. If I were you, I'd eliminate the threat posed by my older sister immediately. Queen of Queens or not, Chancery's heart is dangerously kind. I worry that may get in the way of her taking the proper action against someone who openly attacked one of her supporters."

A supporter who probably caused the attack. "Duly noted."

"You haven't given me your assessment of your sister. From what I hear, you had no intention of allowing her to rule. And yet, when you fought, you could have defeated her. Is it true?" Melisania's tone is light, but her eyes are intense.

"I had no intention of allowing her to defeat me," I say.

"What happened?" Melisania asks.

I can't answer her question. I haven't asked Judica myself. But I realize I have a chance here, as Judica, to entice Melisania to betray me, to admit to her own less than pure intentions—as if I'm offering an under-the-table alliance. "I found out about the prophecy," I say. "Once I knew about it, I had two choices. I could try to fight fate, or I could yield and be her supporter. I decided I'd prefer to be mentioned than overrun entirely."

"So you stepped down voluntarily?" Melisania taps her fingernails against the table. "Curious."

"Have you ever met my sister?" I ask.

She shakes her head.

"Then you don't understand yet. I don't know why she was chosen, truly I don't, because she's kind, she's generous, and she's easy to manipulate."

"Easy to manipulate?" Melisania asks.

I fold my hands in front of me and lean back in my chair.

"You're here because you're really running things?" she asks.

I shrug. "I think it's more accurate to say that my sister allows me to make the difficult decisions so that she can be who she truly is."

Melisania's smile lights up her entire face. "While I had hoped your sister would come herself, as it happens, my main proposal is for you. And after our conversation, I feel even better about making it."

I lift my eyebrows. "For me?"

"I know that Chancery must unite the families, but I can imagine how onerous it would be to decide every little thing that arises. Of course I'd like to be named to care for my current holdings. Beyond that, I'd like a seat on the Council, and a say in major decisions. But unlike Analessa, I don't have aspirations on forcing your sister to choose a Consort of my selection. I don't have any plans to insist on her genetics carrying the stamp of Lenora."

"Since every one of our families has intermarried over and over in the past seven generations anyway?" I ask.

"Precisely. But I do believe that Lenora should be honored, and I believe I have valuable counsel to offer. I do want to make sure my family receives some recognition for its willingness to submit first. A few reassurances is all I ask, so that I can be sure my suggestions won't be totally ignored."

"What reassurances are you requesting, exactly?"

"Well." Melisania smiles again. "Correct me if I'm mistaken, but Chancery isn't the only Alamecha princess who is currently unattached. You're clearly valuable to your sister, currently her heir, and from what I hear, you value skill and savagery. We excel at combining skill and savagery among the ranks of Lenora, my family in particular." The joyful look on her face when she discusses skill and savagery is a little unnerving.

"You want to choose my future husband." My tone comes out flatter than I intended. After all, as far as I know, Judica has been lying to my face since her return. What do I care if she's stuck marrying someone awful?

"That's just it," Melisania says. "I'm young and healthy, and I'm not a monster. For millennia we've sold our sons to the other royal families to provide options for our daughters. This would hardly differ from that. You can marry the next of my sons you take a fancy to, whenever that happens in the next, let's say, hundred years. You can train him in any way you like, or you can direct me to do it for you. You'll have years and years to do literally anything you please. And if anything happens to you, not that I think it's a huge risk, your sister's first daughter can step into your place."

"You know it's very unlikely I'll remain my sister's Heir for very long. She's young and eventually she'll marry, and then I'll be nothing more than a member of her Council. Which means, if you make this deal and she has a child in a year or two, you're stuck with nothing more than a son married to the sister of the Queen of Queens."

"You'll always be a valued, respected, skillful member of her Council. There's a reason things fell out as they did. And because you play a long game, other than your sister, you're the only person mentioned in the prophecy."

"That's it? Your only demand is that I marry one of your sons?"

Melisania leans back, her lips curled up. "And I won't even make you do it for, let's say, one hundred years. Do what you want during that time, but you must marry one of my sons by the end of the timeframe. Although, that's not my only demand."

"What else?" I ask.

Melisania pulls a sheaf of papers from a briefcase and hands it to me. "The devil really is in the details, isn't it? But in this case, I think you'll find my terms aren't outrageous. I want a seat on the Council, access to you and your sister, and time with you each year, to make sure you're carefully considering your options for marriage."

I think about Judica's reaction whenever Roman comes up. I think about how, for the first time, she seems happy. But if she's been ignoring my commands because she's unwilling to let go of her anger against Melina. . . "You could have sent this directly to my sister, you know."

Melisania shrugs. "I wanted to meet with you in person."

"You had no idea who would come," I argue.

She smiles. "But I suspected your sister would come herself, or she'd send you. Either way, I'd learn something—about who she values."

"Before this morning, did you intend to insist on a

marriage between one of your sons and me?" I arch one eyebrow.

She shifts in her seat and leans closer to me. "I knew I would insist my child marry whomever Chancery trusted enough to send here today. But I'm delighted that it was you. Judging from the fight you deflected, you'll be a more than suitable match for one of my children."

I wonder momentarily whether she might have orchestrated the entire attack to gauge my skill level. If I were Judica, I would know whether the attack truly came from Melina. That woman seemed to recognize her. And there were names she mentioned, William and Ambrosia. I wish I knew who they were.

I wish I shared the contents of my sisters' brain instead of just her face.

"In any case," Melisania says. "Communicating an offer of this magnitude, the complete surrender of my entire family, my divine mandate, my power and authority, via electronic message hardly represents the kind of partnership I envision for our future."

"Partnership?" I ask.

"Oh you know how these things work. Of course she will be my leader, but she's so young, so inexperienced. It will be very advantageous for her to have someone like me, someone who isn't overbearing or unreasonable, but who always provides a willing ear. You and I will always be here for her, as a shoulder to cry on, a guiding force to help her when things are vexing. For instance, I would be happy to terminate this older sister as a gesture of goodwill to you, Judica, if that's something you see as an impediment to Chancery's healthy and safe rule. She may squirm about doing what needs to be done, but you and I don't need to shy away from the dirty work, do we?"

Right. Of course not. Why would Judica balk at eliminating someone I don't want dead? I do not flinch, I do not scowl, and I do not allow my heart rate to spike. For once, I keep everything controlled exactly as I ought. "I'll think on what you've said and review the rest." I wave the papers. "It may take me some time to analyze it all, assemble my thoughts, and communicate with my sister."

Melisania shrugs. "I'm not in a hurry."

I am, but there's no reason to indicate that. Besides, I need to see Judica. We have things to settle.

❧ 19 ❧

"The first decision we need to make is whether it's safe to fly home," I say.

Edam shakes his head. "You never should have let that psychopath talk you into trading places."

He's probably right. But I don't love hearing Judica referred to as a psychopath. "We don't know whether anything that woman said is true," I say. "It could all be a lie. In fact, she could be working for Melisania." I cross my arms.

"Melisania did pounce on Melina pretty quick, offering to execute her." Noah leans against the wall. "It was almost too convenient. Do we know whether she and Melina have a history?"

"Of course we don't," I nearly yell. "I'm so young compared to all of them that I don't know anything. And everyone lives so long that they all share huge histories I know nothing about. I don't even know basic information about my own father."

Melina's messenger really landed a blow when she mentioned that my father left Melina the prophecy. I never even met him, and I hate it. I wish I knew what happened between him and my mom. Was he really crazy? And if so, what did he leave Melina?

"I should call Judica," I say.

Edam shakes his head. "Bad idea. Don't call her until you know exactly what you want to say and how you'll drill her to find out what you need to know."

"You need to know whether she's been torpedoing you with Melina," Noah says. "And whether it's only because Melina kidnapped her and she can't let it go, or whether it's part of a more significant plan to keep you in the dark and out of control."

"Thank you, Socrates," Edam says. "And while we're at it, we should ask her if she plans to hand the ring back to Chancery when we land, or if she's hatching a plot to eliminate you and step into the role of Chancery permanently."

Noah rolls his eyes. "Umm, that's not nearly subtle enough."

Edam's jaw clenches.

I stifle a laugh. "I doubt Noah really thought I should call and ask flat out." Although. She wouldn't expect me to do that.

I think about what I know. Judica came home voluntarily when she could have simply disappeared. I'd never have found her, not with the jet and Roman to help her. They could have gone anywhere. She came to me to propose that we swap places, but only to give me what I wanted.

Right?

At the end of the day, I have to trust someone. When I close my eyes and think about the time we have spent since her return, I hear her melody and it's the one I heard before our fight. Melina's people, if they really are her people, have tried to undermine my faith in my twin.

Should I let them? At the end of the day, I have to trust someone, and I'm not a very subtle person. My gut tells me that Judica may be misguided, but she isn't betraying me. If someone is blocking Melina's messages, I don't think it's Judica. She wouldn't have argued so vocally for me to kill her, she wouldn't have fought so hard for me to eliminate her, if she was going to go behind my back and prevent our communication.

No, if that's happening, it's not because of Judica. I think Melina is wrong—there's someone else who doesn't want us to talk. I wish I had asked Melina's last attacker how to reach her. Not that she'd have given the information to Judica, more than likely. She wasn't there to deliver a message—she was there to kill me so Melina's messages could get through.

But I can call one of my sisters. Before Edam or Noah can argue with me, I dial Judica's number.

"How are you?" she whispers.

"I'm fine. Are you okay? Why are you whispering?"

"I'm in your room, but I'm never one hundred percent positive how well people can hear," Judica says.

I laugh. "You're so paranoid." I could probably use a healthier dose of that myself. "Speaking of."

"Melina attacked you."

"She did."

"One of your overzealous newly-pledged minions named Gregory called me. He told me that Melina's fighter, the one with a partially shaved head, accused me of burying her messages so you wouldn't see them."

"Did you?"

"You don't believe that, or you wouldn't have called me."

I don't want to believe it.

"Or maybe you do, and you called me anyway." Judica swears. "You are so absurdly optimistic."

BRIDGET E. BAKER

"I want you to tell me the truth," I say, my voice trembling. "I want you not to have done it."

"I should have killed her that day, Chancery. Even if it ended me, I should have—" Judica swears again. "I haven't hidden her messages, but I'm not the only one who could have done something like that, so she's likely telling the truth. If she's been trying to reach you, there's pretty much no way that your message got through to her. The question becomes—who is working against you?"

A question I've asked over and over now.

"It could be Alora or Inara," Judica says. "Or Balthasar, Marselle, basically anyone on the Council who has top clearance."

Great. My entire Council could be working against me communicating with Melina. "I doubt it's Inara, since she wanted me to reach out to Melina."

"True," Judica says. "But she could be saying that to throw you off."

"But if she had argued against contacting her, and you agreed, I'd have been a fool to ignore you both."

"I'll compile a list," Judica says, "of who has access to outbound and inbound communications. Your guards, if a few of them were working together, might have stopped it. Should I talk to Frederick?"

I don't think he'd be involved, so he might be a good resource, but ultimately, I don't know. "Do you ever feel like we're playing a game of Marco Polo?" I ask.

"Of what?"

"It's that game we played in the ocean," I say. "As young children. I'd yell Marco if I was 'it', and then everyone else would yell Polo. I'd be blindfolded and have to swim toward them."

"I never played games," Judica says. "But I certainly can relate to feeling like I'm making decisions with a blindfold.

Being young as an evian sucks. We haven't witnessed enough for context, and we don't have enough experience to judge."

"Did you know the woman?" I ask. "The one who tried to kill me? Or I guess she tried to kill you. She had a partially shaved head."

"And earrings running up her ear," Judica says. "And yes, we've met twice. I shot her in the face the first time. When she tracked me down the second time, I stabbed her in the leg, and then I cut her throat."

Classic Judica. Good grief. "So basically she's in training to be your new bestie. You must not have had any forks lying around. It's a good thing too, or I might have gotten jealous."

She chokes. It almost sounds like a suppressed laugh. "You're the only person I've ever stabbed with a fork."

"That may be the sweetest thing you've ever said to me."

"You still don't know whether to believe me."

I clear my throat, unwilling to agree with her out loud. "She mentioned some people Melina will kill if she doesn't receive confirmation that I got the message."

Judica inhales sharply. "Billy and Ambrosia. Is that what she said?"

"Gregory could have told her that," Edam says. "It means nothing."

"I hear my fan club back there, singing my praises as usual," Judica says.

"They're simply being logical," I say.

"There's nothing I can say to make you believe me," Judica says. "Just as there was nothing I could do to reassure myself you would welcome my return before I flew home. At some point, you either believe me or you don't."

She's right.

"Be safe," I say.

"I can send you more men," Judica says. "Whether you believe me or not, I'm worried about you right now."

"I've got Edam."

"Who clearly figured out that we switched," Judica says.

"Actually, Noah figured it out."

"You're kidding."

"I'm not."

"Your hopelessly devoted, completely worthless human is the one who realized you weren't me?"

"Noah realized I was far too nice to be you." She can't see my smug smile, but I bet she can guess how I look.

"Well, who knew he was good for more than deflecting stray bullets?"

Noah's right—she wouldn't have agreed to think about the value of humans. "Accept the world as it is," I say softly.

"Let's change it," Judica says.

I hang up. I don't realize until after the phone is dead that I didn't even mention the details of Melisania's offer. Maybe I'm not ready to talk to her about it yet. Because the offer is a great one. Judica has up to a century of romantic freedom, and she can choose from men who are already alive, or any other son Melisania may have.

The whole concept of scoping out babies as possible husbands icks me out, but Judica was the one telling me she'd take the offer and marry Edam in my place. Perhaps she'd like the idea of designing a husband from the ground up.

A memory of Judica holding tightly to Roman's hand on her return surfaces and I close my eyes. She may have encouraged me to take Analessa's offer, but I chafe at the idea of being forced to marry Edam, and I *like* him. Like, really, really like him. What if it was someone I'd never met? And I was already hopelessly in love with someone else?

"Should I tell the guards we're headed home?" Edam asks.

I open my mouth to say yes. It will be a relief to be myself again, but then something occurs to me. Whether it's Judica or not, *someone* on my Council has been covering up the messages Melina sent, and the ones I issued to her.

Which means even if Judica hasn't betrayed me, I have an enemy at home.

"We're not going back to Ni'ihau. Not yet, anyway."

"We're not?" Edam asks.

I shake my head. "We're going to see Melina."

"The woman who just sent all those people to kill you," Edam says.

"No, she sent a squad to kill Judica," I say. "She wants to see me."

"But she thinks you're Judica," Noah points out.

True. But surely I can convince her of who I am, if I can even reach her. I shake my head. "We'll figure that part out, but I'm not ready to fly home and sit in a throne room arguing with people who are supposed to work for me about who I can talk to and what I can do. Now is the time."

"I like this new attitude," Noah says.

"I'm sure your fond stories about her attitude will elicit some poignant tears at her funeral when this proves to be a monumentally bad idea," Edam says.

"I'm the one who's fragile," Noah says. "If I'm willing to risk a side trip, what do you have against it?"

Edam shakes his head, finally sick of arguing, I assume. "I'm ready. Let's go."

Noah takes our orders to the pilot while I explain to Agnes that we're leaving. "Let Melisania know that we're headed home to carefully review her generous proposal. Tell her I appreciate her support, as well as the time she took to meet us here in person."

"It was good to see you," Agnes says. "And please do pass along my support to your sister. Things are always scary and hard at the beginning, but she has more of us behind her than she knows."

"Thank you," I say.

I don't mention to Gregory that we're headed for Austin before we take off. Once we're in the air, I consider waiting a few hours, but I doubt that will help. Besides, I need to plan what to do when we arrive, and I'd like some input. I stand up and walk over to where he's seated. His eyes are closed and his arms are crossed over his chest.

"I wanted to thank you for protecting me back there," I say.

He doesn't open his eyes. "We did our job."

Six of them didn't survive, and I'm pretty sure he blames me for that. It's fair, but in this case, it's not really my fault. "I feel like you ought to know that we aren't returning to Ni'ihau. At least, not yet."

Gregory's eyes open and he sits up abruptly. "That is unacceptable. Chancery tasked us to keep you safe, not to follow you around to who knows where."

I pin him with my bravest stare. "It's time you learned the truth."

Noah shakes his head. Why shouldn't I tell them? Or maybe he's telling me not to tell them why I'm headed to Austin. I'm surprised he thinks he needs to signal me not to share the fact that I have someone working against me. You know, I wish the stupid staridium gave me powers of telepathy.

"Judica and I switched places." I prepare myself to fight

with them. I have a half dozen arguments and explanations on the tip of my tongue.

"Wait," Gregory says.

I'll start with the explanation of why we switched. I can explain that my Council didn't want me to come, but I needed to talk to Melisania myself to gauge how sincere she was. Then I'll move on to why I brought Edam and Noah along.

"I knew it," Ibrahim says. "I told you it wasn't the twin."

Wait. They talked about this?

"Edam wouldn't have lifted a finger to protect Judica, and he certainly wouldn't have fought like he did." Ibrahim smiles. "I knew it."

"Even that little human jumped in front of her," Voron says. "I should have known then."

"And she said that the human gave her a lot to think about," Ibrahim is quick to point out. "I told you that was weird."

Noah scowls. "I have a name, you know. And I'm not little."

"Now I'm really glad I leapt on that bomb. It made an impression, right?" Ibrahim wiggles his eyebrows up and down and beams at me.

"It was very selfless," I admit. "Or it was, until you made it clear that you did it in order to impress me."

He swears under his breath. "But even so, I didn't know whether I'd survive. That must count for something."

I grin. "Maybe a little something." I turn so that I'm facing all of them. "You've all sworn to serve me. We're headed to Austin because I have some sensitive matters to address there."

"You want to talk to Melina before she kills Judica, or Judica kills you," Gregory says. "And you're going now so that whoever has been keeping her messages from reaching you won't try to stop you."

So much for not telling them everything.

"We're totally on board," Ibrahim says. "This doesn't sound nearly as dangerous as jumping on a bomb."

"Although, depending on Melina's true purpose and her total force, it might not be that different," Voron says, and then blinks. "But of course we support you, Your Majesty."

"I think we can all agree on one thing," Noah says. "It's a good thing Chancery's not dreaming of a career in Hollywood, because her acting skills stink."

❧ 20 ❧

We spend the entire flight discussing our options. "I still vote that I walk right up, announce who I am, and she'll let me inside."

A chorus of refusals meets my ears.

"This is why I didn't fly home," I complain. "Because I knew everyone on my Council would protest and whine."

"She's already tried to kill Judica twice that we know of," Edam says. "Let us go and extract her for you."

Basically every single Motherless agrees with him.

"That's a Judica plan if I ever heard one," I say. "Slash, burn, and then take what you want. It's not me. We've already killed enough of Melina's people."

"I normally don't agree with Edam," Noah says softly. "But I'm okay with people dying as long as you aren't among them."

I roll my eyes. "She won't kill me. You heard her messenger. She wants to serve me."

"So she says." Noah shakes his head. "You can't trust her. No one knows her, and she's a complete wild card.

Even your mother banished her. She wouldn't have done that without good reason."

"We land in an hour," I say. "I am not going to agree to let the fifteen of you sprint into some kind of war zone and steal my sister and then—"

"You need leverage," Noah says.

Everyone falls silent.

"I don't know her well enough to have any ideas what might constitute effective leverage." I sigh. "It's a good idea, and if I had more time, or more faith in my own people back home, I could—"

"Marselle is from Austin. She would know a lot about Melina," Edam says.

"We've been over this and over it. She would know a lot, but for that very reason, she's at the top of the list of people who might be blocking my messages." I will not throw a fit like a small child. "We have two options. Mine, where I walk up peaceably and ask to talk to her, and yours, where we go to war with a sixteen-person army. And if you lose, and by lose, I mean if you all die, I'm alone, stranded in Austin, with at least one enemy back home, and Melina knows I'm close and vulnerable."

"And if you do what you want, she could kill you fifteen different ways," Noah says.

"What's your brilliant plan, human?" Edam asks. "Because all I hear is a bunch of objections, which is utterly unhelpful."

"I might have one, actually," Noah says.

"I'm all ears," Edam says.

"I didn't want to say it, but they do kind of stick out from your head." Noah smirks. "Like a fennec fox, actually, but like, not nearly as cute."

"What's your idea, Noah?" I ask, before Edam can punch him.

"What if we didn't walk up and present Chancery like a lamb for the slaughter, but we also didn't attack Melina and drag her out by her hair like Fred Flintstone? What if we infiltrate her organization and nab someone important, and then we invite her to join us for a chat?" he asks.

"Brilliant," Edam says. "And six months from now, we'll have that important sit down. Meanwhile, we're living off of nothing while Judica becomes increasingly comfortable back home on Chancery's throne."

"We know where her base of operations is," Noah says. "And we can watch for someone to leave. At a baseline, we know that the woman with the Mohawk and earrings is important. We could nab her."

"Which would probably be perceived as an act of war," I say. "Or at least a threat."

"Which is so different from how she has behaved toward you, how?" Noah asks. "I mean, you did just kill twenty-five of her people, right? Kidnapping one is practically a love letter by comparison."

I swallow hard. He's right. I did just kill a lot of Melina's troops. I killed them in self-defense, but still.

"What if you could enter without her even realizing it, and then talk to her alone?" Noah asks.

"Uh, yeah, that's like my plan on steroids, but I don't see how it's possible." I lean back in my seat and close my eyes. "We all need sleep. Let's take a break until we reach the hotel."

"Agreed," Edam says.

"If I'm honest, I need way more than an hour of sleep," Noah says. "I think I'm about a million hours deficient right now."

"We agree that you're deficient, at least," Edam says, but his mouth is turned up into a half smile and I'm practically positive he enjoys picking at Noah.

Noah sits on my other side and buckles up. "You should consider my idea," Noah whispers.

"I am," I say. "It's the closest option to mine, and I like it better than going in and destroying Melina's house and people and everything else. I mean, that's basically what Judica would do, so it'll only confuse her. She needs to believe I'm actually me for this to work."

Noah opens his mouth and closes it, his hand fiddling with the cord around his neck.

"What?" I ask.

"Nothing," he says.

"What's that necklace?" I ask. It's strange that I've never seen anything but the cord. There must be some kind of pendant attached, but even when we jumped into the river, I don't recall seeing anything else.

"It's on loan from my dad. Family heirloom, I guess."

"Can I see it?"

He shakes his head. "There are a few things I'm not supposed to talk about." He's agitated, which means his heart should be pounding, but it's not. It's a steady beat, a little slow for a human, honestly.

"What does that mean, there are a few things you can't talk about?" The hair on my arms rises. "Like what?"

He clucks. "Uh uh. That would be telling, and I've already said too much."

Too much? I think about every interaction I've ever had with Noah. He runs nearly as fast as me. He's handsome, despite what Edam delusionaly insists. He's smart, really smart. He never seems to need sleep, his recent protest notwithstanding. He stepped in front of me when I was distracted and the huge evian got around the Motherless, instead of simply yelling and running away. Noah doesn't seem frightened, even surrounded by evians. And his blue, blue eyes are a bizarre anomaly for someone from China.

His father's commanding presence raised a few red flags I ignored. It was odd he landed in Ni'ihau at all, and odder still that he peppered me with so many questions.

But in retrospect, he didn't ask nearly as many as I would have expected from a scared human, like why we had a palace on Ni'ihau, or why we took his son without any signed permission forms. Or why a teenager was leading the company—or at least, directly reporting to a CEO.

How did I not question any of this before? Noah's heartbeat is the obvious answer. I can accelerate my heartbeat, I suppose, but not all the time, not every second of every day. I'd forget. It would drop, and people would notice. Noah's is steady, occasionally a little low, but steadily in the human range. But if I disregard the heartbeat, I realize I don't have much evidence of Noah's humanity.

I've never seen Noah sleep. Not once. He's always been awake when I wake up. Even though humans need double the sleep I do, and four times the sleep of an adult evian. How is he always awake? My hands begin to shake, my body feels trembly, and my stomach feels wrong. Not hungry, not overfull, just wrong.

I've felt this way before, nervous, almost ill—when Lark asked me to commit treason.

I trusted Noah when I didn't trust anyone. I counted on him, relied on him, and I've told him things. So many things. He's my example of a human who has value and adds almost as much as the evians around him. He's my connection to China, the one place evians don't control.

I shake my head. I'm going crazy here, that's all. I'm stressed, I'm nervous, and I'm losing my mind.

But he says he can't tell me things. Is it possible Noah. . . isn't really human? If I ask him, he'll deny it. And the others will hear, and they won't take it well. I pick up my water glass and swirl the ice with the tiny plastic toothpick. It's shaped like a spear, pointed on the end.

I glance to my right. Edam's asleep, or he's trying. His chest rises and falls naturally. I should sleep too. I should cast these absurd questions out of my mind. Noah couldn't possibly be. . . evian. Right? Not after all this time. Someone would have realized it. I would have realized it before now.

But he did escape from the cells in Ni'ihau. It was such a chaotic time that I didn't ever press him on *how*. Why didn't I pursue an explanation? Because I need someone to trust, someone who supports me and doesn't want anything from me. I needed a friend, not another angle that would slide sideways.

But I can't turn a blind eye, not anymore. A sideways glance shows Noah staring at me steadily. Almost as if he's willing me to figure something out. Could he want to tell me the truth, but be unable to do it? I shake my head. That's crazy. Beyond crazy. Noah huffed and puffed, red in the face when we ran. He couldn't keep up with Edam and me.

But we broke that record. The record I shouldn't have broken. Did I break it because I was pacing myself against another evian? I gulp.

And when Alora called me and confessed to betraying me. . . she heard Noah behind me and asked who it was. What if her real betrayal wasn't that staged attack? What if she used that as an excuse to cover another betrayal I hadn't even discovered? What if she enrolled me at Trinity to place me in Noah's path? Have I been groomed this entire time to become his friend so I would trust him? Is all of this just another in a string of manipulations? Is nothing in my life my own?

My hand tightens around the tiny toothpick spear and

my heart hardens. No one else is looking at us. In fact, everyone is nodding off or asleep. Everyone except Noah and me. The human is awake when everyone else is tired. Anger grips me tightly, permeating every cell of my body, and I slam my hand down onto Noah's where it lies innocently on his armrest. I shove the plastic toothpick into the back of his hand and yank it back out again. Noah's face is white, but he doesn't make a sound. Not a sigh, not an inhalation, not a complaint.

Blood bubbles up from the hole and pours over the top of his hand to drip to the floor of the jet.

But it doesn't bubble for very long. The wound closes over quickly, as quickly as mine would. Scenes flash through my mind as if in fast forward. Our first kiss, the time I sheltered him when I was attacked in New York. When he dove after me bravely and we swam to shore. His incredulity when I smashed my arm to show him we heal. I may not be a very good actor, but Noah is a master.

All of it was a lie.

I leap to my feet and run for the bathroom.

Noah's only a step behind me. "I wanted to tell you," he whispers. "So many times."

His pulse slows, the speed matching mine.

Last week my heart shattered, the pieces forever irreparable. So much loss, so much death, so many expectations crushed into rubble. Slowly, piece by piece, I glued it back together. Noah, Edam, Judica, Alora, Inara, they all helped. They all allowed my heart to heal enough to function.

And now it's pulverized again. I fly into the bathroom and slam the door. I sit on the toilet and try not to sob loudly.

"What's going on?" Edam's voice, strong and true, outside my stall.

"Leave me alone," I whimper.

A ragged breath.

A growl. "What the—"

"It's complicated," Noah says.

A body slams up against the wall of the bathroom and it shakes. "Uncomplicate it. Your heart is suddenly beating far too slow. Explain that Noah, and do it fast."

"I have a bad heart."

"And why is Chancery's crying?"

More boots moving toward me, more heartbeats, surrounding Noah. I wanted to hide. I wanted to take a moment to think things through, let my heart bleed out, anything but face this.

But my time out is over, because if I don't intercede, they're going to kill him.

I shove the door open and push past where Edam's hand is wrapped around Noah's throat. "Let him go."

Edam doesn't release him or even loosen his grip.

"I said put him down." I grit my teeth.

"He's evian," Edam says. "Or at least half."

I shake my head. "I don't think he could tell us. I had to figure it out."

"Why?" Edam asks.

The Motherless mutter amongst themselves, most of them scowling.

"I don't know yet," I say. "But I know one thing. I'm not ready for him to die."

"Oh good," Noah chokes out. "Then could Edam put me down?"

Edam punches Noah in his face, hard. It shatters his nose. But Edam finally drops him. "That felt so good."

Noah stands up and wipes his nose on his sleeve, the damage already repaired. His mouth turns up on the corners into a grin. "You think that felt good?" He hits

Edam with a cross to the jaw, and Edam sprawls backward into one of the plane chairs. "I'm sick to death of pretending to be a lightweight."

The Motherless scatter while Edam and Noah go at it: swings, uppercuts, jabs.

Bling, bling. The overhead PA system sounds. "We're on our final approach to Austin. Find your seats and buckle in."

The boys don't act like they heard a single word.

"Hey," I unsheathe my swords. "Do I need to slice some sense into you two, or are you going to knock it off and buckle up?"

Edam pulls up short, and Noah lands a solid uppercut on his chin. Edam scowls but holds.

Noah stumbles back. "You give up?"

"Human or not, you're still an idiot." Edam shakes his head. "Chancery says we're landing. She wants you to sit down." Edam backs up and drops into his seat.

Noah follows his lead, and just like that, I'm sitting in between a traitor to Alamecha and some kind of secret agent, about to land in Austin to face my banished-but-not-banished sister.

That's what I get for thinking things couldn't get any weirder.

21

I don't know what to do about Noah. Part of me wants to attack him like Edam did. He lied to me, to all of us, and he's done it for a long time. He also isn't offering up any explanation for his lie. When Edam realized I knew he had been in contact with his sister, he immediately apologized and explained it was a mistake. He let me decide whether to forgive him with all the information. Or at least, I think he did.

But Noah simply nudged me toward the truth and won't offer any extra details.

On the other hand, he's done nothing but help me. And if he hadn't nudged me in the right direction, I probably wouldn't have figured out his secret at all.

And a small part of me is excited. I'm embarrassed that I'm excited, but it's true nevertheless. I've liked Noah for a long time, but he hasn't been a viable option for me. I value humans and respect them, and I think we need to improve this world for them. I believe my people have lost their way and treat humans all wrong. But no matter how much I value them, I could never marry a human.

But Noah's not human. I suppress the tiny thrill that pulses through me at that thought. Because he may be evian, but he's also a liar.

I have no idea who he's working for or why he finally wanted me to figure out the truth today.

"Why?" I ask him softly. "Why now?"

Noah shrugs. "I can't say. But I can tell you that I have a special skill set. There's a reason I was sent to America. I was always supposed to meet you. You've been my end goal my entire life."

That electric thrill isn't tiny this time. It makes the hair on my arms rise. Again. "The only way I can get past this is if you tell me everything."

"Then I guess I'm doomed. I've made vows," Noah says. "I can't tell you anything. You have to figure things out for yourself."

Or I could kill him and stop the leak. My fingers itch to see whether he'd change his tune with my sword pressed against his throat. I wonder, in this bizarre moment, as the landing gear drops on my plane, whether he's a decent fighter. Edam was angry, but he wasn't really trying to harm him. As much as he might protest, I think Edam likes Noah.

Why would I be his target? "You were sent to find Chancery Alamecha?" I ask. "Or you were sent to befriend the leader of Alamecha?" Something occurs to me. "Or were you tasked to find the Queen of Queens?"

"Is there a difference?"

"I was nobody one month ago," I say.

"Your mother was the empress of the first family of Eve," Noah says. "That's a strange definition of nobody."

"My point is that no one cared what I did, other than my mother and probably Alora." I close my eyes and review my conversation with my sister the last time I was flying with Noah into enemy territory. "Did she betray me. . . by introducing me to you?"

"I can neither confirm nor deny that outrageous guess." But he bobs his head up and down.

She did. "What family do you work for?"

"I'm Noah Wen, from China," he says. "I work for my own family, as I already told you. You've even met my father, my biological, full-blooded father."

His father had a human heart rate too, but perhaps he's the one who taught Noah to control the speed of his heartbeat. "How did you do it? Was it terribly exhausting, accelerating your heart rate *all the time?*"

"You have no idea, princess," Noah says. "No idea. I'm so relieved not to have to act so breakable, either. That was even worse than the constant biological limitations. I wasn't lying when I said the thing I wanted the most was to heal. Actually, whenever possible, I haven't lied to you at all."

Does he really come from China? Maybe one of the banished evians went there and started a family. Probably someone with an agenda. Or maybe Noah made the entire thing up as a cover for the family he really works for—it could be Shenoah, or Adora or Shamecha. He could even be working for Analessa, for all I know.

While the plane lands, my hands grip the armrests so tightly that my knuckles turn white. I don't mind flying, but when this plane stops moving, the Motherless and Edam are going to expect some kind of decision from me about Noah. And I have no idea what to do.

"How did you get away from the cells in Ni'ihau?" I ask. "That day when I had Edam lock you up."

Noah shrugs. "How do I maintain my heartbeat?"

He does something to his body? "You can flatten yourself into a pancake and slip through the crack under the door?"

Noah laughs. "You got it. I'm basically Elasti-girl."

So that's not it. The plane is taxiing. I'm nearly out of time. "You did something that allowed you to exit without anyone knowing. But what?" I think about the guards, about who was on duty that night. Think, brain. It was Blake and Kyle. Kyle is nearly the same height as Noah, and he's got blue eyes.

I can change my eye color. I can change my hair color. I can change my skin color.

What if Noah can change more than that? Could he have convinced one of the guards that he *was* the other guard and been released as a result? I focus on my nose and will it to shift. Nothing. But my eyes begin to twitch from being crossed.

"You're on the right path," Noah says. "If you can figure out how I escaped, you might be able to walk right in to see your sister without any risk, without any war or attack or any more death at all."

He can change his appearance. It's the only explanation. But how? I've never heard of anything like this. But then, two weeks ago, I'd never heard of a prophecy. I'd never heard of Nereus before Mom died. I had no thoughts of ever ruling. And I didn't know evians could accelerate their heartbeats for sustained periods of time to mimic humans.

The plane stops. The Motherless unbuckle.

Edam unbuckles and stands. "What do you want us to do?"

"Restrain him," I say. "And if we have any tranquilizers on board, hit him with them."

"He's evian," Edam says. "They won't last long."

"Yes, thank you, I'm aware." But it will buy me a few minutes to think.

"The restraints are entirely unnecessary," Noah says. "I'm on your side, and I always have been. My actions all confirm that truth. I won't try to escape."

"I have no idea who you are," I practically spit. "Or whose side you're on. I don't know you at all."

Noah holds my gaze without blinking or flinching. He puts up no struggle when Gregory tranqs him. Twice. But he slumps in his seat, and it takes two Motherless to carry him off the plane. I insist he remain in my car on the way to the hotel.

My phone rings almost the second we reach the car.

"Judica," I say. "I hope you're well."

"You're alive, so why aren't you home yet?"

"I'm doing quite well, actually. Thank you for checking in. I'll be home before you know it. If you could simply hold things down until—"

"I can't believe you didn't come straight back. Analessa has not been patient and lately she's been sending me more and more frequent requests for a visit. I'm running out of reasons to delay her."

"You're inventive. Remarkably inventive. Lean into that."

"You're Empress," she hisses. "Not a tourist off to see the big wide world. Get back *now*."

"Luckily, as far as anyone knows, I *am* back."

"Are you even going to tell me where you've gone?"

"I had a pressing matter to deal with," I say. "But since you need something to contemplate, perhaps I should share the terms of Melisania's offer. She will surrender control of Lenora to me, but only if I agree to let her have an apartment on Ni'ihau, a permanent place on my Council, and access to me alone on a weekly basis."

"All of that is completely reasonable," Judica says eagerly. "Did you agree? Do you have the second ring?"

"She had another large condition, and a bunch of small details I haven't combed through yet."

"What was the big condition?" Judica asks.

"Oh, about that. She thought she was talking to you, of course, so this was a hard one. She wants me to agree that you'll marry one of her sons. She isn't picky. There are a few among the Motherless of course, and more scattered around in various places. But she's also more than willing to pop out as many boys as evianly possible to give you options. So many options. A hundred years' worth of options, in fact."

Total silence.

"You did spend quite some time reaming me for balking at similar, but more restrictive terms, when Analessa offered me Edam."

"Are you ordering me to do it?" she asks softly.

Am I? "No."

"Fine, then. Is it up to me?"

"Not exactly," I say. "But you and I will have a discussion about it upon my return."

"Where did you go?" she asks. "What's so important you had to rush off and leave me here even longer, pretending to be all sweet and sh—um. Shiny."

"Please tell me you haven't been swearing. Everyone will *know* you're not me."

"Just tell me where you are," she says. "I know evasion when I hear it."

"Speaking of that, I'm going to need an address from you. I could just call Roman and pretend to be you, but I'm guessing that might be awkward. I mean, are you more of a honey-bunches kind of person? Or do you prefer hotter nicknames, like lover?"

"Do not call Roman."

"Don't call him what? Honey bunches? I was pretty sure that wasn't you—"

"Stop," Judica hisses.

"I will, just as soon as you shoot me the address for Melina's compound in Austin."

"Oh my go—"

"We *just* talked about language."

"You can't go see her. She's unstable. And she killed Mother."

"*You* think she killed Mom, and she definitely wants you dead. But so far, she seems not to want to harm me. And one thing that is in extremely short supply around here is answers. If you follow me out here, or send a strike team, or do anything else like unto or related to those themes, I will remove you from my Council and try you for treason when I return."

"Chancery, this is madness. We have plenty of older sisters who aren't trying to shoot us," Judica says. "Let's pump them for information before we deliver banana nut muffins and a gold-engraved invitation to Melina."

"Wait, does she like banana nut muffins? Because that kind of insight could really help me right now."

Judica growls and hangs up, but she texts me an address. I hope it's the right one, or someone is about to get a very unwelcome amount of evian attention.

"Today has been full of feelings," Edam says dryly.

"I wish I knew how I felt," I say.

"Me too." He slumps against his seat. "I mean, I hate that guy. I'm pissed he's evian. And maybe a little jealous. But also, I liked having him on our side. He has good ideas."

I can't entirely hide my smile.

"What?" Edam frowns.

"You don't hate him at all."

"I thought he supported you. That's it. I don't like him, but I didn't hate him as much as I said. When I thought he was human, anyway."

"Who do you think he works for?" I ask.

Edam shrugs. "Who knows? No family rules China, but doesn't that make it the perfect place for discarded or banished evians to flee?"

I had never thought about it. They don't make waves, so it makes sense I wouldn't have heard, but there's probably some kind of 'exiled evian' organization. If they welcome banished evians. . . they probably take in evians who have half-evian children, which would account for Noah's progressive views on humans. It also might explain his surprising knowledge of pop culture, and his choice to come to America and train at a human school that includes a lot of half-evian students and staff.

What if he's related to me, and Alora just didn't tell me for some bizarre reason? Because I am *so* not a fan of the Luke and Leia thing. Yeesh.

But thinking about Noah being evian. . . I shove the thought away. The whole thing is such a tangle. At its heart, it all comes down to one question: How can I trust someone when I don't know who they really are?

"You don't work for your sister, not anymore, right?" I ask Edam.

He shakes his head. "I only serve you." His eyes are steady, unafraid, bold even.

"I believe you."

"You believe me because my actions support my words." He gestures around. "Have I not always done whatever you asked, even when it's hard for me?"

"Noah has, too."

"He sneaked on your plane right after you were crowned," Edam says.

"Which saved my life."

Edam scowls.

"We need to find out what he'll tell us, and then I can make my decision." I cross my arms. "He's the one who pushed me toward this discovery. He wanted me to figure him out."

"Why?" Edam asks. "Why out himself?"

"Honestly?" I shake my head. "I think he was sick of pretending to be human. But beyond that, there's something he thinks we can use him for now, here."

"Like what?"

"He escaped those cells to come with me on the plane." I think about our setup below the palace. "The question is, how? And why didn't I investigate that breach sooner?"

"I reviewed the tapes," Edam says. "But I didn't conduct a further investigation because he helped you. I figured it was a fluke."

"What happened?" I drum my fingers on the arm rest in the rented suburban.

"Blake and Kyle were the guards assigned to physically watch the cells."

I knew that already. "Go on."

"Usually both of them are required to be present. After all, evians and containment don't mix. Most of us have been trained to escape in any way possible. Once you provide the required amenities, it becomes too hard to prevent escape for an extended period of time."

"Right," I say.

"But Noah was human. We all knew it."

Except he wasn't. And if I'm right, he wouldn't be able to disguise that fact when he slept. His sleeping heart rate drops precipitously, I'm guessing. "And?"

"Kyle hadn't eaten all day and he was starving."

I look at the ceiling in frustration.

"And Blake got a phone call."

"Okay."

"Then before he knows it, he hears the door to the cell clang, and Kevin is inside, shouting for Blake to let him out."

"How was that even possible?" I ask. "Did you see him go inside?"

"Clearly someone spliced the feed."

"But how?" I ask. "Was the date stamp off?"

Edam shakes his head. "I don't know. I would have pursued it more, but I figured Noah lured Kyle over, insisted on getting the door open and then employed some kind of mad millennial computer skills to cover his tracks."

"That didn't concern you?"

Edam shrugs. "Look, everything about him concerned me. But you didn't want me to pick at him, and when I tried, you got defensive. Ultimately, he could have killed you on that plane, or any of a dozen other times. He seems bizarrely motivated to protect you, and I like things that keep you safe. Plus, how great of a threat did a human really pose?" Edam grunts. "His disguise really bought him a lot of latitude."

"But," I say.

"But if we don't know his long term game. . ."

"We don't know when his orders might flip, making me dispensable."

"Exactly," Edam says. "That's a real problem."

"Hey," I say. "What if the feed wasn't spliced?"

"Wait, you mean, what if, instead of going to get food like he said, Kyle actually snuck into the cell?"

I shake my head.

"Good. Because you can see him leave on the camera feed."

"No, I mean, what if it isn't actually Kyle who Blake

released? What did the guys say when you interviewed them?"

"They were as confused as me. Kyle insists he was never even in the cell, and Blake says he let Kyle out. The camera supports Blake's story, so Kyle ended up being removed from the guards and placed on housekeeping detail for six months' probation. I assumed he was lying, because he was embarrassed that a human tricked him."

"Poor Kyle."

Edam shakes his head. "Don't feel bad for Kyle. And Blake didn't get off scot free either. He got a month of scut for being inattentive."

A smile creeps onto my face, but the idea leaves me uneasy, too. "What if no one left that cell?"

"I don't understand."

"What if Kyle didn't go inside, and Blake inadvertently released Noah, thinking he was Kyle?"

"You mean." Edam freezes, not moving a single hair.

"We can change our eye color. We can change our skin color and grow our hair out in any color we choose. What did Kyle's clothing look like when he left the cell?"

Edam closes his eyes and I know he's going over the memory of the tapes he saw. He swears extensively. "It was Noah. The clothing was the same, only he looked just like Kyle, I swear."

"So Noah can shift more than his skin and eye color." I tap my index finger against my lip. "Quickly, too."

"That can't be it," Edam says. "Not just because it's insane, but also, he couldn't have changed his hair color. He didn't have scissors or a knife or anything, and there wasn't any hair on the ground in the cell."

"Is that something you even looked for?" I ask. "What if he hid it well enough that the cleaning crew took care of it the next day? Maybe he tossed it in the trash and no one even thought to check? It's part of their everyday routine to take out the trash."

"I don't—"

"I know it sounds far-fetched."

"It sounds batsh—"

"It sounds crazy, yes. But it also looks like the most likely possibility."

"And what? Noah pointed you at the notion that he's evian. . . So he could lead you down the path to discovering that he can shift his features to look like, well, like anyone at all? How would this help you with Melina?"

"If Noah can transform himself into someone she trusts, he can walk me inside himself."

"You think this is why he hinted that he's evian?"

"All I know is," I say, "I never would have figured it out without his nudge. And now we may have a way to engage Melina without anyone dying."

"But what do we do with Noah?" Edam asks.

I still have no idea.

22

I do not rush things when we settle into our hotel. Judica's in a hurry, but I won't jump the gun on this and die, or worse, let the world end because I'm not there to save it. I'm doing this the right way. It's time I get some answers on what Melina thinks, and why she left, and if she knows anything about our father, I'd like that information, too. Plus, she needs to learn that Judica's my greatest supporter.

Or at least, I really hope she is.

"Gregory and Ibrahim," I say.

"Yes?" They both turn around in a snap and answer in unison. It's a little creepy, honestly.

"Can the two of you do a little surveillance for me? I need information on Melina's operation. Specifically, who's important, who looks like they're issuing orders, and who's following them. If my guess is right, we're going to need photos and images, the best quality we can get, as soon as possible."

They both nod.

"This is dangerous," I say.

"Would you say it's more or less dangerous than, say, leaping on top of a grenade?" Ibrahim asks.

The other Motherless all groan, but I think he's kind of funny. Like an overeager puppy that can't stop scratching his ear. "Pick a few others to help you and go."

After they leave, it's time to wake Noah.

Which I am longing to do and dreading at the same time. I check my watch. I should have another half hour at the dosage he received, but usually they can be poked awake earlier. I have Edam lay him on a bed, and ask everyone but him to leave.

The Motherless do not approve.

"You should keep us in here," Voron says. "You need protection." He eyes Noah. "He's not a human. He lied."

I put my hand on his beefy arm. "I appreciate your sentiment, but he slept in my room the other night, ostensibly to keep me safe. I passed out first. He didn't do a thing, so I doubt he'll suddenly become homicidal."

"We should be here in case he does." Günter's face is set, his jaw locked.

"You may leave two men, no more, no less, just outside the door. The others will only be a room away. These aren't evian rooms, so I'm sure you'll be here quickly if he causes any trouble."

After a lot of huffs and grumbles, they go.

"Did any of them pay attention when Melina attacked in Hong Kong?" Edam asks. "I did all the work there, and I'm not leaving."

"In their defense, they just witnessed you and Noah rolling around on the floor like brothers, with neither of you coming out on top." I smirk. "Maybe they're worried about your dedication."

Edam's eyes flash. "If I think you're in danger, ever, I won't hesitate. Surely you know that."

I cross the room until he's only inches away. "I do. That's why I sent them away." The heat from his body radiates, like he's a tiny walking furnace. It also draws me toward him one more step.

"Things have changed," Edam says softly, his breath blowing over my lips.

"They have," I say.

"But my feelings for you remain the same." His head lowers over mine.

And just like our first kiss, I'm drawn to him in a way I can't explain. My lips set fire. My belly burns. My right hand curls up, my nails biting into my palm. Because I want Edam. In so many ways, he's exactly what I want. Generous, supportive, kind, ferocious, talented, brilliant, exceptional, and of course, handsome.

Plus there's a heat between us like a raging inferno.

When he kisses me, my knees go weak and my brain melts into my head.

He pulls back to say, "I'm glad you kicked those Motherless out. I've been dying to do this for longer than you can know. And this time, Noah's not coming out of the shower."

Oh my goodness. Noah. I force myself to stumble backward.

Edam swears. "He did it again. Except this time, I'm the one who mentioned him."

"We need to wake him up and interrogate him," I say. "I can't be making out with you right now."

Edam smiles. "But you wanted to."

I always want to. That thought floods my cheeks with color, which is a distraction I can't afford. I walk across the room to stand in front of the other bed and shake Noah gently. "Hey, wake up."

"You don't have to treat him like he's broken anymore. He's evian, remember?"

Edam strides across the room and yanks out a dagger.

"Whoa." I grab his arm. "Let's take things back a few levels."

Edam rolls his eyes and jabs Noah in the thigh. At least he doesn't slice through the clothing or worse, into his skin. Just because we *can* heal doesn't mean we should have to do it.

Noah bolts upright and his eyes fly open. "Where am I?"

Edam brandishes the dagger. "We're in Austin, *friend*, and we have a few questions for you."

Noah scowls. "Why's he waving a knife at me?"

"To make sure you don't attack our dear princess. You've always been far too perceptive, and I let it slide because, hey, Noah's harmless. But now that I know you're a counteragent, I mean to find out who you're working for."

"Hello pot. I'm kettle, but I like to pretend I'm not exactly the same as you." Noah winks at Edam.

I kick him. "Both of you, quit. And Edam, go sit down. I'll be asking the questions."

"I like this arrangement much better," Noah says. "It's always good to let the bad cop scowl a little, but good cop is the one who gets the results. Skip right to that." Noah shifts and swings his feet over the side of the bed. He pats the space next to him. "Now what did you want to know? I'll warn you, there are quite a few things I'm not allowed to say."

"Fine, then question one, why aren't you allowed to say so many things?"

Noah tilts his head sideways. "Duh. That's the first thing I can't tell you."

"We know there's a large group of evians living in China." Or we assume it, thanks to Edam's brilliant mind.

Noah's eyes widen. Bingo.

"Obviously they've been deftly blocking all attempts by the families to take over for years," I extrapolate, "and using the human regime as puppets."

"I wouldn't call them puppets," Noah says. "More like human shields."

It's my turn to be shocked. "But you like humans."

"Absolutely I do," Noah says. "But they're very capable of doing and saying aggressive, military-minded, and stupid things all on their own. We simply nudge them in the right direction."

"So you do belong to a band of outcasts?"

Noah puts a fist to his mouth for a moment. "I didn't admit that. But if there was one, they wouldn't struggle to manipulate the regional governments."

"What about half-evians?" I ask. "Loads of those, too?"

He shrugs. "Can't really say."

I do not scream, but I can't hide my exasperation either. "Noah, what can you say?"

"Probably not much," he says. "But hey, you celebrate Christmas, right? It's a delightful human tradition. Pops never agreed to celebrate it, but I picked up a few things while I was at Trinity. And lots of my friends played this game. Their parents would hide the presents, and then they had to try and find them. They could use their parents' responses to guide them. 'Hey, how about we go skiing this weekend?' they would ask."

"What does this have to do with anything?" I ask.

"Let me talk," Noah says. "So they'd ask about skiing, knowing the ski stuff is in the hall closet, next to the blankets. If good old mom and dad agreed to go, the kids knew there wasn't anything there. So they'd suggest a rousing game of golf before the first snowfall. But clubs have already been put in the attic."

"And if mom and dad didn't mind," I say.

"Nothing is hidden in the attic." Noah nods. "Now you're getting it."

"So you can't tell us anything," I say. "But you can look squeamish and uncomfortable if we guess something ourselves."

Noah puts his finger on the side of his nose.

It's like the dumbest game of charades in the world. I sigh. "Fine. Then tell me. Did you somehow make yourself look like Kyle and fool Blake into thinking you *were* Kyle in order to get out of the cell the night I fought Judica? Is that how you escaped?"

"Who the heck are Kyle and Blake?" Noah asks.

Edam walks toward him.

I hold out my hand to stop him. "That's not how this game is played, Edam, and we'll try it his way first."

Edam grumbles, but he steps back.

"I should have specified," I say, "seeing as they weren't likely to have shared their names. There were two guards who were physically down in the cell with you on the night of my fight with Judica. I told them to detain you. I didn't mean for them to lock you in a holding cell, but they were confused. I would have fixed it, but I was in a rush."

"And might I add," Noah says, "if I'd been the pathetic human I was pretending to be, after you died in that fiery explosion, the one that my idea prevented, I'd have been stuck there to rot and then die."

He's not wrong. "Look," I say. "I appreciate what you've done. Your advice has always been sound, but I need some answers here." I close my eyes so I can think without distraction. Noah can't answer me head on. He can't admit to anything, but I need to pry some answers out. Inspiration finally strikes, and I yank a knife from my boot.

"What's that for?" Edam shifts from foot to foot on the plush, beige hotel carpet.

"I'm not carving him up. If we get to that, I'll let you do the honors, I promise. But I've had an idea." Before I can stop myself, and before they can stop me, I cut off the end of my own nose.

Ohmygosh it hurts. After watching the last half inch of my nose drop to the ground and blood soak the front of my shirt, my vision blacks out and I wobble on unsteady knees. The image replays in my mind over and over, but I will not puke. I. Will. Not. Puke.

I focus on my nose, willing it to regrow. The pain is unlike any other wound I've ever healed. Agony claws at my face. Anguish streaks downward, suffusing my entire body with waves of pain in a way I've never felt. I nearly pass out, but I push past it, focusing on growing my nose longer. Longer than it was before, and pointier too. I push, I push, and I push.

It grows, slowly. I cry out several times, practically choking on the blood from my nose that has run down the front of my face and down the back of my throat. Edam rushes to the door to reassure the Motherless they aren't needed as I moan and whimper. I feel confident that Noah couldn't possibly have done this in a cell without anyone noticing.

Unless he had done it over and over and over before.

Ohthepain. I bunch up the comforter in my hands, my nails shredding the fabric, but I keep on growing my nose. It actually grows faster than I imagined it might, but the toll on my cellular structure is great. My hands tremble, not from fear, but from fatigue. My stomach growls and my eyes focus and unfocus.

But finally it's done. I pat the end of my nose and it's healed. I walk slowly toward the mirror, wiping the blood away as best as I can before I look at my reflection. Now that it's done, I'm actually excited to see my long, pointy nose.

Except it's not.

I look exactly like I looked before, other than the seeming buckets of blood covering the lower half of my face and my neck.

I spin around and pin Noah with a glare. "You can't tell us anything, but tell me this. Is that what you did?"

Noah bites his lip. "Well, you didn't actually do anything. You didn't think it would be easy, did you? Nothing that's worth it is *easy*."

In that moment, I want to claw his eyes out.

But I'm also amazed. Because he didn't deny it, or laugh, or mock me. Which means he probably did just exactly what I did, only he was better at it. It took me several days before I could change my eye color the first time. I'm beginning to think we may not know the half of what evians can do. But I don't have weeks to perfect this. I need to see Melina, make my decision, and fly back home.

"If I find out what someone close to Melina looks like, can you . . . look like him enough to get me inside?"

"Oh, absolutely not," Edam says. "There's no way that Mr. Chameleon here is going to escort you alone into Melina's compound."

Noah grins. "Relax, Rambo, I'll take you both."

✣ 23 ✣

"See what I did there?" Noah says. "Rambo's not very smart, and he's old."

"His sense of humor is the same," Edam says. "And I find that it annoys me exactly as much as it did when I thought he was human."

"Wait," I say. "How old are you?"

"I'm nineteen. Still a much more suitable age for you, if I do say so myself," Noah says.

"You say a lot of things yourself," Edam says. "This whole line of discussion is stupid. We should be discussing our plan to reach Melina so Chancery can decide how to handle her."

"I can get you inside," Noah says. "I can get you to Melina. But once you're there, if she's set on killing you and we're right in the middle of her entire compound. . ."

"That's why we're bringing Rambo," I say. "I have confidence that he can—"

"Oh I bet he can carve himself out," Noah says. "But I'd prefer not to be in a body bag next to him. Melina's team was evian. Her people will be evian. They won't be easy to kill."

"That's part of what the guys I sent will be finding out," I say. "Exactly how dangerous a situation we're facing. But I don't think it will come to that. She's been sending me messages, and she believes that I am the Eldest, the prophesied ruler."

"But will she believe you are who you say you are?" Noah asks. "I mean." He points at my clothing. "Her team *did* just try to kill you, earlier today in fact. Or was that yesterday? With the time changes and the jet lag, oh and the tranquilizer darts, I'm all sorts of disoriented."

"I do need a different outfit," I say. "But I'll make her believe me. At the end of the day, if she takes the time to talk to me, I think it'll be pretty clear who I am." I wish I'd brought my ring, but that would have left Judica with a very hard sell back home.

"So we wait for the guys to return, with the expectation that men with zero training as intelligence officers will have done effective reconnaissance." Noah sits down and exhales slowly. "You should have sent me."

"Yes, our trust in you is at an all-time high," Edam says.

"But your faith in my ability to infiltrate should be pretty strong," Noah says.

He's not wrong there.

"Believing a dog will go after a ball is one thing. Expecting him to bring it back to you, that's another." I cross my arms. "We have no idea who you really are, or who you're working for. I've been lucky so far that your interests have apparently aligned with mine, and I trust you to get me inside to see my sister because I don't see a better way. But after that. . ."

"I'm kicked to the curb?" he asks.

"I don't see why your dad can't send one of his many jets

to pick you up here," I say. "Because I think my ability to trust you is shot." Saying the words breaks my heart. But a broken heart heals. A severed head, on the other hand. . .

"I knew I wasn't likely to retain my job," Noah says. "Human liaison seems to require, well, a human. But I thought you might want to keep me around." His eyes are shadowed, unsure. It's not something I'm used to seeing.

"If you would just tell me—"

He shakes his head. "I'll be in enough trouble as it is. You're not the only one who likes his head where it is."

"So if you tell us who you are, your family, or your boss, or whoever, will what? Kill you?" I ask.

Noah shrugs. "Maybe that was just an expression."

But I don't think it was.

"Edam told me he had to do some training in intelligence before he came back to security, right?" I ask.

Edam shrugs. "All of the Motherless in Alamecha did a rotation. Not sure about the other families."

"So maybe they won't be hopeless at it," I say. "Really, how complicated is it? We're asking them to hide in the bushes and see who comes and goes. Look for someone important. I doubt Melina is expecting us to turn up on her front porch. That's sort of the whole idea. Judica wants her dead. Apparently Melisania agrees that's my best play. But I am not a shoot first and ask questions later kind of person. I want to talk to my sister, even if she tried to smother me when I was a baby. I want to know why she did that, and I want to know why she's trying to kill Judica now."

"She might just be nuts," Noah says. "That happens sometimes, even with evians."

"She could be. But everyone is the hero in their own story. I want her to have the chance to explain her story to me," I say.

So we wait. After a few minutes, I walk down, with an

escort, to the hotel shop and buy some new clothing. Then I try my hand again, unsuccessfully, at badgering Noah into answering questions on accident. The whole situation results in a lot of pacing on Edam's part, and a lot of irritated looks on mine.

"Are you the youngest in your family?" I ask.

Noah nods.

"Ah, you actually answered something."

He shrugs. "I'm not trying to keep my life a secret, princess. But I was sent to Trinity to do a job, and I can't talk about the details, not without permission."

I hand him my phone.

"What's that for?"

"Get permission."

"Uh, I can call my commanding officer," he says nervously, "and I can tell him you've figured a few things out. I can ask him what I'm able to tell you." Noah shrugs. "But I might get called home. Or they might order me to do something else I don't want to do."

"What exactly *do* you want to do?" I ask. "Can you tell me that?"

Noah looks me dead in the eye. "I want to stay by your side. I want to help you out in any way that I can. Now that you know I'm not human, I might be able to do a lot more. Standing in the corner, pretending to hide when people were attacking you? That was the lowest point in my life so far, and my life hasn't been as easy and pampered as I led you to believe."

I think about my mom dying, Lyssa's death. My dogs dying. Unbearable pain. Slicing the end of my nose off earlier today is the closest physical pain I've ever suffered to the emotional pain of those days, and he's theoretically done what I just did on more than one occasion, or something very similar to it. "Hiding in the corner was your low point?"

His voice drops to a bare whisper. "I wasn't lying, what I told you after my dad left. If I thought I'd get permission, I'd leave my position forever to be with you."

"And if you don't get permission?"

He looks away. "I don't know."

"You have a strong sense of honor and duty. I respect that."

"It's not only that," he says. "I wish I could explain everything, but I'm not allowed to say anything else." He drops his voice again. "But I think you need me. I think you'll need *us* before this is through."

"What does that mean?" I ask. "Who is us?"

He shakes his head. "I can't say anything else. But I wish you would believe me when I say we aren't enemies. We aren't a rival family, and we don't want anything from you. At least, nothing you wouldn't give yourself."

"Then just tell me who you are," I beg. I want to believe him. I want it so badly that I worry it's coloring my decision. My entire life is a series of gambles, but the real gamble I take every day is who to trust. I thought Noah was human, and I know now that he manipulated things to come into my life, and yet he's been there for me when I needed him. He's helped me whenever I was in trouble. He may not be helping me for no reason at all like I thought, but it doesn't mean he didn't render help when I needed it. If he would tell me who he was, maybe I could come to terms with it, like I have with Edam. "Please tell me something, anything."

"I can't. It's not my secret to divulge."

"You're such a tease," Edam says.

"You're one to talk. You didn't tell her about your sister, either."

"I cut my sister off the second I walked on that plane to New York City." Edam's eyes flash. "I never looked back. I didn't hesitate. I threw my lot in with Chancery the second I had the chance, and I've never regretted it for a second. You dance around, making promises we can't verify, and hinting at things we don't understand."

I open my mouth to stop this, since it's hardly helpful, but the door to the room opens.

Gregory and Ibrahim are back.

"Any news?" I ask.

Ibrahim looks practically ill. His mouth is clamped shut, his skin pale.

"Oh my, are you alright?" I ask.

"We might have done something stupid," he says.

Oh good. That's what I need to hear. "What happened?"

Gregory lifts his chin and exhales heavily. "We saw a chance, and we took it."

I close my eyes. "Please tell me you didn't kill anyone."

Ibrahim's eyes light up. "No, we didn't kill anyone."

"Just tell me what happened."

They widen the door, and a struggling person comes into view. A man with ink black hair, shaved into a Mohawk, and earrings climbing his ear. He looks surprisingly similar to the lady Judica says she shot in the face. "We saw this guy embrace your sister," Gregory says. "And then he left. Alone."

I close my eyes. "You kidnapped him?"

"No one saw," Gregory says. "We're sure of that."

"That's way better than a video," Edam says. "And we can ask this guy anything we want."

"Plus, did you hear the part where we said he hugged your sister?" Ibrahim asks. "Because it was a pretty long hug."

"Fine, undo his gag," I say. "Let's hear what he has to say."

That might have been a little premature. The string of profanity that spews from his mouth makes my ears ring. I cross the room and slap him. "Knock it off. Your girlfriend tried to kill me yesterday, and under false pretenses. She thought I was my sister, Judica. I'm not. I'm Chancery, and from what I heard, I think she's been dying to talk to me."

He closes his mouth with a click and nods.

"Now, I want to talk to Melina, but I can't think of a way to get inside."

"I'll take you," he says.

I consider it. He could take me, and he could immediately order his people to bind me, and then they could kill me. He knows who I say I am, whether he believes it or not, and he knows Melina's true position. Something I don't yet know.

I shake my head. "I have a better idea." I turn to Noah. "Is this something you can work with?" If I take Noah, I have an extra assurance we can get out. All we have to do is take our friendly guy "hostage" and escape slowly, at which point we can release Noah and he can return with us. It's the prudent play. I may not trust Noah entirely, but I trust him a heck of a lot more than I trust this guy.

Noah says, "I can do it, yeah. It'll take me a minute, and I need some privacy to prepare."

"Can you use the bathroom?" I ask.

He bobs his head. "But I'll need his clothes and earrings."

The man stumbles back against Ibrahim.

"Don't worry," I say. "We'll let you change into something else. I don't want anyone hanging around naked." That doesn't seem to reassure him, but luckily, I'm not worried about how safe and secure he feels.

He struggles while Ibrahim forces him out of his jacket, and then his shirt.

"Tell me," I say. "Do you happen to have a sister?"

He blanches.

"I'm not threatening her, idiot," I say. "I'm not even threatening you. You're a means to an end. But the woman who escaped the attack on me in Hong Kong looked a lot like you. You could be twins, almost."

"Three years apart," he says. "You have a good eye."

Gregory throws a pile of clothing at Melina's friend and he wastes no time in putting them on. Edam takes the man's clothes to the bathroom and drops them in front of the door.

"What's your name?" I ask him.

He presses his lips together and shakes his head stubbornly.

"It's Paolo," Gregory says. "I heard that much."

I notice the bathroom door open a crack and watch as Noah's hand snatches the clothing.

"Thanks, Gregory. Appreciate the information," I say. "Look, Paolo, I'm not a monster. I didn't kill my mother, and I don't threaten to kill babies in their cribs, or capture and murder people. But your girlfriend, or wife, or boss, or whatever, she does do all of those things. So I don't need you to cringe away from me. I'm actually here so that she can explain her side of the story. As you might imagine, my sister Judica wanted to bomb her off the face of the earth. I have the means to do that, and you should believe me when I tell you that no one would blame me. In fact, no one would so much as chastise me for doing it. So you might want to talk. Because if I die today, my sister Judica takes control of the family. And you and your friend will be chased down like a fox in an old English hunt, but with more explosives and torture."

"Melina loves you," he says. "None of this is necessary."

"I hope that you're telling the truth," I say. "That will make this all much easier, but I watched a video where she tried to smother me. When she failed, stopped by dear old Mom, she threatened to kill Mom, too."

"All of that was a misunderstanding. Melina can clear all of that up. In fact, I can call her right now and ask her to meet me somewhere. Anywhere you name. Then you don't have as much risk in talking to her, and you can relax."

I narrow my eyes at him. "Why would you do that?"

"Because I know my sister-in-law. She doesn't mean you any harm."

Sister-in-law. If Melina is married to his brother, he knows her pretty well. She should trust him. I think about Mom. If Judica's right, Melina killed her. She certainly tried to kill Judica. Is it possible she's no threat to me? And if so, what does justice demand for our mother? And what about for her attempts to eliminate Judica? I don't think I can decide, not without knowing her motivation.

"Make the call," I say. "Tell her to meet us in the fountain in front of this hotel. Tell her to come alone."

Edam hands his phone to Paolo, who dials a number and hits talk. A few seconds later, the call connects.

"Hello?" a deep alto answers.

"Melina," Paolo says. "It's me."

"I thought you'd be back already. You were just leaving to grab—"

"I've run into a spot of trouble. I really need you to meet me. I'll explain when I see you."

"You what?" she asks. "Paolo, what's going on? Why are you calling from this number?"

"Unfortunately, I don't have time to explain my issue. It's not anything terrifying, but I need you to be the one to help me. Trust me on this. I'm safe and you'll be happy with me when you arrive, I promise that much."

"Okay," she says, clearly unsure.

"I'll be waiting near the entrance to the Four Seasons. Come now."

"Who should I bring?" she asks.

"That's your call," he says. "But you're not in danger."

"Okay. I can be there in ten minutes."

"I'll see you then." He hangs up. Unless they have some kind of hidden code that I couldn't detect, he didn't warn her of anything. I won't rest easy until I've had the chance to talk to her myself and I'm safely on my way home, but it's promising.

Three seconds later, the toilet flushes. A beat after that, Noah walks out of the bathroom, or at least, I assume it's Noah. He looks identical to Paolo in every way. I blink. Then I blink again, but not a hair seems off.

Paolo loses it. Another string of impressive curse words, several of which I've never heard used together, erupt from his mouth. "Who is that?" he asks. "Is he a cyborg?"

Without missing a beat, Noah-Paolo stiffens his arms and legs. "I am the Terminator, sent from the future to kill Sarah Connor."

"What's he talking about?" Gregory asks.

"I never have any idea," Edam says. "I was hoping he'd stop, now that we know his secret, but I guess not. Just ignore it."

"You people need to get out more," Noah-Paolo says.

I can't stop staring at Noah-Paolo. No screaming, no howling, no sounds of agony at all, and yet here he is. A clone of the guy who was just singing Melina's praises. "We'll take my friend who looks an awful lot like you downstairs in your place," I say. "I feel like it's safer for me that way."

BRIDGET E. BAKER

When Paolo objects, Ibrahim and Gregory restrain him.

"Relax," I tell my sister's gagged brother-in-law. "We're not going to hurt her. But I can't have you stabbing me in the back while we talk."

Edam leaps to work like a pro. We all head downstairs, leaving only two Motherless to watch over the real Paolo while Noah-Paolo follows us down. Edam hides men in a dozen different places, but he stands with me, next to a bench in the hotel lobby. Noah-Paolo waits alone with his hands clasped in front of him, near the drive where a visitor would approach.

Minutes tick by.

Actually, they kind of drag. I glance at my phone. It's been fourteen minutes since the call. Maybe she hit traffic. Maybe she's not coming. Maybe Paolo somehow told her to run. Maybe I will have to harm him after all.

A red Jaguar roars around the corner, and somehow I know it's her.

She kills the engine and hops out, long limbs, bouncing mahogany curls, burnished skin, almost painfully high cheekbones. She strides up the pavement separating her from Noah-Paolo in knee-high, black leather boots. "What's wrong? You look fine."

Noah-Paolo smiles. "Everything is fine."

The hair on my arms rises. He sounds just like the real Paolo. I wouldn't have any idea it wasn't him.

But something is clearly off, something maybe only someone who had known him for years would even spot. She stops and looks around, acknowledging something I've heard all along. Almost twenty evian heartbeats in a fifty-foot diameter. Her shoulders hunch, her eyes dart, her heart rate spikes. "Who are you, and where's Paolo?"

I step forward, waving. "I'm Chancery," I say.

308

She freezes, her eyes widening with what looks a lot like alarm.

She scowls at me. "Judica."

I shake my head. "I'm Chancery, not Judica. You sent a team to kill me in Hong Kong, believing the ruse I planned to keep myself safe while I met with Melisania." I practically choke thinking about how badly that went down. "I didn't want to kill your people, but they were relentless in trying to kill me."

"No." She shakes her head. "That was Judica. I received confirmation."

I shake my head. "I got your message. I assume it was your sister-in-law who delivered it, and she's likely the one who confirmed the attack was on Judica. But it wasn't. And maybe it's for the best things fell out the way they did. I might never have believed Judica's claim entirely if I hadn't seen you try and kill her with my very own eyes."

"You don't understand," she says.

"Then tell me," I say. "I'm here now, and I'm listening."

She looks around warily. "Not here, not in the open like this."

I cross my arms. "I almost came to you in your lair, you know. That was my plan. Until your brother-in-law ducked outside and my men nabbed him."

"I can't believe I'm talking to you right now," Melina says.

"On a scale of one to ten, how disappointed are you that your smothering attempt failed?"

Her whole face falls. "I'm so sorry about that. There's more to that story than you know. But the prophecy—"

"I'm all too familiar with that cursed prophecy," I say. "It has ruined my entire life, but I'm trying to do the best I can in the wake of that disaster."

"I saw the video right after Judica escaped," she says. "I was very proud of you. Mother would be too."

I can't listen to her talk about Mom. Not until I know what role she played in Mom's death. I open my mouth to accuse her, but it feels like the wrong time and place. "I need you to come back with me," I say instead.

"Judica will kill me." Her voice is flat.

"She might try," I admit. "She's not a fan. But do you blame her? You held her captive in her underwear, and told her you meant to kill her. Just as soon as you could confirm that Mom had named me Heir because she believed me to be the Queen of Queens, you would have done it."

"I might have taken things too far, but you don't know everything. You have so much you need to learn. You only have part of the prophecy, for one thing."

"Your sister-in-law mentioned something like that," I say.

Melina's mouth opens and then closes again. She shakes her head. "My sister-in—"

"Look, the point is that we need to talk, but you don't want to do it out in the open, and I don't feel safe following you to your compound."

"We do need to talk. Urgently. Eve's prophecy had two parts," Melina says. "It was given to the bearer of the key, to Eve herself, at the same time that the stone was cut from the mountain. And the first half was inscribed on the top of the stone. The second half was carved into the key itself."

"And the half I have?" I ask. "Which part is that?"

"That's from the engraving on the stone. Eve wrote that down."

"And the other half?" I lift my eyebrows.

"The keeper of the key has it. No one else."

"That's convenient. So you don't have the second half? The one you're telling me I need."

Melina shakes her head. "But I know the gist of what it says."

"Perfect," I say. "Since you don't have it, but you know the gist, I can just do whatever you tell me to do. That seems like my safest bet, actually. How about you follow me home, and you can be my boss from now on."

"I don't want to order you around. I want to help you," Melina says. "It's my life's purpose. I've always known that."

"There are a lot of things I've always known," I say, anger stiffening my limbs, burning in my belly, enlivening my soul. "And you destroyed every single one when you killed Mom." Tears fill my eyes and streak down my cheeks. "What makes you think there's any world in which I'd let you guide me or tell me anything at all? Why would I listen to the person who ruined *everything?*" Wow, I'm a lot madder at her than I realized.

Her eyes widen and she stumbles backward. Noah-Paolo stabilizes her and she snatches her arm away from him. "Get your hands off me, imposter."

Noah-Paolo's eyebrows rise. He's impressed.

"I didn't kill our Mother," Melina says. "Neither did Angel."

"Why should I believe that?" I ask.

"Look, Mother begged Angel for a promise before she died."

I lift one eyebrow.

"She told her she thought she might be poisoned. She didn't feel well. She was worried about you, about Alamecha. She told Angel hard times were coming and she needed Angel to do whatever was necessary to safeguard the family."

"And that helps me trust Angel, how?"

"That's why Angel took Judica. We both believe she's the biggest threat to you. Angel loves Judica as much as her own children. She helped raise Judica and took an active interest in her training. They bonded in the kitchen, and Angel says Judica showed a real aptitude for intelligence and interrogation and logical analysis. I tell you that so that you understand that it pained Angel to bring Judica to me, but she agreed that you must succeed. There's too much at risk, and Judica's brilliant, strong, and amazing." Her voice drops to a bare whisper. "But she's also a wild card."

The irony of Melina calling Judica a wild card appears to be lost on her.

"I'm supposed to simply believe Mom's dying wish prompted Angel to kidnap Judica and take her to you— after I had already defeated her in a challenge, I might add —but you two had nothing to do with Mom's death?"

"I wish I knew who did it. I was angry with Mother for a very long time, but I always assumed we would reconcile eventually. That's one of my biggest regrets. When Judica flung the accusation at me, it didn't feel necessary to refute it, since I had every intention of killing her. Perhaps my attempts have been misguided, but I don't believe so. At the very least, she's been keeping you from me since her escape. And any way you look at things, she poses a very real threat to you. From what I know of that prophecy, you might have to die to save the world. The only one who can prevent that eventuality is your strongest supporter."

Noah-Paolo flinches next to her. Edam's whole body goes rigid next to me.

"If you truly believe that's meant to be Judica, that's fine," Melina says. "But it must be someone you trust when you trust no one else. It must be someone about whom you have no doubt, someone willing to make any sacrifice necessary, someone who values all life, including those worth less than their own. Is that Judica, do you think? Is that your twin?"

I can't think of a single person who I trust explicitly, not anymore, and no one else seems to value human life. Noah's an evian of unknown origin. Edam was committing treason, but insists he's reformed. Lark's Mom was killed by mine. Alora betrayed me to Noah. Which makes me wonder whether she can cast some light on his family. But that's a distraction.

If I need to locate someone I can trust, and someone I also believe is selfless, well, that's not Judica. She almost killed me last week and may have been blocking messages from Melina up through yesterday. I'm not entirely certain she hasn't seized the throne in my absence, and I don't understand much about her motivations, but I'm pretty sure she's not willing to sacrifice everything to save the humans of the earth.

Perhaps I can trust Inara, but if I need to trust someone down to my bones, I'm already doomed. The only person I trusted that much is dead. My heart contracts in my chest at that thought.

I don't trust a single person on earth. Not one.

"I can see that frightens you. But it shouldn't. You will learn who you can trust by our actions. I'll prove myself to you, I swear I will. And on top of that, I've dedicated the past eighteen years to tracking down every snippet of information about the Garden of Eden and the keeper of the key."

"Have you found either?" I ask.

She shakes her head. "Not yet, but I'm close. Very close. And I haven't had the resources of Alamecha behind me. I also couldn't leave Austin. Without those restrictions, I can find both for you quickly, I know it."

"No one would admit to having killed Mom," I say. "Why should I believe your denial?"

She frowns. "I have no evidence that I *didn't* do something, but taking Judica isn't evidence that I did."

"What does the name Nereus mean to you?" I ask.

She blinks. "Nothing. Should it mean something?"

Her heart didn't accelerate, and her breathing didn't alter. She exhibited no signs of shock or worry. Of course, it's hardly conclusive, but you'd think she'd react in some way other than blinking in confusion. "Nereus is the code name for the person who killed Mom," I say. "But it looks like you have nothing to add there."

"Take me with you," she says. "Let me serve you. We have a lot to discuss, and I have a lot of bridges to rebuild."

I want to ask Edam and even Noah what they think. I want to look at this from a dozen angles, but I don't have time for any of that. I came, I found what I wanted, and she's offering me exactly what I've been pursuing: answers. If nothing else, we can put her on trial for Mom's murder. Maybe that will help Judica sleep better at night.

"Agreed," I say. "You can come back with us. Our jet has enough space for eight more."

She shakes her head. "I'll need to bring several of my people, of course. I can't just abandon them here. I'll come with you, but in my own jet."

"Fine."

"And you'll lift Mother's ban on my travel?" She lifts her eyebrows. "Because right now, there are people that watch to ensure I don't leave Austin. They've been given orders to kill me if I do."

I nod. "I'll call home and make sure Marselle and Balthasar have any restrictions removed."

"Oh good. We can do this the easy way." She beams and motions to the bushes. Three dozen guards stand up behind mine and walk toward us. "I always prefer a peaceful resolution whenever possible. Did everyone hear that? We're headed home—to Ni'ihau."

24

"How did we not hear them?" Edam draws a sword.

"Sound muffling vests," Melina says. "You should look into them. They're all the rage with the banished right now, but put that monstrous sword away. It's unnecessary." She glances at me. "Is that Edam?" She purrs. "Nicely done."

Heat rises in my cheeks. "Well, I'm glad we're doing this the easy way."

"Me too, but it's always good to be prepared." Melina glances around. "Speaking of, where's my actual brother-in-law, and who in the world is this abomination?"

Noah-Paolo grimaces. "I'll go get him and change back. Be down in five."

When he heads upstairs, I realize I'm in for an awkward wait. Paolo's sister strides right up to Melina's side. "I'm Aline." She extends a hand.

I reach mine out and clasp her forearm. She clasps mine in return. "Chancery."

"I'm Paolo's sister," she says. "I hope he's unharmed."

I nod. "He's fine."

"I'm relieved. He can be a real pain, but he's a pretty good brother." Aline slings an arm around Melina's shoulder and my sister leans into her. Obviously they're close, but it makes me wonder where the husband is.

"I'm sorry my twin shot you in the face," I say, glancing at Aline's perfect features. "But it looks like you've recovered pretty well."

"I try," she says.

"Is your husband around?" I ask Melina. "I'd like to meet him."

Melina glances at Aline and they burst into laughter.

"I missed the joke," I whisper.

Edam shrugs.

"I have no husband," Melina says.

"But Paolo is your brother-in-law." Oh, no. Her husband must have died. "I'm so sorry. I didn't know."

"You're excused," Melina says. "It's not common with evians, I know."

Wait. It's not common? We live a long time, but people die frequently. Too frequently.

"I think we might be talking at cross purposes," I say. "Is your husband dead?"

Melina and Aline laugh again, but this time when the laughing dies off, Aline's hand drops and Melina's arm shifts so that their fingers interlace.

Oh.

"I'm married to Paolo's sister," Melina says.

"But evians can't marry—"

"Humans allow it now," Melina says. "We were married in Boston the second it was legal."

I have no idea what to say, but I believe her statement that we have a lot to discuss. There's no way Mom would have taken this very well. In fact, I'm pretty sure I understand the flaw Mom mentioned.

Melina meets my eye and holds my gaze. "Please forgive me for being so wrong when you were born. I was grieving. My father and I were very close and he had only just died, and I had recently told Mother the truth about Aline. It was a bumpy few weeks."

I inhale quickly. I can relate to a sequence of miserable days. "I've been there," I say. "I mean, the last two weeks have not been among my best. And you may have been the first sister to try and kill me, but you weren't the last. In fact, if I killed every relative who tried to end my life, I'd have far fewer sisters."

"And it appears that you've forgiven Judica," Melina says. "For things I would have thought would be unforgivable."

I shrug. "I'm a forgiving person. It's one of many character flaws."

"Your mercy is practically legendary already. It's not a common trait among evian rulers." Melina drops her voice to a whisper. "I believe it may be the reason God chose you."

Judica wasn't kidding. She throws the word God around pretty freely. "Perhaps."

She smiles. "You don't believe?"

"I don't know what I believe."

"I can teach you," she says. "Father was a believer, you know. A great believer. He believed we have strayed far from our true purpose. It was his life's work to bring evians back to the way—the path to their destiny."

"What did he think our destiny was?" I ask.

"We're meant as the protectors for the entire race of Eve. We were never meant to hold ourselves above others. Our DNA doesn't make us better, it makes us better able to serve."

Conviction bursts inside of my chest and spreads

through my entire body, as though she's spoken the most *right* thing I've ever heard. I won't admit anything, not to her, but I'm desperate to hear more. I want to know what my dad believed, what drove him, and ultimately, what killed him. No one has ever told me that, but I have a feeling Melina will.

"Do you miss him?" I ask instead.

She nods abruptly and then she sniffs sharply. "Every second of every day."

She loves him like I love Mom. A longing to meet him sharpens inside of me. It's impossible, I know, but Melina is the closest I'll come. "I'm sorry."

She shakes her head. "I'm sorry for you. He was—" She chokes. "He was like no one I've ever met. He loved and longed and burned for a world that was different from the one we know. He was the epitome of our family motto."

"Accept the world as it is," I say.

"He was burning with the desire to change it," Melina says.

"Is that what got him killed?" I ask.

"Time enough for that," Melina says.

I nod, dumbly. Time enough, I suppose. Although lately it seems like there's never enough time. My eyes sting from lack of sleep.

"You're tired," Melina says. "You should be sleeping much more than you are."

"Too many things to do," I grumble.

"Like coming here to retrieve me," she says. "And I appreciate it. But you won't survive what's coming if you aren't strong. I'm going to insist that you sleep enough. I'll pull whatever weight you need, I promise you that." The corner of her perfect mouth turns upward and my heart lifts.

What if she's for real? What if she's not crazy, just

misguided? Oh, how I hope for that. If Inara, Alora, Judica, Melina, and I all united, what couldn't we do together?

"You're such an optimist," Melina says. "It's written across your face, carved into your mouth, plain in the glint in your eye."

Edam smirks. "You don't know the half of it."

"What does that mean?" I scowl.

"I can see the reflection from all the happy images forming in your young mind. Kum-ba-ya, hand holding, sisterly support." Melina shakes her head. "Don't delude yourself. No one will be happy to see me, except for maybe Inara."

I lift my eyebrows. "Are you two still close?"

"We were inseparable when I was young." Melina's face is almost wistful. "She took me everywhere. She taught me everything."

"Wow, she said—" I stop. I have no idea what Inara really wants now. Better not to get her hopes up. "She mentioned how fond she was of you, but didn't elaborate."

Melina waves her hand. "It was a long time ago, and I hurt her badly when I left."

"But you think she'll welcome you back?" I ask.

She nods. "I do, but Alora and I were never close. She didn't like my father, not at all. Or, I guess I should say she disliked our father. I'm surprised she took to you. I hear you're together quite often."

"We were," I say. "She understood me, my oddities, my eccentricities, I think, more than anyone else."

"Understanding is what we're all looking for," Melina says. "In the end."

Noah, his face back to normal, walks through the front doors carrying my bag, his own, and Edam's. The other two Motherless are with him, and walking alongside the three of them is the real Paolo.

Melina's face lights up. "Oh good."

Paolo jogs across the drive and hugs both Melina and Aline. I can't believe I didn't see it before. I'm such an idiot.

"We have a lot to do and not much time," Melina says.

"You aren't unhappy with me, then?" Paolo asks.

She shakes her head. "Never. You did just as you should have."

"What was your code?" I ask. "How did you know there was something off?"

"Ah, ah, ah," Melina says. "You can't ask me to betray my family." She winks at me. "You and I will develop our own history. But some things shouldn't be shared with others." She looks at Edam and lifts her eyebrows. "You'll learn soon enough."

Noah drops the bags. "Or maybe not."

"Ah," Melina says. "Do we have a rival?"

"Some things shouldn't be shared with others," I say. "And at the present, that includes my love life."

Melina shrugs. "All in good time."

"I'll be ready to leave in an hour and a half," Melina says. "Will that work for you?"

I nod. "We'll be waiting."

Once Melina leaves, the adrenaline filters out of my body and I want to collapse. "We have an hour and a half. The airport is what? Ten minutes away?"

Edam nods.

"Great. I'm going to take a nap on an actual bed." I pin Noah with a glare. "You didn't check out, did you?"

Noah steps backward, nearly tripping over his bag. "No, I just carried the bags down."

I sigh and hold out my hand.

He slings my bag over his shoulder and gestures toward the room. "By all means, let me carry it back up for you."

I nod. "Fine." I turn back to look at Edam. "Send some room guards, but do you mind getting everyone else ready to go and notifying our pilot?"

"Of course."

Noah and I head for the elevator. "I'm actually glad for a moment with you," Noah says.

What now? I can't handle much more today.

"I know it's already been a weird day," he says. "But I wanted to make sure you're okay with me. . . You know. Shifting."

I stop and pivot on my heel. "What do you really look like?"

"I could ask you the same thing," he says.

I shake my head. "Don't do that. This is what I look like. You saw me after the explosion, so you know. I healed up exactly as I look now. This is me. I can shift my skin color, sure, my eyes, my hair color even. But that's it. My face is my face, my hands are my hands. What you did." I shudder. "It's not normal."

He sighs. "You had your training, and I had mine."

I wonder what his childhood was like. He's so easygoing and amiable, I just assumed it was good. What if he's covering up untold misery? Maybe his life was even harder than Judica's. "Okay, I'll try and reconcile myself to it."

He starts walking again.

"I mean, maybe I'm a little bit jealous. I mean, that hurt. It really hurt, and nothing happened."

"If it helps," he says. "I don't lop the end of my nose off." He snorts. "That was a little drastic."

"Oh?" I lift my eyebrows. "What do you do?"

"When we reach Ni'ihau, I can show you."

"But you didn't answer," I say.

"What you see is what you get." He looks down at his feet.

"Except for what?" I ask.

He meets my eyes, and I gasp. His eyes are a deep, dark, velvety chocolate brown.

"Why would you change just your eye color?"

He shrugs. "Why do you change yours?"

"I don't know. Change of pace?"

"Well, I had to be an evian among humans who no one knew was evian. The evians all thought I was human, including Logan. They had to, or I was toast. I had to be unexceptional in every way. But I wanted one interesting feature." He ducks his head. "It seemed harmless enough, and then I kind of liked it."

I touch his arm. "I like your real eye color better." I notice he doesn't change it back, and that makes me smile.

When I reach the room, two of the Motherless are already waiting. Edam must have made them sprint up the stairs. Noah takes up guard near the door, too. "Uh, what are you doing?"

He frowns. "You need to sleep, and I'm trained, you know. Not just as a spy. I've got almost as much combat training as Edam. You just haven't seen me in action."

"Well color me impressed," I say.

"What color is that, exactly?" he asks. "Yellow? Red?"

"I think yellow is happy, and red is angry," I say. "How about green?"

"Jealous," he says. "So I don't think that's your color either."

"Noah," I say.

"What?"

"I have plenty of guards. I don't need more guards."

He steps inside the door and closes it behind him. "What do you need?"

"I don't know yet."

"You didn't object to me coming upstairs," he says.

322

"I need to sleep," I say.

He practically races across the room.

I hold out my hand to stop him and my fingers splay against his chest. "Don't."

"Don't what?" he asks, pushing against my hand, drawing nearer to me, inch by inch.

His chest is more muscular than I recall. I wonder whether he can shift his musculature. Whether he's been stronger all along, but downplayed it. "I can't," I say. "Not now, not with what I know."

His eyes meet mine, desperation hiding in their depths. "You never said no when I was human."

"That was a lie," I whisper. "Everything up until today was a lie."

Pain rolls over his features, his eyes widening, his lips opening, his mouth compressing. "I never lied, not about that."

"You never told the truth."

"I want to tell you everything," he says.

"You told me you *loved* me," I complain. "How can you say that, and stand in front of me, not telling me who you work for? Who you really are? I don't even know your name."

Anguish. It's the only word for what rolls across his face. "I do love you, but my love for my family." His head thrashes back and forth and he steps backward. "I can't betray them, Chancery. Can you understand that? I made promises before I ever met you. If I break them, I don't know who I'd be. Not someone deserving of love. I know that."

"Then when we get back, you call your family and you tell them what you want. I can't do this anymore, Noah. Not now. The stakes are too high. I've called the world to bow down before me. You're either with me, or you aren't."

He grabs my hands and twists them up in his. "I'm with you, I swear I am."

I gulp. "But you aren't. Not yet."

He kisses me then, but it's not a claiming kiss. It's a goodbye. I can feel it. He's preparing himself for a no from his parents, or his boss, or whoever controls him. He doesn't know what he'll be allowed, and he's not willing to cast his family aside, not for me. Not for us.

And at the end of the day, if I can't trust that he'll choose me above all others, I can't trust him at all.

I pull away after that, and curl up in the center of the bed. The room isn't cold, but I'm shivering anyway. Mom centered me, and Lark, and Alora. But Lark's broken, Mom's dead, and Alora's not who I thought she was. She might even be tangled up in this Noah mess.

I've been holding off on doing what I should have done all along for the wrong reasons.

"Go downstairs, Noah," I say. "I can't sleep with you here."

That's a lie, but he doesn't know it. He leaves. And I pick up my phone. I dial Analessa's number. Three rings before she answers.

"Hello, Analessa. It's Chancery."

"Chancery," she trills. "I've been just dying to hear from you."

"Have you?" I ask. "Well, that's great news. Because I think you'll like what I have to say."

A very quiet tap at the door precedes someone entering with a key. It's Edam, come to make sure I'm okay, probably. He pads across the floor soundlessly, taking everything in and meeting my eyes with a quizzical expression.

Your sister, I mouth.

His eyes widen.

"What's your answer, then?" Analessa asks.

"I'm sure this might disappoint you," I say, "but I'm not quite ready to get married, not yet."

"I'm not delighted to hear that, no."

"I'll agree to all of your other terms though," I say. "And I have a counter offer for you on the wedding."

"You do?" she asks. "What exactly is your counter?"

"How about an engagement to Edam? It can be as formal as you'd like, of course. We can even do a ceremony if you want, and I'll give him a title, like Consort-to-be or something."

Analessa pauses. "I'll need to think about it."

"You will?"

"There's no precedent for this. And until you're married, you can call it off. Which means there's absolutely no chance I'll hand over my ring to you."

"Of course not. And if I called off the engagement, I'm aware it would crumble the alliance."

"So then, what's the point in this stop-gap measure?" she asks.

"I need allies right now, Analessa. I need you, and I think you know I'm the queen from the prophecy. You have this one shot to get in on the bottom floor. You'll want to preserve some of your sovereignty, and you should take the opportunity to do that while you can. And if you think Edam and I are so perfect for each other, an engagement should be good enough for now."

"You make a good point." I hear Analessa tapping something through the receiver. "Alright, I accept. I'll draw up some papers and send them over for your signature."

"So it's settled?" I ask. "You've surrendered Malessa to Alamecha? I'll be ruling both families?"

"You will, my dear, assuming you don't break your word to marry my little brother. Can you pass my congratulations along to him?"

"Of course," I say.

When I lay down for my nap, my fiancé curls around behind me, keeping me warm, making me feel safe. When we wake up and walk downstairs, Noah's waiting. His eyes meet mine momentarily, before scanning downward to where my hand is clasped in Edam's.

"We're engaged," Edam announces to the Motherless. But he and I both know he announced it for Noah's benefit.

The pain on Noah's face is exactly what I hoped it would be. But for some reason I don't feel any better. This should be the happiest day of my life. The day I become engaged to marry a man I adore, a man who takes care of me. And Edam's beaming like his horse won the big race, like his lottery ticket just paid off, like his first child was just born.

The beauty of his smile takes my breath away. His hands clasp my waist and spin me around and around. When my feet finally touch the ground again, his lips cover mine and the moment is almost perfect. His joy is so abundant that it spills out and down and all over me.

It's almost enough.

I try to forget about the almost and focus on what's right about my decision. I've gained control of a very powerful ally, which I'll need with the fourth, fifth, and sixth families all in open rebellion. And it's not like Noah is even willing to tell me anything about himself. I'm doing what my family needs, same as him.

It's certainly something he should understand, but for some reason whenever I glance his way, he doesn't seem to understand.

Not at all.

And I know just how he feels.

❧ 25 ❧

"**A**bsolutely not." Judica's brandishing my swords and her eyes are flashing when she meets me on the jet way.

Maybe I shouldn't have radioed ahead to tell her that Melina was coming for those banana nut muffins. But at least Roman's not waiting for me at her side, ready to lay a big old kiss on me. I was a little worried about that.

"Yes," I say, a little relieved that she's only upset about Melina and not contesting whether I'm me, and she's herself. "I spoke with her, and I think we at least need to hear what she has to say."

"She's going to try and kill me." Judica sheathes her swords, thankfully, but her nostrils flare when she yanks the ring off her finger and slams it into my palm. "You know that, you have to know that."

"I had a front row seat to her last attempt," I say. "But she promised not to move against you at all while she's with us."

"Oh," Judica practically yells. "She promised, wonderful."

Wow, where is her signature calm and collected demeanor? "You might have been trying a little too hard to channel your inner Chancery," I say. "Because you need to cool down."

"You are so freaking naive," Judica says. "If a viper promises not to bite you, you'd snuggle it into your Hello Kitty pajama shirt."

"Good pop culture reference," I say, pointedly ignoring her insults. Obviously she's crabby that I've been gone so long.

I head for my room, and she strut-stomps along next to me.

"She won't take your place," I say. "You're my twin. No one else is at once both more and less like me than you. But she knows about our father, among other things, and I want to learn about him."

Judica's face tilts upward. "I don't. I want exactly nothing to do with him or stories about him or anything else affiliated with that man."

"What's your deal?" I ask. "You have to be curious."

"Mother told me he was deficient. I don't need to know the details of how and why so I spend the next nine centuries worrying I'll turn out like him."

I actually understand. "Then you don't have to know, and we'll station guards around Melina. Guards you can choose, if that will ease your mind, but I invited her, and you'll be civil."

"Civil?" Judica practically spits. "I want her to spend a few days in a cell in her underwear. And I want to kick her in the ribs while she's in there. Several times. And then I want her to have to risk her life trying to escape in an unknown place. And then I'll get creative with the rest."

I laugh, I can't help it. She implied I wear Hello Kitty pajamas, but she's the one who wants to inflict exactly the same amount of indignity and pain on our sister that she endured. "I think we can arrange that, but perhaps not this very moment. She's coming with an entourage."

"Of course she is," Judica mutters.

"Listen." I grab Judica's arm. "I need to thank you. I asked you to step in for me, and you did it. I doubted you back there, when Melina's people accused you of blocking their messages to me."

Some of the fire goes out of Judica's eyes and her shoulders relax. "Do you doubt me now?"

I swallow. "I don't want to, and we're making solid progress."

Judica nods.

"I know what I'm asking you to do is hard, but Melina isn't the only sister who has ever made the mistake of trying to kill her sibling." I arch one eyebrow.

My twin scowls.

"If I can forgive. . ."

She growls. "I never meant to kill you, you know."

"Not when you almost impaled me with a sword the morning I reacted to Mom's ring?"

She shrugs.

"Or what about when we fought in the challenge?"

She won't meet my eye.

"Look, all I'm saying is that our family is complicated." I punch her shoulder. "Let's see if there's anything here we can heal. If not, we cut her loose."

Judica shakes her head. "She killed Mother."

"I'm not sure she did," I say. "I want justice, I really do, but the last time I was absolutely positive one of my siblings killed Mom, I was wrong. Death is permanent. Let's make absolutely sure before we hang the wrong person, okay?"

"I want a trial," Judica says. "And I want Angel to come back. She has a lot to answer for."

I should have made that a condition of Melina's arrival. Judica's a better leader than me, clearly. "She does. I'll summon her, and I'm sure Melina can apply some pressure."

That seems to mollify my twin, at least a little.

"Also," I say, "I have a little news."

Judica's brows draw together. "Good or bad?"

"I don't know. Complicated."

"I'm tired of everything being complicated."

Now she's singing my theme song. "Me too."

When we reach my door, Judica stops me from opening it. "As it happens, I have a little present for you as well."

"Yes?"

"Death potty-trained your stupid mutt."

"Red Bull?" I ask.

Judica laughs and the sound startles me, I'm so unused to hearing it. "You are horrible at choosing names for pets. Like, epically bad. You should never ever choose a name for a pet again."

"Says the woman whose dog is named *Death*."

"That's a great name for a Doberman. And on top of his skillset, he's my taster. He will either cause death to my enemies, or prevent my death with his own." She shakes her head. "I am as good at pet names as you are bad."

I may never understand Judica. I walk through the door and Red Bull immediately barrels into my arms and licks my face.

"So, you had news for me?" Judica asks.

I hail my guards. "When my sister Melina arrives, tell Larena to put her in the north cottage. There should be room for her people there with her. Then come and let me know. I'll go and check on her first thing." When Barrett nods, I close the door.

"Out with it," Judica says. "What's this complicated news?"

Start with the first piece, I suppose. "Noah's not human."

"Excuse me?" Judica asks.

"He's been pretending," I say. "He's evian as you and me, from what I can tell."

"No way."

I nod. "I was shocked too."

"How did you find out?"

"I stabbed him with a plastic toothpick."

"Uh, what?" She opens her mouth and closes it again.

"I only did that because he tipped me off. He felt like he had to do something, I suppose. I was planning on sneaking into Melina's compound myself and asking to talk to her."

"Terrible plan."

"Pretty much everyone agreed with you, although as it turns out, I think it would have been fine."

"Agree to disagree," Judica says. "But explain how that led to the toothpick stabbing?"

"Noah didn't think my plan was safe. He wanted to go in to talk to Melina for me, but disguised as someone she knew. Only, he couldn't tell me that himself. It violated some kind of vow he made. So he kind of . . . hinted at it. I stabbed him to confirm my suspicions."

"He saw you growing closer to Edam and didn't like it," Judica says.

I shake my head. "No, he wanted to help."

"Help himself to a level playing field. That boy was sick of being overlooked." Judica whistles. "I don't blame him, either."

My jaw drops. "Judica, you're not listening."

"Because you have no insight. Geez, for someone with two guys trailing her, you don't know anything about them."

I have no idea how to reply to that.

"And? Did you kiss him after you found out? Did it feel different?" Her eyebrows bounce up and down like an impatient toddler.

Our kiss certainly wasn't better. It broke my heart. "Look, that's not the point."

"Isn't it?"

"Well if it was, it backfired. I called Analessa and took her offer," I say flatly.

This time it's Judica's jaw that drops. "You didn't."

I nod.

Judica swears. "You're getting married?"

"Well, I told her I'm not ready to set a date, so we're engaged for now."

"Still." Judica sits on my bed and whistles. "I did not see that coming. I really thought Noah would give Edam a run for his money. You know, now that he can actually hope to keep up."

"He won't even tell me who his family is," I say softly. "He won't explain who he works for."

"That's rough, but if you had orders, you wouldn't go against them, would you? Not without permission? There's some honor in that."

"He says he's going to call his people now that we're back," I say. "To tell them that I know."

"This may be the world's shortest engagement." Judica grins.

I shake my head. "I've made up my mind."

"You're way too keyed up about Noah for me to believe that fib," Judica says. "Nice try, though."

"I think he's working with a group of outcast evians who have made China home."

Judica's eyes widen. "That makes sense. It might even be a large group." She stands up. "They might have been fending off all attempts by the families to take over for years, to keep their haven safe."

"I think so, yes."

"He could be the key," she says.

"Oh stop," I say. "Not everything is about China." She's like a dog with a bone.

"No, I suppose not," she says. "But I can't believe I never even thought about that, not seriously anyway. I'm such an idiot. I should have been nicer to him."

"Yes, if you had called him idiot five hundred and ninety-nine times, instead of six hundred, maybe he would have told you everything he so carefully concealed."

"You're grouchy," Judica says, "for a recently engaged woman. Shouldn't you be gushing and glowing and I don't know, like spinning and pirouetting?"

"Speaking of, we should discuss Melisania's offer."

"I've been thinking about that," Judica says. "Has she considered that you'll likely produce a new heir with Edam?"

I can't even think about that. "I mentioned that possibility, although I hadn't yet agreed to marry him at that point."

"Well."

"She knows you won't remain my heir, yes. And you should know that I'm going to let you think about it, Judica."

She doesn't meet my eye.

"But."

Judica swallows.

"I'm not going to force you."

Her eyes shoot up toward mine and widen. Her breathing is shallow.

"I've never seen you happy, you know. Not in eighteen years."

She shakes her head. "That's not true."

"It is," I say. "Except for the brief interactions I've witnessed between you and Roman."

She inhales sharply.

"I won't take that from you, not even if it means war."

"One person's happiness—"

"If it's part of the prophecy," I say, "we will find another way."

Tears well in Judica's eyes. "He and I might break up in a month. Or in two. You should take the deal. We'll figure something out. We have a hundred years to solve that puzzle."

"We can't do the wrong thing and hope that somehow the wrinkles will iron themselves out. Life doesn't work like that, or it shouldn't." I pull Judica close and hug her. "I won't do that to you. I care for Edam a great deal. I don't know whether I love him, or exactly what I feel, and it's messy and complicated, but I care for him. That makes my situation very different from yours. I won't rip away the only good thing that's come into your life. Not for any reason."

"Roman's not the only good thing in my life," Judica whispers.

For the first time in days, my heart says I'm on the right path. I breathe a huge sigh of relief for making the right decision. And I believe I was right to trust her. Melina asked me if I trust Judica more than anyone in the world, and in this moment, I might.

So of course, there's a tap at my door. "Melina has landed, Your Majesty."

"Thanks, Barrett," I say.

"Shall we go and chat with our dear sister?" I ask.

"No time like the present," Judica says. "But can I change first?" She eyes my black boots and pants longingly.

I hand her my suitcase. "Meet you in the hall in five minutes."

I change too, happy to be out of all the black. I lop my hair off and regrow it dark and shift my eyes to grassy green. Maybe I miss Trinity. Maybe I'm not sure who's staring into that mirror anymore. I don't know, but I can't waste time psychoanalyzing myself. Not right now.

Judica's hair is back to normal when she returns, and she looks a million times more comfortable in her own skin now that she's wearing solid black again.

We walk down the hall, headed for the north exit of the palace. We're only a few feet away from the door when Balthasar's voice calls to me.

We both turn at the same time.

"Wait up." Balthasar jogs toward us. "We're under attack."

"Excuse me?" I ask.

"This just arrived from Adika." He hands me a letter.

I read it.

Chancery,

You turned my daughter against me. You've caused our own sons to openly rebel. You're destroying our people, our future, everything that matters.

Your threat will not go unanswered. Shenoah declares war on Alamecha, a war that will not end until Alamecha is free of your despotic rule and radical changes.

Adika

"Dramatic, anyone?" I ask.

Balthasar frowns. "She has gathered up hundreds of Alamecha citizens in each of her holdings. Yesterday she killed one thousand of them. She will kill another thousand every single day until you surrender your demands, issue an apology, execute the Motherless for treason, and pay her reparations for turning Vela against her. She also wants Judica to take the throne in your place."

"She wouldn't."

"The first thousand have already been executed." Balthasar hands me a list. "Men, women and children. She only included ten evians, as a courtesy I assume. She will double the number of evians each day, or that's her claim."

My stomach churns angrily and my hands shake. "Interrogating Melina is going to have to wait," I say. "We have a war to stop."

❧ 26 ❧

A thousand people dead—my fault. Utter destruction. A thousand more today—my fault. Utter destruction. A thousand more the next day —my fault.

How am I not the very plague Mom thought I would prevent?

I should never have agreed to support Vela in a coup against her mother. At first, the fallout didn't seem so bad. I mean, the Motherless came over to my side. Edam and I aren't the only ones who see that practice as barbaric. It was validating.

But now things are spiraling out of control.

I'm sitting in my mom's records room. Actually, if I'm being honest, I'm *hiding* in my mom's records room. I've been bawling like the baby that I am for far too long. But one thing has become quite clear to me. My entire coronation was a mistake. I shouldn't be Empress. I can't be Queen of Queens. I don't know how to manage my own Council, much less the entire world.

I read Mom's words to me again, the rest of the letter blurring through my tears.

As queen, you can never make any mistakes.

Except, I'm pretty sure that's all I've done since taking Mom's place. I did one thing right—trusting Judica, surrendering to her. That landed me the crown, the ring, all of it.

It's all been downhill since.

I don't even want to rule. Once I learned Judica didn't kill Mom, I should have abdicated. All I've tried to do is what Mom wanted me to do, but she's gone. How should I have any idea what she wants?

Oh, Mom, what were you thinking?

I have no idea who killed her, which means there's still a serpent among my own family.

In light of that, the proclamation was a catastrophically bad idea. I have no idea whether this prophecy, the cursed prophecy that caused all of this, is even talking about me. Am I the Eldest? Who even knows? The earth seemed to be doing just fine until I started meddling in things I don't understand, screaming that I'm queen of the hill.

I have no idea why Analessa and Melisania are considering supporting me.

Although. I close my eyes. *Are they really?* It's just as likely that they're offering to support me, but making plans to betray me and take over Alamecha for themselves. In fact, that could be the reason Edam's supposed to marry me. It would certainly be easy for him to kill me once we're married—and if they play their cards right, they could rule Alamecha, Lenora, and Malessa, whoever topples me.

I don't think Edam would do something like that, but with as bad as my judgment is, who knows? I thought Noah was a human this entire time. Even with piles of clues, I was completely oblivious.

I should have been working with Balthasar on ways to

protect my people. Instead, I was flying all over the world pretending to have better insight into people than anyone on my Council. I should have delegated everything to the people who know far better than I do.

Possibly worst of all, I went behind Adika's back and hatched a plot with her Heir. Now she's so upset she's slaughtering my people by the thousands. Literally. And I have no idea how to stop her.

I force myself to read Mom's words again, even though they're already practically tattooed on my brain.

As queen, you can never make any mistakes. I'm going to say that again: You never make any mistakes, Chancery. This will be especially difficult for you because you're naturally receptive to correction. It has made you an exceptional student. You take whatever criticism people dish out and then apply it. It's one of your strengths, but with all things, our strengths are also our weaknesses.

And oh boy, is this my weakness. I'm too weak, and I have no idea whether good judgment can even be learned. But hiding in here isn't helping anything. I force myself to square my shoulders and stand up. I will walk out of here, and I will not tell everyone that I ruined everything. I will not proclaim my flaws, but I won't compound them either. I will delegate, delegate, delegate. Everyone on my Council knows better than me. Everyone in my family could have handled things better.

Fine, then I'll let them handle it.

When I emerge, Edam, Judica, Inara, and Balthasar are all waiting in my room. Before anyone can ask anything, I hold up my hand. "You will each do your jobs. Balthasar, you will develop, under Judica's direction, the details of our response to Adika."

"I've begun already," Balthasar says. "And Marselle provided a lot of invaluable Intel on the region. But we can't simply defend, not in light of her demands."

"No, we can't," Judica says. "It's time for Alamecha to finally take its rightful place. We've wasted too much time in diplomacy. Playing nice hasn't helped us. We've always been the first family, the strongest, the best. It's time the others feel the might of our rage. She's threatening us?" Judica's smile sends a chill up my spine. "We will destroy her."

I don't want to destroy anyone, certainly not an entire family. What will the ramifications of that be for her people? I open my mouth to object, and then I remember.

I shouldn't be making any decisions. All of mine have been bad. Every single one.

I sit down at my desk and stare out the window while the others talk. My only hope of making the right decision is if I don't make one at all. My Council has this under control. Armies, strike teams, embargos, the conversation swells all around me. It's all wrong, so wrong, damaging to the people of Shenoah.

Which is how I know it's probably right.

Anything that feels totally wrong to me is probably the right move. That should be my new barometer. If I think it's the right move and everyone disagrees, ignore my gut. Do whatever they say.

"Adika hasn't left her home base according to our reports," Balthasar says. "None of this will end until she's dead."

"That's one hundred percent right," Inara says. "All of the rest of this is simply cover. We need to take her out. Immediately."

"I'll call Analessa," Edam says. "She has a large force outside of Rome. I'm sure she'll let me lead it, and I'm confident we can breach Adika's defenses on San Marino. The Piazza del Liberta has always been a joke, tactically. They allow private citizens to tour it, as if that washes away her sins in her other holdings. When I'm done with her, I'll bring the ring back for Chancery." He actually smiles at me. "Which is sort of like a human engagement tradition, right?"

Except humans don't cut the ring off of another woman's corpse. *Do not puke, Chancery, don't do it.* All of this feels so wrong. Human armies. Human collateral damage rising with every leg of this attack plan. Evian strike teams, including my fiancé. All so that I can wrest control from someone who has run her own sovereign holdings for five centuries.

And we're justifying all of this with words written on an old piece of paper.

Utter destruction.

I should stop this somehow, but I can't see a single way to do it. And besides that, every single move I've made has been wrong, so wrong. It's not like some magical solution I fabricate will fix anything. It would only make things worse.

"Where's Noah?" I finally ask. "What did you do with him when we returned?"

Edam's face blanks.

"He's under constant guard," Judica says. "Non-stop line of sight."

"He can't even pee alone," Balthasar says with a grim smile. "Kind of brought that upon himself."

I suppose he did.

"Has he called. . ." I don't know who he needs to call. "Whoever it is he meant to call?"

Edam shakes his head. "I wasn't sure if you really wanted him to do that. He knows a lot, which means he can share a lot of information."

He does, and that's all my fault too. How much worse could things get if some kind of rogue evian group begins attacking us too? "This is all such a mess." My shoulders slump.

Inara, Balthasar, Judica and Edam stare at me.

"What?" I ask.

"This isn't a mess," Inara says slowly. "We're doing quite well. Alamecha has long held far more than one sixth of the power on the globe. And to have Malessa on our side, well, we easily already represent at least half of the power on the grid. Shenoah is small potatoes."

Even Inara? She doesn't see the cost of this? She thinks we're doing well? I blink. Wait. Do any of them realize quite what I've done? How much I've messed up? "A thousand people died yesterday." Thanks to me.

"There are almost eight billion people on the earth," Balthasar says, "if you include all of the humans. And there are close to a million evians."

"Are we just reciting random facts?" Judica asks.

I shake my head. "Another thousand will die today, if we don't fix this."

"We can't possibly be ready to go before tomorrow," Edam says, his eyes gentle.

So those people are dead, too. I close my eyes.

Inara pulls a stool up next to me and sits down. "You can't fault yourself every time someone dies. You'll go mad that way. And far more than a thousand people die each day. Many of natural causes."

"I've been focused exclusively on the people whose death I've caused," I say. "Should I feel that a thousand deaths a day is reasonable? Does it indicate I'm doing a good job, do you think?"

"Adika caused those deaths," Judica says. "Not you."

"Fine," I say. "Fine. I need to talk to Noah." I stand up.

"I'll accompany you," Edam says.

I shake my head. "No, it's fine. You should keep planning. You have a lot to do, and you shouldn't delay any more than we must. Call Analessa, do whatever you need to do. I'm the only one who can decide how to handle Noah."

I walk through the door and down the hall before I realize I'm not sure quite where they're holding Noah. It might be the regular cells, or it might not. I stop and turn toward my guards. Luckily, it's Frederick and Arlington. They're rapidly becoming my two favorites. "Freddy, do you know where Noah's being kept?"

He nods. "He's our only official prisoner at the moment, so he's below."

"Official?"

"Melina's being treated as an enemy of the state, per Judica." Frederick shrugs.

"What does that mean, exactly?" I ask.

"Around the clock surveillance and tactical teams keeping eyes on her people."

I can't fault her for that, seeing as Melina has tried to kill her now, twice. "I'm going to see Noah," I say. "And I'll want some privacy for our conversation."

"Understood."

I wind around the corner and down the hall toward the holding cells. This is Noah's second visit to Ni'ihau's holding cells. I wonder if he finds this one more frustrating, now that we know his secret.

Laughter drifts upward when I round the final corner and I glance at Frederick. He shrugs.

"No, I'm not even kidding," Noah says. "I'm at the zoo, right? And I'm staring at this poor Tibetan mastiff. The sign on the pen says it's a *lion*, and I ask the attendant, 'Um, is the real lion like on a break or something?' Like maybe this dog is just filling in. . . But the staff looks at me like they don't even understand the question."

Gregory laughs. Voron laughs. Horace and Nina are both laughing so hard tears are leaking from their eyes.

"Uh, hello," I say. "Am I interrupting something?"

Noah sits up immediately. "Princess. How are you?"

"What's going on?" I ask.

Gregory salutes me. "Nothing, Your Majesty. We're watching Noah every second, as directed."

"While he regales you with stories about wacky zoo misadventures?" I raise my right eyebrow.

"There was a zoo that had a bunch of animals mislabeled," Nina says. "They were passing a mastiff off as a lion to the people who—" She cuts off when she sees my face.

"I need a minute," I say. "I trust you can entertain yourselves for a few moments while I interrogate the *prisoner.*"

Frederick ushers the guards, apparently including two of my Motherless, outside and closes the door behind him. I use my palm to open the door to his cell and slip inside, leaving the door cracked so I can leave again without calling for help.

"What's going on, Noah?"

"I could ask you that. I thought you were going to let me call home."

I hand him my phone.

"I can't do it with you standing there, obviously."

"Why not?" I'm sick of things being obvious to everyone but me.

"Because I can't speak freely, and you'd be able to hear everything they say."

"Oh, right. You need to make your call to my enemies in private, so you can decide what details about my plans to share with them and which things you share to relay back to me." My hands ball into fists. "Lying to me and having completely free rein for the past few weeks wasn't enough. You need me to *knowingly* allow you to be a spy."

He shakes his head. "It's not like that. I want to ask for permission to tell you everything."

"Then do it in front of me, Noah." It occurs to me for the first time that Noah probably isn't even his real name. "Should I be calling you Fred or, I don't know, James Bond or something?"

Noah grins. "I do like the idea of being called James Bond. But my family members all call me Noah."

"Is it your name?" I ask.

He licks his lips.

So it's not—more like a nickname. Which means I really don't even know his name. I close my eyes. "Just make the call."

He takes me in, his eyes traveling from my hair to my face, and down to my feet, and back up to my face again. No one else noticed anything was off, no one else asked if I'm okay, but Noah sees. "Something's wrong. What is it?"

I slump against the wall and drop to the floor, hugging my knees up against my body. "Everything is wrong." And telling Noah about any of it is more of the same. I shut my mouth with a click before I can compound my past mistakes.

"You came here to talk," he says. "So talk."

I shake my head. "Wouldn't you just love that? You're such a good spy that even after I know you're full of it, I still come crying to you?" In spite of my horror, tears spring to my eyes.

Noah gathers me against him, my head pressed to his chest. "I wouldn't love anything that has you crying or sad. You should know that, at least."

I shake my head and push back against him. "Why should I know that? Why? How can I know anything about you? I don't even know if that's your real face, and you won't tell me your real name."

"My name isn't spoken, princess, not even by my family, okay? I can't tell you more than that." His breath warms my face and my hands.

I want to believe him, but nothing he says makes any sense. "We only have names so they can be spoken. It's literally the entire point of names. The spoken signal of who we are."

"The name my family uses when they call me, the only name my family and friends have ever used for me, is Noah, the same as the name you use when you're talking to or about me."

I want to scream. I want to shred something or hit something. And I realize, I can hit Noah. He's not break-able, not anymore. So I do. I smash him in the face, my hand connecting against his nose with a satisfying crunch.

Noah's eyes widen with shock, but he leaps to his feet with a blood-smeared smile on his face. "You're upset? That's fine. I can handle that." He gestures for me to proceed, to attack him.

I jump to my feet. Because I do want to hit him again, badly. My general self-pity transforms somehow, in a slip-pery way I don't comprehend, into rage. I rain blows against him, and he blocks them all. Infuriating. I pull a nasty eight inch knife from my boot and toss it to him, and then I pull my sword.

Noah grins wider than I've ever seen. "Oh, now we're talking," he says.

I slash at him without fear, knowing he won't die from any injury I inflict, knowing he can take it. And he does. He blocks with the dagger, spinning my hacks into wide blows. He even manages to slice my thigh once before I halt him.

"Enough." I collapse back into the corner, but this time I'm not huddling. And I decide that like always, I can talk to Noah. He'll understand. "I've ruined everything."

He slides down to the floor next to me. "You've ruined nothing."

"You're wrong. You wouldn't know yet, but Adika has declared active war on us, thanks to Vela's misguided loss." I close my eyes. "She wants me to kill every Motherless. She wants me to surrender my demands. And for every day that I don't, she's going to kill a thousand people."

"Okay," Noah says.

"Okay?" I'm sick of people acting like it's not a big deal. "You may be evian now, but I thought you'd still care about humans. And she's killing some evians, too."

"It's a temper tantrum," Noah says. "A terrorist threat, by someone who can't hope to actually defeat you."

"She's defeating me every time she kills one of my people. I can't save them, not without killing others. I'm not sure how many it will take to stop her. Maybe hundreds of thousands. And in *taking* her ring, by *stealing* her sovereignty, I'm still failing, Noah. I hoped that you might see it, even though no one else does."

He shakes his head. "You think it's a failure, but you had to know when you sent out a video of you blasting a fireball out of thin air that you'd face opposition. You had to know that you can't prevent utter destruction without some messiness."

"There isn't even a threat right now," I say. "Which means I'm creating 'messiness' for no reason other than my own greed for power."

"You're not responsible for the evil things Adika does."

My laughter sounds a little unhinged, even to me. "Of course I am. She wasn't killing anyone before I issued my demands."

"But you didn't attack her—not yet anyway—and you

aren't attacking her now. This killing, this unprompted cavalier attitude with human life, this is what makes her an unsuitable ruler across the board. I'd have encouraged you to remove her, even before the proclamation, for actions like this."

"Edam and Balthasar and Judica are ensconced in my bedroom, devising a plan of attack right now," I say. "They're basically plotting world domination."

"Isn't that what you want them to do?" he asks. "I mean, it's kind of what you demanded."

He's right. Which is why this is all my fault. "I have no idea who might die in their attacks." Including my sisters, my fiancé, and all of my mom's oldest supporters.

"It's a risk they're all willing to take," Noah says. "I know we aren't sure yet what the utter destruction refers to, but there's a reason for the prophecy, you know. Something is coming. Something that we'll need you to protect us from."

"You believe it?" I ask. "That I'm the Eldest, that there's something coming?"

Noah's jaw locks and he won't meet my eye, and I realize that he knows. He knows exactly what's coming.

"Call your boss, your dad, whoever. Do it now."

Noah swallows and nods. He picks up my phone and dials a number, and then enters a long sequence of numbers.

"Son," the voice says. He glances my way and shakes his head.

"Father."

"This isn't a scheduled check in, and it's not your typical phone." The voice pauses. "She knows, doesn't she?"

"She knows what I can do, yes."

Silence. An exhalation of pure disgust.

"I had no other choice," Noah says.

"There's always a choice. We told you not to share that information."

"I didn't share it. She figured it out."

"She's in the room with you right now."

Noah gulps and straightens his shoulders like somehow his dad might see it. "She is."

"You've handled this all wrong. I should bring you home immediately."

"I won't go." Noah juts his chin outward. "I won't leave her."

"You're a fool."

"I request permission to tell her everything."

"Permission denied," Noah's father says. "Flatly denied. Do you hear me? You will not tell her a single thing. Unlike you, I was not impressed with her."

"I will not return," Noah says. "You can't forcibly recall me. Not from here, not in her home base. And I'd rather serve her than you. She may not know everything, but that isn't her fault. I did what you told me to do, and I gave you my evaluation ages ago. She's the Eldest. She'll do what needs to be done. You can trust her."

"We took your evaluation under consideration, but we believe your assessment is compromised."

Noah gulps again.

"You will come home immediately and make a full report. You must be tried for the decisions you've made. They've gone far beyond the approved scope."

"I will not come home, Father, not until you allow me to tell her everything."

"You love her."

"I do."

"You're a fool."

"You've said that."

"You do not have permission to share anything," Noah's father says. "Do you hear me?"

"I do."

"And if you refuse to return, I'll remove you. Permanently."

Noah's face blanks.

I snatch the phone from his hand. "You're a horrible father. And that means something coming from me, because I didn't have a father at all."

"We all have fathers, young woman, whether we know them or not."

"I never met mine, and by all counts, he was a louse. But even so, he wasn't as bad as you." I wish I could punch him through the phone line.

"It was a pleasure meeting you," Noah's father says. "Although I wish now that we'd been a bit more forthright with one another."

"You started the lies," I say.

"Did I?" he asks. "After all, you told me my son had received an internship."

"For a human, working with my organization is better than an amazing internship. You're the one who made me believe he was human from the start."

"That was Noah's idea," his father says. "One of his better ones, actually, but now it's time for him to come home."

"I don't think so," I say. "Noah failed to mention that he's being held here as a prisoner."

Noah's father laughs. "There's not a prison on earth that can hold my son. If he's staying, it's because he wants to stay."

"Just tell me who you really are," I say. "Who are you working for? What's your real goal?"

"Ah, ah," Noah's father says. "Beggars don't get to

choose. I'll tell you when I'm ready. Tell my son he's made a grave mistake." He hangs up.

Noah's face has drained of all color behind me.

I feel exactly as bad as he looks. I'm sick of making people do things they don't want to do. I'm sick of never knowing who is truly on my side. I don't even want him around if I don't know who he works with or why. "Just go home."

Noah immediately focuses on my face. "No."

"Yes. Just leave, okay? I'm sick of all of it."

Noah's face brightens again. "My dad was right about one thing."

"Oh?"

"I would leave if I didn't want to be here."

I think about the laughing guards, his power to transform. I imagine he's likely right. There's no prison that can hold Noah, not for long. But he wants to stay here with me. I may not know much, but I know this. Noah loves me, and he's staying at great personal cost.

Maybe I'm not doing everything wrong.

27

With my eyes closed so I'm not distracted by Noah's handsome face, I review in my mind every single interaction I've had with Noah. We met at Trinity, which Alora knew would happen. He invited me join the track team, and I went to a party at his house. He went for a jog with me that ended in an attack—was the attack intended to help us draw together?

"You knew Alora," I say. "You're the betrayal she apologized for."

Noah's lips compress into a tight line.

"You can't admit it, perhaps, but I know. When she called me on my way home, she wasn't going to confess anything, until she heard your voice. She only admitted to betraying me because she thought I knew."

"I didn't know your sister," Noah says. "But she owed my father. I can't say more, except that she was supposed to arrange an introduction between us as a favor."

Which is why Alora called to invite me out for a visit before Mom got sick, before the ring reacted to me. Before my twin challenged me.

"I was nothing then," I say.

He shrugs. "You were my 'in' with the family. If I met you and impressed you, I might get to know your entire family. That was the plan."

"And then it just so happened that I became the new Heir, and when you realized I was the Eldest, it was a bonus."

Noah's eyes are sad. "I never cared about that, but yes, that's all true. Except I don't believe in luck. I think there's a reason that the member of the royal family I thought might grant me entree to the rest turned out to be the very person—" He cuts off. "I can't say anything else."

But he wants to tell me more. "I don't want to keep you locked away." And it's beginning to feel totally pointless. "But I don't have any way of knowing when your interests will fall out of alignment with mine."

"I can swear you an oath," Noah says. "I can't control my family, and I can't betray them. But obviously I take my oaths seriously."

Or this is yet another manipulation. "What did you have in mind?"

"I will swear that I will never do you harm, and that I will tell you if I ever discover that someone else means you harm."

Trust. It's almost a dirty word to me right now. Ever since Mom's death, I've been painfully short on anyone I can count on, anyone I believe is on my side. And I shouldn't trust Noah at all—he acknowledges that he has lied to me since our very first meeting. But betraying his employers would be so much easier, and he won't do that. Conversely, his loyalty to them in spite of what I believe is real love for me confirms that he's trustworthy.

"You don't worry that an oath like that might conflict with your family directions?"

Noah beams. "I can't explain how, but I swear to you that there is no way that keeping you safe will ever conflict with my family's directions. It literally cannot."

"Your family wants to keep me safe?" I lift one eyebrow.

"They do. I swear it."

"Fine. Then make your oath."

He does, exactly as he offered, with his hand resting in the middle of his chest, just below his neck. I have no idea whether that has any significance, or whether it's simply a cultural thing.

"I accept," I say.

"Does that mean I can leave?"

I fling the door to Noah's cell open, and several guards round the corner, including Frederick. "I've decided to free Noah," I say.

Because I either have to kick him off the island or decide to trust that he truly means me no harm. I'm not ready to kick him off the island, so.

I expect the guards to argue with me. After all, we have no idea who's pulling his strings. But Frederick simply nods, and the other guards shrug. I'm beginning to wonder whether they would have even tried to stop him before I decided to let him go.

"Will I keep my old room?" Noah asks.

"And your spot on the Council," I say. "Except instead of the human liaison, you'll be my Unaffiliated Evian Liaison."

"Oh, I like the sound of that," Noah says.

"Speaking of which," Frederick says. "Judica came by while you were inside. She said they're still hammering out details of the attack, but she'd like a moment to speak with you."

I don't even bother trying to puzzle out what she might

want. Instead, I stop by her room on the way back to mine and tap on her door.

Death's barking tells me Judica's there.

She looks past me to Noah before she pulls the door open. "I take it that you've forgiven your favorite pet?"

I shake my head. "Not exactly, but there's no point in guarding someone who can come and go as he pleases."

"There's no point in keeping him alive, knowing what we know—he could be anywhere, discovering anything. But that's not my decision to make, I suppose." She scowls at Noah. "I'm going to need to see a demonstration later of this ability my sister tells me you have, but for now, I need to talk to her alone." Judica swings her full attention back to me.

"I'll wait outside with the guards," Noah says, stepping back and shutting the door.

"Is everything okay?" I ask.

"I might have overstepped." Judica looks at the toes of her boots and won't meet my eye.

My sister is never nervous. What could make her nervous? Oh, no. She's killed Melina. "What did you do?" My stomach lurches.

"I was worried Melina's people would—"

"Tell me you didn't kill her." My tone is flat.

"Of course not! I appropriated one of the family jets to bring some people to Ni'ihau, without your permission."

What in the world? "Who?"

"Your human isn't a human, so I thought you might need some candidates for the empty Council position."

"I think I literally have millions of good options for that," I say.

"Oh." Judica sits down and pats Death's head. He looks as shocked by her affection as I am, but he recovers quickly and leans against her hand.

"Who did you bring?" I don't ask how Judica met a human and why she cares, but that's what I really want to know.

"Melina threatened some humans who helped me out when I escaped in Austin. Gregory mentioned it, and then I worried about them."

My sister was worried. . . about humans? Enough that she sent a *jet* to pick them up? "You had them brought here?" It must be the William and Ambrosia Melina's wife threatened. I scratch my head. "Where Melina is currently in residence?"

Judica squeezes Death's ear a little too hard and he yelps. "I'm also here. I can make sure they're safe."

Oh Judica. She uprooted two humans from their homes, their families, and their lives because she thinks they'll be safer here, living in a den of vipers. "Look, I don't mind you making friends. Far from it, but I think with friends, you would typically ask their thoughts and feelings on something like this before—"

"Oh, we aren't friends," Judica says. "I just didn't want them to *die.*"

I don't bother explaining that not wanting someone to die is kind of the ultimate bedrock of every good friendship. "Alright. Well, I'm going to recommend that you discuss with them whether they remain or head back home. Then you need to honor their wishes. After that, you can go back to doing your actual job."

Judica bobs her head. "The plans are nearly in place. It's a solid framework. It will work."

"Oh good."

Noah and I head back to my room, where Edam and Balthasar are still hashing out details.

"Whoa, what's he doing free?" Edam eyes Noah.

"My call," I say flatly.

Edam's nostrils flare, but he drops it. Mostly. "I want to walk you through this plan, but is it wise to have him here for this?"

"We trust him or we don't," I say.

"We don't," Balthasar and Edam say at the same time.

"We have no idea who he might report back to, and this is sensitive."

"Fine." I wish I could get his feedback, since he's had surprisingly good ideas on all the other plans we've prepared, but I don't have the energy to fight. "Outside." Noah goes to stand outside the door with my guards without complaint.

Edam and Balthasar walk me through the rudiments of the plan. An attack force comprised of mostly humans will take out one of Adika's biggest holdings. At the same time, we'll launch an air strike on another position, one that's closer to her home base. Judica will coordinate our human forces. Edam and Balthasar will each lead strike teams from opposite directions to take out Adika herself on her own soil. We're assuming she's still in residence in her palace in beautiful San Marino. Our reports confirm that, anyway. The thought of destroying a big piece of history like that makes me cringe, but not as much as sitting on my hands while she slaughters more and more of my people. Half the force will be provided by Analessa from nearby France and Monaco. Half we'll fly in ourselves.

"How will you get there?" I ask.

"It's not like the rest of Italy knows it's at war," Balthasar says. "I imagine Adika is rolling out a phased plan, and at some point she'll boycott or set up rerouting, but Italy's part of the EU. Blocking the borders is harder to do than it used to be. No protocols in place to prevent flights yet."

"The 'more freedom for your workers' concept has its

drawbacks," I say. "Especially when you want to foster trade."

"Exactly," Balthasar says. "And for most of her holdings, Adika has refused to allow her humans much freedom. But Italy is flourishing with the economic incentive to produce, and she's reticent to lose that. Which helps us."

It helps us because it makes her easier to kill.

"You will stay here for once," Edam says. "But you'll have total operational control over all levels, and current technology will allow you to see in real time exactly what's happening with each of the phased attacks." Edam points at my desktop. "You can monitor each of us on a split screen, or tap whichever you want and zoom in to see exactly what's happening."

"I'll be so far away that it won't matter what I think." I frown. "There will be nothing I can do. And if communications go out. . ." I sigh. "May as well sit at home and pray while clutching at my pearls."

"Look, Analessa said you'd be welcome to come to Monaco with me," Edam says. "You can stay there and watch from a much closer location, but you told me and Balthasar to run this op. Our top priority is your safety."

"Then I'm coming."

"To Monaco?" Edam asks.

I shrug. "Fine."

He smiles. "I can deal with that." He crosses the room and touches my face, tilting it upward. "What's the point of having all these warlords if you take all the risks yourself?"

"Feeling like a fiancé?" I whisper.

He bites his lip. "Maybe."

"I guess that's okay," I say.

"Good." He leans down and brushes a kiss against my mouth. "And I'll rest a little easier knowing you're close enough to me that if something goes wrong, I can reach you quickly, too." His hand wraps around mine, our fingers interlocking.

I lean my head against his chest and hope that I'm doing the right thing by backing off and letting my Council make these decisions. When I review my long list of mistakes again in my head, I feel positive I am.

"Wheels up in an hour, even for lovebirds." Balthasar winks at me and ducks out.

Noah clears his throat from the doorway. "I better go get packed."

"Oh, you're not coming," Edam says.

"You should do a thorough analysis of his skill level when this is over," I say, "but Noah's a warrior, Edam. I think having him with me would be an asset."

Edam sighs. "You're kidding."

"You're leaving me to go who knows where."

"He could betray you while I'm gone," Edam says.

"I would never do that," Noah says. "And my father and I aren't currently speaking."

"Super," Edam says. "Well if he's not currently talking to his handler, then it's probably fine."

"Good," I say.

Edam throws his hands in the air. "I'm kidding."

"We're taking the Motherless?" I ask.

"They'll all insist on coming with you," Edam says.

"And will you allow them to come?" I ask.

He shrugs. "Do I have a choice?"

"They've sworn an oath to me, a strong one, a lifetime oath."

"Okay," Edam says. "But people break oaths."

"Noah doesn't break his," I say softly. "And he swore one to me, and I accepted it. I'd feel safer having him with me."

"Fine," Edam says. "Whatever you want, Your Majesty. I suppose I'll have to get used to it."

"To what?" I ask.

"To you having friends and supporters I hate." He crosses his arms.

"If it makes you feel better, pick the forty or so Motherless you trust the most," I say. "And bring them with me too. That way I'll be amply prepared if Noah does something dire. We can also keep him under surveillance the entire time so that we know he's not contacting anyone else."

"Yes, that will make me feel better," Edam says. "Now get your stuff together. I'll see you on the jet in a few."

"Thank you," I say. "For doing this. For handling everything."

Edam frowns. "It's my job. And you're the one calling the shots. We just assembled a plan to accomplish what you need."

"I know."

Edam ducks out, leaving only Noah to stare at me.

"He has no idea."

"Excuse me?" I ask.

"He has no idea you blame yourself for how everything has gone down."

"Not exactly. It's more that he doesn't think anything has gone wrong," I say. "He thinks we're right on track."

"Are we?" Noah asks.

I sit on my bed. "I don't know anymore."

Noah sits next to me. "You're worried that you're greedy for power?"

I shake my head. "Is that it? Maybe. I don't see anything that poses a threat. There's no utter destruction yawning before us, other than the destruction I've created."

"What about this Nereus?"

"The person who bought the poison that killed my mom?" I ask. "Sure, I want to find him or her. And as soon as we're done with this battle, I'll pitch all my resources into it. But I'm not sure that's a harbinger of the end of the world."

Noah breathes in and out slowly.

"What do you know?"

He shakes his head slowly. "I can't tell you. But I will tell you that you should take some time and talk to Melina."

I jump off my bed and start throwing things into my bag. "I don't have time. You heard Edam. We leave in less than an hour."

"Maybe you let them handle this, and you stay here to talk to your sister."

I can't do that. "I need to be close."

"Why?"

Mom's ring flashes on my hand and like I knew to duck, I just know. "I can't sit here on my island throne while they attack an empress on my orders."

"Fine. The second we return, then," Noah says.

"What do you think she knows?" I ask.

Noah shrugs.

"The second prophecy?" I ask. "Is there really a second one? And does it explain what the destruction is?"

Noah pretends to zip his lip.

"Look, you picked my side. Just tell me what you know."

"I wish I could do that," Noah says. "But my family's complicated, and they have their reasons too. I'm not in charge, Chancery. I'm not the one who decides that stuff— and my dad's the only one who can decide what risks to take. Once you've done what you need to do with Adika, maybe I can set up a meeting. A proper meeting, where he could tell you things you need to know."

"Fine."

Noah leaves to grab his things with one of my guards following him, and I wonder whether he'll find a way to contact his father. I wonder whether he's really on my side, or if this is yet another fake out. He could make himself look like Edam right now. He could be passing our plans off to his family. He could be calling Adika.

Maybe I should send him away.

The thought of that makes me want to cry, but what if I'm making another catastrophic mistake? I need to think this all through, but it will have to wait until a thousand people aren't hoping Adika doesn't execute them. I sling my bag over my shoulder and walk out the door, my remaining guards falling in behind me. The rest of my Council matches my steps as I walk toward the airstrip. I used to be the one trotting after everyone else.

It's a little disconcerting.

Alora squeezes my hand. "This will work."

I haven't seen Alora since before I realized Noah wasn't who he said he was. I don't have time to confront her, but I can't act like nothing's wrong either. I pull my hand away and ignore the wounded look in her eyes. Noah can't tell me a thing, but she's my sister. She should have come clean.

I don't look forward to dealing with her when I return.

"I'll keep things running smoothly here," Inara says.

"I know that right now Adika's our priority," Marselle says, "but I wanted to tell you that I've been pressing on my leads for information on your Mother."

How could she know how guilty I feel for making no progress there?

"I'm hoping to have some new information when you return," Marselle says.

I want to ask her what she thinks about Melina standing trial, whether she believes Angel could have been involved. But now isn't the time.

"Wait!" Someone yells from across the courtyard.

We all turn toward the sound.

As if she knew I was thinking about her, Melina sprints toward us. "I need to speak with you Chancery."

My guards would probably have perceived anyone sprinting toward me as a threat, but they're especially suspicious with her. By the time she reaches my side, a dozen people are pointing blades at her.

"Where are you going?" Melina glances around at my guards, and then registers the presence of Alora and Inara. "You're both here, but you haven't come by to see me?"

"I'll only be gone for a short time," I say. "And I'll come to see you the second I return, but we have some very pressing issues to deal with right now."

"I don't need a lot of time," Melina says. "But this is more urgent than I thought. Remember I told you—"

"This can't wait," Alora says. "Alamecha is at war. It may not be something you've needed to worry about over the past twenty years, but it's our reality."

Melina snaps her mouth shut. "Fine, but Chancery?"

"Yes?"

"The second you're back, come see me," Melina says. "Swear it."

"I will."

She nods and takes a step back. "Fine. Be safe, be quick, and don't lose sight of your true purpose."

"I'll try not to," I say.

But I fear I already have.

Noah's already waiting on my jet, but Edam saved me a seat. I walk past Noah and Moses to sit by my fiancé. "Where's Judica?" I ask.

"We're taking eight jets," Edam says. "Yours boasts the heaviest firepower, but we put Judica and Balthasar on separate planes. No reason to give anyone a single target. Besides, Judica's not going to Monaco."

"Right." I think about our multi-layered attack. "Do you think Adika might attack us en route?"

Edam shakes his head. "I doubt she's expecting us to retaliate this quickly, but that doesn't mean we don't plan for it."

I lean back in my chair. "I hate this."

He takes my hand in his. "I know you do."

"The thousand?" I swallow. "Did she?"

He nods and says nothing else.

I swallow hard. "At least we're responding as quickly as we can."

"No one could accuse us of delay."

"Will the attack happen today? Or tomorrow?" I ask.

"We land in the middle of the night. We move at first light tomorrow."

I read Balthasar's recent instructional manual on air and ground strike patterns and then fall asleep on Edam's shoulder.

When I wake up, we're landing in Monaco. I glance down at my jeans and pink t-shirt. I probably should have dressed a little better, since Analessa may be meeting us on the runway.

"I need to run to the bathroom," I say.

Edam presses a kiss to my forehead. When I reach for my bag, he tilts his head. "Everything okay?"

"I thought I might change clothes," I say. "I wasn't thinking when I picked this."

"Analessa won't be here," he says, "if that's what you're worried about."

Wait. "Why not?"

"I told her not to come. I didn't want to worry about her allegiances or keeping you safe with her around."

"Oh." A wave of gratitude rolls over me. I may not know what Noah's goals are, and I may not know who he really serves, but Edam, he's on my side. All the way. "Thank you."

"So if you want to change clothes, feel free. But you look amazing in that, and no one in Monaco will care what you're wearing."

I sink back into my seat. "Thanks."

"I got you," Edam says.

And I realize, he really does.

"I'm glad you slept on the flight," Edam says. "Because things are about to get crazy."

He's right. When we land, everything happens all at once. Analessa has prepared a lot of things for us, but there's still so much to coordinate. Edam leaves almost immediately to meet with his team. Balthasar disappears at the same time to prepare his crew.

And I'm stuck working on tech support. It's amazing that we have so many pieces of technology these days—I can communicate in real time with every branch of our attack. Anthony, our chief of technology in Ni'ihau, walks me through the details of the interface I'll be using to track the various angles of attack over the phone. Suddenly, Judica's feed goes live. "Oh, it worked," I say.

"Hey, Chancery," Judica says.

Hey, she says, like she's not about to launch several attacks that will kill thousands upon thousands of humans.

"Hello Judica. How are you feeling?"

She shrugs. "Fine. A little bored, honestly."

I nod. She's always bored when she's not hacking at someone. "Roman with you?"

"He's on site to manage the air strikes. I'm on location to handle the ground movements."

"Sorry."

She raises one eyebrow. "For what? This isn't some kind of couples retreat. We're at war." She can't keep the smile from creeping onto her face.

"That's a bad thing," I remind her.

"I know you think that, but it's really not. Adika handed you the impetus you needed to get this done. You'll be Empress of Alamecha and Shenoah in the next twenty-four hours."

If all goes according to plan, she's right. "Then I guess I should wish you good luck."

"This part is routine," Judica says. "I don't need luck."

Sometimes I wish I'd been trained the same way Judica was. Then maybe this would feel routine to me, too. "Well, I'll see you afterward."

"Be safe, sister." Judica hangs up.

Noah and Moses set up tables and chairs on either side of me. They even have their own monitors. "My two lieutenants," I say.

"I wasn't going to ask," Moses says. "But I can't seem to help myself. Who is this guy, exactly? He's not human." He frowns. "I didn't understand why you had a human liaison, and now that we know he's been lying to you, why is he here at all?"

"Noah wasn't honest with me when we met," I admit. "He has continued the false pretense of being a human for quite some time. It's an impressive feat, but it undermines my willingness to trust him. Don't doubt that."

Moses scowls at Noah.

"But he has offered help and provided exactly what he offered every step of the way. He has never tried to force me to do anything, and his advice has been pretty solid."

"I heard he gave you a jet."

I nod.

"No offense, but you have jets. You didn't need his," Moses says.

"You weren't here yet, so you might not know that if it weren't for him, I'd be dead. Before I returned to Ni'ihau, my sister sent bombs toward China. I left to stop them, but the only way I saw to do that would have killed me."

"Noah saved you? How?" Moses asks.

"He did." I think about the advice he offered. It was good, almost too good. Almost like he knew what I could do with my ring. But that's not possible, because no one knew I had reacted to it at all, other than my mom, Inara, and Judica. "He has continued since that time to offer me advice, solid advice. He hasn't been able to share every bit of information about his life with me yet, but I believe him when he tells me he would if he could."

"Don't kill him then, but keeping him this close is a mistake," Moses says.

"I took you at face value," I say. "I didn't know you when you showed up on my doorstep with Vela. I haven't done a DNA test to confirm you're my brother." Not that I need to with his eyes. They're clearly Mom's. "But you took a vow to protect me, and you gave up your past life. I'm in the same quandary with the Motherless. I don't know them, not individually, and yet I trust that their vow to serve me was genuine."

Moses looks Noah up and down and nods. "That's true."

"I'm not asking you to trust Noah," I say. "I'm asking you to trust my judgment."

"Fair enough." Moses sits down and refocuses on his interface.

Edam comes by a few moments later. "We're about to leave. I need to be ready to go when the sun rises."

I stand up, not sure what to do. Forty people in this

room, and all of them are looking at us. I step toward him. "Please come back," I whisper.

He closes the gap between us and wraps his arms around my waist. "I will," Edam says softly. "And I'll bring you a ring when I do."

"I don't care about the ring."

"I do. It's your destiny."

I shake my head. "Perhaps, but you mean more to me than a rock. Don't forget that."

Edam smiles and leans toward me, but instead of kissing me, he touches our foreheads together. His next words are so soft I can barely make them out. "I know this isn't how you wanted things to go, with the ruling people, and the fighting wars, and the subjects dying. But no matter how life happens, I will fight for us. Every day. Against your enemies, against my family, against anyone who means you harm, I will fight."

I lift my chin and kiss him, softly, briefly. "I know you will, and I love that about you." It's not a declaration of love, not quite, but it's close.

Edam's smiling when he marches out of the room. I wish I felt half his optimism. Even if we win, I fear I'm losing.

"You know that he has to kill her," Noah says.

I wish it didn't always feel like he was reading my mind. "Yes."

"Good," Noah says. "Because you like to spare people, and she can't be spared."

I go back to my screen, tapping through the various feeds.

"Adika certainly doesn't have clean hands," Moses says.

"Why?" I ask, sick of them acting superior. "Why does she have to *die?* It may be the evian way, but I don't think it should be." I think about Mom chopping off Lyssa's head, and I shudder.

That's not me, and it never will be.

"Adika is killing a thousand people a day," Noah says. "Just to get your attention."

"She's misguided, clearly," I say.

"She's insane," Noah says. "And she's been in power so long, she thinks she deserves it. She thinks people live to serve her, not the other way around."

"I agree we need to stop her. I even agree that we need to use force." I snap my mouth shut. Arguing with Noah and Moses is pointless. The decision is made in any case, and not by me this time. So why do I still feel guilty about it?

"You wish you could spare her, or better yet, reform her," Noah says. "You always want to fix everything. Some things can't be fixed."

"Her people will never follow you if you aren't savage enough to eliminate your rival," Moses says. "Shenoah is a strong family, but they're brutal. They would never accept anything less than total defeat."

I don't say anything else because I'm sick of fighting about it. Without any conversation, the minutes crawl painfully by. In the moments before dawn, I click from one feed to the next frenetically.

Noah puts a hand on my arm. "You're going to get click finger."

"That's not a thing," I say.

"It is."

"I'm worried," I say. "This is my first attack."

He shakes his head. "Melina's attack was your first attack, and you were in mortal peril. This is a simple maneuver, and we're going to win."

He's right. Of course he's right. I slow my heart and

regulate my breathing. Then I watch as the steps of the plan fall into place, one by one. Judica initiates her strike at the same time as Roman. I force myself to watch the effects of the air strike. Buildings explode. People scream. Then I refuse to turn away as Judica orders her troops to roll forward. She and Roman are far enough back that I'm not worried about them, but the carnage sickens me.

I hate war.

I hate everything about it. Having the biggest guns doesn't make it any better.

"We can turn these off, you know," Noah says.

Moses taps on the screen and it goes blank.

"No," I say. "I need to watch it."

"Who says self-flagellation died in the fourteenth century?" Noah asks.

"Stop. Both of you." I turn the screens back on.

Our attacks go exactly as planned. Every single step.

Balthasar launches his strike, his team scaling the sides of the main city. Edam's team begins five minutes later. They both arrive at the precise moments intended, meeting exactly the resistance we expected. My unease grows with every part of the plan that follows our expectations. My right foot taps and taps.

Edam fights like a lion, which isn't a surprise. He leads every charge himself, killing double the number of anyone else on his team. Balthasar's only a step behind him.

"Just watching them wears me out," Moses says. "Your guy's like a Tasmanian devil."

"The old man's holding up pretty well, too," Noah says. "I mean, I figured he'd be a little slow. He's over nine hundred years old, right?"

"Nine hundred and twenty-three, I think," I say.

Adika's troops put up an admirable fight, but eventually Edam and Balthasar reach the top of Monte Titano and scale the walls of the Guaita Fortress where Adika's throne room rests. The battle fervor increases. Edam's camera moves so quickly it's hard to follow. He's spinning, slicing, parrying, ducking, and no matter how hard he fights, new opponents continue to appear. I worry for his team, and for Edam, too. If he's killed. . . I can't think about it. I can't.

Balthasar roars from the other side, and Edam presses, the two of them joining in front of the broad doors and finally clearing through the opposition. They successfully breach them and walk inside.

But the throne is empty.

In fact, no one is inside the central chamber of Guaita Fortress at all, but there's a box on the seat. Edam approaches at a run. I yell for him to stop, but it's too late.

The box explodes and I lose both video feeds at the same time.

The ring on my hand flashes angrily, and I leap to my feet. I run for the doorway, calling to Moses and Noah as I move. "I'm leaving now. You'll air drop me over the tower."

"It's a no fly zone," Moses says. "We can't do that. They'll shoot us down before we could get anywhere close."

If that stupid prophecy has any elements of truth to it, I'm the only person I know for sure will survive this attack. I should never have let them plan things without me. I should never have stepped back at all. Ignoring my instincts, sitting back and letting others do everything. . . that may have been my biggest mistake to date. But I'm done whining about it.

"Let them try," I say.

28

Analessa's pilot tells me I can't take her jet. "Get out of my way," I say.

"I'm sorry, but you're not authorized to take her Cessna," Finnigan says. "We're allies, but taking her aircraft—"

I slice his throat, shove him to the side and point at the Super Grand Caravan. "I assume you can fly that?"

Moses nods.

None of Analessa's other men offer any protest, not while Finnigan's still spasming on the floor. I step over the puddle of blood and climb the steps into the jump craft. "It seats nineteen," I say. "Pick your best men. We leave immediately."

Moses shouts names of his selected Motherless, and we board in less than three minutes. We're wheels up five minutes after that, but it feels like an eternity. I have no idea if my men are alive or dead.

Including Edam.

My cell phone rings on the ascent. I can barely hear over the engine, but I answer anyway.

"Chancery," Adika says.

"Adika," I practically growl.

"I have your boyfriend."

"Is he alive?"

"He came to kill me," Adika says. "I should separate him from his head immediately, but I haven't yet. I thought I'd give you another chance to agree to my terms."

"If he's still alive, you should watch your back," I say.

Adika laughs. "You have a very high opinion of him, but it's unfounded. He and Balthasar fell right into my trap. I'm looking at them right now, held in place by a very powerful electric fence. They dropped right into my throne room, as if I'd lounge around in there with a target painted on my chest."

She's there. They're there. And I'm coming. I just need her to hold tight until I arrive.

"I argued with my Council, you know," I say.

"Did you?" Adika asks. "Did you want to surrender?"

"I wanted to spare your life," I say.

"And now, now that I've captured your boyfriend and I *haven't* killed him, now what? You're so enraged that you've changed your mind?"

"I thought you and I could come to an agreement."

"We will never agree. I'm a queen. I'll never surrender to a little girl, no matter how flashy her jewelry. And trust me, even if your little fireballs aren't all computer animation, they won't help you."

"You called to what, then?" I ask. "Gloat?"

"You have one hour to think about your options, and how far into quicksand you've sunk with your warlord and your boyfriend both captured," Adika says. "In an hour, I'll remove both their heads and ship them back to you. And tomorrow, because you've pissed me off, I'll kill ten thousand of your people."

I can't pay as much attention as I'd like to Adika's threats, because Noah's waving at me frantically.

"I'll be in touch." I hang up and turn to Noah. "What is so important?"

Noah points at the cockpit. "We're not quite to Florence yet, but we're being hailed."

"And? What do they want?" I walk toward the front of the plane.

"It's the Italian military," Noah says.

I listen long enough to realize they're ordering us to turn back.

"Bongiorno," I say. "We have a dive set up this morning."

"We have orders not to allow anyone to fly in this direction," the man says, "not for any reason. If you don't turn around, we will be forced to shoot you down."

I smile. "That's truly unfortunate. I hope you'll reconsider."

I reach down into the well inside my head and pull on every bit of energy accumulated there. I shape it into the largest ball I can create, and then I wait for the energy to begin refilling. I grab that too, and then enlarge the ball.

"Umm, not to badger you," Noah says, "but if you're planning to do something, it might be a good time." He points out the windshield of the plane. Two fighter jets on the horizon.

"That guy was serious. They really do intend to shoot us out of the sky." I shake my head. I had hoped I wouldn't need to do anything.

"What's our plan?" Moses says. "Because my only defense in this Cessna is to hope and pray."

"We have almost the same idea," I say. "Because I'm hoping and praying I can pull this off." I push outward with the same part of my brain that feels the well and realize that I can sense the area around our plane. I let go of the ball long enough to shove out past it, and it works. I hope. I focus on the enormous ball of energy I've shaped, and I expand it, and then hit it with everything I have, exploding it outward in every direction. The power tears from me, my shoulders slumping as it pulses outward. It feels like someone stuffed my skull with cotton balls. I shake my head to try and dissipate the fog, but it doesn't help.

I'm not sure how it was such a difficult concept for me before, widening the center of my blast radius, but I suppose comprehension comes with time and practice.

Moses swears when the jets shudder and descend rapidly. "Whoa, what just happened?" He glances over at me. "Are you okay?"

"I've knocked out the planes, and probably most of the electronics around Florence," I say. "I'm pretty sure."

"How?" he asks.

"It's a long story," I say. "But we're close to San Marino, right?"

"We are," Noah says. "And we need to talk about our plan."

"You're going to fly over," I say. "And I'm jumping out over Adika's fortress."

"I'm going to guess this will be your first jump," Noah says.

"I've gone before," Moses says.

"So have I," Noah says. "But if the princess hasn't ever done it, she'll need some help."

"Monte Titano is around 2500 feet or so," I say. "If I jump at thirteen thousand, that gives me almost sixty seconds to fall."

"Plus parachute time," Noah says. "Which is the slowest bit."

"I'll tandem with Chancery," Moses says. "That way I

can provide cover fire while she does whatever she needs to do to make sure the guys are free when we land. I'm assuming that's your plan?"

Power slowly trickles into the bottom of my energy well, and the fog is dispelling incrementally from my brain. "Yeah, something like that." I hope.

Moses calls one of the Motherless to handle the piloting and follows Noah back into the cargo bay. Noah helps Moses and me suit up, and then he preps himself.

"You can stay on the plane," I say. "You don't have to jump."

"You're crazy if you think I'm sitting this out," Noah says. "Especially since we have no idea whether Adika's even telling the truth about Edam being alive."

That possibility hadn't even occurred to me. I'm not sure whether it's the suit, the altitude, or the idea that Adika might be lying, but I struggle to breathe.

"Are you ready?" Noah asks.

No time for a panic attack. The plane is losing altitude, preparing for us to jump.

"Your Majesty," Gregory says. "Not to bug you, but we're close, and we have incoming. Again."

I glance at the horizon. Another fighter jet approaches from the north.

My power isn't recovered, and my head still feels strange, but it's coming fast.

"We may need to wait a bit," I say. "I have to hit San Marino and that jet at the same time."

"I hope you all packed your clean underwear," Gregory says.

The jet fires a missile our direction.

Voron opens the door so we can jump. I snag a tiny bit of energy and form a fireball. I fire it out the door and toward the open field below, hoping it'll draw the missile.

It works.

The explosion beneath us shakes the entire plane, and I grab the wall next to me.

But now I can see it. San Marino is just ahead. The jet is circling back around to hit us again. It's time.

I reach down into the well of power again. It's only three-quarters full, but it'll have to do. I yank out the power and shape it, expanding around our aircraft again. I finish it and hold. "Are you ready?" I ask Moses.

He nods and lines us both up at the door. "We jump on three," he says. "One."

I yank on the extra drips and drops that have funneled in and shape them into the smaller power ball, expanding it slightly.

"Two."

Then I expand the power outward, spreading the ball as thin as possible, pushing in the direction of the jet and the opposite direction toward San Marino.

"Three." I hit that ball with all the force I have, sending another shock wave outward.

Moses jumps, dragging me along with him. The wind hits us like a wall. I'm hurtling through the air, and all I can think about is the pilot in that jet I just destroyed.

This time I can practically smell the exhaust from the fighter as it nose dives. I have a front row seat when it crashes beneath us. I close my eyes and focus, because I need to pay attention to Moses, not worry about someone who was trying to kill me.

I struggle to remember what he said I should do and when. We're hurtling toward beautiful San Marino, and I glance backward to verify the others made it. Gregory, Noah, Flynn, and Voron are spread out behind and around me, and I choke in a tiny breath just so I can exhale with relief.

The pressure of the air against my skin feels like a wind tunnel. My hair and clothing are plastered against my face and body. Moses angles downward and I follow his lead, heading for Monte Titano like a torpedo.

"Now?" I ask.

"Hold," Moses says.

Noah pulls his. Then Gregory, then Flynn.

"Hold," Moses says. "We're headed straight for the top tower."

Voron releases his chute, and we are still powering toward the earth.

Finally Moses pulls his, yanking us upward.

"Now me?" I ask.

"Not if you want to land first," Moses says.

I release my chute a few seconds before we hit the ground, the tandem harness yanking harder. We were aiming for the highest tower, but the wind doesn't help us. We crash into a tree right off the path along the top of the wall. I dislocate my right shoulder, break my right shin, and shatter at least three bones in my left wrist.

"Ahhhhhhh," I moan. "That landing was not fun."

"We're here, though." Moses slices the harness and I fall another dozen feet to the ground.

It takes me a moment to recover, healing my injuries as quickly as I can. A few seconds after I hop to my feet, Noah lands next to me, softly, quietly, like a freaking cat. "Not bad for your first time, princess."

"Shut up." I unsheathe my swords and take off at a sprint for the main tower we missed.

"Never run with your sword out," Moses says next to me, panting slightly.

"Do I get a sword?" Noah asks when he catches up.

I toss him my second blade without breaking stride and he catches it.

"I'm so glad not to be human anymore," Noah says. "This is way more fun."

Running up a mountain toward armed guards and a rival empress after air dropping from a plane? I guess he's right.

The other Motherless fall in next to me one at a time during our sprint to the top. I'm prepared for an epic battle when I reach the barricaded front gate, with ten men to support me. Adika's waiting for us, sword drawn, at the clearing in front of the enormous doors. I walk toward her and meet her stare with a glare of my own. "I came, but I'm not surrendering."

"I can see that," Adika says. "But tell me this. If you're the queen of prophecy, meant to save us all. . . What exactly are you saving us from?"

I shrug. "Not sure."

"You're a fraud."

"Maybe I am," I admit. I hope it's not true, but I fear she's right.

"You aren't your sister. You don't even want control. So why not surrender your claim?" she asks.

"We've gotten lost as a people," I say. "It's time we regained our purpose."

"Are you asking me? Or telling me?" Adika gestures in a circle and her guards step forward, falling into a semi-circle behind her. The Motherless step up behind me. "What purpose did we lose?" She comes at me then, swinging her blade toward mine.

I deflect and turn easily. "We should be making the world better for all the descendants of Eve, not just those we consider good enough."

She sneers. "So this is all about your love for humans?"

"No. I don't love them, not any more than I love evians. The point is that we're the same. All of us are Eve's people, not just those we deem pure enough."

"And what about your sheltering of these *Motherless?*" she asks. "You think you'll keep Alamecha pure without providing appropriate options for your children?" She comes at me again, this time with a sequence of blows. Her men seem content to stand and watch, for now at least.

"I think that's been the justification for a lot of injustice over the past six thousand years," I say, blocking her blows, but not attacking yet. "But I won't do terrible things to preserve the bloodline."

"So you'll keep all your children and raise them in love?" Adika laughs, but she comes after me in earnest.

It takes all of my attention to fend off her attacks. "Yes. I'll keep all my children."

"But the youngest will be Heir," she says.

"Yes," I say.

"You're so young and stupid." Adika ducks below one of my strikes and surprises me with an unexpectedly rapid upswing, slicing my side.

"I'm young." I spin away, buying time to heal my side. But it doesn't heal, and my arms and legs slow down too. Her blade must've been coated with something. "Your sword's poisoned." My words stumble out slurred, and I blink to try and clear the haze from my vision.

"And stupid." Adika smiles, showcasing an entire mouthful of beautifully white teeth.

A dagger flies from a window and lodges in my chest, slicing my heart nearly in two. I stumble backward and fall onto the ground on my butt.

Adika walks toward me slowly. "I don't play fair. I never have. Expecting justice from the world and taking unnecessary risks is the province of the innocent."

Kirabo, Adika's daughter and Heir now that Vela's gone, jumps to the wall. She clearly threw the dagger. I blink again, hoping to make more sense of what's happening. Two minutes ago, I was on top. Two minutes ago, I was going to save Edam and Balthasar and win this fight. Now I'm on the ground, my heart foundering, a wound in my side festering.

I'm about to die, and Edam and Balthasar may already be dead. Adika couldn't be more pleased.

"Chancery plays fair," Noah says softly behind Adika. "But I don't." He swings the borrowed sword downward swiftly, cleaving Adika's head from her body.

As if they're following an order, the Motherless attack Adika's guards. I yank the dagger from my chest, and I nearly black out in the process. Noah reaches my side a moment later and applies pressure to the hole near my sternum. "Focus," he says. "You can heal this. You're young and strong, not young and stupid." He grins at me and my diced heart hammers. Blood gushes over his hand.

Removing an evian's heart kills them, but does slicing it in half? My eyes drift, scanning the melee and beyond, to where Adika's Heir is watching and probably preparing to hurl another dagger. Maybe that one will finish the job.

Edam leaps onto the wall behind Kirabo while I'm trying to repair the ventricles of my heart and knocks her to the ground. I try to sit up to see what's happening, but Noah shoves me down. "Stop. Heal first, stand up later."

A bloody Edam bounds up to me a moment later, as I repair the right ventricle. Noah's scrubbing at the wound on my side. It's burning like fire, and it still isn't healing. I cough and spray blood all over the cobblestones.

"Kirabo's dead," Edam says.

"But I got Adika." Noah puffs his chest out. "While you were still penned up like a dog."

Edam drops a hand on Noah's shoulder. "Thank you."

I don't die of shock, but I do fall back to my elbows again. Edam leans over Adika's body and tugs at it. He stands back up and holds up her ring. "Told you I'd get this for you." He beams at me above the black rock.

"So you did." I finish healing my heart. I may not be sure whether we can heal a severed heart, but a mostly severed one—that can be repaired.

"What's going on with her side?" Edam asks, crouching next to me.

"Adika poisoned her blade," Noah says.

Edam swears under his breath. "Wish she was still alive so I could kill her again."

"It's not healing," Noah says.

"I want to go home," I say. "Right now."

Edam scoops me up, his arms sliding under my shoulders and my knees. "Then let's do it."

"You may need to smooth a few things over with your sister," I warn him.

"Like what?" Edam asks.

"I cut her pilot's throat and stole her plane," I say. "Think she'll forgive me?"

"Oh please," Edam says. "She'd have been disappointed if you did anything less."

"She *wanted* me to maim her pilot and steal her plane?"

"No, she wanted you to race off to save your fiancé." He presses a kiss to the side of my head and then jogs with me down the wall. The fighting around us is winding down, not because the Motherless are killing the guards so much as the guards are surrendering. It looks like Balthasar and Edam may have been right after all. Kill the monarch, secure the throne.

Moses catches us and salutes. "You fought well," Moses says. "Don't let Adika make you feel bad about fighting with honor."

Like me, Moses is young and stupid. I laugh at the thought, but it sends a bolt of pain through my side. "Since you know the people and the lay of the land here," I say, "I'd like to leave you in charge until I can appoint a regent."

Moses sighs. "I was afraid you might ask something like that."

I reach over and pluck a stray branch out of his hair. "Thanks for your help today. I couldn't have made that jump without you."

"I'm sorry, what jump?" Edam asks.

I ruffle his hair with the arm on my good side. "See that tree?" I point. "See how the limbs on the right side are totally ruined?"

Edam follows my fingers and takes in the devastation of the huge old tree. "You did that?"

"With my own body," I say. "But don't worry. It'll survive, and so will I."

"You did more than survive," Moses says. "You did very well today. Mom would have been proud."

We killed an Empress and her heir, and I'm terribly afraid he's right.

"I'm not sure the people here will accept a male interim leader," Moses says.

"You trusted that I trusted Noah," I say.

Moses frowns. "And he saved you."

"I trust you, too," I say. "Tell the people that I'll be back within a week to introduce myself and do a presentation, but that for now, my *brother* is more than capable of acting as my Regent."

❧ 29 ❧

I take a miserably cold shower in San Marino before boarding the plane home. I was so bloody after that heart-splitting dagger that I needed something, and since I knocked out the entire power grid, none of the water heaters are working. Reap what you sow and all that. But my side still isn't healing. Now that I'm clean, I can see the wound. It's six or seven inches long, and the edges are black, the skin almost necrotic.

"You need to bandage that," Edam says.

I drop my shirt like it burned me.

"It's going to keep bleeding."

I nod tightly, and allow him to do it for me. His hands are light, but sure, as he presses gauze against the wound, and surrounds it with white first-aid tape.

"How do you know what you're doing?" I ask. "It's not like you've ever bandaged anyone before."

Edam shrugs. "It's pretty intuitive. All we need to do is keep your clothing clean until Job can figure out how to remove the toxin so your side can heal."

I hope he's right.

"Are you going to put it on?" Edam asks.

"Put what on?" I pretend I don't know what he's asking.

"A lot of people died to secure that ring," he says.

I pull it out of my pocket and study it for the millionth time. The staridium is smaller than Mom's stone by half. It's just as black as Mom's gets when I'm not wearing it.

"Would you care to give it a try?" I ask.

Edam frowns. "Don't tempt me."

"You're seventh generation, same as me." I extend it toward him, carefully holding only the metal so that the stone doesn't touch my skin.

"You're afraid of it."

"Maybe," I admit. "When I tried on Mom's, the whole world imploded."

"Also, you knocked out the entire island's power." Edam shakes his head. "Maybe neither of us should put it on while we're twenty-thousand feet in the air."

"Good call." I wrap it up in the tissue again and slip it back into my pocket.

"I think Moses will handle things really well," Edam says. "And I believe he's totally loyal to you. But do you really think we need to pick any more fights?"

"What does that mean?" I ask.

"Evians have been ruled exclusively by women for six thousand years," Edam says. "And Moses left Shenoah a few days ago after being driven away by Adika herself."

"I'm going to start in the way I mean to continue." And I realize that I mean it. I issued a proclamation telling the world I was the Queen of Queens, but I didn't explain what that meant. It's time they know what they're signing on for, and if that causes Analessa and Melisania to change their minds, so be it.

I pull out a piece of paper and start to write.

1. Royal children will meet and choose their own spouses. No more sales of sons.

2. Females will no longer be preferred. Equality between males and females will be written into all laws. My youngest child will rule in my place, whether it's male or female. This goes for humans, too. No more suppression of women in human communities.

3. Humans have value and will not be mistreated by evians. A bill of rights will be created and enforced for all subjects, evian or not. This includes half-humans, too. Half-evians will not be banished, and remaining with your family is no longer treason.

4. All citizens shall participate in the search for the Garden of Eden. It's the only way, per the prophecy, to save the world, and I intend to do it.

I look up at Edam. "What am I missing?"

He laughs. "You never do things halfway."

"People need to know what I stand for. Adika thought my attack was a power grab, but I need to make sure it's not. I have things to fix, and it's time to fix them. No more waiting."

Edam and I discuss the variants of the evian law on the way home, crafting ways to modify them that will keep our people secure but right the worst wrongs. Noah sits behind me the entire way without making a single comment, snide or otherwise. Just before we land, I decide to kick the anthill.

"Why so quiet back there?" I ask. "What do you think about all of this?"

"I'm proud of you," Noah says. "You were unsure before, confused. You didn't know what was right or wrong, but somehow that win galvanized you. You're going to need that energy in the days that are coming, I think."

Edam scowls. "What does that mean?"

"It means you should enjoy this moment, and prepare for the future."

"Lenora is nearly on board," Edam says. "Malessa already is. We just took out the sixth family. Unless I'm messing up the math here, only Adora and Shamecha are opposing us. Things couldn't be better."

"You're good at math alright." Noah nods. "If this were simply about securing the six evian rings, or even merely about ruling the world, you'd be in great shape."

I wish I knew everything, but I'm not going to fret about it. Not now. I'll talk to Melina when I get home, and then I'll press Alora. Between the two of them, and Noah touching his nose and nudging me in the right direction, I'll figure this out. "I'm glad you approve of my plans."

"What?" Noah asks. "No complaining about how I won't tell you what's coming?"

"Arguing with someone who can't tell me anything is pointless." My new Zen attitude notwithstanding, a wave of exhaustion rolls over me as we prepare to land. I wish I'd slept a little more and talked a little less. "After I'm done talking to Melina, I'll go back to haranguing you."

"I can always break his kneecaps," Edam says. "Or shove bamboo shoots under his fingernails. He may be evian, but I'm confident I can break him."

I shake my head. "Funny."

When I land, I turn my phone back on. I shouldn't have turned it off for the flight, but my side is burning and my eyes are heavy, and I didn't want to deal with anything else. Just for a few hours, I wanted some peace. It bings with lots of messages the second it reconnects. I start scrolling through them. Analessa tells me not to worry about stealing her plane for a second and congratulates me on taking Shenoah. She hasn't offered to manage it for me yet, but I'm sure that's coming. Judica sends four texts, which for her is essentially blowing up my phone, telling me she's happy I'm alive.

Balthasar's jet is behind ours but should be landing soon, and Judica's will arrive within an hour of that. I'll breathe a hearty sigh of relief when my entire Council has made it home safely.

"Ready to try on that ring yet?" Noah asks the second my feet touch the ground.

I promised to head straight for Melina, but a few minutes won't make a difference, I suppose. Inara, Alora, and Larena are waiting to greet me at the edge of the runway.

"You did it," Alora says.

I force myself to smile at her. I'll save my interrogation for a more private place.

"You scared me," Inara says. "When those feeds went black, yours did too." She touches her throat.

"I'm sorry to stress you out," I say. "But. Maybe you'll forgive me when I show you what I brought home." I pull the second stone carefully from my pocket.

"What does it do?" Inara asks, her eyes eager.

I shake my head. "I haven't checked yet."

Alora's eyes widen. "I'd love to watch when you do."

"I second that," Gregory says. "Because watching as she knocked out the power grid in most of the Western side of Italy was one of the high points of my life."

"That has been all over the news," Inara says. "And five of their air craft went down, too."

Which means there were more fighters after me than I even saw.

"A Typhoon, a Reaper, and three Leonardos," Marselle says from behind me. "If the early reports are to be believed."

Frederick and Arlington jog along behind her.

"I saw the Reaper and the Typhoon near Florence," I say. "And I can confirm that I took out a Leonardo near San Marino. I didn't see any others, but that doesn't mean they didn't get hit."

I feel a little bad about that, if they weren't tasked on me. Collateral damage? Ugh.

Marselle bites her lip and her eyes sparkle with excitement. "Did you manage it without knocking out your own aircraft?"

"My jumper plane?" I ask. "Correct, I set off the EMP beyond it. I'm learning."

"You are," Inara says. "Mother would be quite proud."

"I'm going to jog a few hundred yards from here," I say, "so that nothing happens this close to the compound or the planes. Then I'll try on the new ring."

"I'll come," Edam and Noah say.

"Me too," Alora and Inara say.

"You're all welcome," I say, "but I have no idea how this might go down, so brace yourselves. Last time was an EMP and a fireball."

"At least you're prepared," Inara says.

"Not really," I say. "I mean, how can you prepare for something completely unpredictable?"

I take off at a jog, happy to be home, but a few steps in, my side starts screaming at me. I wish it would just heal, already. I gulp in huge breaths of Hawaiian air, my lungs finally expanding fully for the first time since I left. I run further than I intended, mostly because it feels good to stretch my legs. It's encouraging that the rest of my body seems to work fine, even if my side won't heal.

I'm home, surrounded by family, and about to do something monumental. Life is good.

This time, I won't blow anything up, or set anything on fire. This time, no one I love desperately will die. I finally stop near the crest of the ridge overlooking the north-eastern shore. The wind blows over my face, soothing me, calming my anxiety. Inara, Alora, Noah, Edam, Marselle, Frederick, Arlington, and Gregory stop behind me, a dozen or so paces away. I pull the ring from my pocket and unwrap it slowly.

I hold it up so they can all see it. Mom's ring flashes brightly on my right hand. Edam jokingly called this my engagement ring, so why not? I slide it onto the ring finger of my left hand.

Just like last time, nothing happens. It sits inert, lifeless. A smaller lump of black similar to the large one Mom left me.

But then I feel it. The trickle I couldn't feel before, the sensation I didn't recognize that first time. Only now I know what to expect. My hands shake. It's not filling the same bucket as Mom's ring. It's a new hole in my head, a new well. It's not larger or smaller, it's just *different*.

"I feel it," I say softly. "It's there."

"The stone is black," Inara says.

"Give me a minute," I say. But when the bucket fills, it simply stops. No explosion like last time. No fireballs or EMPs. It's simply full.

And the Shenoah ring finally begins to flash. Light from Mom's flashes almost routinely, like a light house. But Shenoah's stone pulses more erratically. It speeds up and then it slows down, but I can't quite figure out why.

"Did it do anything? Can you do anything with it?" Edam asks.

"There's power there," I say, still watching the play of light. I hold up the ring and show it to them and the flashes slow down. "But I'm a little worried about using it."

"Try it," Alora says. "We're all dying to know what it might do."

I lower my hand and the pulses accelerate again. I lift it up again, and it slows. I lower it, and it accelerates. I crouch down on the ground, lowering the ring as much as I can, both my hands next to one another, resting on beautiful Hawaiian earth. The Shenoah ring pulses frantically.

I realize it's not the height that's making it pulse more quickly. It's the proximity to Mom's ring. The Shenoah ring. . . likes Mom's stone.

Oh, if only Mom were here to tell me that my conclusion is ridiculous.

It's time to see what it can do. I stand back up and dip my mind into Mom's ring's bucket, and pull out some energy. I turn toward the ocean and fire off a small ball of molten energy. It smashes into the ocean and creates a plume of steam.

"It makes fireballs?" Noah asks. "Same as your mother's?"

I shake my head. "No, that was Mom's. I thought I'd make sure it still works."

"Okay," Frederick says. "Looks like it does. Now try the new one."

"Look," I say. "I know you're all impatient, but I'm not going to do this wrong, not this time."

I think about my friends and supporters. They're trying to help, like always, but they are pushing me on this and they don't understand it. Their impatience is kind of pissing me off. I shouldn't do this mad, so I focus on the ocean waves. Whatever else happens, I don't want to hurt anyone. In fact, I sort of wish they hadn't come. They're making me way more nervous.

Mom was the only person to witness this last time, and she's dead.

I shake my head. That won't happen again. It won't. I won't let it. I dip my mind into the new well of power and lift my hands. Energy flies away from me without control, without form, without shape.

Nothing happens.

Cries behind me yank my attention backward. My friends are lying on the ground dozens of yards further away than they were.

"Whoa," I say. "What happened?"

"You hurled us all backward." Edam leaps to his feet. "That's what happened. Did you mean to do that?"

I shake my head. "No."

Inara stands up and brushes off her pants. Her grin is wolfish. "Do it again, but on purpose this time."

Everyone else stands up too, looks of shock on their faces.

"Yeah, again," Noah says.

"I'd like to see you try," Arlington says.

I reach back into the well and fling more energy.

They fly even further out this time, several of them breaking bones. This is fun. And this well fills faster than the one for Mom's ring.

"We're going to need to work this into your training," Edam says. "Now that you have something practical for combat."

"Hello, fireballs," I say.

Edam shakes his head. "Too destructive of property to do much training with it. It's more of a blunt force tool. But a telekinetic pulse? That's great."

I guess so. I move my hands closer together and watch as the Shenoah stone pulses frantically. I separate them and it slows.

It's strange. I wonder what it means, until I remember that they supposedly came from one big stone. A stone that was cut from 'the mountain,' whatever that is, and then shattered by Eve. I pull the new ring off my finger and the stone dies back to black.

Noah walks toward me. "What's going on?"

"There's something weird about it," I say. "It's like. . ." I trail off, since saying the Shenoah stone is calling to Mom's stone sounds insane.

I pull out a dagger and use the sharp point to pry the stone from the ring setting.

"Whoa," Edam says. "What are you doing?"

The others converge. "Not a good idea," Alora says. "Let's not scratch or break the shiny new chunk of staridium on the first day it's ours."

I pry Mom's stone out of its setting too.

"Or, you could ignore all of us and do whatever you want, like always," Noah says.

I roll my eyes and focus on the stones. I've never studied them free of a setting. Both stones flash in my hands, Mom's erratic, the Shenoah stone with increasing frequency.

If Mom's voice wasn't mocking me in my head, I'd say it looks eager.

I slowly bring the stones closer, feeling for the roughest part on Mom's stone, the ridge that feels like the carved part of a key. I feel something on the edge of the Shenoah stone that could be the inverse.

I press the stones together, fitting those two places into one another and power explodes outward. A hundred times the size of a fireball. A million times the size of the blast I sent toward my friends. I fly backward through the air, clutching the newly joined stone in my hands tightly. My back slams into the surface of the ocean and I sink, lower, lower, lower.

The water is black, so black, and cold. Much colder than I expected it to be. I thrash in the water, thrash and thrash, not sure which way is up. I choke on water and nearly drop the stone, but I don't. Finally my mind clears enough to look for bubbles. There's almost no light, but when I blow bubbles with the last of my breath, I see them, faintly. I follow them up, my arms and legs stiff, but still thrashing. When I finally surface, I gasp and splutter, working to refill my lungs with the oxygen they need.

What happened to everyone else? I look around, frantic. The shore is hundreds of yards away. I'm lucky I was thrown toward water. What about anyone tossed against something less forgiving? I shake my head to clear the gruesome images that form unbidden. I have no idea where my dagger went, but my swords are still lashed to my back. I hope the dagger didn't impale anyone when we were thrown.

I focus on the task ahead, swimming to shore. I knot the stone into my shirt and then knot it again. Then I set to swimming, checking every few strokes to make sure it's still there.

I finally reach the shore and crawl out of the surf and on to the sand.

No one is anywhere in sight. I untie the stone and slide it into my pocket. Then I run, barefoot, back toward the palace, my sense of unease increasing with every step. What made me combine the stones? I'm an idiot.

I just hope my stupidity didn't kill any of my friends.

❧ 30 ❧

I'm met by a half dozen frantic Motherless a few hundred yards from the palace. It feels like someone ran a hot poker down my side. With every step more rocks replace the powdery sand, their jagged edges tearing my bare feet.

"Your Majesty," Ibrahim calls.

"Have you heard from Alora or Inara?" I ask. "Noah or Edam? What about Frederick or Marselle?"

Balthasar races past Ibrahim and envelops me in a hug. "You're alright."

"I'm fine," I say.

"We were so worried," he says.

"How did you even know—"

Balthasar points at where I was standing on the ridge a few moments ago. I couldn't see it before, thanks to the tree line, but now it's in plain view.

The entire side of the cliff is missing. Presumably the blast sheared it off. My eyes track downward where there's a colossal pile of rubble on the beach below that stretches out into the waves. I swam to shore just around the corner from all of it. If I hadn't been thrown clear, I could be buried under hundreds of tons of rock. My heart accelerates. "The others?"

"We haven't found Noah yet," Balthasar says. "Frederick, Marselle, Alora, and Inara were blown back, but they're alright. Edam and Gregory are being checked by Job, but we believe they'll be fine. Edam wanted to rush off to look for you, and he's not very pleased that Job didn't allow it."

"You could at least try to say that without smiling," I say.

"It wouldn't be funny except that you're okay." He pauses and then lowers his voice. "I hear you joined the stones." Balthasar looks down at my hand. His eyes widen when he realizes my fingers are bare. "Did—" He clears his throat. "Are they lost?"

It's not like I could have had the joined stones set into jewelry already. He's obviously not thinking. "I did join them, and I didn't lose them. Or I guess I should say 'it' at this point." I pull the large, black rock from my pocket. It brightens when I hold it, light rising from its depths, just as it did from Mom's stone before. The pulses are erratic, but more regular than the Shenoah stone. As I take a closer look, I realize I can't even see where the two stones were previously separated. "It healed, like an evian."

Balthasar reaches for it and then pulls back. "It's miraculous."

I nod. "I'll feel better once we've recovered Noah."

"I'll send the men out to sweep the beach," he says. "Immediately. There are already crews shifting the rubble." Balthasar exhales loudly. "I'm relieved you're not underneath."

"I need a shower," I say. "And a meal." And I really hope Noah, or whoever he is, isn't buried under a load of rock.

Balthasar frowns. "There's something a little more pressing, I'm afraid."

My stomach sinks at his words. I'm standing barefoot, in ragged, salty pants. My hair is stringy around my face, and I'm exhausted deep down in my bones. Something is so pressing, other than Noah being missing, that I can't shower and eat. "What's wrong? Just tell me."

"I think you should see it for yourself."

I gulp and follow him at a hobbling jog. We don't go far. The housing I selected for Melina is around the bend, and Balthasar slows to a brisk walk when it comes into view. My stomach lurches. It can't be Melina. Oh, what if Judica killed her? Or what if she killed Judica? I should never have brought her back. I'm as stupid as Adika said. "What happened?" I ask. "Just give me the broad strokes."

"We aren't sure." Balthasar stops in front of the door to her five-bedroom cottage. He turns to face Ibrahim and Voron. "Wait outside." He inhales deeply and then exhales, and then he opens the door and steps through.

I follow him, closing the door behind me. Bodies cover the floor, and heads, but they're all separate from one another. I want to run and hide. I want to pretend I never stepped into this cottage, but I force myself to look. I count heads. I walk from room to room, checking in every corner. Twenty-four people dead, all of them Melina's people, including her brother-in-law. At least I don't see her wife. I close my eyes and shake my head. "Melina?"

"She's gone," Balthasar says. "I don't know where or when or how she could have left. There's no record of any of our planes or helicopters leaving."

"Could she have left by boat?"

"Or she left on something we don't have a record of. There's been a lot of chaos."

Understatement of the year. "How long have they been

dead?" I hope my experimentation with the stupid rocks didn't provide the perfect cover for this massacre. What if it's somehow my fault that this happened? Did my bringing them here cause it? Or would this have happened no matter where Melina had been?

Balthasar shrugs. "Job has been so busy with your explosion, he doesn't even know about this yet. Only you, Remington, and I have even seen it."

I lean against the wall and close my eyes. "Pull the security feed. Before you talk to anyone else, I want to see what it shows. Actually, I'll follow you to the control center. I want to see it now, before anyone can tamper with it."

"The only camera we have on this cottage shows a view of the front porch," Balthasar says.

"We'll see what we see," I say.

We don't speak on the way back, but I can't help feeling like it's my fault—somehow my reaction to the stones caused this. Every single time I touch a new one, the bottom falls out of my world. I touch the first, and my mom dies. I reunite them and Melina's people all die and she disappears. Certainly not a good sign.

I try not to think about the fact that Noah's missing.

An hour ago I was on top of the world. I want to run to my room and lock the door. I want to cry in my shower for a week. I want to run away and never think about any of this again. When my breathing grows ragged, a predecessor to tears, my side screams at me. Somehow, the pain feels fitting, like it's what I deserve. A reminder of how stupid and young I am.

But I'm not the girl who lost her mother two weeks ago. I'm not the child who runs and hides when things overwhelm her. I'm not what Adika called me. I am Chancery Divinity Alamecha, ruler of Alamecha and Shenoah, and daughter of Enora. I walk with my head high through the halls of my palace. I follow Balthasar's broad shoulders to the main security office.

"I'm sure you've seen things much stranger than this," I say. "In the past nine centuries."

He pauses over the keyboard and looks up at me. "Actually, sweetheart, I've never seen anything like that."

Oh.

"It's like they didn't even fight back. I have no idea how or why, but it looks like those trained evian warriors stood still while someone killed them, one-by-one."

"It probably took a huge force—"

"They would have been congregated by the door," Balthasar says, "if it had been a large group of attackers. Or the fallen would have defensive wounds that didn't heal after their heads were removed." He inhales deeply. "Those decapitations were all done at the same angle, and I bet Job tells you they were all done by the same blade."

One person? He thinks one person killed twenty-four evians?

I feel sick thinking it, but is it a coincidence that Noah's missing? Could this literally be my fault? Could I have brought the homicidal warrior who killed them all to the island? He can do other things no one understands, that no one can replicate. Is it such a stretch to think he could be capable of worse?

But the timeline is impossible. He was blown to kingdom come the exact time as me, and there's no way he could have made it to Melina's cottage in time to do this. He was with me until moments before. It couldn't have been Noah. Relief washes over me, followed by guilt that I'm more worried about Noah's innocence than the truth.

"Let's see the feed," I say.

Balthasar presses one more button and a video pops up. He fast forwards and I lean closer by the second, watching an empty front porch. Finally, an hour and two minutes ago according to the time stamp, a cloaked figure approaches. I can't tell whether it's a man or a woman.

Melina answers the door herself, and I'd bet my crown that she knows the hooded figure. Her face relaxes and she smiles. "I was wondering if you'd come," she says. The words are faint, but combined with the movement of her lips, I understand. She opens the door and the hooded figure enters.

Time is a funny thing. It's one of the few constants in life, and yet it feels inconsistent, more so than any other measuring tool. Seconds pass, rolling over on the clock one at a time, and finally, after three minutes and forty-six seconds have elapsed with the door closed, it opens again.

The hooded figure has pulled the cloak further down over his or her face and is dragging Melina along behind. She grabs at the doorframe and then the railing, but the hooded figure pulls her inexorably forward.

"Stop," Melina sobs. "Stop. Why? Why would you do that?"

"I had no choice," the figure growls. "My hand was forced from the first day. It had to happen, and this does too, so stop struggling."

"You're Nereus," Melina says. "You must be. Which means *you* killed her."

The hooded figure snarls and slams Melina against the doorframe and then shoots the camera. The feed goes blank.

I swear. Then I swear again. Nothing I say will bring Melina back. Nothing I say will clean up the digital feed, or shine a floodlight on the person who massacred an entire room of evians and stole my sister before I could even get to know her.

But I will find this Nereus. I will. I'll bring Nereus to justice if it's the last thing I do.

❧

Grab Melina's story, misUnderstood. And the next volume in Chancery's epic journey, Disavowed, releases May 15, 2020.

Also, read on for a sneak peek at Marked, book one of my other YA series, available now in Kindle Unlimited. That entire series is complete, so you won't have to wait for the next.

Finally, if you'd like a free full length novel, you can grab Already Gone, a romantic suspense I wrote for FREE if you join my newsletter at www.BridgetEBakerWrites.com.

APPENDIX: THE SIX FAMILIES

1. ALAMECHA: United States of America, England, Ireland, Scotland, Canada, Cuba, Puerto Rico
    Eve
    Mahalesh 3226 BC
    Alamecha 2312 BC
    Meridalina 1446 BC
    Corlamecha 553 BC
    Cainina 273 AD
    Enora 1120 AD
    Chancery 2002 AD
    H. Judica 2002 AD

2. MALESSA: Germany, France, Netherlands, Switzerland, Norway, Sweden, Finland, Australia, New Zealand, Papau New Guinea, Iceland
    Eve
    Mahalesh 3226 BC
    Malessa 2353 BC
    Adorna 1451 BC
    Selah 618 BC

Lenamecha 211 AD
Senah 1022 AD (Denah dead twin)
Analessa 1820 AD
H. DeLannia 1942

3. LENORA: All of South America (including Chile, Argentina, Brazil), Mexico, Spain, Portugal
Eve
Mahalesh 3226 BC
Lenora 2365 BC
Ablinina 1453 BC
Leddite 652 BC
Selamecha 379 BC
Priena 460 AD
Leamarta 1198 AD
Melisania 1897 AD
H. Marde 1987

4. ADORA: India, Japan, Korea, Indonesia, Thailand
Eve
Mahalesh 3226 BC
Adora 2368 BC
Manocha 1461 BC
Alela 590 BC
Radosha 192 BC
Esheth 638 AD
Lainina 1444 AD
H. Ranana 1967

5. SHAMECHA: Russia, Mongolia, Kazakhstan, Pakistan, Uzbekistan, Philippines
Eve
Mahalesh 3226 BC
Shamecha 2472 BC

Madalena 1639 BC
Shenoa 968 BC
Abalorna 299 BC
Venoah 333 AD
Reshaka 936 AD
Melamecha 1509 AD
H. Venagra 2000

6. SHENOAH: Continent of Africa, Saudi Arabia, Iran, Iraq, Turkey, Greece, Italy, Jordan, Afghanistan
Eve
Shenoah 3227 BC
Adelornamecha 2385 BC
Kankera 1544 BC
Avina 670 BC
Sela 467 BC
Jericha 135 AD
Sethora 399 AD
Malimba 708 AD
Adika 1507 AD
H. Vela 1990

❧ 31 ❧

BONUS CHAPTER: MARKED

I'm a big fat coward.

I've known this about myself definitively since one month before my sixth birthday. The night I lost my dad.

Case in point: I'm just shy of seventeen. I've been in love with the same guy for almost three years. Even though I see Wesley a few times a week, I haven't said a word. But tonight I have the perfect opportunity to do what I've always feared to try. Tonight, to celebrate our upcoming Path selections, all the teens in Port Gibson play a stupid, risky game.

Spin the Bottle.

I glance around as I walk toward the campfire in front of me. Only thirty-five kids turned seventeen in the past year, so of course I know them all. My best girl friend, Gemette, waves me over. I try to squash my disappointment at not seeing Wesley. When I played this scene in my brain earlier, I was sitting by him.

"You gonna scowl at the fire all night, Ruby?" Gemette pats a gloved hand on the slab of granite underneath her.

"You couldn't have saved us one of those seats?" I point at the smooth, flat stumps on the other side of the fire. I sit down and shift around, trying to find a flat spot.

"I think what you meant to say was, 'Thanks, Gemette. You're the best.'"

Her straight black hair reflects the campfire flames when she tosses it back over her shoulder. It's against the Council's rules for hair to cover your forehead. Gotta make it easy to see anyone who might be Marked. Except tonight, no one's following the rules. Everyone's wearing their hair down, and Gemette's silky locks frame her face beautifully. I envy her sleek hair almost as much as I covet her curves.

"My bum's already hurting on this," I mutter.

"If you weighed more than eighty-five pounds soaking wet, it wouldn't bother you so much."

Instead of curves, I've got twig arms and a non-existent backside. I shift on the huge slab, trying to find a position that doesn't hurt. I arch one eyebrow, not that she can see it in the dark. "I weigh ninety-two pounds, thank you very much."

Gemette snorts. "That proves my point, you bony butt."

She leans toward the fire and picks up the glass bottle lying on its side. She tosses it a few inches up into the air before catching it again.

"Be careful with that." That bottle's the only reason I'm sitting here, sour-faced, stomach churning.

Slowly the remaining seats around the fire fill up. Wesley shows up last. There aren't any seats left, but before I can convince Gemette to squish over, he grabs a bucket. He turns it upside down and takes a seat a few feet away from everyone else. I guess that's fitting. His dad's the Mayor of Port Gibson and a Counsellor on the CentiCouncil, so Wesley's in charge by default tonight. He'll probably take over for his dad one day, which isn't as glamorous as it sounds since less than two thousand people live here.

He looks around the fire, and his gaze stops on me. He bobs his head in my direction, and I shoot him a smile. I'm glad he can't hear the thundering of my heart.

Although we're all huddled around a campfire, and I've known most of the kids here for years, we maintain carefully measured space between us. Tercera dictates our habits even when we're rebelling. Which we're only doing because it's a tradition.

Maybe Tercera's made cowards of us all.

"Are we starting?" Tom's sitting to my left. His parents are both in Agriculture and he's Pathing there, too. He has broad shoulders and tan skin from working outside most of the day. Gemette likes him, and it's easy to see why. Of course, he's nothing to Wesley.

I glance across the fire in time to see Wesley stand up. He straightens the collar of his coat slowly and methodically, like his dad always does before a town hall meeting. Wesley loves doing impressions, and he's usually convincingly good at them.

"I'd like to take this opportunity to welcome you all to the Last Supper." His voice mimics his father's, and he touches his chin with his right hand in the same way his dad always rubs his beard. Wesley himself is tall and lean with long black hair that he's wearing down, for once. It falls in his eyes in a way I've never seen before, and I feel a little rush. I want to touch it.

Wesley smirks. "I know you may be less than impressed with the culinary offerings for our gathering, but as I always say, Tradition has Value." He cracks a grin then, and everyone laughs. "Seriously though." He drops the impression and returns to his normal voice, which I like way better anyway. "I know the food sucks, but this whole thing started with a bunch of teenagers who were sick of rules and ready to throw caution to the wind for a night."

I look down at the three or four-dozen nondescript metal cans with the tops peeled back, resting on coals. Another few dozen are open but sitting away from the fire. Presumably they contain fruit or something else we won't want to eat hot.

Wesley leans over and snags the first can, his gloves keeping him safe from the heat. "I hope you'll all forgive me, but this was what we could find."

"This is a pretty crummy tradition." Lina reaches down and grabs a can with mittened hands. Her dark brown hair falls in a long, thick braid down her back, like it has every single time I've seen her.

"Traditions matter, even the silly ones. They help pull us together as a community, which is valuable when fear of Tercera yanks communities apart. We're stronger when we aren't alone. Thinking every man should look out for himself hurts all of us." Wesley takes his first bite right before Lina. I grab a can of baked beans.

The food really is as bad as it looks, but at least it's not spoiled.

Wesley talks while we eat.

"As you already know, we come from a variety of backgrounds. Before the Marking, Port Gibson housed approximately the same number of people, but not a single person who lived here before the Marking survived. We cleaned out the homes, burned some to the ground and rebuilt, circled the city with a wall, and made it our own. The Unmarked who live here are Christian, Muslim, atheist, black, white, Hispanic, Russian, German and Japanese. I could keep going, but I don't need to. Before the Marking, these differences divided humanity. Now, we know that what truly matters is what we all share. We embrace the traditions that bring us all together, because we're more alike than we are unalike."

I swallow the last spoonful of baked beans from my can and set it down on the ground by my feet. I'm almost the last one to finish eating, but several half-full cans are scattered around the campfire. A few people grab a can of fruit. I prefer the stuff my Aunt and I process and can ourselves, so I don't bother.

I rub my hands together briskly. Even in mittens, my fingers feel stiff. It's usually not too cold in Mississippi, even in January, but a late freeze has everyone bundled up. The Last Supper's supposed to be a chance to rebel, but I'm grateful that everyone's as covered as possible. It means I won't look as cowardly for keeping my mittens on. My aunt is Port Gibson's head of the Science Path, so I know all about how Tercera congregates first in the skin cells, even before the Mark has shown up on the forehead in some cases.

The wind moans as it blows through the trees, and we all huddle around the meager fire. Even though the flames have died down to coals in most places, it burns hot. My face roasts while my back freezes. The bottle lies stationary on the weathered flagstones by the fire where Gemette set it, light glinting off of the dingy glass at strange angles.

The quiet conversations die off and the nervous laughter ends. Eyes dart to and fro among the thirty something teenagers gathered.

"So." Evan's voice cracks, and he clears his throat. "Who goes first?"

"Thanks for volunteering," Wesley says.

I suspect no one else asked for just this reason. All eyes turn toward poor, gangly, redheaded Evan.

Evan gawks momentarily. Even though he and I work in Sanitation together, I don't know him well. I haven't been there long enough to guess whether he feels lucky or put upon. He sighs, and then leans forward and tweaks the bottle. It twists sharp and fast and skitters to the right, spinning furiously.

I really hope the bottle doesn't stop on me, and I doubt I'm alone in that thought. Evan's funny in a self-deprecating way, but he isn't smart, and he definitely isn't hot. I bite my lip, worried about what I'll do if it does stop on me.

It slows quickly and finally stops pointing to my left. I sigh in relief, which I belatedly hope no one heard.

Tom gasps, and then in a raspy voice says, "No way. I mean, you're nice and all Evan, but I'm not . . . I don't . . ."

"Yeah, me either. Chill, man." Evan laughs. "So, does it pass to the next person over?" Evan raises his eyebrows and glances at me.

I want to protest, but my throat closes off and I look down at my feet instead.

Evan stands up. "So Ruby . . ."

He may not have saved me a seat, but Wesley jumps in to save me now, thank goodness. "That's not how it works. If you get someone of the same gender, and neither of you . . . well, then your turn passes to him or her. Which means you sit down Evan, and you spin next, Tom."

"Who made these rules?" Evan grumbles as he sits.

Gemette smiles. "They make sense, Evan. I mean, it's not spin the bottle and pick best out of three. Your way, you'd basically pick someone in the circle who's close and kiss whoever you want."

Evan shrugs and glances at me again with a smile. "Sounds pretty okay, actually."

Tom snorts. "I don't hear Ruby complaining about Wesley's rules. I'd say that's your answer, man."

I look back down at my shoes, but not before I see Tom's wink. Jerk. Evan must feel idiotic, and I definitely want to sink into the ground.

I bite my lip again, this time a little harder. Tom's an obviously good-looking guy, but I have no interest in kissing him. I hope his wink was a joke about Evan and not some kind of message.

Cold air blows past me as Tom leans forward to spin the bottle, his body no longer blocking the wind. One thing jumps out at me as he reaches for the glass bottle. In spite of the cold, Tom isn't wearing gloves. He must've taken them off at some point. He's either a daredevil or an idiot. I'm not sure which.

Tom spins the bottle less forcefully than Evan and rocks back and forth as the bottle circles round and round. His eyes focus intently on the spinning glass as if he can somehow control where it stops. I wonder who he's hoping for and look around the circle for clues. Andrea seems particularly bright-eyed. My eyes continue to wander. One gorgeous, deep blue pair of eyes in the circle stares right back at me. Wesley. I've looked at him a lot over the past few years, but this feels different somehow. A spark zooms through me, and I quickly stare at my feet.

No luck for Andrea tonight, or Gemette. The bottle comes to rest on Andrea's best friend, Annelise, instead. She and I were in Science together a long time ago. Her dark brown hair hangs loose, framing high cheekbones and expressive chocolate eyes. She frowns. Tonight doesn't seem to be going right for anyone so far.

"Now what?" Annelise's voice shakes. "We just kiss, right here in front of everyone?"

"No, of course not," Gemette snaps.

"Who made you the boss?" Evan frowns. Judging by his sulky tone, he's still mad about losing his turn earlier.

"Unfortunately, I'm the boss," Wesley says, "and she's right." He points to a dilapidated shed at the top of the hill. "You two go up there."

"Romantic." Tom rolls his eyes as he stands up. He rubs his bare palms on his pants. Gross. At least I know I'm not the only nervous one here. Tom and Annelise trudge a path through clumps of frozen brown grass toward the rundown tool shed.

What a special memory for their first kiss.

Gemette sighs and I pat her gloved hand with my own. I'd feel worse for her, but Gemette likes every decent looking guy in town, including a few boys a year younger than us. She'll recover from missing out on a special moment with Tom.

I glance again toward Andrea, an acquaintance from my time in Agriculture. She and Tom trained together for years. She may have liked him as long as I've liked Wesley. She looks into the fire while her foot digs a messy hole in the soil. I wonder how I'll feel if Wesley spins and gets Andrea. Or worse, Gemette. I'll have to sit here and twiddle my thumbs while I know he's in there kissing a friend. My stomach lurches. Coming tonight was a stupid idea. I clearly didn't think this through.

No one speaks to distract me from my anxiety. The shed isn't far. We could easily eavesdrop on them if the wind would shriek a little less.

"How long does this take?" Evan asks.

"Who the heck knows?" Gemette points at the bottle. "Impatient for another crack at it?"

Kids around us chuckle.

After another few awkward moments, Gemette grabs

the bottle and gives it a twist. "No reason we have to wait on them."

"Sure," Wesley says. "Whoever it lands on can go next."

"Wait," Evan asks, "whoever it lands on goes next as in it's their turn to spin? Or goes next as in Gemette's going to kiss them?"

The bottle stops before anyone can respond, pointing directly at Wesley. His perfectly shaped brows draw together under disheveled black hair. Gorgeous hair. His lips form a perfect "o". His bright blue eyes meet mine again.

My heart races and the baked beans sit like a lump in my belly. I shouldn't have come. Of course Wesley will want to kiss her. Gemette's gorgeous, curvy, and smart. Ugh. Am I going to have to sit here while my best friend kisses the guy I like twenty feet away? This is all my fault. If I'd only told Gemette, she'd beg off.

I bite down a little harder on my lip and taste blood this time. I really need to kick this particular habit, especially with kissing in my future. Maybe. Hopefully. I'm such an idiot.

Wesley clears his throat. "I think I'm going to sit this game out. I'm more of a moderator than a participant."

"No," I blurt out. "You can't. You're here, you're seventeen, you have to participate." What am I doing? Why am I shoving him at my friend? But if I don't make him play, I'm flushing my chance to kiss him down the toilet. I want to cry.

"Well, then I guess it's my turn to spin." His deep voice sounds completely different than any of the other kids here tonight. My stomach ties in knots when I hear him speak, which is ridiculous because I've heard his voice a million times.

I glance at Gemette. She looks disappointed and I want

to cry with relief, but I don't blame her. He could've kissed her but didn't pursue it. I imagine most any girl here would be disappointed. He glances up and his eyes lock with mine again. Caught. I start to shiver and try to stop it. This look is different somehow from any before, like something shifted. Wesley clears his throat, looks down at the bottle, gracefully reaches over, and snaps it between his fingers.

It spins evenly, not moving to the right or the left. It spins on and on, and I wonder if it'll ever stop. It slows, whirling a little less with each rotation, the butterflies in my stomach swooping and swirling with each pass.

Until it finally stops. On me.

My eyes snap up reflexively, wide with shock. Wesley doesn't even seem surprised. He simply stands and inclines his head toward the shed.

"Isn't it still..." I clear my throat. "Umm, occupied?"

"We can wait over there." He gestures at the hill to the right of the shed. One side of his mouth lifts in a smile and I feel an answering grin form on my lips. Which makes me think about what we're about to do with our lips.

Swarms and swarms of butterflies flutter in my chest.

"Sure," I say.

I stand up and without even thinking, I wipe my palms on my jeans. They aren't even sweaty and what's more, I'm wearing mittens! I really hope no one noticed. Okay, more specifically, I hope Wesley didn't notice. Gemette holds something out to me when I stand. I can't tell what it is from feel alone thanks to my thick mittens, and in the dark I have to squint to make it out at all. A tube of something. "What—"

"Lip gloss," she whispers. "A gift from my mom. I was going to use it, but looks like you need it more, you lucky, lip-biting brat." She winks.

I'm glad Wesley's still across the fire from me and that

it's dark. Maybe he somehow miraculously missed both the palm wipe and her wink.

I walk as slowly as I can toward the old shed, partially to avoid tripping, but also so I won't look overeager. I try to hide my face while I apply the fruit-scented lip-gloss so that Wesley won't notice. It's dark, but I don't want him to be put off by dry, scratchy lips, or worse, dried blood. Gemette's a good friend. I feel guilty for overreacting earlier when I thought she might kiss Wesley. Not super guilty, but you know, a little.

Neither of us speaks a word, but I feel the eyes of the other teens follow us toward the shed. We're only a few crunching steps away when the swinging door flies open and Tom and Annelise barrel out. I jump when it bangs shut behind them.

Tom looks as ruffled as I feel, his eyes darting back and forth. He ducks his head and reaches down to take Annelise's hand. They walk out and away from the fire and the rest of Port Gibson's teens. I can't tell where they're headed, but somewhere far away from here.

"Did you know almost a third of the couples in town trace their start to the Last Supper?" Wesley asks.

"No way."

He shrugs. "We've only been an Unmarked town for seven years, so it's even more impressive. Not all of them are matched up from a bottle spin, but I think the game helps people realize how they feel."

A thrill rushes through me. Does Wesley feel the same as me?

My hand reaches for the door handle and collides en route with his. I'm wearing mittens, of course, and he's wearing shiny, brown gloves, but a thrill runs through me when we touch, even through layers. He doesn't move his hand away, but instead draws my hand in his and pushes the door handle back in one fluid movement. My heart skips a beat and time stops. When the door's completely open, he slowly releases my hand. I lower my eyes and step over the threshold into the rundown little building.

Although there's clearly no power, and consequently neither heat nor an overhead light, the walls at least cut the wind. It's at once both warmer and quieter. Two tall candles burn softly on a pile of rusted metal boxes in the corner. Someone prepared this dump, I realize. I wonder whether it was Wesley. The flames provide enough light that I can see his face. His dark brows are an even more startling contrast to his dark blue eyes than usual, accentuated by his hair falling in his face.

"So," I say. "Here we are."

Wesley looks at me from less than a foot away. The shed's small and crammed full of moldering farm implements. The air around us practically hums, but that isn't new. It's always like the moments right before a lightning storm when he's near. Supercharged almost, like the electrons around my body might fly off at his slightest touch. The difference is that here, away from the town's work projects, away from my family and his, it feels like anything really could happen.

Wesley's so close I can smell him, the same citrusy, woodsy smell I've secretly savored for years. It's even stronger tonight, like he put on more of whatever it is he usually wears. I breathe deep, and all the memories of him re-imprint on my brain. Scrubbing, sanding, painting, digging, cleaning, hammering. Projects his dad made him attend, but I suffered through to be near him. When I'm with him, I belong somewhere for the first time in a decade.

When we become adults next week, Wesley's mandatory attendance at work projects ends. Wesley steps into his role as an administrator, and I'll become part of Port Gibson's janitorial crew. It's now or never if I want to make any kind of permanent place with Wesley.

I never thought I'd be close to him like this, and I know I may never be again. I lean toward him and tilt my face upward, eyes closed, ready for what comes next. Maybe I'm even a touch impatient. I have waited for this for years.

Except I keep waiting, and then I wait some more.

Not a single thing happens. The trouble with being ridiculously small is that Wesley, who's on the tall side anyway, towers over me. Even with my face angled up, his lips are pretty far away. I can barely make out his expression, but it looks guarded.

Maybe he doesn't know how to do it?

No way. Wesley must know. I mean, it's not hard, right? You just push your lips onto the other person's mouth. Why isn't he doing anything? This is the moment. THE moment!

Until it passes. And then another moment falls on top of it, and another. All passing. Even the butterflies in my stomach get bored and go look for flowers elsewhere.

I'm not sure exactly how much time has elapsed, but the seconds drag, heavy with my growing frustration. Soon, someone will bang on the door. "You've been in there forever," they'll say. "Make room for the next couple."

I want to smack them in their eager faces.

I know I don't have much time, and I want to say something, anything. I need to tell him how I feel, say the words, take a gamble. But like it always does, my tongue shuts down. My throat closes off. The words stick inside my throat. Why am I such a coward? Our perfect moment withers and dies. Tears well up in my eyes, and I can't breathe.

Wesley isn't similarly affected. He steps back and says,

"We don't have to do this, Ruby. It's not safe at all. I don't know why my dad even lets these dinners happen."

"Why'd you spin the bottle in the first place?" I hear the desperation in my voice, but the words pour out in spite of myself. "I know you, and you know me. How's it dangerous for us?"

He takes another step back, his expression registering surprise. "People get Marked, Ruby. It still happens. Every few weeks, in fact. Maybe I'm Marked. You don't know. It happens, even here, even with all our rules. It may take years to die once you're Marked, but it's inevitable."

I roll my eyes. "Well I'm not Marked, if that's what you're worried about." I point at my forehead. "See? Clear."

"We shouldn't be taking these risks." Wesley scowls. "Not now, not right before our real lives begin. This whole thing's supposed to be a time to say goodbye to being a kid, not act like an idiotic five-year-old, breaking rules for no reason."

Our real lives? Maybe he never thought it felt right, the time we spent, the way we are together. Maybe I never belonged with him at all. "Why'd you even come, then? Why follow me in here if you're not going to kiss me?"

Was he hoping for someone else? Was he stuck with me and looking for any excuse to bolt? Am I Evan in this scenario?

I look up, but I'm too close. The hair cascading over his face obscures my view. I want to touch his hair; I want to kiss him; I want to tell him I love him, and that I always have. My fingers and toes and everything connecting them zings in spite of the bitter cold, in spite of the indifference of his words. Energy spins round and round in my body, a closed circuit with nowhere to go.

"Look, Ruby, I don't know what to say . . . but the thing is . . ." He sounds torn, confused.

Suddenly, I don't want to hear "the thing," whatever it is. I've been talking to Wesley for years, talking and talking, and working alongside him, but I don't want to talk to him anymore. I know what I want and I'll never have a better chance to play things off as part of a game, if he feels like I now suspect he does. The notion of an excuse appeals to my cowardly heart. I can't speak the words, but I won't stand here and do nothing, not anymore, because he's the real life I've longed for.

I stop thinking and step toward him instead. He tries to step back and slams up against the back wall. I quickly take one more step and use my gloved hand to pull his head down to mine. I push my lips against his. In my haste, I push too hard and pull a little too fast. Our teeth smack into each other and my tooth knocks against my own lip, splitting it wide open again.

It's the opposite of magical.

I look up at Wesley instinctively. He has blood on his mouth, but whether it's his, or mine, I can't tell. And if it's not awful enough already, Wesley stiffens from head to toe like I mauled him, like I forced him into something torturous.

A tear rolls down my cheek and I inhale deeply. I won't cry over this. I can't, because there's no way I can play it all off as a game if I bawl my eyes out. I turn away from him. If I can't stop the tears, at least he doesn't need to see them. When did this go so wrong? I should be calm, cool, in control. I need to laugh it all off and tell him friends can't be expected to kiss well. Whoops.

Except my heart won't listen to the screaming from my head. I'm not calm. I'm the opposite of cool. I've lost all control.

He grabs my shoulder and tugs me around. I turn, but

my eyes stay glued to the ground, too ashamed to meet his gaze.

"Ruby, look at me."

He puts two gloved fingers under my chin and lifts. His head comes down then, but slowly, too slowly. My heart stops pumping and I worry it might never beat again. His lips brush mine gently, then with more pressure. I ignore the discomfort of my torn lip and lean into him, connected to him in a way I can't explain. I need more air, but I want less, because that means more space between us. If this never ends, maybe it'll erase the moments that preceded it.

Suddenly, he lets me go and steps back. Emptiness fills the space where he stood. I reel again, sucking air in and blowing my breath back out to steady myself.

When I raise my eyes, our gazes lock. All my sorrow from before is gone, replaced with a feeling like I'm flying, soaring, floating on top of the world. His sapphire blue eyes reflect candlelight back at me. He's breathing as deeply as I am; he's as affected as me. I can't look away from his strong, almost hawkish nose, his square jaw, his flashing eyes and thick black lashes. I continue to stare as Wesley reaches up and brushes his unkempt hair away from his eyes.

I almost faint.

Such a simple movement. Small in the grand scheme of things, but also vast, earth shattering, all encompassing. My dreams crumble. My world spins out of control. He moves his hair off his forehead, and suddenly things make sense. His reticence to touch me, his skittishness, but also his quick recovery. Once he knew it was too late, he didn't hesitate to kiss me.

Because we'd already touched.

A tiny rash mars his otherwise perfect forehead. Before the world died, it wouldn't have mattered. Before the

Marking, no one would have cared about a few bumps. It would be harmless: acne, a bug bite, or a reaction to hair product. It shouldn't matter that his forehead has a blemish. It shouldn't terrify me, but it does. Because that small rash means Wesley is Marked, and in under three years, he's going to die terribly.

And now, so am I.

Grab Marked here.

ACKNOWLEDGMENTS

My husband Whitney is a ROCK STAR. Okay, he actually has no musical talent. But he's better than a rock star in so many ways. We have five kids and he does mountains of laundry so that I can write. He also cooks and cleans and plays with our kids and takes care of my horses, all to support my writing.

My mom is amazing too. She cheers me on, she recommends my books to all her friends, and she helps me work through things when I get stuck.

Also, my kids are so supportive. They are always beaming about my books. They read them, they push them (haha!) and they tell me how much they love them.

My ARC team is amazing. Have I mentioned how much I love you lately? I do. Thank you for being excited and making time to read my books and leave me positive feedback right away. It helps me so much.

And to my readers: I love you all. Truly. When you get excited about characters and their decisions and lives, it makes me beam from ear to ear.

Thanks to my writing friends and my editors. Peter, Carla, and Mattie—you are AMAZING. Thank you so much for helping me make this book as good as it can be.

ABOUT THE AUTHOR

Bridget loves her husband (every day) and all five of her kids (most days). She's a lawyer, but does as little legal work as possible. She has two goofy horses, two scrappy cats, one bouncy dog and backyard chickens. She hates Oxford commas, but she uses them to keep fans from complaining. She makes cookies waaaaay too often and believes they should be their own food group. To keep from blowing up like a puffer fish, she kick boxes every day. So if you don't like her books, her kids, her pets, or her cookies, maybe don't tell her in person.

ALSO BY BRIDGET E. BAKER

The Almost a Billionaire clean romance series:

Finding Faith (1)

Finding Cupid (2)

Finding Spring (3)

Finding Liberty (4)

Finding Holly (5)

Finding Home (6) July 2020

The Birthright Series:

Displaced (1)

unForgiven (2)

Disillusioned (3)

misUnderstood (4)

Disavowed (5)

unRepentant (6)- September 2020

Destroyed (7) - November 2020

The Sins of Our Ancestors Series:

Marked (1)

Suppressed (2)

Redeemed (3)

A stand alone YA romantic suspense:

Already Gone